Hello!

I hope you'll enjoy *All I Ever Wanted!* I think, like a lot of us, Callie feels that if she just does everything right, she'll get the results—and the man—she wants. She tries so hard, but life seems to have other plans. Her challenge now: get over the guy who doesn't want her, even though she thought they were pretty perfect together.

One of the things I love best about this book is how the hero and heroine meet. We've all had moments where we've seen people at their worst, not to mention those moments in our own personal histories we wish we could erase! But Ian and Callie see something in each other that no one else does, and in some ways, that's the essence of a romance novel. It was awfully fun to write two characters with such different personalities, and I love the way Callie and Ian bump up against each other again and again. She wants to help him out so much! And he thinks he's just fine on his own. But sometimes in life, what we want is not really what we need, don't you think?

As always, you'll find a quirky family (I especially like Noah), a great dog and a beautiful little town, this time in the form of Georgebury, Vermont. I visited the Northeast Kingdom part of the state last year and was especially fond of the Cabot's Dairy tour, the rushing rivers and the faint smell of syrup that tinged the air.

Hope you'll have a lot of laughs and a few deeply satisfying tears with *All I Ever Wanted*. And of course, I'd love to hear from you! Visit my Web site at www.kristanhiggins.com.

Happy reading!

Kristan

KRISTAN HIGGINS

all i ever wanted

HQN™

ISBN-13: 978-1-61664-644-8

ALL I EVER WANTED

Printed in U.S.A.

This book is dedicated with love and gratitude to Carol Robinson, who has been my great friend since I was just a little kid. Love you, Nana.

Acknowledgments

Thanks as always to Maria Carvainis, my brilliant agent, as well as to Keyren Gerlach, my wonderful editor, and everyone else at HQN for their overwhelming support and enthusiasm.

Many thanks to my incredibly nice vet, Sudesh Kumar, DVM, MS, PhD, for answering a hundred questions, and to Nick Schade, owner of Guillemot Kayaks and boat builder to the gods. Visit www.guillemot-kayaks.com for a peek at his breathtaking craftsmanship. For the use of their names, thanks to Annie, Jack and Seamus Doyle; Jody Bingham; Shaunee Cole; and my lovely friends, Hayley and Tess McIntyre. Adiaris Flores helped me with a few Spanish phrases... *gracias,* sweetheart! Thanks also to Lane Garrison Gerard for inspiring Josephine's somewhat dubious taste in music.

I have been blessed with the support and friendship of many fellow writers, and though I can't name them all, here are a few: Cindy Gerard, Eloisa James, Susan Mallery, Deeanne Gist, Cathy Maxwell, Susan Andersen, Allison Kent, Sherry Thomas, and Monica McInerney. Thank you. Truly.

And lastly, all my love to my husband and kids. You three are everything to me.

Also available from

KRISTAN HIGGINS

and HQN Books

The Next Best Thing
Too Good to Be True
Just One of the Guys
Catch of the Day
Fools Rush In

all i ever wanted

CHAPTER ONE

AS THE MAN I LOVED approached my office, the image of a deer being hit by a truck came to mind. I was the deer, metaphorically speaking, and Mark Rousseau was the pickup truck of doom.

But here's the thing. The deer always freezes, as we all know, hence the expression *like a deer caught in the headlights.* The deer and I (Callie Grey, age thirty as of 9:34 this very morning) are well aware that the pickup truck is going to hit us. But we just stand there, waiting for the inevitable, whether it's a pickup truck (in the deer's case) or a man walking athletically toward me (in mine), perpetual smile in place, his brown hair carelessly curling, those gorgeous, dancing dark eyes. I waited, doe-eyed. It was all really too bad, because outside of Mark's influence, I was not at all a deer about to be run down. I was much more of an adorable, perky hedgehog or something.

"Hey." Mark grinned.

Bam! We have impact. The sunlight streamed through the windows of the old brick office building in which Mark and I worked, illuminating him so that he looked like something painted by Michelangelo. To make him even more appealing, he was wearing an old sweater vest his mom knitted for him years ago, shapeless and faded but something he just couldn't part with. A good son *and* a sex god.

It was as if there were two Callies…the smarter, more sensible self (I pictured her as Michelle Obama), and the dopey, in love part…Betty Boop. Would that Michelle could give Betty Boop a brisk slap, followed by some vigorous shaking. Alas, Betty just sat there, enthralled, as the First Lady snorted in disgust.

"Hi," I said, feeling my face warm. You'd think that four years of seeing him almost daily would have built up some tolerance in me, but no. My chest prickled with longing and love, my throat turned Saharan, my feet and fingers tingled. Though I was trying hard for Intelligent Coworker, my expression was probably somewhere around Pathetic Adoration.

Mark leaned against my desk, which meant his crotch was, oh, let's see, about a foot and a half from my face, since I was seated. Not that I noticed, of course. "Happy birthday," he said, making it sound like the most intimate, most suggestive phrase in the world.

Face: nuclear. Heart: racing. Callie: half inch from orgasm. "Thanks."

"I got you a present, of course," he murmured in that voice… God, that voice. Low and soft and velvety…the same voice he used in the bedroom, as I well knew. Yes, Mark and I had been together. For five weeks. Five *wonderful* weeks. Almost five and a half, if you really analyzed it. Which I had.

From his back pocket, he withdrew a small, rectangular package. My heart flopped as my brain raced with contradictory thoughts. *Jewelry?* Betty squealed. *That means something. That's romantic. So romantic! Oh!*

My! God! On the other hand, Michelle advised caution. *Calm down, Callie. Let's just see how this plays out.*

"Oh, Mark! Thank you! You didn't have to," I said, my voice breathy.

On the other side of the glass-bricked wall that separated our offices, Fleur Eames slammed a drawer. The wall only went up ten feet; the ceilings were twelve, perfect for eavesdropping, and I guessed she was trying to snap me out of my daze. Fleur, a copywriter here at the firm, knew about my crush. Everyone did.

Clearing my throat, I reached for the package in Mark's hand. He held onto it for a minute, grinning before he let go. It was wrapped in cheerful yellow paper. Yellow is my favorite color. Did I tell him that once? Had he filed away that little fact the same way I filed away everything he ever told me? I mean, really, it could hardly be coincidence, right? He smiled down at me, and my racing heart stuttered, stalled, then revved into overdrive. Oh, God. Could it be? Did he finally want to get back together?

I'd worked at Mark's firm for the past four years. We were the only advertising and public relations agency in northeastern Vermont. Our staff was small—just Mark and me; Fleur; the office manager, Karen; and the two pale computer geeks in the art department, Pete and Leila. Oh, and Damien, Mark's personal assistant/receptionist/willing slave.

I loved my job. Excelled at my job, as proven by the large poster on my wall, which had very nearly won a Clio, the Oscar of advertising. Said Clio ceremony took place eleven months ago out in Santa Fe. And in that beautiful, romantic city, Mark and I had finally hooked up. But the timing wasn't right for a serious relationship. Well, at least that's what Mark had said. Honestly, has a woman ever said that? Not a lot of twenty-nine-year-old women truly have timing issues when it comes to being with the man they love. No. It had been Mark's timing that wasn't right.

But now…now a gift. Could it finally be that the time was right? Maybe now, on the very day that my thirties began and I entered into that decade where a woman is more likely to be mauled by a grizzly bear than get married…maybe today really was the start of a new age.

"Open it, Callie," he said, and I obeyed, hoping he didn't notice my shaking fingers. Inside was a black velvet box. Squee! I bit my lip and glanced up at Mark, who shrugged and gave me that heart-stopping smile once more. "It's not every day my best girl turns thirty," he added.

"Oh, gack," sniped Damien appearing in the doorway. Mark glanced at him briefly, then turned his eyes back to me.

"Hi, Damien," I said.

"Hi." He stretched the word into three syllables of contempt… Damien had once again broken up with his boyfriend and currently hated love in all its forms. "Boss, Muriel's on line two."

Something flickered across Mark's face. Irritation, maybe. Muriel was the daughter of our newest client, Charles deVeers, the owner and founder of Bags to Riches. The company made outdoorwear from a combination of plastic grocery bags and natural fiber. It was our biggest account yet, a huge deal for Green Mountain, most of whose clients were in New England. I'd only met Muriel once, and then only briefly, but Mark had been flying back and forth to San Diego, where Bags to Riches was based. As part of the package, Charles had asked

Muriel to come to Vermont and work as the account exec, so he could have someone close to him keeping tabs on things. And, since Charles was paying us gobs of money, Mark had said yes.

Mark didn't answer Damien, who was quivering with the joy of running Mark's day. "Boss?" Damien said, a bit more sharply. "Muriel? Remember her? She's waiting."

"So let her wait some more," Mark answered, tossing me a wink. "This is important. Open the damn box, Callie." Damien sighed with the heavy drama that only a gay man can pull off and hustled down the hall.

Cheeks burning, I opened the velvet box. It was a bracelet, delicate silver strands that twisted and turned like ivy. "Oh, Mark, I love it," I whispered, running my finger over the intricate lines. I bit my lip, my eyes already misting with happy tears. "Thank you."

His expression was soft. "You're welcome. You mean a lot to me. You know that, Callie." He bent down and kissed my cheek, and every detail was immediately seared into my brain—his smooth, warm lips, the smell of his Hugo Boss cologne, the heat of his skin.

Hope, which had been lying in ashes for the past ten months, twitched hard.

"Think you'll make it to my party later on?" I asked, striving for perky and fun, not lustful and ruttish. My parents were throwing me a little bash at Elements, the nicest restaurant around, and I'd invited all my coworkers. No use pretending: I was turning thirty; might as well get some presents.

Mark straightened, then moved a pile of papers from the small couch in my office and sat down. "Um… Listen, I need to tell you something. You met Muriel, right?"

"Well, just that once. She seems...very..." Hmm. She'd worn a killer black suit, had great shoes...kind of intense. "Very focused."

"Yeah. She is. Callie..." Mark hesitated. "Muriel and I are seeing each other."

It took a few seconds for that to register. Once again, I was that stupid deer, watching mutely as the pickup truck hurtled down the road. My heart slammed to a halt. For a second, I couldn't breathe. Michelle Obama stood by, shaking her head sadly, her fabulous arms crossed in regret. I realized my mouth was open. Closed it. "Oh," I heard myself say.

Mark looked at the floor. "I hope that doesn't cause you any...discomfort. Given our past involvement."

There was a white, rushing sound, like a river engorged with snowmelt and hidden debris. He was seeing someone? How could that be? If the timing was okay for Muriel...why not... Oh, crap.

"Callie?" he said.

Here's the thing about being hit by a truck. Sometimes those deer keep running. They just bound into the woods, sort of like they're saying, *Whoo-hoo! That was close! Good thing I'm okay. Um...I am okay, right? Actually, you know what? I'm feeling a little strange. Think I'll lie down for a bit.* And then they wake up dead.

Mark's voice lowered. "The last thing I want to do is hurt you."

Say something, the First Lady commanded. "No, no!" I chirruped. "It's...just...no worries, Mark. Don't worry." I seemed to be smiling. Smiling and nodding. Yes. I was nodding. "So how long have you been...together?"

"A couple of months," Mark answered. "It's…it's fairly serious." He reached out and took the bracelet out of the box, then put it on my wrist, his fingers brushing the sensitive skin there, making me want to jerk away.

In the many years I'd known Mark, he'd never dated *anyone* for a couple of months. A couple of weeks, sure. I thought five was a record, quite honestly.

Ah. My body was catching on to the fact that I'd just been slammed. My throat tightened, my joints buzzed with the *flight* response to danger, and a sharp pain lanced through my chest. "Right. Well. You know what? I have to get my license renewed! I almost forgot! You know…birthday. License. Renewal." *Breathe, Callie.* "Okay if I zip out for lunch a little early?" My voice cracked, and I cleared my throat again, studiously avoiding Mark's dark and now sorrowful eyes.

"Sure, Callie. Take all the time you need."

The kindness in his voice made me feel abruptly murderous. "I won't be long," I chirped. "Thanks for the bracelet! See you in a bit!"

With that, I grabbed my oversize pink hobo bag and stood up, excruciatingly careful not to brush against Mark, who still sat on my couch, staring straight in front of him. "Callie, I'm sorry," he said.

"No! Nothing to apologize for!" I sang. "Gotta run. They close at noon today. See ya later!"

THIRTY MINUTES LATER, I stood in line at the Department of Motor Vehicles, and the effects of being emotionally run down by the man I loved—and now hated—but still loved—were catching up with me. Michelle Obama had abandoned me, regretfully acknowledging that I was beyond help, and Betty Boop was clamping her lips together and blinking back tears. Trying to keep the choo-choo train of despair at bay, I glanced around. Gray, grimy tile floors. Dingy white walls. I stood in the middle of a line of about ten people, all of us listless and lifeless and loveless…or so it seemed.

The whole scene was like something out of some French existentialist play… Hell is not other people. Hell is the DMV. Robotic clerks shuffled behind the counter, clearly hating their lot in life and contemplating the easiest form of hari-kari or embezzlement so they could leave this grim place. The clock on the wall seemed to taunt me. *Time's a'wastin', kid. Your life is passing you by. Happy fucking birthday.*

My breathing started to quicken, my knees felt like a hive of angry bees. Tears burned in my eyes, and on my wrist, my stupid birthday present tickled. I should just rip it off. Melt it down into a bullet and kill Mark. Or myself. Or just swallow the bracelet whole and let it get tangled in my intestines and require emergency surgery and then have Mark come to the hospital and realize just how much he really loved me after all. Not that I would have him now. (*Yeah, sure, Callie,* said Mrs. Obama, making a reappearance. *You'd eat a baby if it meant having him.*)

Well. Maybe not a baby. But the idea that Mark was *with* someone…for a couple of months, fairly serious…ah, shit! Panic loomed like the jaws of a great white shark, terrifying and unexpected. Stupid Muriel with her black hair and white skin, like some vampire in fabulous shoes…when the hell had they started dating? When, dammit?

Oh, crap. Should I go? No. I had to get my license

renewed. Today was the last day I could do it without incurring a fine. I'd picked out this wicked cute outfit, too—red-and-white printed blouse, short red skirt, big gold hoops, and my hair was perfect today, all shiny and swingy... Besides, what could I do? Sit in my car and wail? Kick a tree? Strangle a moose? I really wasn't the type. The only idea that held any appeal was that of sitting in my rocking chair and eating cake batter.

A dry sob raked my throat. Shit. Shit on a shingle. Shit on rye.

"Next," called one of the DMV drones, and we all shuffled forward six inches. The man behind me heaved an audible sigh.

Without another thought, I fumbled in my purse for my cell phone. Where was it? Where was it, dammit? Tampon...no. Book on CD...no. Picture of Josephine and Bronte, my nieces...even their beautiful faces failed to cheer me. Where was the phone? Ah. Here. I scrolled down to *Annie Doyle*. Damn! I got her voice mail. Somehow, it felt like a personal insult. How could my best friend be unavailable in my time of need? Didn't she love me anymore?

Clearly the choo-choo was chugging faster now, so I scrolled down for backup. My mom? God, no...this would just be confirmation that the Y chromosome should be erased from humanity. My sister? Not much better. Still, it was someone. Mercifully, Hester answered, even though I knew she was at work.

"Hester? Got a minute?"

"Hey, birthday girl! What's up?" My sister's voice, always on the loud side, boomed out of my phone, and I held it away from my ear.

"Hester," I bleated, "he's seeing someone! He gave me

a beautiful bracelet and kissed me and then he told me he's seeing someone! For a couple of months and it's fairly serious, but I still love him!"

"Jesus, lady, get a grip," muttered the man behind me. Without thinking, I whirled around and glared. He raised a contemptuous eyebrow—jerk—but okay, yes, heads were starting to turn. Miraculously, no one I knew was here today…the DMV was in Kettering, the town next to Georgebury, so at least there was that.

"Is this Mark we're talking about?" Hester asked, as if I'd discussed any other man for the past year. Or two. Or four. Ah, shit!

"Yes! Mark is dating Muriel from California! Muriel, the daughter of our biggest client! Isn't that lovely?"

The man behind me cleared his throat in a very phony and noticeable way.

"Well, I always thought Mark was a smug bastard," Hester said.

"You're not helping!" I bit out. Why hadn't Annie answered her phone? She was so much better at this sort of thing. She was normal, not like Hester.

"Well, what should I say? He's a prince? Where are you, anyway?" Hester asked.

"At the DMV. In Kettering."

"Why are you at the DMV?"

"Because my license is about to expire! It was on my calendar—*renew license*. And I had to get out of there…I just didn't know what else to do." A sob caught in my throat. "Hester…I always thought…" I took a shuddering breath and tried to lower my voice. "He said it was just timing. He's never been serious with anyone before. And they've been together for *months*." The betrayal, the *shock* of those words made my chest actually hurt, and

I pressed one hand against my swollen heart, feeling hot tears slice down my face.

The woman in front of me turned around. She had the leathery, lined face and broad shoulders of a dairy farmer. "You a'right, theah, deah?" she asked, her Vermont accent as thick as overboiled maple syrup.

"I'm fine," I answered in a shaky and rather unconvincing voice, attempting a brave smile.

"I ovahheard you, you poah thing," she said. "Men can be such ahssholes. My husband, Nahman we're talkin' about, he sits down to dinnah one day and says he wants a d'vorce on account a' he's been banging the secretary down at the creamery. And this when we've been married fahty-two yeahs."

"Oh, my gosh, I'm so sorry," I said, reaching out to hold her hand. She was right. Men *were* assholes. *Mark* was an asshole. I shouldn't be heartbroken over him. Except I loved the rat bastard. Oh, blerk!

"Hello? I'm still here, Callie," my sister reminded me sharply. "What do you want me to say?"

"I don't know, Hes... What do you think I should do?" I asked.

"Step outside?" suggested the man behind me.

"Damned if I know, Callie," she sighed. "The longest relationship I've ever had lasted thirty-six hours. Which you know," she said, her voice turning thoughtful, "has worked really well for me."

"Hes," I said wetly, "I'll be seeing them together every day." The notion made my heart clench.

"That's probably gonna suck," my sister agreed.

"You poah deah," said the older woman, squeezing my hand.

Work would never be the same. Green Mountain

Media, the company that I helped build, would now be home to Muriel. *Muriel.* That was such a mean name! A rich girl's name! A cold and condemning name! Not like Callie, which was so bleeping friendly and cute!

A sob squeaked out, and Mr. Intolerant behind me grumbled. That was it. I whirled around. "Look, mister, I'm sorry if I'm bothering you, but I'm having a really shitty day, okay? Is that okay with you? My heart is breaking, okay, pal?"

"By all means," he said coolly. "Please continue with your emotional diarrhea."

Ooh. The bastard! He looked like the stick-up-the-butt type…dressed in a suit (and you know, please—this is Vermont). He had a boring military-style haircut, cold blue eyes and disdainful Slavic cheekbones. I turned back around. Clearly *he* didn't understand what love felt like. Love gone bad. Love rejected. My tender and loyal heart, broken.

That being said, maybe he had a point.

"I'd better go," I whispered to my sister. "I'll call you later, Hes."

"Okay. Sucks that it's your birthday today. But listen, if it's having babies you're worried about, don't bother. I can get you pregnant in a New York minute. I know all the best sperm donors."

"I don't want you to get me pregnant," I blurted.

"For God's sake," muttered Mr. Slavic Cheekbones. The older woman who'd been cuckolded looked questioningly at me.

"My sister's a fertility doctor," I explained. I closed my phone and wiped my eyes with the back of my hand. "She's very successful."

"Oh, that's nice," my dairy farmer friend replied.

"My daughter did in vitro. She's gawt twins now. Foah yeahs old."

"That's wonderful," I said wetly.

"Next," droned the robot. *Shuffle shuffle shuffle.* The man behind me sighed again.

Images of Mark flooded my mind—our first kiss when I was only fourteen. Years later at work, him bending over my computer, his hand companionably on my shoulder. Getting nearly drunk on maple syrup just last week at a farm we were pitching. Our first kiss. The fateful airplane ride to Santa Fe. Did I mention our first kiss?

Hot tears leaked out of my eyes, and I sucked in a shuddering breath.

Suddenly, a neatly folded handkerchief appeared at the side of my head. I turned. Mr. Intolerance of the Cruel Cheekbones was offering me his handkerchief. "Here," he said, and I took it. It was ironed. It may have been starched. Who did that anymore? I blew my nose heartily, then looked at him again.

"Keep it," he suggested, looking over my head.

"Thank you," I squeaked.

"Next," one of the drones called from behind the counter. We shuffled forward once more.

An eternity later, I finally had a new license. Insult to injury...for however many years, I would look like an escaped lunatic...mascara puddled, face blotchy, smile wobbly and insincere. So much for my spiffy outfit.

As I fished my keys out of my bag, I saw the older woman standing near the exit, putting on those vast black sunglasses old folks wear after cataract surgery. My heart went out to her...at least my husband didn't cheat on me. Leave me after forty-two years. Crikey.

"Would you like to get a cup of coffee?" I asked.

"Who, me?" she asked. "No, sweethaht, I've gawt work to do. Good luck with everything, though."

On impulse, I gave her a hug. "Norman's an idiot," I told her.

"I think you're one smaht cookie," she said, patting my back. "That boyfriend of yaws doesn't know what he's missin'."

"Thanks," I answered, tears threatening again. My new friend gave me a wave and went out to her car.

My phone bleated. Mom. Great. "Happy birthday, Calliope!" she sang.

"Hi, Mom," I answered, wondering if she'd pick up anything from my leaden tone. She didn't.

"Listen, I have news. Dave just called. Elements burst a pipe and flooded."

Being housed in a 150-year-old industrial building, Elements was somewhat prone to this type of thing. "That's fine," I said. "I'm not really in the mood anyway." At least I wouldn't have to endure a birthday party. I could just go home and eat cake batter.

"Don't be silly," Mom trilled. "I've already called everyone. We're having your party here."

My heart sank. "Here? Where do you mean, here?"

"At the funeral home, honey. Where else?"

CHAPTER TWO

"HARD TO BELIEVE you're thirty," my mother said that evening, giving my hand a little squeeze. "Mr. Paulson's family is receiving visitors in the Tranquility Room," she added as a well-dressed couple halted in confusion upon seeing my birthday balloons.

"How can our little girl be thirty, Eleanor, when you don't look a day over twenty-five?" my father murmured from my other side, giving me a bear hug and nearly causing me to spill my second cosmo. Mom ignored him, as was her custom lo these many years since their divorce. Dad took it like a man. "Callie, I fell in love with you at first sight. You were such a beautiful baby! Still are! So beautiful!"

"Has...*your father*...been drinking, Callie?" my mother asked, not deigning to look at dear old Dad. "If so, please ask him to leave." In this house, *your father* was synonymous with *that shithead*.

"Have you been drinking, Dad?" I asked amiably.

"Not too much," he answered with equanimity. "Not enough, I should say," he added in a lower voice.

"Hear, hear," I murmured, taking a slug of my pink cocktail. Given that (A) the man I loved, etc., etc.; (B) Verdi's *Requiem* was playing in the background, and (C) my party was being held at a funeral home, I'd decided to (D) ring in my special day in the company of Grey Goose and cranberry juice.

Irritated that she'd failed to insult my dad, Mom shot me an evil look. I snapped to attention. "This party is lovely, Mom," I lied, giving her a big smile.

Mollified, she gave me a little smile. "I've always thought this was the most beautiful building in town," she said. "Well, better go check on Mr. Paulson." With that, she bustled off to check on the wake in the next room.

Misinski's Funeral Home *was* an impressive building, a large Victorian with the first floor serving as the business end, the second and third floors as living quarters for Mom and, recently, my brother, Freddie. I'd grown up here. The basement, of course, was where all the yucky work was done. To my mother, there was absolutely nothing odd about having a birthday party next door to a wake; this funeral home had been in her family for three generations, and the whole *death is a part of life* philosophy was indelibly tattooed on her soul. So what if at age three, Freddie wouldn't take his nap anywhere but in a casket? So what if Mom used to store the Thanksgiving turkey in the same fridge that kept the clients fresh?

Outside, the sun was shining, as Vermont was enjoying her two weeks of summer. The sky was rich and blue, the air fresh with the scent of pine. In here...not so much. The funeral home was like a time bubble in which nothing ever changed. The smell of lilies, the sounds of sad, classical music, the sight of the heavy, dark furniture...the caskets...the dead people. I sighed.

"So how's my pretty girl?" Dad asked. "You got my check, right?"

"I did, Dad. Thank you so much! And I'm doing

great." It was always my habit to be cheerful around my parents, even when that meant lying through my pearly whites.

"Can I tell you a secret, Poodle?" Dad asked, waving at someone on the far side of the Serenity Room.

"Sure, Daddy," I answered, putting my head on his shoulder.

"Now that I've retired, I'm going to get your mother back," he said.

"Get her back for what?" I asked, assuming this was a revenge thing.

"Get her back as in woo her. Court her. Seduce her."

I straightened abruptly. "Oh. Yeah, um…no. In case you forgot, she…uh…she hates you, Dad."

"No!" He grinned. "Well, she might think she does. But your mother is the only woman I ever loved." He gave me the wink that served him so well. Dad was a good-looking guy, silvery hair, dark eyes, dimples. I looked a lot like him, minus the gray. (*Which is just around the corner!* Betty Boop sobbed. *And Mark's with someone else!*)

"That's not a good idea, Daddy," I said, taking another sip of my drink.

"Why isn't it a good idea?" Dad asked, unsettled by my lack of enthusiasm.

"Maybe because you cheated on her when she was pregnant with Freddie. I'm just throwing that out there, of course."

He nodded. "Not my best moment, I'll admit. The cheating, I mean." He paused and finished off his drink. "But you understand, Callie, sweetheart. It was a mistake, I've spent twenty-two years paying for it, and it's all water under the bridge. She'll forgive me. Hopefully."

"You really still love her, Dad?"

"Of course I do! I never stopped." He gave me a squeeze. "You'll help me, right?"

"Ooh. Not sure about that. The wrath of Mom...you know." Having Mom mad at you was the emotional equivalent of standing in the path of a category five tornado...lots of big things flying around ripping great chunks out of you.

"Oh, come on, Poodle," Dad cajoled. "I thought we were the same. We're romantics, aren't we? God knows I can't ask Hester."

"True, true." After all, Dad's bad example was the reason my sister specialized in getting women pregnant without benefit of the physical presence of a man. "But, Dad...really? Do you really think you can get past all that...stuff?"

For a second, the expression on my father's eternally smiling face flickered. "If I could do it all again," he said quietly, looking at his drink, "things would be so different, Callie. We were happy once, and I...well." His eyes went dark, like a light was turned off.

"Oh, Daddy," I whispered, unable to stanch the sympathy that swelled in my heart. I was eight when my parents divorced, aware only that my world was falling apart. Years later, when Hester illuminated me as to the why, I was shocked and dismayed with my father...but he'd already been punished for so long. Hester had barely spoken to him for years, and my mother kept the emotional knives sharpened, as was her right. But for whatever reason, it wasn't in me to hate my father. His infidelity was a mystery best left unexplored. To the best of my knowledge, and despite his Cary Grant charm and crinkly eyes, Dad had been alone ever since he left my mother. Certainly, I had never met a girlfriend or heard a tale of even a dinner companion. Indeed, it seemed as if Dad had been atoning since before Freddie was even born.

"She loved me once," Dad said quietly, almost to himself. "I can make her remember why."

Yes. Squirreled away, separated from the memories of Mom sobbing on the couch or spewing curses at my father as my infant brother screamed his way through five months of colic, were a few little gems. Mom sitting on Dad's lap. The two of them dancing in the living room without benefit of music when Dad returned from a long business trip. The sound of their laughter drifting out from behind their bedroom door, as comforting as the smell of vanilla cake, fresh from the oven.

"Will you help me, Poodle?" Dad asked. "Please, baby?"

I took a deep breath. "You know what? Sure. It'll be an uphill battle, but sure."

Dad's expression changed, and he once again became a sparkly George Clooney. "That's my girl! You'll see. I'll get her back." He smooched my cheek, and I couldn't help smiling. Twenty-two years should be enough time served, right? Dad deserved another chance at love.

And so did I. Dammit, so did I! Betty Boop stopped crying and seemed to look up at me. *Really? Honest and true?*

"Want another drink?" my father asked, and without waiting for an answer, trotted to the makeshift bar in the back.

Suddenly, I felt better. My father was going to try again to reclaim the love of his life. I should try, too. Mark had chosen me once…maybe I'd been too…sappy or clingy or whatever during those five weeks. I'd been mooning after him ever since Santa Fe. Maybe, just by going back to myself, that cheerful, smart, likable person I was, Mark would see that I was the one for him, not Muriel. And if he saw me with someone else, maybe that would be the kick in the butt he needed.

The—what had the man at the DMV called it?—ah, yes, the *emotional diarrhea* had been purifying. Life was good, as the T-shirts said. Or it could become good, right? I could find someone else. Even if Mark didn't want me—I winced, but kept going—if that was true, then I'd find someone else who did. I would! No more Debbie Downer, no more Bitter Betty. I was Callie Grey, after all. Former prom queen, I'll have you know. Everyone liked me. They really did.

"Doesn't it look so pretty, Auntie?" asked Josephine grabbing my hand. Today, my five-year-old niece was dressed like a tiny, trashy pop star, fishnet vest over leopard leotard, ruffled pink skirt and flip-flops.

"So pretty," I answered, smiling down at her. "Almost as pretty as you." She beamed up at me, showing me her adorable, tiny teeth, and I touched her button nose.

The Serenity Room was strewn with pink and yellow streamers. Matching balloons drifted lazily past the stained-glass window depicting Lazarus coming forth from the tomb, and a table holding my birthday cake sat up in front, where the casket usually went. Bronte had made a big sign that said, "Happy 30th, Callie!"

The room was filled with an array of friends and relatives, as well as a couple of rather confused-looking people who were probably here for the wake in the Tranquility Room. There was Freddie, my brother, who was taking a year off from Tufts University, where he seemed to be majoring in skipping classes and drinking. He raised a glass to me and I waved fondly. My sister, built like a strong rhino, towered over him in full lecture mode, judging from the glazed look in his eyes. Pete and Leila, my fused-at-the-hip coworkers, surveyed the cheese tray (thank God for Cabot's!).

"Happy birthday, Calliope," came a low and very silken voice behind me. My uterus seemed to shrivel as my blood ran icy cold. "You look very beautiful today. Perfect, in fact."

"Thanks, Louis," I murmured, immediately glancing around desperately for a sibling or parent or friend (or priest, just in case it was true and that Louis was a ghoul who needed to be exorcised by an agent of Christ).

Louis Pinser was my mother's mortuarial assistant, and quite beloved by Mom and Mom alone. Since her children had all refused to go into the family business, she'd had to look elsewhere. Elsewhere (somewhere damp and underground, I imagined) yielded Louis, a tall, chubby man with a receding hairline, slightly bulging green eyes and the requisite deep and soothing (and terrifying) voice of a funeral director. Once I'd overheard him in the bathroom reciting, "I'm so sorry for your loss, I'm so sorry for your loss." Needless to say, he found me *very* attractive. All the weird ones did.

"I'd like to take you out to celebrate properly," he murmured, dropping his gaze to my breasts. He held up his drink to his mouth, and his tongue darted out, seeking but not finding the straw as he continued to stare at my boobs. Blerk!

"Ah. Well. That's nice of you," I said. "But I'm so…it's been a crazy…you know. Work. Stuff. What's that?" I pretended to hear something. "Yes, Hester? You need me? Sure!" With that, I bounded out into the foyer, where my sister had just gone, and took a few deep breaths. Being around Louis always made me want to run out into the sunlight and play with puppies.

"No, you can't straighten your hair," Hester was saying to her older daughter. "Next question?"

Bronte turned to me. "Don't you think a teenager should be able to do what she wants with her hair?" she asked, hoping for solidarity.

"Um...Mother knows best?" I suggested.

"You try being the only black kid in school," Bronte muttered. "Let alone having this stupid name."

"Hey," I said. "You're talking to Aunt Calliope here, named for Homer's muse. No sympathy on the name."

"And I was named after the slut in *The Scarlet Letter*," Hester said. "At least you have a cool author's name. Which, once again, I didn't even pick, as you well know." Bronte had been seven when Hester adopted her. Though my sister was a fertility doctor and could've had her children the old-fashioned way (artificial insemination, that is), she'd adopted both her children. Bronte's biological father had been African-American, her birth mother was Korean, and the result was a stunningly beautiful girl. But as Vermont is the whitest state in the union, she felt her difference keenly, especially since she'd hit adolescence, when looking like everyone else is so important. Josephine, on the other hand, was white and looked very much like Hester, which was pure coincidence.

"Well, I'm changing my name to Sheniqua when I'm sixteen," Bronte said, narrowing her eyes at her mother and me.

"I love it," Hester answered calmly, which caused Bronte to flounce off. My sister glanced at me. "You doing okay?" she asked.

"Oh, sure," I lied, though the question made my heart squeeze. "Much better. Thanks for listening earlier."

At that moment, my mother came out of the Tranquility Room. "Did you girls happen to see Mr. Paulson?" she asked, referring to the man whose wake was currently under way. "Gorgeous work. That Louis is so talented." She bustled off.

"Happy birthday, Callie," said Pete, emerging from the Serenity Room, his lady love firmly welded to his side. "We'd love to stay…"

"…but we need to go," finished Leila. She glanced nervously at the other room, where we could just glimpse Mr. Paulson in his casket.

"Thanks for coming, guys." I smiled gamely.

"Callie, when does Muriel start?" Pete asked.

At the name, my face ignited. "Don't know," I said, feigning a lack of interest. The young lovers exchanged a look. *Poor Callie. Let's pretend we don't know about her and Mark.*

"See you Monday, Callie," Pete said at the same time Leila murmured, "Have a nice weekend."

Off they went, into the sunshine and fresh air. Before the door closed, a most welcome sight appeared.

"Come on outside," my best friend said. "I have wine, and it's gorgeous. We're not sitting in a fucking funeral home on your birthday." Despite the fact that Annie was a school librarian, she swore like a drunken pirate when young ears were not around, which made me love her all the more.

The air was dry and sweet outside, and Annie was indeed clutching a bottle and a few paper cups. She gave me a quick hug, then trotted around the side of Misinski's to the pretty backyard of my childhood.

"Hallo, what've we got here? Nipping off? Abdicating the throne, Callie?"

Annie grimaced. "Hi!" I said. "Join us, Fleur. It's so nice out."

Fleur and Annie were both my friends. Well, Annie was in a different class, as we'd known each other for eons. But she'd married her childhood sweetheart at the age of twenty-three and had Seamus, my darling godson, a year later, and was blissfully happy. Fleur was single, like me, and we occasionally had drinks or lunch and commiserated over the single life. Due to three weeks spent in England during college, Fleur spoke with a varying British accent and could be quite funny. The two women didn't quite like each other, which I found rather flattering.

The three of us sat at the picnic table Mom still kept under the big maple in the backyard, though to the best of my knowledge, no one ate out here anymore. A wood thrush sang overhead, and a chickadee surveyed us wisely.

"So. Fuck all about Mark and Muriel, eh?" Fleur lit an English Oval and took a drag, then exhaled in a stream away from Annie and me.

"Yeah," I said, gratefully accepting the paper cup of wine from Annie.

"You're better off without him," Annie said firmly, handing Fleur a cup, then pouring one for herself. She'd endured a long e-mail from me earlier this afternoon with all the details of my misery. "He's an ass-wipe."

I sighed. "The thing is, he's not," I told Annie.

"He's really not," Fleur echoed.

"Callie, I'm sorry. I hate him. He dumped you, made up some bullshit line about timing, and now he's seeing another woman! Ass. Wipe." She glared at Fleur and me over her gold-rimmed glasses.

"Okay, you have a point," I conceded. "But those are just the details. Mark's...he's..." I sighed. "Kind of perfect."

"Christly, you're defending him," Annie muttered. "You're pathetic."

"You sound like my grandfather," I said.

"Right, well, not everyone gets to marry their little Prince Charming from third grade, yeah?" Fleur said to Annie. "For the rest of us, there's a limited pool. Mark's pretty great compared to what-all else is out there. And if he's the love of Callie's life, I say go for it, Callie. Take no prisoners."

"Well, I think you can do much better," Annie said loyally. "And Fleur, I forget. How long did you live in England?"

Fleur narrowed her eyes. "A good bit of time," she said tightly.

"You just have to get out there, Callie. Find someone else," Annie said.

"Or better yet," Fleur said, "win him back. Remind him of how fab you are. Find some man, make Mark screamingly jealous and bam! You're back in."

Though I'd thought the same thing earlier, I said nothing.

"Nope. Leave him in the dust, Callie," Annie countered. "You deserve better. Write that down and tape it to your mirror. 'I deserve better than the ass-wipe formerly known as Mark.'"

"You need to get laid, Calorie?" my brother asked, appearing at the back door. "My buddies back at school think you're hot. You could be a cougar, how's that?"

"I'm too young to be a cougar," I said. "I'm only thirty! Besides, I want someone who doesn't live with his mom." I turned to my friends. "Is Gerard Butler single?"

"Setting your sights a *bit* high," Fleur murmured. Hmmph.

"How about Kevin Youkilis?" Freddie suggested, joining us. "Then we could get Sox tickets."

"Nah," Annie said. "He has a lightbulb head. Consider your nieces and nephews, Freddie. Oh! How about the center-fielder, the cute one. Ellsbury? Now *he's* hot!"

As my friends and brother suggested increasingly ridiculous choices for my new boyfriend, my brain was busy. Annie was right. I had to get over Mark. For months now, a stone had been sitting on my heart. I'd shed a lot of tears over Mark Rousseau, lost a lot of sleep, eaten a lot of cake batter. Somehow, I had to move on. Work would be hell if I didn't shake loose from the grip he had on my heart. I most definitely didn't want to keep feeling this way, alone in a love affair meant for two.

Even if he'd felt like The One. Even if I'd always thought we'd end up together. Even if he still had a choke chain on my heart.

CHAPTER THREE

UPON RETURNING HOME that night, I tripped over an appendage, an all too common experience for me. "Noah," I called out, "if you don't start picking up your legs, I'm going to bludgeon you with one of them."

My grandfather's rusty voice came from the living room. "That's right. Pick on the poor cripple."

"You think I'm kidding, old man?" I asked.

Bowie, my husky mutt, came leaping into the kitchen, singing with joy and canine love, his tail whacking me, great clumps of fur falling to the ground. "Hello, Bowie," I crooned back at him in my special dog voice. "Yes, I love you, too! Yes, I do! I love you, handsome!" When Bowie had licked me, nipped my chin and turned in a dozen or so frenzied circles, he raced back into the living room. I picked up Noah's leg and followed my faithful dog.

"The doctor said you need to wear this," I said, bending to kiss my grandfather's bearded cheek.

"Fuck the doctor," Noah said amiably. His stump was propped on some pillows.

"Watch your language, Grumpy," I said. "Is your leg giving you trouble?"

"My lack of leg is giving me trouble," he retorted. "But no more than usual." He rubbed the stump idly, not taking his eyes from the television screen.

Noah was a boat builder, the founder and sole operator of Noah's Arks (a name I'd thought up when I was four and something I was still pretty proud of). His boats were the stuff of legend—beautiful wooden rowboats, kayaks and canoes, each one made from Noah's design, by Noah's hand, selling for thousands of dollars apiece. Up here in the Northeast Kingdom, where the rivers ran wild, he was pretty much a god.

Unfortunately, he'd suffered a small stroke two years ago. Even more unfortunately, he'd been holding a running radial saw at the time, and the result was a cut so bad that his leg had to be amputated just above the knee. At a family meeting, the doctor had recommended an assisted living facility for seniors. Noah, who'd lived alone since my grandmother had died years ago, had gone white. Without forethought, I found myself offering to live with him for a while 'til he got used to his new situation. And though the curmudgeonly old bastard would never say so, I liked to think he appreciated it.

Noah was watching a *Deadliest Catch* rerun. We both loved reality TV, but this one was our favorite. As the hardy Alaskans battled it out on the Bering Sea, I sat on the couch, Bowie leaping neatly up beside me and laying his beautiful gray and white head in my lap, blinking up at me in adoration. My dog had one brown eye, one blue, which I found very appealing. I made a kissing noise at him, and his ridiculously cute triangle ears swiveled toward me, as if I were about to tell him the most important news ever. "You," I said, "are a very good dog." Because really, what message could be more important than that?

Glancing around, I saw that Noah, as usual, had ignored my pleas to keep our place tidy. Newspapers were strewn around his chair, as well as a bowl filled with a puddle of melted ice cream and an empty beer bottle. Yummy.

Noah and I lived in an old mill building, half of which was his workshop, the other half our living quarters. The downstairs housed the kitchen, a den and a huge great room with forty-foot ceilings and massive rafters. The great room was circled by a second-floor catwalk, off which were two bedrooms. My own was quite big and sunny, with plenty of space for my bed, a desk and my rocking chair, which was set in front of two wide windows that overlooked the Trout River. I also had a gorgeous bathroom, complete with Jacuzzi and separate shower. Noah was down the hall from me and mercifully had his own bathroom. There's only so much a granddaughter will put up with.

At the commercial break, Noah hit Mute. "So? You have a good time?"

I hesitated. "Um…well, the party was at the funeral home. Mom and Dad were there. It was fine."

"Sounds like a shit bath to me," he said.

"You were right to stay home," I confirmed. Noah avoided family get-togethers as if they were hotbeds of ebola. He wasn't exactly close with my father, his son. Dad's brother, Remy, had died in a car accident at age twenty, and I gathered from the little Dad said that Remy was the type of son Noah had expected: rugged, quiet, good with his hands. My father, on the other hand, had spent his life schmoozing people as a drug sales rep. And, of course, there was my parents' divorce. Noah, who had adored my grandmother and nursed her through the horrors of pancreatic cancer, fiercely disapproved. "I brought you some cake, though," I added.

"Knew I kept you around for a reason," he said.

"Here." He reached into his shirt pocket and withdrew a little hand-carved animal...a dog. A husky.

"Oh! Thank you, Noah!" I gave him a kiss, which he tolerated with a mere grumble. He'd been making his grandchildren—and great-grandchildren—these little animals all our lives. I had quite a collection.

"You seem down," Noah observed. This was deep in Dr. Phil territory from a man who didn't spend a whole lot of time navel-gazing...in fact, Noah was the least sentimental person I'd ever met. He never spoke of my uncle Remy, but there was a picture of him in Noah's room, the one thing that never needed dusting. When Gran died—I was six at the time—Noah didn't shed a single tear, but his sorrow was palpable. I'd drawn him a card every week for months to try to cheer him up. Even when the bandages came off his leg for the first time, his only comment was, "Fuckin' foolish." No self-pity, no maudlin mourning of his limb. To comment on my emotional state...shocking.

I stared at him, but he didn't look away from the muted television set. "Um...no. I'm fine." I glanced at my wrist. Still wearing Mark's gift, loser that I was. "Noah, I'm thinking I should probably find a..." the word *boyfriend* sounded so lame "...a special someone." Ooh. Not much better. Far worse, in fact. "Care to share the wisdom of your long life?"

"Don't do it," he said. "Nothing but heartache and misery." Underneath his white beard (Noah looked like a malnourished, possibly homeless Santa), his mouth twitched. "You can live here forever and take care of me."

"And I do so love taking care of you," I said. "How about a nice enema before bed?"

"Watch your mouth, smart-ass," he said.

"Hey. Be sweet to me. I turned thirty today," I reminded him. Bowie licked my hand, then turned on his back so I could see that his big white belly was just lying there, all alone and unrubbed.

"On second thought, 'twouldn't hurt for you to get a move on with life, Callie," Noah said unexpectedly. "Don't have to stay here forever."

"Who else would put up with you?" I asked.

"Got a point there. You gonna talk all night, or can I watch Johnathan save this guy?"

"I'm going to bed. You need anything?"

"I'm fine, sweetheart." He dragged his eyes off the TV. "Happy birthday, pretty girl."

I paused. "Wow. It's that bad?"

His beard twitched. "Cahn't say I didn't try."

A few minutes later, washed and brushed and in my comfiest jammies (pink-and-yellow striped shorts, yellow cami), I was sitting in my rocking chair. Turning thirty was a momentous event in a woman's life. Also, I needed to…I don't know. Process things. And there was no better place to process anything than my Morelock chair, which I'd received twenty-two years ago to this very day.

There are two halves of Vermont—Old Vermont and New. Old Vermont was made up of crusty, rugged people who dropped their *R*s and owned the same American-made pickup truck for thirty years, didn't feel the cold and were immune to blackflies. Noah was Old, of course…he might not speak to his neighbor, but he'd cut and stack five cords of wood if that neighbor became sick. New Vermont…well, they were people who drove Volvos and Priuses, owned expensive hiking boots and hung out their laundry as a political statement as much as to get the clothes dry. They were friendly and cheerful…not like Noah at all, in other words.

Like my grandfather, David Morelock was Old Vermont. He was a furniture maker and Noah's longtime compatriot. One summer, a reporter happened to be vacationing in St. Albans, where Mr. Morelock lived, and stumbled upon the furniture shop, learned Mr. Morelock had no formal training and didn't even use power tools…just went out to his barn each day and worked. Two months later, the *New York Times* featured a story on Mr. Morelock, and bingo! He went from local craftsman to American legend. Suddenly, all those New Vermonters *had* to have a piece of Morelock furniture, and just like that, the old man had more work than he could manage. Before the story in the *Times,* his pieces had cost a few hundred dollars apiece. After the story, they sold for thousands, much to the amusement of their maker.

The day I turned eight was a bleak one in my personal history. Dad had moved out the week before, and in all the distress, my birthday was kind of forgotten. Mom was not only pregnant, heartbroken, furious, but also trying to manage a double funeral for a couple who'd died of carbon monoxide poisoning. Hester was away for the summer at some mathlete camp, and the end result was that Mom had hurriedly poured me some Cheerios, then shuttled me over to my grandfather's. Noah popped me in his truck and drove to St. Albans. I don't remember the reason.

At any rate, the two men got talking, and I wandered around the drafty old barn, picking up scraps of wood, drawing my initials in a pile of sawdust, trying not to be bothered by the fact that no one remembered that I was eight years old, because even then I understood that grown-ups had a lot of problems. Then I saw the chair.

It was a rocking chair, the type meant for a front porch. Made from honey-colored tiger maple, it was truly a work of art, elegant and slender, almost glowing from within. With a glance at Noah and Mr. Morelock to ascertain that they were too busy to notice, I gave it a little nudge, and it glided back soundlessly. Could I sit in it? There was no sign saying I couldn't. I sat. The seat and back were perfectly proportioned, curving in all the right places, and when I rocked in it, the movement was as gentle and slow as a quiet river.

Even then, I recognized that the chair was special. It was so…graceful. And so happy, somehow. Just sitting in this chair would make a person feel better. Even if her daddy didn't live at home anymore. Even if her sister was far away. Even if her mom hadn't baked a birthday cake. This was a chair that promised a better time ahead. The tightness that had wrapped itself around my throat the day my parents told me they were getting divorced seemed to ease as I rocked, the motion somehow tender and deep.

Closing my eyes, I pictured, perhaps for the first time, what I'd be like as a grown-up. I'd have a rooftop apartment in Manhattan overlooking the entire city. There'd be a garden up there with lemon trees and glorious flowers, and I'd work all day on the *Today* show, and at night, I'd come home and Bryant Gumbel, my husband, would bring me a drink that contained alcohol, and we'd hold hands and talk about really adult things, and he'd never leave me, a fact I'd know beyond a shadow of a doubt.

"You like that chair, little one?" Mr. Morelock asked, and

I jumped in guilt and opened my eyes, feeling my face burn.

"It's…it's very nice," I mumbled, unsure if I was in trouble.

"Your grandpa here tells me it's your birthday," he said. I looked at Noah, surprised that he was aware of the date. My grandfather winked at me.

"Yes, sir. I'm eight," I said.

"How'd you like this chair as a present?" Mr. More-lock asked, and suddenly, my eyes were wet, and I looked down at my lap and nodded, unable to speak. Then Noah picked me up and gave me a bristly kiss, told me not to go all sloppy on them, and did I thank Mr. Morelock? I wiped my eyes and did as I was told.

When Noah took me home that evening, he carried the chair up to my room. "You take care of this chair, young lady," he said.

"It's my happily-ever-after chair," I said, quite pleased with the title. The chair gave my room an entirely new look, and suddenly my ruffled pink bedspread and unicorn poster seemed quite passé. Noah chuckled and ruffled my hair, then left me to worship my new treasure.

David Morelock died later that week. For some reason, his death hit me hard…it was like losing Santa or something, and I was raw anyway. Noah told me that my chair was the last one Mr. Morelock made, and more special and valuable than ever. I took Noah at his word. I didn't want anyone to sit in it, even me… I saved it for those moments when I felt in need of the most comfort.

Like now. And as usual, the chair was working its magic. From outside came the rushing and gurgling of the Trout River. A distant owl called out. I rocked, the long, smooth glide always a shock of sweetness. Dear

Mr. Morelock, how I loved him that day! Sending up a silent thank-you to my chair's maker, I felt the tension in my shoulders surrender bit by bit.

Somewhere out there was the guy for me. Bryant Gumbel, alas, was spoken for, but somewhere in the Green Mountain state was a man who'd see me and love me and think I was the most wonderful person on earth. We'd get married, and there'd be days when I'd come home and we'd sit on the front porch, and all I ever wanted would have come true.

And so, shoving aside the feelings of sloppy misery and humiliation and summoning the relentless optimism I'd wielded all my life, I took a deep breath, causing Bowie to snap to attention as if I were about to announce something momentous and hugely brilliant. "Bowie," I said, loath to disappoint, "let's find you a daddy."

CHAPTER FOUR

THURSDAY MORNINGS MEANT Senior Citizen Yoga. Granted, I was forty or fifty years younger than most of the other attendees, but since I was extremely unlimber and therefore made them feel good about themselves, I was welcomed. The fact that I brought my famous chocolate chip cookies was just gravy.

I never really got yoga. Indeed, I often dozed off during deep meditation at the end and had to be nudged back into consciousness by a classmate. Leslie, the instructor, often shot me disapproving looks as I blinked sleepily. Then again, I'd been getting those looks ever since I beat her out for prom queen. But I loved yoga class, because I loved the ladies and figured the exercise and chakra alignment (whatever that was) couldn't hurt. Still, it was a little embarrassing to be the only one grunting as we moved into Upward Laughing Monkey.

One of the far-too-many reasons I loved Mark was that he was a wonderful boss. He gave us a flexible schedule, figuring happy employees worked harder, and so I could always squeeze in a yoga class or chaperone a field trip for one of my nieces. Besides, Mark encouraged his employees to be active in the community; like me, he was a Georgebury native, and we often did pro bono work for various nonprofit groups, including the Senior Center.

We'd helped with the fundraising drive a couple of years ago, and I'd made some nice friends during that time.

I confess, I also enjoyed being fussed and cooed over. It was a commonly held belief that I was a *jewel* and destined for a wonderful romance with a wonderful man. I often heard things like, "You're smart to wait for the right man, Callie, sweetheart. You don't want to end up like my daughter/granddaughter/niece/sister/neighbor/self." Then the horror stories would begin, and though I probably shouldn't admit it, I *loved* hearing them. Jody Bingham (who could do a full split at the age of seventy-six *and* had better legs than I did) knew a woman who married a man who already had a wife, possibly two. Letty Baker's daughter married a "crackhead pot-smoker" who was arrested during the wedding reception. Elmira Butkes's daughter Lily was twice divorced—the latest ex was a poet, and the shocking news was that he didn't make enough to feed an ant. He was suing Lily for alimony…insult to injury.

"Honestly, I don't know what's wrong with her," Elmira said as we smoothly transitioned into Downward Looking Giraffe (well, some transitioned smoothly. Others looked like Downward Dying Giraffe, but I was trying). "Why can't she find a normal man with health insurance and a decent haircut?"

We all murmured in sympathy, getting a dirty look from Leslie, who frowned on chatting during class. "Well, anyway," Elmira said, "I took Mr. Fluffers to the vet this week, and he's single—the vet, that is, not Mr. Fluffers—so I called up Lily right away and said, 'Lily, the new vet is single. Why can't you go after someone like that?' Well, of course she didn't listen to me…"

"You should give him a try, Callie," Jody said, sliding

into her trademark split, the show-off. "A vet's almost as good as a doctor." She smiled up at me and gave me a wink as I struggled into a distant approximation of her position. How Jody could smile while doing that was a mystery of physics and superior genes.

The new vet, huh? I thought. Very promising indeed! I'd worked for Dr. Kumar, the old vet, back when I was a teenager. Everyone adored Dr. Kumar. He offered coffee and doughnuts in the waiting room, gave out his home phone number and sang to nervous animals until they were literally eating out of his hand. He was so tenderhearted that he often cried more than the pet owner when Roscoe or Tabby had to be put down. He'd retired recently and had great plans to take the lovely Mrs. Kumar to Branson, Missouri, where they were eager to tour the wax museum and ride the duck boats.

This new vet...hmm. If Dr. Kumar had sold the practice to him, the new guy had to be a real sweetheart. Already, we had so much in common! Vets loved animals...I also loved animals! With a hopeful note ringing in my heart, I contorted myself into Westward Twisting Heron and made a mental note to call for an appointment this very day. It was worth a shot, and I was taking all the shots I could find.

Last night, for example, I'd registered on eCommitment. Annie had been more excited than I was, since her last first date had been at age 14. Several friends, including Karen, our office manager, had met their husbands online, so what the heck. Yes, it would be nice to meet someone the old-fashioned way...my maternal grandparents, for example, had met over a cadaver in mortuary school. Well, okay, maybe that wasn't the epitome of romance I was going for, but still.

In the past, before Mark and I were together, I'd had

a relationship or two. I wasn't a troll or anything. In fact, men really liked me. I was quite attractive, if I do say so…smiley brown eyes, shiny brown hair (it ought to be shiny, considering the number and cost of the hair-care products I used). A dimple in my left cheek…adorable! I'd grown a little chubby in the past year, courtesy of trying to bribe my heart into a good mood by eating cake batter, but still fell in the pleasingly curvy range. My Wonderbra and I could manage some very impressive cleavage. Men's heads still turned. I was popular with the River Rats, a local boating club who worshipped my grandfather. I met clients who, occasionally, were single, normal, age-appropriate males.

Despite my parents' wretched example and Hester's utter revulsion of the idea of marriage, despite the fact that Noah had been gutted by the loss of my gran, I'd always been an optimist. Love made you a better person. Made you feel protected and precious and *chosen*. Chosen. Such a lovely word! And in loving someone else, you became better…noble and generous and beneficent.

I stretched my arms wide in Gentle Gorilla and tried to embrace my karmic blessings, as Leslie was telling us to do. The new vet, huh? Employed. Educated. Smart. Someone who could definitely compare to Mark. No doubt this new vet was also tender, loving, funny, probably a fabulous cook with Ryan Reynolds abs. Ryan Reynolds everything, maybe.

Not that I was getting ahead of myself, of course.

I MANAGED TO GET an appointment to see Dr. McFarland late in the day, telling Carmella Landi, the longtime receptionist, that poor little Bowie wasn't himself and I figured he should be checked out. "Got it," she said, her voice short.

"I think he ate something weird," I added, trying to be convincing. This was half true…Bowie ate something weird at least once a day…a sock, a chunk of wood, a bag of frozen lima beans. Once he ate one of Noah's feet…the rubber kind that was attached to the end of a particularly ugly prosthetic.

However, as we got ready for the appointment (I'd gone home to fetch my dog, of course, and freshen up a bit), Bowie looked in fighting form, all glossy and gorgeous and yipping and singing, his unusual eyes winking at me as I adjusted my cleavage. Should I change my shirt? Yes. Pulling on a pale green short-sleeved sweater, I unbuttoned the top two buttons. Should I go for three? No, three was slutty.

"Try to act calm, at least, Bowie," I said. "You don't have to lie, but you don't have to do somersaults, either." I switched my earrings to match the sweater, added a green and blue beaded necklace, then smiled winningly at my reflection. "You're adorable," I told myself. "Come on, Bowie."

Ordinarily, I'd have ridden my bike… Bowie, being a husky, was born to do one thing, and that was pull. Noah and I had rigged up a terrific little harness to hitch onto my bike, and my dog loved nothing more than towing me up the hills of our fair city. Today, however, I'd have to drive Lancelot, my green Prius. Couldn't have my dog pull me three miles out of town if he was allegedly under the weather. I felt a pang at the untruth and said a quick prayer to St. Francis, patron saint of animals, as well as to Balto, the legendary sled dog whose heroics had given birth to the Iditarod, so that Bowie would remain in the pink.

It was humid today, the sky an unconvincing blue, and the forecasters had predicted heat in the mid-eighties, which was about as hot as Vermont was going to get. Mosquitoes, the Vermont state bird, were out in force, so it was just as well that I was driving.

Georgebury was a typical Vermont city—well, typical for the Northeast Kingdom part of the state, where the mountains were too small and too rough for skiing and the gobs of money it infused into the economy. No, Georgebury was scruffy, and we residents liked it that way. The downtown was set into a hillside, a few blocks of shops and offices and restaurants, the aging brick architecture from a more caring age, when builders left a legacy of arching windows and intricate details, high ceilings and wide-planked floors. Green Mountain Media occupied a Flatiron-style building on the V-shaped intersection of Allen and River Streets.

I glided past the office and headed up the hill to the more upscale, residential area of town—huge Victorian homes built by the mill owners in the town's heyday, the beautiful town green, the athenaeum and town hall, the private boarding school. Misinski's Funeral Home was here as well, tastefully painted in shades of dark green, yellow and rust, the long awning and hearse in the driveway marking the building's function.

Though it certainly wasn't necessary, I turned onto Camden Street. Just sightseeing, I lied to myself, looking for a car with rental plates. Almost against my will, I slowed.

Mark's house was a place I'd always loved, a grand Craftsman with a stone front porch and a huge copper beech tree in the back. Of course, I'd pictured myself living here. Eleven months ago, I'd spent four nights here in Mark's house, in Mark's bed. My chest tightened as I looked at the yard. Our kids were supposed to have played there. *Not gonna happen,* the First Lady reminded me. *He didn't choose you. Move on.* "Right, right," I muttered. She had a point. Besides, no one seemed to be there. Maybe Muriel was staying elsewhere. Maybe this whole *seeing each other* was a lot less serious than it sounded.

With a sigh, I eased past Mark's, heading down the other side of the hill.

The vet's office was located out on Route 2, four or five miles from downtown. I pulled into the parking lot, grabbed Bowie's leash and unclipped him from his doggy seat belt. "Let's go, boy," I said, trying not to stagger as Bowie lunged for the door. He adored Dr. Kumar, of course, and would often sing along as Dr. K. serenaded him. Bowie chugged right up to the counter. "Hey, Carmella," I said. "Bowie's here for a check."

"Right," she said, raising a knowing eyebrow.

"He ate something, I think," I reminded her.

"Mmm-hmm." Again with the eyebrow. "That seems to be going around." She jerked her chin, urging me to look. I did.

Ruh-roh.

The waiting room was…gosh, it was pretty full, wasn't it? And not just full. Full of women. Many of them *young* women. And um…you know…like me, sort of decked out, sort of shiny. Sort of *single.* Crap. There was Lily Butkes, who had apparently heeded Elmira's advice, holding a very large Persian cat, which eyed me contemptuously. Aimee Wilder, who'd been a year ahead of me at school, clutched a trembling Chihuahua. "Hey, Callie," she said, smiling. Dang it. She was quite attractive, very tall and lean and supermodelesque.

"Hi, Aimee, nice to see you!" I answered merrily. Also in the waiting room were two women I didn't know, one with a hugely overweight terrier, the other with a ball python coiled around her arm. There was Jenna Sykes, another old schoolmate, who gave me a confident smile. A golden doodle puppy snoozed on her shoulder like a baby. Okay, that would be hard to beat. A puppy was an unfair advantage in man-seeking, especially if the man was a vet. I wondered if that was Jenna's strategy. Not a bad idea when I thought of all the money we women invested to get a man—haircuts and color, makeup and moisturizers, minimizers, maximizers, lingerie, clothes, shoes, waxes…crikey! And all we asked in return was that they be semi-clean. At least Jenna's investment would love her back.

"Have a seat, Callie," Carmella said, taking out Bowie's chart and clipping it to a board.

"Thanks, Carmella. Come on, Bowie." I tugged and nudged my dog as he tried to sniff every square inch of floor, his curling tail wagging madly, sending clumps of husky fur through the air. "Come on, Bowie, be a good boy," I reminded him. He sniffed the python owner's knee, then, finding it to his liking, tried to lunge in for her crotch. "No, Bowie! Stop it! Please stop!" I commanded. "Sorry," I said to her, reeling in my ridiculously strong dog. "He's a people person." She gave me a cold look from her reptilian eyes, and made a big point of brushing Bowie's fur from her knee. You know how they say people resemble their pets? True.

"Jenna, you can go into Room 3," Carmella said. "Aimee, Room 2." Jenna stood up, still cradling the sleeping puppy, and shot me another confident smile. Aimee also rose, hips swinging in a passable runway walk as she strolled down the hall. I heard the rumble of a masculine voice, then Aimee's giggle.

I sat and waited, the minutes ticking by slowly. *This could work,* I reminded myself. *Men love us.* Ball Python Woman was next, and frankly, I was glad. That snake had been staring unblinking at Bowie. *I may not be big enough to eat you,* the creature seemed to be thinking. *Yet.*

From where I sat in the waiting room—the coffee service was gone, much to my disappointment—I couldn't see Dr. McFarland. And okay, clearly I wasn't exactly original in bringing in my doggie for a quick once-over. But a girl had to try.

Ruh-roh. Here came Jenna, looking quite miffed as she held the now awake and squirming puppy. She scowled at Carmella as she settled the bill, then caught my eye. "May as well go to Dr. Jones in Kettering from now on," she grumbled. "This guy's a dick. Didn't even give me the time of day." With that, she stomped past me to the door.

"Bye," I said. Hmm.

A few minutes later, Aimee came out with her Chihuahua, who still seemed extremely stressed. Aimee handed her credit card to Carmella, sighed loudly, then caught my eye. "Good luck," she said flatly. "If you're here for why I think you're here, that is."

"Thanks," I said, frowning.

Finally, it was my turn. I brushed a clot of Bowie fur from my skirt (I'd craftily worn white as camouflage), squared my shoulders and walked down the hall.

"Hi, Callie!" It was Earl, a tech who'd worked here for ages.

"Hi, Earl!" I said, giving him a hug.

"Don't tell me Bowie's sick," Earl said.

"Oh, just a little," I said, blushing.

"Ah," he said knowingly. Too bad Earl was in his sixties. I'd always loved him.

I went to Exam Room 4 and took a seat on the hard little wooden bench. Dr. Kumar used to have pictures hanging up…that series where the dogs are playing poker or pool. Those were gone now, but the walls had been painted a nut brown, which was kind of nice. Otherwise, the place was as bland as any veterinarian's exam room—metal table, small fridge for the vaccines, scale and a poster about tick-borne illnesses. It all made me kind of sleepy. Bowie seemed to share the sentiment— he yawned and flopped down at my feet, panting rhyth- mically.

Being at the vet's brought back a lot of happy memories, a few sad ones as well. We hadn't been allowed to have pets as kids…we tried having a cat when I was about nine, but it had crept into an occupied casket one day and reappeared during the wake, much to the horror of the family of the departed, so Mom sent Patches to live on a nice farm.

But I always loved animals, and when I was fourteen, Dr. Kumar let me come work here cleaning cages and, as I got older, washing dogs. When a pet died, Dr. K. would sometimes ask me to handwrite the Rainbow Bridge poem so he could mail it to the owner. Ah, the Rainbow Bridge. Oh, blerk, I was getting all choked up just thinking about it.

The Rainbow Bridge poem says that when your pet dies, he goes to a wonderful, sunny place full of meadows and woods and doggy and kitty friends. He's young and healthy again, and very happy. There's a beautiful rainbow bridge nearby, but your dog never crosses it. No.

He just plays and eats steak. But then one day…one day, your pet goes on alert. He sees something in the distance. He starts to tremble. Can it be? He breaks into a run. He runs and runs and runs…toward…you! Yes, it's you, you've died and you're coming to heaven, and for all these years, your pet has been waiting for you. He runs to you and licks your face and wags and wags his tail and you pet him and kiss him and hug him. You're so, *so* happy to see your old friend…and then, finally, you and your beloved pet cross the Rainbow Bridge together into heaven proper to live for all eternity.

I seemed to be sobbing. "I love you, Bowie," I squeaked, leaning down to pet my pup. Bowie was only three, so hopefully he and I would have a long, long time before I had to think about any rainbow bridges. Bowie licked my cheeks happily and sang me a little song— *Rurrrooorah.* "I love you, good doggy," I repeated wetly.

The door opened and I quickly blew some dog fur off my lips. "Hello," I said, wiping my eyes hastily as I looked up.

Oh, shit. Shit on a shingle. Shit on rye.

It was the guy from the DMV. The *Jesus, lady, get a grip* guy.

He was studying Bowie's chart and didn't see me at first. Then he said, "Hi, I'm Ian McFarland," and looked at me. His expression froze. "Oh."

"Hi," I muttered, feeling my face ignite.

"Are you all right?" he asked, frowning.

"Yes," I said. "I'm fine. Well…I was crying a little. You know that poem about the Rainbow Bridge? I was just thinking about it…well. Got a little weepy! You know how it is." I wiped my eyes again, then fumbled in my purse for a tissue. Crap. Didn't seem to have one.

"Here." His expression stony, Ian McFarland once again handed me a handkerchief.

"Thanks," I said, standing up. He took a quick step backward, as if my *emotional diarrhea* might be catching.

He wasn't particularly good-looking...well, maybe he had a rough appeal. Sort of a Russian gangster look with sharp cheekbones, short blond hair and Siberian blue eyes. The overall effect was...let's see. Disapproval. Great. This guy did not look like a tenderhearted vet who'd cry over the Rainbow Bridge or ask me to dinner. He looked more like the type who'd know how to kill me using only his little finger.

"Hi," I said again, remembering that I should probably speak. "I'm Callie. Callie Grey."

At the sound of my name, Bowie whined and thumped his tail as if telling me I was doing *great*. Dr. McFarland glanced at the chart. "What seems to be the problem?" he asked. Bowie, sensing a belly rub somewhere in the very near future, rolled over and offered himself. And oh, how adorable. My dog was...you know. Excited. Interested. Aroused.

Tearing my eyes off the display of canine *amour,* I swallowed. "Um...well, Bowie ate something this morning. Which is not uncommon. Bowie, get up." He *was* neutered, of course, but just because he couldn't father any cute little puppies didn't mean he didn't have urges, and apparently Dr. McFarland was his type. My dog didn't move, just lay there, exposing himself.

"What did he eat?" the vet asked.

"Uh, the newspaper? But he does that a lot. He's probably fine."

"You should be more careful about where you leave the paper." He made a note on the chart—*Bad pet owner,*

I imagined—then looked up at me. Yep. Disapproval. "How's he acting?"

Horny? "Um…he felt, well, he seemed to be a little, ah…blue? Not himself? So…" I smiled weakly. *Roooraahroh!* Bowie sang, wagging his tail.

The vet glanced at Bowie, then shot me a look that bespoke gobs of cynicism.

I swallowed. "I just figured it's never the wrong thing to do, you know, double-check on your dog, see if everything's okay. He seemed a little…down."

Bowie took this as a cue to flip to his feet in that agile and speedy way huskies have. He stared at me with his wide, different-colored eyes, tilting his head and giving a single yip, as if saying, *And then? And then? What happened next, Mom? I love this story! It smells good here! Can I have some meat?*

"He seemed down," Dr. McFarland repeated.

"Off. He seemed off." I looked at the floor.

He sighed, then set the chart down on the counter. "Miss Grey," he said, folding his arms and giving me the full power of the Arctic stare. He paused for a moment. "Let me share something with you. You're the eighth woman this week to come in with a vague complaint involving a pet eating something he shouldn't have." He paused. "Seven of those women were single. And as I seem to recall from our morning together at the Department of Motor Vehicles, you're single as well."

D'oh! as Homer Simpson would say. "Wow. Someone has an ego," I murmured, pulling on Bowie's leash as he inched closer and closer to Dr. McFarland's leg.

"Two of the dogs supposedly ate dishcloths. When I told the owners that this was cause for concern, as cloth can be very damaging to an animal's intestinal track, they rather abruptly amended their stories. A parrot may or may not have eaten a plastic toy. One cat allegedly ate a ring. When I recommended an X-ray, the owner found the ring in her pocket. And four dogs, Miss Grey, seem to have eaten a newspaper and were feeling a little off."

"What a coincidence," I said brightly.

He raised an eyebrow, slowly. Mr. Darcy could take put-down lessons from this guy. Jenna was right. He *was* kind of a dick.

"You know what, Dr. McFarland?" I chirped. "You're actually a little bit right. Here's the thing." I paused. He waited. I waited, too, for something good to come to me. "Bowie did eat the paper this morning. I'd been meaning to come see you anyway, and since my dog felt a little *blue,* I figured what the heck." I cleared my throat. "See, the thing is, I used to work for Dr. Kumar, did you know that?" Dr. McStuck-Up shook his head, looking utterly uninterested. "I washed dogs, cleaned up, was generally helpful."

Dr. McFarland sighed and glanced at his watch.

"Anyway, I work in advertising and public relations now…um, and I know how friendly and sweet Dr. Kumar was, and you have big shoes to fill and all that. So I was thinking maybe you needed some…I don't know. A little help in getting the word out that you're just as sweet as Dr. K. Because I'm guessing that even though you're seeing a bump in the single-women-pet-owning population right now, business might die down a little."

Ah-ha! He frowned—frowned more, that is—and I kept talking. "You might not know this, but there's another veterinary practice in Kettering, which is only fifteen minutes away, and it's not really much farther for the people who live east of Main Street, so you know…

I wondered if you might be interested in a little PR, so I figured I'd drop in and offer my services."

Well! That was as unexpected as pigs flying out of my butt, as my dear grandfather would say. *Not bad,* Michelle said. *Though I don't approve of lying, of course.* "Why?" I asked. "Did you think I was checking you out?"

Dr. McFarland regarded me steadily. "I'm sorry," he said. "I'm not looking for an advertising agency."

"This would be more public relations," I said. Bowie wagged encouragingly and added a yip.

"No, thank you," the vet said. "Now. Would you like me to examine your dog or not?"

"Sure!" I said. "Might as well, right?" He didn't roll his eyes, but I sensed it was close. The vet knelt down next to Bowie, who immediately tried to mount him for a little dry humping.

"Off," Dr. McFarland said. Bowie obeyed, surprisingly, and licked the vet's face, getting a little smile as a reward. A smile. Something hot and unexpected darted in my stomach. Dr. McFarland…Ian. Nice name. Ian McFarland. Yes. I liked it. Dr. Ian took a stethoscope out of his pocket and pressed it against Bowie's side, gently holding my dog's head with one hand so Bowie didn't lick him again.

"So, the women of Georgebury have been through, huh?" I said, just to show I was not one of *them,* the desperate hags of northeastern Vermont. "I guess you can't blame them. Hard to meet people up here, I suppose. It's funny, seven people with—"

"Miss Grey?" He looked up at me with those blue eyes, and suddenly I felt that liquid, flashing heat again. Those were some very pretty eyes, and he was looking so deeply at me, as if maybe…maybe he kind of felt something? Something for me?

"You can call me Callie," I said, and my voice was a little breathy. "Short for Calliope. Homer's muse."

"Callie, then."

Your name! He said your name! Betty Boop's eyelashes fluttered. "Yes?" I sighed.

"I can't hear your dog's bowel sounds if you don't stop talking."

"Right! Bowel sounds. You keep going. Do what you need to do. You're the doctor. Examine away. Good boy, Bowie." I closed my eyes, closed my mouth and sat still, imagining the First Lady sighing yet again.

After a minute, Dr. McFarland said, "Everything sounds fine." He stood up and scribbled something else on the chart. "Try not to leave newspapers where your dog can get them. Please see Carmella on your way out."

"Right. Nice to meet you," I said, blushing once again.

"Same here," he lied.

I followed him out of the exam room. Bowie yipped, then lunged, causing me to crash into Dr. McFarland's back. He turned, scowling. "Sorry," I muttered, hauling Bowie back from the object of his interest—an unleashed and extremely beautiful Irish setter. When she saw us, she sat immediately and wagged her plumy tail.

"Wow, that is one gorgeous dog," I said. "Is she yours?"

"Yes," he answered. He eyed my whining dog the way a father eyes his teenage daughter's boyfriend.

"Bowie, stop," I ordered, tugging on the leash. My dog was getting aroused once more. "What's her name?"

"Angie."

"Angie," I immediately crooned in a whispery voice. The old Rolling Stones song was a favorite of mine,

"'Aaaangie, you can't say we never tri-ah-ah-ied.'" Bowie joined right in with a whining howl, and Angie wagged appreciatively. Her owner said nothing. "Did you name her after the song?"

"No. Her name is Four D Mayo's Angel," he answered in what I'm sure he thought was a patient tone. "I shortened it."

"Oh, so she's one of those purebred AKC dogs, is that it?" I asked.

"Yes."

Apparently unable to stop talking, I kept going. "Bowie's a mutt."

"Yes. I'm aware of that."

"Right. Because you're the vet." *For heaven's sake,* Michelle said. *Shut it, Callie.*

"Angie, go lie down, girl," the good doctor said. His dog wagged at me once more, then walked off down the hall. Bowie crooned a mournful goodbye.

"Well, see you arou—" I offered to Dr. McFarland, but he was already going into the next exam room to deal with the obese terrier and its owner.

I looked at my dog, who stared back, ready to hear whatever gem I was about to impart. "That did not go too well," I whispered.

Up at the front desk, Carmella took pity on me. "Divorced," she said. "Not over his wife, I think."

"Oh," I murmured. "Too bad."

My trip to Humiliationville cost me $75. Michelle told me I'd learned a valuable lesson in not wasting other people's time. Betty mourned the shoes that money could've bought.

In the parking lot, Ball Python Woman was sliding her pet into the passenger seat, which made me wonder what the heck the snake did while she drove around. "Well, that was a complete waste of time," she announced as I opened the door for Bowie.

"You're telling me," I answered.

BACK HOME, I CROSSED *New Vet* off my list and checked my e-mail. Yesterday, when Annie was supposed to be getting ready for the new school year, she had instead screened several candidates, thoroughly enjoying her foray into Internet dating. *This guy is gorgeous!* she'd written, complete with a link to his info. Doug336. What did those numbers mean, anyway? That there were 336 Dougs in the world, all of them looking for love? That was a lot of Dougs. I sighed and turned to look at the framed photo I really should toss.

It was taken at last year's company picnic, two months before that fateful foray to Santa Fe. Mark had organized one of those team-building exercise retreat things involving paintball and physical exertion, and though there had been grumblings about why the heck we couldn't have gone on a booze cruise instead, I'd had a great time. Especially during the Chicken Challenge. Oh, I *loved* the Chicken Challenge! It was basically a game of piggyback chicken in a lake, and guess who got to partner up with the boss? Me, that's who, and Pete had snapped a photo of the two of us, soaked and triumphant, me on Mark's back, my arms around his lovely neck. That was a happy, happy day. I'd been so sure Mark was feeling it, too…

Get rid of the picture, Michelle advised.

I didn't. But I dragged my eyes off it and clicked the link. "Okay, Doug336," I said. "Let's make a date."

CHAPTER FIVE

I HAD KNOWN MARK SINCE I was a kid and, like most of the kids I knew, admired him from afar. I might have been pretty and friendly, but *he* was older by two years. *He* was the mayor's son. *He* lived up the street, right on the town green, and not in a funeral home, but in a house where, rumor had it, he had an entire floor to himself. He was an only child, he was tall, he was athletic, he was handsome. In my young eyes, Mark Rousseau and Leonardo DiCaprio both had the same appeal and the same unattainability...they were fun to look at, sure, someone to swoon over...but someone you'd talk to? No.

And then came Gwen Hardy's fourteenth birthday party. Boy-girl, rec room, a closet...the classic scene. Despite the fact that several classmates were well into the world of horny teenage groping, I had not yet so much as held hands with a boy. Jake Fiore had asked me out in sixth grade, but I told him my parents were very strict and old-fashioned...not that my parents were paying a lot of attention, but because it seemed easier than nego-tiating the murky waters of adolescent love.

Anthony Gates approached in seventh grade, and again, I flashed the parent card, apologizing profusely and telling him I thought he was an awfully nice guy, but my dad…gosh, but thanks so much, I was really flattered. (I mastered the art of the nice rejection early in life, as you can see.)

The truth was, I believed in Love. After my father moved out, I resolved that Life Would Still Be Happy. I was helpful with my baby brother, cheerful in the mornings to counterbalance Hester. I made sure I always skipped out to my dad's car when he came to pick us up for his nights and pretended to love bowling because *he* loved bowling. Made Mom tea when she came in from work. Always kept my room neat. Smiled when I felt like crying, and when I did cry, made sure I went into my closet so no one would hear.

Love would be my reward. I *yearned* for love. I'd have it, and not with any ordinary boy, either. It would be overwhelming, undeniable, *meant to be* Love with a capital *L.* The kind that caused Johnny Depp to swing from a rope outside the mental hospital in *Benny & Joon.* The kind that made John Cusack hold up the boom box in the pouring rain so Peter Gabriel could do the talking for him. My parents had obviously failed miserably on that front, but I would never make their mistakes (whatever those were). Hester was cynical and bitter, having been sixteen when Dad left and all too aware of why our parents' marriage failed. She took the other extreme a child of divorce might embrace—swearing that she'd never let a man have so much as a toehold on her heart. She'd roll her eyes as I wept at romantic movies and advise me to stop being such a putz, but I wouldn't stop. Didn't want to.

Okay, so back to Gwen's basement. Her parents were upstairs watching *Seinfeld,* and we were playing some variation of Truth or Dare that involved a boy and a girl going into a closet and making out. Prior to the party,

Annie and I had spent roughly a thousand hours discussing whom we'd most want in the closet with us...her vote was the extremely cute Jack Doyle, the man she'd end up marrying. Me...I didn't really have a leading contender. Until the actual night.

Gwen lived four doors down from the Rousseaus, and she'd worked up the nerve to ask Mark to stop by her party. For some reason, Mark agreed. It was a huge triumph for Gwen...Mark was sixteen already! He had his driver's permit! He was on varsity lacrosse *and* soccer! He *shaved!* Mark, as we all knew, was dating Julie Revere, and Julie's little sister rode the bus with Corinne Breck's cousin, and Corinne, who was in our class, said that her cousin said that Julie's sister said that Julie said she might let Mark go *all the way.*

We were all hugely aware of him...not one of the girls had touched the giant bowl of Cheeto balls for fear of getting orange gunk stuck in her braces, and most of us were sipping Diet Coke instead of the far too childish punch. I was so glad I'd worn my denim miniskirt with the cropped pink angora sweater. And yes, Mark had checked me out ten minutes earlier when he'd come in (thank you, padded bra!), causing me to blush furiously even as I pretended not to see him.

When Mark's turn came during Truth or Dare, I didn't hear the question he was supposed to answer. A roaring sound filled my ears. My face burned. I adopted a casual pose, and when Mark's dark eyes stopped on me, I gave a little smile, even though my heart raced fast enough to make me sick. He stood up, crossed the circle and held out his hand. "Okay, kid. Time to go slumming with me," he said with the crooked grin that would torture me for the next decade and a half.

Gwen and my friends Carla and Jenna fell silent with the wonder of it all, jealousy stamped clear on their faces, the idea of me being chosen as bitter to them as it was miraculous to me. Annie didn't look at me, for which I was grateful…would've broken into squeals if she had—but her face glowed with excitement just the same. I stood up, brushed off my skirt and took Mark's hand. Followed him into the closet, practically floating with the surrealism of the moment. Mark Rousseau was holding my hand! Taking me into a closet! It was more than I ever dared to dream.

The closet was crowded; an air-conditioning vent ran through the space, so we had to stand close. Mark smelled wonderful—a mix of soap and sweat—and I could hear him breathing. He took my other hand. My palms were sweaty, but his were warm and dry, and my body temperature shot up well into fever range, sweat dampening my forehead. "You're cute, Callie," he whispered…the first time he said my name, and I almost threw up with the thrill of it all.

"Thanks," I whispered back, swallowing a little bile. My heart thudded so fast and hard it was a wonder he couldn't hear it.

"You ever been kissed before?" There was a smile in his voice, though I couldn't see it in the dark.

I bit my lip. "Um…not really," I whispered.

"Is it all right if I kiss you now?" he whispered back.

"Sure," I managed.

It was a soft, gentle, wonderful kiss, chaste and perfect, his lips soft and warm. Something flipped in my stomach as his mouth moved against mine, and suddenly, to my mortification, a little moan escaped from my throat. *That* kind of moan. An *oh, baby* moan. Dang it! Mark laughed quietly, pulling back.

"Was that okay?" he asked.

"Mmm-hmm," I answered, too horrified to say anything else.

Then he kissed me again. This wasn't a magical, perfect first kiss. This was…oh, it was warm, and mature, deeper and, oh, Lord, *hot.* My knees weakened in a near painful rush. The pit of my stomach *tingled.* Mark's hands slid down to my ass, and he pulled me against him. Oh!

Then he stopped. "Okay. We're all set, then," he said casually, the way a cool guy would. He stepped back and opened the closet door, the bright light and giggles from the other kids like the rude buzzing of an alarm clock calling me from a soft and lovely dream.

My first kiss! My first kiss was from Mark Rousseau, and it had been perfect. And that second one—holy crap! I floated back to my place in the circle, next to Annie. She asked me something, and I murmured some nonsensical syllables in response, but I didn't hear, couldn't see, was absolutely heedless of the sharp and curious glances from my friends. My heart pounded and kept pounding, faster and faster, the rhythm repeating over and over, *Mark Rousseau kissed me. Mark Rousseau kissed me.*

Of course, I fell crazy in love with him. Made a point of appearing in his path here and there, noting when, during a football game, he might head to the concession stand and hustling there myself so we'd innocently run into each other. He always said hi, sometimes even using my name. I began riding my bike past his house occasionally (well, four or five times a week, to be honest). I even joined the cross-country team because they warmed up near the lacrosse team.

Mark didn't break up with Julie. Didn't hold up a boom box under my window and play Peter Gabriel songs. Didn't swing outside my window to get a glimpse of me.

But he did say hi, and when you're a freshman and a high school junior says hi, that's pretty huge. The next year, he went off to college—and I didn't date anyone until he did…I was so hoping he'd notice me and wanted to be free just in case. But he didn't; he left for the University of Chicago after high school. I dated a nice boy or two. Went to college myself. Had a relationship. Even fancied myself in love, sort of, though the feeling lacked that capital *L* feeling.

After college, I lived in Boston for a few fun and impoverished years, but in the end, it wasn't for me. My job at a large PR firm was pleasant enough, though the pay was mediocre at best. I had some great friends, we had fun, I dated a bit, but I missed Vermont. Missed my family, especially Bronte and baby Josephine. It was time to go home. Settle down. Find some guy and get married. Find Love with a capital *L*.

Back to the clean air and rushing rivers of Georgebury I went, back to the funeral home, back to the sweet light of a Vermont summer. Mom and Dad both seemed pleased that I was home. Freddie, whose IQ was in the genius range, was often bored in school and welcomed the chance to torture me. I babysat for my nieces, hung out with Annie and Jack, got a job covering town meetings for the little local paper and waited tables at night, figuring some job opportunity would present itself.

It did. Mark returned from Chicago, where he'd been working, and opened up Green Mountain Media.

It seemed like it was meant to be, didn't it? I mean,

come on! Of course I applied. So did three *hundred* other people. Jobs like that were rare in our corner of the state, and it was big news in Georgebury. I wore my favorite skirt and sweater ensemble, bought on Beacon Street in Beantown, trying to look creative and funky and professional. Spent even longer on my hair that day, practiced my answers in the mirror.

When I walked into Mark's office, the old attraction came crashing back. He was better-looking than ever, more manly, broader in the shoulders, and he was as nice as could be. Asked me about college and my job in Boston…most of my work there had been trying to make "oily discharge" sound less horrific on drug warning labels, something I acknowledged honestly, getting a good laugh from Mark. He told me he loved the Back Bay and tried to make at least one Sox game a year, chatted about us both moving back to Georgebury. I, in turn, made sure to ask questions about his company, talked about my creativity and excellent work ethic, and agreed that the Sox were looking great.

"I have to tell you, Callie," he said, glancing again at my résumé, "you're one of the most qualified people I've had in here. This looks really good."

"Thanks," I beamed, my toes curling in my new shoes.

"I can't say for sure, since I have a few more people to interview, but…well, I think you'll be hearing from me. By Friday at the latest."

"Excellent," I said. "But take your time. It's an important decision. You want to make sure you have the right mix of people."

He nodded, pleased. "True enough. Thanks for coming in."

"My pleasure," I said.

I made it to the door, quite thrilled with the interview, not to mention the *stir* Mark's physical presence still caused, when he spoke again.

"Callie?"

I turned. "Yes?"

"Didn't we make out in a closet once?"

Bam! My face ignited. "Um…you know, I…don't…"

He raised an eyebrow and grinned, slowly. "Callie, Callie. You haven't forgotten your first kiss, have you?"

I gave a mock grimace. "Okay, you caught me. Yes, we kissed in a closet. I wasn't sure I should bring it up in a job interview."

He laughed. "I can't see how it would hurt." And then he smiled at me, a smile that went straight to my groin, and I held on to the door frame and hoped I didn't look quite as ruttish as I was suddenly feeling.

"I seem to remember it was quite…nice," he added.

"I seem to remember that, too," I said, and my heart knocked around in my chest. "Well. Great seeing you again, Mark."

"I'll call you soon."

And he did call. I got the job, and though I reminded myself that I was no longer fourteen, that I didn't want to screw up a really great career opportunity and that romance had no place in a new company, I fell right back in love. He was a great boss—energetic, hardworking, appreciative of the efforts of his small staff. I loved the work…because we were so small, I worked on every project at first, and Mark quickly realized he'd hired the right person, something he often said out loud. He flirted occasionally, told me often that I looked pretty, something he also said to Karen and Leila and, later, Fleur. But he never crossed the line, no matter how hard I psychically ordered him to.

Until last year, when we were nominated for a Clio.

We'd landed a job for a children's hospital, a coup for us, since we were just a few years old, and we wanted to hit a home run. For two days, Mark and I sat in the conference room from morning until well past dinnertime, working through lunches, guzzling coffee, wadding up pieces of paper, talking ourselves blue in the face. What were the advantages of this particular hospital? How we could show people they didn't have to fly down to Boston to get top-rate care? What did a parent really want in a hospital? Why would they pick this one?

And then, somewhere in the afternoon of the second day, I got it. Mark was blathering about hospital statistics or something, and I held up my hand to silence him. Then I said the line aloud, very slowly. Did a rough sketch on my notepad and looked into Mark's dark eyes. His mouth fell open and he just stared at me. "That's it," he said in a near whisper.

A week later, we did the shoot. I chose the kid, who was an actual patient, and the doctor, scouted out the room where I wanted the picture taken and talked to Jens, the photographer, about what I had in mind, the lighting, the focal point.

The final poster was a close-up of a three-year-old boy in the arms of a doctor. The boy's head rested on the woman's shoulder, and he looked straight into the camera. The doctor's face was turned away, so all you could see was her gray hair and the stethoscope draped around her neck. The boy's shirt was white with thin red stripes, the doctor wore a white lab coat, and the wall behind them was also white. The focal point of the shot was the boy's face…his huge, trusting, remarkable green eyes looking straight at the camera, a slight smile curling his lips. The tagline had been simple: ...*as if he were our own.* Beneath that, *Northeast Children's Hospital.* And that was it. The chairman of the hospital board got tears in his eyes when he saw it.

When the Clio committee called, we were ecstatic. Of *course* we'd both be going to the ceremony. It was huge! A three-day festival with the best advertising agencies in the world, and we were one of them. Holy guacamole!

An hour or two into our flight, Mark dozed off. A permeating fog of lust enveloped me, and tenderness, too. What could be more wonderful than watching over the man you love as he catches up on much-needed sleep? Sigh! For once I didn't mind the fact that the airlines jammed passengers in like packaged herring. For once, I could study him without fear of discovery. His dark hair curled at the neck, his lashes were sooty and long. Even the way his chest rose and fell under his pale blue oxford was a turn-on.

And then, somewhere over the Midwest, the captain's amiable, Texas-twanged voice came over the PA. "Folks, we're gonna run into a few bumps here. Please stay in your seats and buckle up tight. Trays up, too. It's gonna be pretty rough. Flight attendants, take a seat."

I obeyed, making sure Mark was buckled, putting my laptop back in its case. And then, I was being shaken like a rag doll. The plane lurched and shuddered. People screamed as one, myself included. My seat belt cut into my stomach, my hair whooshed up. It was like being bucked off a horse, rough and unpredictable, and a horrible whine pierced the air. The oxygen masks tumbled out, and it was so loud! Mark, abruptly awake, threw his arm out across me, automatically trying to shield me from harm. "What the fuck?" he yelled over the noise.

The plane shuddered again and rolled to the left. I clutched Mark's arm as we tilted, feeling my laptop slide past my feet. My mind went white with terror. The plane wobbled unevenly, people were screaming and praying, the engines roared and shrieked. Mark's eyes met mine. Then the plane seemed to drop, cups and trash and purses flew up and hit the ceiling. More screams. I couldn't seem to speak—I gripped the headrest in front of me with one hand, and with the other, I held Mark's. The plane shuddered again.

"Folks, Captain Hewitt again. We're having a little bit o' difficulty," the captain called out, sounding as calm as if he were watching corn grow. "Hang on tight." As he spoke, the plane fell a few more…feet? Yards? God, we were trapped in a hunk of metal and falling from the sky! My mouth opened but no sound came out.

"Fuck, fuck, fuck," Mark muttered.

"Oh God, oh God help us, please Lord Jesus, save us!" the woman in front of me wailed. The plane bucked again, there was another mass scream. *We're going to die,* came the small, quiet thought in the part of my brain that wasn't roaring in panic. Behind me, someone vomited and my own stomach lurched. *We're crashing, oh, God, this is it.* Fear electrified my legs, and my eyes, stretched too wide, saw everything…the man across the aisle hunched over, his hands over the back of his head. "Hail Mary, full of grace…" Trash was everywhere. Who knew there was so much trash? There was a little girl two rows ahead on my right sobbing, "Mommy, make it stop, Mommy!"

Someone else threw up, people were sobbing into their cell phones—"Baby, it's bad, I love you, I love you so much"—but Mark and I just held on to each other as the plane dipped and shivered. Mark pushed my head down—crash position, Jesus God, I was in crash position, who survived a plane crash? I shook violently, my face was wet with tears… Josephine, Bronte, Hester, Freddie, my parents. Who'd take care of Noah? What about Bowie? Would my sweet dog somehow know that I was gone?

The plane bucked again, tilted, righted. And then, amid the chaos and terror, I saw lights down on land. We were getting lower, descending, even as the plane still shuddered. The wings wobbled, then straightened, the sound of the landing gear locking in place was the most reassuring and beautiful sound that had ever reached my ears.

"We're gonna make it," Mark said, his voice strained. My hand, clenched in his, had gone numb. "We're gonna make it. We're gonna make it."

When the screech of rubber against tarmac sounded, the plane burst into cheers and sobbing. "Welcome to New Mexico," came the captain's voice, shaking now that we were safe. "Sorry for the rough ride." The white-faced attendants stood, and people flung off their seat belts despite the rules of waiting, desperate to be off the plane, many still crying, still swearing, and all of us miraculously alive.

I turned to Mark, and we looked at each other. Then he kissed me, his hands cupping my tear-streaked face. He was drenched in sweat. "We're fine," he said hoarsely. I nodded, my throat still too clamped from terror to allow a word to escape. I'd almost died, but I hadn't. I was alive. It was so strange. We were falling from the sky, and somehow we made it.

Standing in the aisle, waiting to get out, shaking like

a junkie in heroin withdrawal, I found it so bizarre to do those mundane tasks like find my purse and laptop, straighten my shirt. People were already talking on their cell phones, assuring loved ones of their safety, opening the overhead compartments and retrieving their carry-on luggage. I didn't speak. "Callie, you okay?" Mark asked.

I nodded. Realized I was crying. When we filed past the captain and crew, I hugged each of them, my God, I loved them so much. When I came to the captain, it was clear he was God's right hand, not some middle-aged blond man with a mustache. "Thank you. Thank you so much," I wept.

"Well, now, we all made it down safe and sound, no matter what it felt like, right?" He patted my shoulder. "Thanks for flying with us, little lady."

So, okay, you don't almost die in a plane crash every day, do you? It's life-affirming to walk off a plane that had been shuddering and dropping through the sky, to breathe fresh air and feel the ground under your feet again. And you know what else is life-affirming?

Sex.

Mark took my hand once we were off the airplane, and he didn't let go of it. We didn't speak, just got into a cab. Held hands. Got to the hotel. Held hands in the lobby as we checked in. Held hands in the elevator. Our rooms were on different floors, but he only pushed nine, which was where his room was. Led me out of the elevator, down the hall, the two of us bumping as we towed our suitcases, our hands still linked. Went right into that generically pleasing, wonderfully safe room, and the second the door closed, Mark pulled me against him and kissed the stuffing out of me, and let me tell you, we put that king-size bed to good use.

And it was wonderful. I'd never been in love—not like this. The shaking of Mark's hands as he unbuttoned my shirt, his weight on top of me, his mouth on mine, that crooked smile...this was Love. The kind of Love I always knew I'd find, and it was just breathtaking.

The next morning, Mark suggested we blow off the conference, as we only needed to show up for the ceremony, and now that we'd nearly died, we realized how silly all this really was. We strolled through beautiful Santa Fe, admiring the little bungalows adorned with chili pepper wreaths, bought Native American souvenirs for Josephine and Bronte. When the heat got to us, we ducked into a movie theater and made out like teenagers. Had dinner at a tiny restaurant, discovered that green chili sauce was in fact nectar of the gods and wondered how we'd lived without it for so long.

On Thursday night, our poster won the bronze. Not bad, but it seemed so petty in light of everything else. We had each other. We knew what really mattered. That's what I thought, anyway.

Clearly, this was the beginning of a very meaningful, heading-for-marriage-and-they-lived-happily-ever-after relationship. After all, I had known Mark most of my life. I worked with Mark...I worked *for* Mark. He wouldn't sleep with me if it wasn't serious. And the whole near-death experience...it had made him (finally) aware of me in a life-altering way. Faced with the vision of our deaths, he realized that I was, as the saying goes, The One. Priorities were made clear. Right?

Well...no. Actually, no.

At the end of the conference, Mark told me he'd meet me in the lobby. So I went back to my own room...that was one sign I'd ignored...though I'd slept in his room,

I hadn't been invited to actually *share* it, so all my showering and getting ready and stuff was done in my own space. Which made sense, of course, since we'd already paid for two rooms. Packing up my stuff, I hummed away. Josephine would make the cutest flower girl ever. Bronte could be a junior bridesmaid. I'd have to ask both parents to give me away to avoid any show of favoritism. Winter wedding with a Christmas theme, or the more traditional June? Mark and Callie. Callie and Mark. Sounded great together, didn't it? I sure thought so.

When I met him in the lobby, he was engrossed in his iPhone, barely looking up as I approached. I forgave him. In the cab ride to the airport, he called a client. No problem. As I expressed my nervousness at flying again, he said (just a tad impatiently), "Callie, the odds of us experiencing something like that again are minuscule. Don't be silly." I smiled gamely, agreed that he was right, told myself not to be such a Betty Boop. On the flight back, he worked on his laptop. That was okay. We were busy. I pretended to work, too, even though I kept listening for engine failure. I tried to embrace Michelle Obama, the practical and intelligent side of myself. Tried to ignore my clattering heart.

For the next five weeks, I tried to feel happy. I had Mark…sort of. He loved me…or so I thought. For five weeks, I ignored the signs. Pretended that the increasing distance between us didn't exist, tried harder than ever to be perfect, adorable, fun. Forgave him his ever-shorter answers. Until night #38 of our relationship, when he invited me over.

When I first walked in from the cold autumn air, I was pleasantly surprised. The table was set, he'd cooked dinner, there were candles. A fire snapped and hissed in the fireplace. *Huh,* I thought. *I guess he just needed to adjust to things. Clearly, he wants to be with me, or else why would he go to all this fuss? Maybe he's got something special planned! Like an engagement ring!* For the first time since Santa Fe, I relaxed. Of course Mark loved me. Of course he did.

Mark poured some wine, offered Brie and crackers and then broke up with me.

It was the timing, see. Things were really crackling at the company, and a serious relationship…not the right time. He was sure I understood and indeed, felt the same way.

"Oh," I said faintly. "Right." I paused. "So…I guess we should take things slow, huh?"

Mark looked at me with those liquid, dark eyes of his, a searching, soulful look. "Callie, you're so…um, amazing. But I'm not really at a point in my life where I can invest what you deserve. And you deserve it all. It's not that the feelings aren't there…of course you're special to me. You know that, right?"

"Sure," I whispered, my eyes stinging. "So…we'll just play it by ear and reevaluate in, what…six months?"

The fire popped. Mark looked down at his plate and began breaking a cracker into pieces. "To be honest, I can't even look that far ahead. I really wish I could, but…well, I can't ask you to wait around until I can make a commitment."

"No, no! I don't mind waiting!" *Oh, the humanity!* Mrs. Obama said. "I mean…Mark, this whole time in Santa Fe, it was…" My voice broke a little. "It was so…special."

"It really was," he acknowledged, then added in a terrible Bogart impression, "We'll always have Santa Fe."

Oh, God. That sounded horribly final! Desperate, I stammered and blathered, hoping to change his mind. "I—I just feel like we have...something...we have this incredible bond, and I..."

All of a sudden, I understood the phrase *hopelessly in love.* Michelle's voice was kind in my head. *You're not supposed to have to convince him, hon.* I ignored her. "I just don't think we should...I don't think we should throw away what we feel for each other, Mark."

How I hated saying those words...and yet, I had to. I had to beg, even as I detested myself for being so...weak. So helpless. So willing to throw out dignity, so ready to trade that for whatever scraps Mark could give me. But dignity was thrown out just the same. "Please, Mark."

"Uh...well," Mark said slowly, crushing his cracker fragments into crumbs. "Callie, you're just fantastic, and I really wish I was in a different place in my life right now. But I'm not." He gave me a James Dean sort of look, lowered head and sheepish grin. "We'll be okay, right? We're friends still, I hope. I mean, I hope you'll stay for dinner. I cooked for you."

Don't stay. Have some self-respect and walk out of here.

I swallowed. "No, of course we're still friends, Mark," I said. "Of course!"

"Great," Mark said, setting aside his plate of crackers and cheese. "I knew you'd understand, Callie. Thank God you're not one of those hysterical women who can't handle being alone, right?" He grinned. "I'm starving. Wanna eat?"

"You bet," I said. I found myself standing and following him to the dining room table. For the next hour, Mark chatted about his parents and their cruise to Norway, a couple of clients, the unfairness of the Yankees winning yet another World Series. The entire time, I murmured and nodded and even ate my damn dinner as my mind whirled. How the hell… Did I just…*agree?* Somehow, I'd just signed on the dotted line to accept this situation…this un-situation, more like it. Mark had cleverly orchestrated this so there was no scene, no real breakup, no crying…nope, we just sat down and ate, back to colleagues and coworkers. He handled it well, I had to admit.

By the time I got home that night, I'd convinced myself that Mark had been sincere. Timing…a perfectly acceptable answer! Everything he said…true! Mark was right! I did deserve it all! For the next little while, Betty Boop and I held out hope. Tried to be perky and waited for Mark to notice me again and be ready and in a place in his life where he could give me what I deserved. But the days slid past, and my lifelong optimism eroded bit by bit, until even I couldn't deny the truth. He didn't want me.

I should've hated him, but that was impossible. First of all, I loved him (the devil's in the details, right?). He was funny and talented and a great boss, loved his work and valued his employees. He'd send me goofy e-mails or links to odd news stories, sometimes texted me during a meeting with a comment about a client, called me at home if something occurred to him. When he complimented me on my work, I'd feel such a rush of pride and joy…joy that faded to a chalky residue moments after he left.

Those three days in Santa Fe had been so perfect that I just couldn't get past them. I should've called Annie, gotten drunk on chocolate liqueur candies, made lists of why I hated Mark. But I didn't. I was my father's girl, and if I could've gone back in time, I would've endured that flight all over again, just to have those happiest moments back again, when I'd had all I ever wanted.

CHAPTER SIX

ON MONDAY, I HAD A date to meet Doug336 for lunch. We'd taken our relationship to the next level…that is, we'd exchanged a few e-mails, allowed each other to view a photo, checked out each other's Facebook pages, the usual cyber rituals that masqueraded as human interaction these days. Annie was very confident. "You need to get out there," she said, as if she knew all about heartbreak from the six hours she and Jack had been apart during eleventh grade. "This will help. You'll see. Mark will be a distant memory any day now."

It was possible, I thought, picking out my clothes even more carefully than usual. Not only was I meeting the guy who might be The One—it was Muriel's first day of work at Green Mountain Media. The very thought had my stomach cramping.

"No, no," I instructed my reflection. "It's all good. And you look very cute." I definitely needed some positive affirmation today, needed to look the part of Young Professional Cool Creative Director. Today's choice was an adorable, sunshiny yellow dress paired with killer red heels. Red-and-orange beaded necklace, orange suede bag.

Damien watched as I struggled through the office door with a tray of scones. "Can you help me out here, Damien?" I said.

"I'm busy," he returned, evidenced by the single sheet of paper he held.

"You're such a putz," I growled, finally making it into the lobby. "No scones for you."

"I'm on a diet," he said, then lowered his voice. "She's here."

I paused. "Okay. Great! Super."

Damien pulled a face—half sympathy, half disgust—and sat down at his desk.

Green Mountain Media was shaped like a triangle. Damien's domain was the foyer, a large, sunny space filled with framed prints of our work, several large ficus trees and a couch and coffee table across from Damien's glass-topped desk. Next came the art department, an open, cheerfully cluttered space featuring large-screen Macs, printers, scanners and miles of cable and cords. Here Pete and Leila reigned, speaking in their computer-geek acronyms. As the triangle narrowed, there was the conference room, then Karen's office, which was large and dark due to the perpetually drawn blinds (we suspected Karen was part vampire, as she hated mornings and sunshine). Across from Karen was Fleur's office. As creative director, I got a bigger office, closer to the apex where Mark held court in the point of the triangle. Now, the previously empty office directly across from me held our newest employee. Muriel.

As I approached, my heart tightened. Mark was leaning in Muriel's doorway. "Hey, Callie," he said, smiling as if this were a normal day.

"Morning, boss," I said, reassured that my voice sounded normal. I paused, the tray of scones growing heavier. My purse slipped off my shoulder. "Hi, Muriel. Welcome."

She stood next to Mark, one bony hip tilted out.

"Hello," she said, giving me a quick once-over. Her nostrils twitched. "How are you, Calliope?"

"Great!" I answered. "How about you? Getting organized?"

"Already done."

Muriel was beautiful, I couldn't deny that. Her hair was black, pulled back into a severe twist, revealing her narrow, ice-queen face. Glittering pale gray eyes, white, white skin with two fiery spots of pink glowing on her cheeks, as if she were burning from fever. She wore a very fitted black suit—Armani maybe, sleek and vicious—and a black silk shirt. Couldn't have been more than a size two, and I instantly felt quite large and very soft. "Well. I should put these scones—"

"Do you have a moment?" she asked.

I glanced at Mark, who looked blandly back. "Um…sure! Of course."

"I'll leave you girls alone," Mark said, standing aside to let me by. "You look nice today, Callie."

"Thank you," I said. He smiled and closed the door. Setting the tray down on the only available surface— Muriel's desk—I felt a little sweaty. Muriel's perfume suffused the air.

"It looks great in here," I said, forcing a smile. Great if you liked sterile, that was. Over the weekend, her office had been redone—the standard-issue desk had been replaced with something modern and white. A sumptuous white leather chair sat behind it. On the walls hung black-and-white Ansel Adams prints—well, given the de Veers money, they were probably originals. Black bookcases, white walls. There was a picture of her and Mr. de Veers in ski gear standing on some mountaintop. I seemed to remember that Muriel's mother died when she was young.

Muriel sat behind her desk. "Have a seat," she said, looking at me with those glittering eyes. I obeyed, feeling like I'd been called to the principal's office (something that had never happened in real life, let me assure you).

"Would you like a scone?" I asked. "I made them this morning."

"No, thank you," she said, folding her hands primly.

"So," I said. "What's up?"

Once again she looked me up and down as if surveying a bug. "I thought you should be aware that Mark's told me about the little…fling…you two had last year," she said.

Fling? Is that what he called it? My heart flinched. All of me flinched, apparently, because she smiled, an evil little Cruella De Vil smile. "I didn't want you to think you had to hide that information," she said. "It must be quite hard, still having feelings for your employer."

"Oh, no," I lied. "I'm fine. I've known Mark most of my life, and we're very good friends. Thank you so much, though." I tried to match her cool tone, but it was hard when my face was practically bubbling with heat.

"Mmm-hmm," she murmured, raising a silken eyebrow. "Well, I commend you for not letting it get in your way. I'm not sure I could work with the man I loved if the feeling wasn't mutual."

Wow. I mean, really. *Wow!* It took balls of steel to say that. "I'm fine, let me assure you," I said, though my throat was tightening.

"Well! Good for you, Callie," she said. "Now, you'll have to excuse me. I have work to do."

I stood up, my legs unsteady, and walked to the door, hoping not to look as shaken as I felt.

"Callie?" Muriel called, writing something on a pad.

"Yes?"

She didn't look up. "Don't forget your snack."

"They're for everyone," I said defensively. "I always bake on Mondays. Production meetings." She didn't answer, just shot me a dubious look, as if she knew I'd be galumphing across the hall with my scones and stuffing all twelve of them into my mouth.

Taking care not to accidentally let the tray, oh, I don't know...hit her in the face, I picked it up and left, closing the door quietly behind me.

THE NATURE OF ADVERTISING is to make people yearn for something. As creative director, my job was basically to come up with a concept...the big picture, the general idea of an ad campaign. But it was more than that, too. To me, there was something magical about my job. When I had an account, I got the chance to repackage something, to focus only on its good qualities, to convince others to like it, want it and need it. In essence, I focused on the positive. That had always been a strength of mine.

Mark was the account exec on all of our clients, though I knew Fleur had high hopes to move up the food chain. For the time being, she worked under me, doing the grunt work of writing the copy before giving it to me for approval and tweaking. Pete and Leila took care of the graphics side of things, the layout and fonts and color schemes and all that fun stuff. Karen booked ad space, paid the bills and dealt with our vendors, and Damien answered the phones, made appointments and worshipped Mark.

And now there was Muriel. We'd never had anyone work on just one account before, but then again, Bags to Riches was our biggest client. They wanted to do a huge national ad campaign—radio, television, Internet, print, billboards, everything. This morning, Muriel was supposed to give us the lowdown on what the client wanted, and then we'd finesse some ideas. I already had a few mock-ups prepared.

And so, ten minutes later, the entire staff filed into the conference room. I set down the tray of scones in the middle of the table.

"God loves you, Callie," Pete said, lunging for one, then breaking a bit off and feeding it to Leila like a male cardinal.

"Those look great," Mark said, grinning at me. "Muriel, Callie's an incredible baker. Want one?"

"Oh, absolutely," she said, smiling up at him. "I'm starving."

"Bloody hell, don't tell me you're that thin *and* you eat carbs. Life's so unfair. Hi, I'm Fleur Eames." Fleur stopped dunking her tea bag and stuck out her hand. "Sorry I'm late. You wouldn't *believe* what happened to me on the way in. Fucking deer almost smashed my windscreen, yeah?"

"You hit a deer?" I blurted.

Fleur glanced at me. "Almost. I had to pull over and settle down, though. Have a ciggie, calm my nerves."

"Nice to meet you," Muriel said.

"*Great* meeting you," Fleur said. "Heard oodles of good stuff about you."

"Ass-kisser," Damien whispered, taking his customary seat next to me.

"Okay," Mark said. "Let's get down to business. Everyone's met Muriel, we've got Callie's great scones…" He smiled at me, and I forced a smile back. Good old Callie, scone baker. "Muriel, want to get us rolling? Tell us everything we need to know about Bags to Riches."

"Absolutely. And let me just say I'm thrilled to be here." She smiled at each of us in turn, then cleared her throat and reached for her notes. "Bags to Riches is an outerwear company that makes clothing out of a unique blend of cotton and plastic grocery bags."

Her voice was confident and loud, as if she were addressing a stadium. "Our demographic is young, affluent people who enjoy outdoor activities, such as hiking and biking." She paused, and made eye contact with each one of us, her expression grave. Damien kicked me under the table. "Our goal is to reach these people in a variety of media and increase sales. Thank you."

With that, she sat down. Mark gave her a confused look, but she just smiled demurely and looked at her hands. "Um…okay. Great, Muriel," Mark said. "Well, Callie, any ideas?"

I glanced from Mark to Muriel. What Muriel had just told us was something so basic a fourth grader could've presented it. Usually, Mark would give us much more detailed information…how long the campaign would last, which markets were underselling, which were doing great, product tie-ins, etc. "Are you…um, are you all done?" I asked her.

"Why, yes, I am, Callie," she answered. "Mark said you were presenting some ideas. May we see them?"

"Of course," I said, glancing at Pete, who shrugged. "Well, obviously what makes this company unique is the grocery bag element, and that's something we'll definitely focus on."

"Obviously," Muriel murmured.

I looked at her. "My first idea is geared toward male consumers, college grads, twenty-five to forty years old, earning more than fifty grand a year." I reached down next to my chair, grabbed the first poster (PowerPoint was fine, but I was a little old school in presentations) and read my tagline aloud. *"Kick some butt, save the planet. BTR Outerwear."* The poster showed a good-looking, sweaty guy, his backpack next to him, standing at the top of a mountain, overlooking a vast wilderness.

Mark smiled, and the usual tingle of pride fluttered in my stomach.

"Oh, nice work," Leila said.

"Delicious," Karen murmured, taking a bite of scone. "Him, I mean." She jerked her chin at the poster.

"I'm thinking all our ads should be shot in national parks," I continued. "If BTR coughs up some money, we can say we're a proud sponsor of the Yellowstone Foundation or what have you, and—"

"He's not even wearing Bags to Riches clothes," Muriel protested. The rest of us paused.

"It's a comp, Mure," Mark said, patting her hand. "It's a mock-up." At her look of incomprehension, he continued. "It's not the real ad…it's just the idea for the ad."

"Oh," she said. "Well." She squinted at the poster. "The name of the company is Bags to Riches, not BTR."

"Right," I said. "Well, that's another thing. I think Bags to Riches is a little…off. See, it implies that someone's getting rich off this, and while I'm sure that's quite true—" everyone but Muriel laughed "—I think we should abbreviate."

"I doubt my father will go for that," Muriel said, scribbling something in a notebook. "Moving on, Callie, do you have anything else?"

I glanced at Mark, who was looking at the surface of the table. "Yes, I do, Muriel," I said. "Female demographic." I moved to the next comp, something I was quite proud of. It was a stock photo of a woman rock climbing somewhere in Bryce Canyon, dangling from a precipice, teeth gritted in concentration, dripping with sweat. *"Redefining 'bag lady.' BTR Outerwear."*

"Oh, that's fantastic, Callie!" Pete cheered.

Mark nodded approvingly. "Bull's-eye," he murmured.

I smiled. "Now, I'm not sure how much we can afford, but I'd love to use a couple of celebs who champion the environment—Leonardo DiCaprio, for example."

"Why would we use him? Does he hike?" Muriel asked.

I paused. Looked at Mark again, who was suddenly engrossed in doodling. Glanced at Damien, whose eyes were very wide. "Well, if we get a well-known face, especially one associated with a cause, we brand BTR—"

"Bags to Riches," she corrected.

"Right." I paused. "Okay, well…people want to be like celebrities, right? That's why J. Crew sells out of whatever Michelle Obama's wearing."

"J. Crew is not our competitor, Callie," Muriel said condescendingly. Leila winced.

"I know that," I said. "What I mean is, the First Lady has influence. Which is true in any ad campaign that uses celebrities, whether they're hawking milk or Nikes. So if we had Leo in a BTR ad, I'm sure we'd see a bump in sales."

"Hmm," Muriel said. "Interesting."

No one made eye contact. This was Advertising 101. I glanced at Mark, who was looking at Muriel with a very tender expression. He leaned over and placed his hand over hers.

"It's a lot to take in," he said. "Well, this has been great. Thanks, Callie. We'll get back to you and talk about next steps. Oh, and by the way, the BTR people are coming out later this week. We'll be doing an event on Friday. Participation mandatory."

"What kind of event?" Damien asked, immediately suspicious.

"A little hike so Charles can see the beauty of a Vermont sunset," Mark said, ignoring Damien's stricken expression. "Drinks and dinner afterward."

JUST BEFORE LUNCH, Fleur slipped into my office and closed the door. "What the fuck-all was Mark thinking?" she hissed. "Yeah, he's shagging Muriel, but did he have to hire her? She doesn't know a bloody thing!" She flopped onto my couch.

The thing about Fleur was that when she was truly upset, her accent slipped, something she was completely unaware of. Her accent was in full force now. I suspected she wanted gossip.

"It's Mark's company," I said calmly, turning away from my computer. "And I'm sure Muriel will…" I paused. "Well, she'll catch on. Obviously, her dad wants her on this account."

"Callie," Fleur whispered. "I've got much more experience than Muriel." Accent gone, revealing shades of New York. The truth came out. "Just because my father doesn't own the company doesn't mean I should have to take orders from that frigid and ignorant bitch."

"Listen," I said quietly, "don't go there. Just do your job well and trust that Mark will work things out."

"She's making more than me. More than you, too, as a matter of fact. Karen told me."

"Karen shouldn't have—"

"All right, all right, she didn't tell me. I just happened to see some paperwork when I was in there for something else." She sighed. "Figured you should know. You and Mark were…well. Whatever."

The accent was back. I glanced at my watch. "I have to run, Fleur. I'm sorry. I'm meeting someone for lunch."

"Oh, right!" she said. "The plan!"

"What plan?" I asked, closing a file on my computer.

"The plan to make Mark green with envy!" she whispered gleefully.

"Oh, I'm not really going—"

"Now, now, no need to explain! I'll walk you out."

Sighing—Fleur could be a bit much—I grabbed my bag and we walked into the foyer, where Mark was signing something for Damien. "Have fun on your date!" Fleur called loudly as I pulled open the door to leave. Mark and Damien looked up.

"You're going on a date?" Damien asked, as shocked as if I'd just announced I was getting a sex change.

I blushed. "Well, I'm just meeting a…a friend, that's all. For a quick lunch."

Mark's eyes were…knowing. Smiling, too, the type of smile a man uses when a woman…when he…ah, shit, I was losing my train of thought. His eyes were warm, as if we shared a secret, and his generous mouth pulled up at one corner. For a second I—

"How thrilling," Damien drawled. "Toodles."

"Have fun," Mark said. His eyes wandered down to my legs, and when he looked up again, he gave me a little wink, and my dopey heart leaped.

"See you in a bit," I said. *Get over him,* Mrs. Obama said. *I'm trying,* I answered silently.

Doug336 and I were meeting at Toasted & Roasted, one of the three restaurants in our fair city. It was a little café known mostly for its coffee, the usual endless variety of lattes, mochaccinos and chais, but it also served soup and sandwiches for lunch. It was a pretty space with brick walls and lots of plants, the old tile floor intricately patterned. "Hey, Callie," the owner called as I came in.

"Hi, Guy," I answered. "What's good today?"

"Got some nice hot pastrami and Swiss on rye," he said. "Also a Philly cheese steak special."

Both sounded fantastic...but both were dangerous date foods, requiring much chewing and many napkins. They were really more of an "alone" type of food, where you could get grease on your chin and really enjoy. First impressions were so important, though, and I didn't want Doug336 to have a mental image of me with a cheesy wad of steak on my bosom. "I guess I'll have a cup of the soup," I said regretfully.

"Coming up," Guy answered cheerfully.

At that moment, the door to Toasted & Roasted opened, and in came my mother. And Louis. Upon sighting me, Louis's pale face lit up with creepy delight.

"Well, well, well," he said. "Someone looks good enough to eat."

"Hi, Mom!" I said brightly, giving my mother a kiss and making sure she stood between myself and Voldemort there. "Hi, Louis."

"Hello, honey, fancy running into you. And you do look nice. Louis is right." A Grinchy grin spread across Louis's face, and he stepped a little closer to me. Oh, God. He'd obviously come right from work.

"Louis, you're...you still have your gloves on," I said, swallowing against the images that leaped with unfortunate clarity into my brain. Latex gloves meant he was...preparing someone.

"Oopsy," he said. Without taking his eyes off me, he peeled off the gloves, slowly, as if doing a striptease, then did a throat-scraping snort to clear his postnasal drip. Dear God.

"Calliope, did you know *your father* has been calling me?" Mom asked, frowning as she surveyed the take-out choices of the day. "Of course, I don't pick up. Does he have a brain tumor or something I should know about?"

"Um, nope, no brain tumor, Mom. He has more time now that he's retired. Maybe he just…needs to talk." She gave me a dubious look and said nothing.

"I was just thinking about you today, Calliope," Louis murmured. "How I'd…*display* you." His anemic eyebrow rose.

"Come on, Louis!" I blurted. "That's a horrible come-on line, not to mention terrifying!" He said nothing, just smirked. "Well, I'm meeting a friend, so I'd better run," I added, backing away. "Have a nice lunch!" With that, I scampered into the corner and took a seat.

Toasted & Roasted started to fill up with the lunch crowd. I waved occasionally, since I knew just about everyone in town. There was Shaunee Cole, one of the River Rats. Dave, Annie's brother, was on his phone. "Hey, gorgeous," he called to me, pausing in his conversation. I waved back. Always loved Dave.

In four more minutes, Doug was going to be late, I noted, glancing at my red Hello Kitty collector's edition wristwatch. I figured I'd give him ten minutes, then leave. Granted, I'd have happily waited hours for Mark…had, in fact, waited for months, if not years. I squelched the small lance of pain that thought caused and texted Annie to distract myself. *Am meeting Doug336. Please choose color of your dress as maid of honor. Will call with a report.* Annie was taking quite the interest in my love life, determined that I, too, should end up as smugly happy as she and Jack were.

Ah-ha! Here was Doug336 coming in right now. I waved (not too vigorously, didn't want to seem psychotic or desperate). He didn't see me. Alas, the guy behind him did, and that guy was Ian McFarland, veterinarian. He froze, then gave a small nod before fixing his attention firmly on the specials board.

Oh, calm down, I thought. *I'm not here for you.* I stood up and walked over to greet my date. Ian didn't look away from the board, reminding me of Josephine's early years, when she'd cover her eyes to become invisible.

"Hi, there, Doug." I smiled my hundred-watter and noted from the corner of my eye that Ian McFarland let out a sigh of relief. For heaven's sake!

"Hi, Callie! Great to meet you," Doug said.

"I got us a table in the back," I said. "Do you want to order?"

"Nah, I'm not here for the food," he grinned. "Lead away."

Ooh! I liked Doug336! He was cute! And how nice for Dr. Stuck-Up to see that a man liked me! So there! "Hello, Dr. McFarland," I said.

"Hello, Miss Grey," he said, not taking his eyes off the specials board.

"Can I call you Ian?" I asked, just to be a pain.

He cut his eyes to me, then looked back at the menu. "Of course."

"Have a wonderful day, Ian," I said, turning away to my date. *That's right, Ian. I have a date. And he's cuter than you.*

"You're even prettier than your picture," Doug336 said as we sat down.

I smiled. "Thank you, Doug." He was quite attractive, with longish dark hair and hazel eyes. Nice build, jeans, T-shirt, a woven bracelet made of some shiny fiber.

I hadn't been on a first date in a long, long time. In fact, I'd never been on a date with someone I didn't know pretty well. "So," I said, grinning so my dimple showed, something that always worked well for me. "Where shall we start? I have to admit, you're my first Internet date ever."

"An Internet virgin," Doug murmured. "Nice." I blinked. "How about a basic exchange of information?" he suggested.

"Sure," I agreed, suddenly hesitant. "Well, I work at an ad agency. Um, I have an older sister and a younger brother. Lived in Vermont most of my life, though I went to college in Pennsylvania and lived in Boston for a few years. Never married, no kids, two nieces."

"Do you live alone?" he asked.

"No, I live with my grandfather, actually. He's um…" I paused, not wanting to share Noah's issues with a stranger. "We're very close."

"I have a housemate, too," Doug answered. "She's kind of a shrew, but it's her house, so what can you do?"

"Oh, that's too bad," I said. "Are you looking for another place?"

"Well, it's my mother, so I'm stuck."

Strike one. "Why don't you move?" I asked.

"I'm broke," he said with a deprecating smile.

Strike two. Not to be financially prejudiced, but a broke thirty-three-year-old who lives with his mama…the positive indicators were not exactly raining down. *Mark and Muriel,* Michelle Obama reminded me. *You're moving on, remember?* Right. Plus, the surly vet had just sat down nearby, and for obvious reasons, I wanted him to see me interacting successfully with a male of my own age.

"So what do you do for a living, Doug?" I asked. Out of the corner of my eye, I could see Ian unfolding the *Wall Street Journal.* Before Doug could answer, my mother and Louis approached, brown bags in hand.

"Callie, are you on a *date?*" Mom asked, not bothering to keep the shock and horror from her voice.

"Hello," Louis said, standing much, much too close to our table. Doug and I both looked up. "I'm Louis. Calliope's special friend."

"He's not," I said. "Mom, Louis, this is Doug. Doug, my mother, Eleanor Misinski, and Louis Pinser, her assistant."

"Nice to meet you," Doug said.

"What are your intentions toward Callie?" Louis said in that silky, serial-killer voice. "Is this serious? Should I be concerned, Calliope?"

"Okay! Bye now," I said. "Bye, Louis. You may go. Off with you now."

My mother took Louis's arm and pulled him back a few steps. "I hope you have fun," she said in that sympathetic and somber tone she used at work. She sighed tragically—poor woman, had her daughter learned nothing?—and guided Louis out the front door.

I took a deep breath and refocused on my date. "Sorry," I said, smiling sheepishly. "You were about to tell me what you do for a living."

"I'm an artisan," he said, his face lighting up. "I use organic materials in unexpected applications to try to get people to pay more attention to our natural gifts." It was clearly a recitation Doug used often. He leaned back in his chair and grinned.

"Oh," I said. "Ah." I tried not to hold the whole granola/artisan/crunchy Vermont thing against him... after all, you couldn't go forty feet in this state without tripping over a potter or a weaver or a sculptor. My own grandfather was quite an artisan, though I was fairly sure Noah would stick a fork in his eye before using that particular label.

"So what do you actually make?" I asked, taking a spoonful of soup. Ah. Broccoli and cheese. Delicious.

"I make plant holders out of human hair," Doug said, and I choked. Grabbed a napkin and wheezed away, coughing, tears in my eyes, swallowing convulsively. My eyes dropped to his bracelet. Blerk! It was hair! Someone's hair! I wheezed harder, horror and hilarity thrashing in equal measure.

"Wow," I managed. Ian McFarland shot me a glance, and I tried to smile, gave him a feeble wave.

"You okay?" Doug asked.

"Oh, sure," I said, finally getting my breath back. "So. Human hair. Wow."

"I know," Doug said proudly. "No one's really doing that these days, so I've cornered the market."

"There's really a market for human hair macramé?" I asked. "Um, I mean... Human hair. Wow."

Steee-rike three! I suppressed the urge to do that cool little punching thing the home plate umpires do, but come on! Doug336 of the human hair craft corner was not the kind of guy to replace Mark.

Appetite slain, I tried to tune out Doug as he waxed rhapsodic about the strength and versatility of different types of hair…red, brunette, the rare natural blond. Glancing surreptitiously to my left, I saw that Ian was engrossed in an article. Nice way to spend a lunch, reading and eating, two of my favorite pastimes. And he'd ordered the pastrami, lucky bastard. It looked fantastic.

Across from me, Doug laughed at something he said, and I snapped to.

"So…" I paused, and curiosity got the better of me. "Where do you get the hair? From a salon or something?"

"No, not a salon. I have my sources," he said. His eyes rose to my head. "You have very pretty hair, by the way." I swallowed. "Want to go back to my place?"

"So you can scalp me?" Here I'd thought Louis was creepy! I couldn't wait to call Annie.

"No." He laughed. "So we can fool around. My mom's a heavy sleeper."

"Jeesh!" I blurted. "I'm sorry, Doug. This isn't going to work. I'm sure you're very…uh…creative and, um…fun, but I don't think there's a…a future here."

"Fine! Thanks for wasting my time." Doug stood up and left, just like that, stomping like a sullen three-year-old. Heads turned. I wondered if anyone noticed his bracelet. Or his bald spot, which caught the light as he went outside.

I glanced at Ian McFarland. He was looking at me with his icy blue eyes, the way you'd eye roadkill. "Everything all right, Callie?" he asked.

"Oh, everything's great, Ian," I answered. "How's your lunch? The soup was wonderful. Whoops, look at the time. Must run. Have a wonderful day."

CHAPTER SEVEN

STEPPING INTO NOAH'S workshop was like entering a cathedral.

The old mill building had once been part of the lumber industry on which Georgebury was founded. The ceiling was forty feet high, so the place echoed like a canyon. The walls were rough-hewn brick, the floor made from uneven, unvarnished wide-planked oak, worn smooth as glass and stained nut brown from more than a hundred years of footsteps. Along one wall was Noah's workbench, lit by an old copper pharmacy light; in the corner was a hideous plaid recliner where he sometimes napped and which the health department really should condemn. Fifty feet long, forty feet wide, the room was suffused with the smell of a century and a half of wood.

There were other smells, too, of course…polyurethane, smoke from the woodstove on the far wall, the pleasant, oily smell of Noah's tools and occasionally that of wet dog, since Bowie stayed with Noah during the day. But lording over everything, the strong, wonderful scent of wood, cedar and pine and oak. Even when I lived in Boston, the smell of freshly cut wood had me turning to look for my grandfather.

At the moment, Noah had three boats in various stages of completion. One was a kayak, the type that had made him quite revered in the world of wooden boat paddlers. Long, sleek and lean, the bow so slim that it would slice through the water, this one was for ocean racing. Another one was, in Noah's terms, "for idiots like yourself, Callie," by which he meant for people who enjoyed paddling around a lake looking at the pretty birdies and trees. Very hard to tip, that model, but still graceful and lovely. The third boat was quite pretty, too…this one was an Adirondack fishing boat, and even though it was only half finished, I could picture Jay Gatsby in it, casting a line over the side while he yearned for that shallow tramp, Daisy.

"Noah?" I called. Bowie's head popped up, and he yipped twice as he leaped to his feet, trotting over to see me. "Hi, boy," I said, petting his big and beautiful head. "Where's Noah, huh?"

"Right here, right here," my grandfather grumbled, emerging from the back room where he kept his supplies. "What do you want?"

"I'm great, thanks! You're so sweet to ask." He rolled his eyes, unamused. "I just wanted to remind you, dear Noah, that everyone's coming here for dinner, so you should come in and wash up."

My grandfather scowled—Santa with a pounding hangover. "Do I have to?" he asked. "Seem to remember I can't stand half the people in my own family."

"Stop whining," I said. "Yes, you have to. And it's not half. It's more like a third."

"Fine, fine," he muttered. "Who's coming?"

"The usual suspects," I said. "Freddie, Hester, the girls, Mom." I paused. "Dad."

"What?" Noah said. "Both your parents? Does your mother know?"

"No," I answered. "I figured it'd be better as a surprise."

"That son of mine is a fuck-up," Noah grumbled, shaking his head. "And your mother! She'll gut him with her fork. What are you thinking, Callie girl?" He ran a gnarled hand through his thatch of white hair and gave me a look.

"Well, here's the thing, Noah." I took a deep breath. "Dad wants to get back together with Mom, and he asked me to help him out…"

"He never should've left her, the stupid fool. I never even looked at another woman once I met your grandmother."

I smiled. "I know," I said. "But Dad's…well, he's trying, anyway."

"He's still goin' over jackass hill, if you ask me," Noah said, referring to my father's eternal adolescence.

"Well, he's always been a good father," I said. It was true. If you discounted the cheating-on-Mom part, that is.

"A good father loves his children's mother," Noah said.

"Okay, well, everyone's still coming."

"I'll take dinner in my room."

"Oh, no, you won't," I said firmly. "This is a family dinner. Even Freddie's coming."

"Speakin' of jackass hill," Noah grunted. "Hasn't he finished college yet?"

"No. He's taking a year off to figure out what he wants to do, as he's told you eighteen times. Hester's coming with the girls, and of course, me, your favorite. So you're eating with us." I steered him out of the shop and into the kitchen, where the smell of roast chicken greeted us warmly.

"I still have sanding to do," he objected.

"You know I'll do it for you later, old man. No excuses. You're eating with us."

"You're so cruel, Callie," Noah said, sitting down to unstrap his leg. "Bowie, your mama, she's a mean one."

I straightened from checking the chicken. "Mean? Didn't I just clean this entire house, including that terrifying abyss you call a bedroom, where, by the way, I found four dirty plates and six glasses, not to mention the bottle of Dewar's you think I don't know about. Don't I cook you dinner every night, old man? Don't I sand your boats when you complain that your arthritis hurts when we both know that you really just hate sanding? And get that leg off the table."

"All right, all right, I take it back," he said. "You're not half-bad."

I HOSTED A FAMILY DINNER about once a month, though I alternated parental invitations. Still, my mother didn't object when she came through the door an hour later and saw dear old Dad standing there, grinning sheepishly at her as he hugged my brother. No. She smiled, which was much more terrifying.

"Tobias," she said in a mellifluous and deadly tone. If a cobra could speak, I'm sure it would sound exactly like my mom.

"Eleanor," Dad said. "You look beautiful tonight."

"Attaboy, Dad," Freddie said, helping himself to some wine. "Flattery's a good place to start." Apparently, Fred was in on the plan as well.

"Thank you, Tobias," Mom said. "You yourself look—" she scanned him up and down "—very well. How's the syphilis?"

"I don't have—" Dad began sharply, then remembered he was wooing his lady love. "I'm 100 percent healthy," he said in a gentler tone. "How are things with you?"

"Wonderful," Mom answered, not blinking. I swear the air temperature dropped five degrees.

"Hi, Mom," I said, kissing her on the cheek.

"Calliope!" she exclaimed. "Thank you for having us." Her dark eyes narrowed. "So nice to include…*your father.*"

"I'm scared," Freddie whispered, grinning at me. "Hold me, Callie."

"Would you like some wine, Mom?" I offered.

"Absolutely."

"How are things at the funeral home?" I asked, hoping to score points with a subject near and dear to her heart.

"Wonderful," she said, her tone a bit less terrifying. "Louis just did a reconstruction on a man who was hit by a rogue tire iron. His head looked like a bowl of SpaghettiOs."

"What exactly is a rogue tire iron?" Freddie asked, fascinated. "Shit, that must've been a mess!"

"Oh, it was," Mom said, warming to her subject. "You couldn't even tell where his—"

"Stop!" I yelped. "Please, Mom!"

"Callie, how can you be such a wuss when you grew up in a funeral home?" Mom wondered. "Death is in your blood, after all."

"Death is *not* in my blood," I said impatiently. "And it's not like I got to choose where we lived."

"Anyway," my mother said, giving me a cool look before turning her attention back to her son. "His face was—"

"Oh, look, Hester and the girls are here!" I announced. "I'll just run out and help." With that, I galloped into the rainy evening.

"Is that Dad's car?" Hester said, heaving herself out of her Volvo with some difficulty, a reminder to me to go easy on the cake batter.

"Hi, Auntie!" Josephine said, flinging her arms around my waist. "Want to braid my hair? Guess what? I'm in the school chorus! We're singing 'Greensleeves'! Braid my hair!"

"That's great, honey! I'll braid your hair in a little while, okay?" I said, smooching my younger niece. "Hi, Bronte, sweetie-pie."

Bronte glared at me, her earbuds firmly in place. "Hi," she grumbled. Ah, adolescence.

"I'm so happy to see you. I love you. You're gorgeous and brilliant," I said.

"Calm down, Callie," she said, but she gave me a kiss and trudged inside, Josephine prancing at her heels.

"Is that indeed Dad's car, Callie?" my sister repeated.

I sighed. "Yes. I thought it would be nice for all of us to get together."

"Nice, Callie? As in, 'It would be nice to have my kidneys torn out by a lion while I'm still alive?' That kind of nice?"

"Yes! Exactly what I was going for!" I answered. "Let's not exaggerate, Hester. It's not like they're never together."

"Public events only," Hester said. "With lots of other people to distract and confuse and block." She looked at me in exasperation. "You're an idiot, you know that? What are you doing? Trying to get them back together?"

"No, no," I said. "Well…Dad…um, never mind."

"Dad what? Is he dying?"

"No! You and Mom…he's not dying. He just…he wants to make amends with Mom, that's all."

"Fuck," Hester said. "Listen, why don't I leave the girls here, and I'll go and lie down on the highway and hope to get run over instead?"

"Well, as fun as that sounds, get your ass inside and stop complaining," I said. "I made a gorgeous dinner. Come eat."

My sister obeyed. I took a cleansing breath of the cool, damp air, said a little prayer for peace and followed her inside.

Family gatherings were…um, let's see, what's the word I'm looking for?… Hell. They were hell. Being the middle child, I served as referee and confidante, hostess and martyr. Did I feel we should get together once in a while? Sure. Did I *want* my family all together? Theoretically, yes. In reality, dear God, no.

But Dad had asked, and even though his odds were probably that of a baby chick surviving a stroll across the Daytona 500 Raceway, I had to help him out. If I didn't, no one would.

For years, Dad had exemplified the sheepish charmer…*I know, I was so bad, but don't I have the twinkliest eyes? Does anyone need a new car?* Mom, on the other hand, was the ice queen, never letting Dad forget just how little she'd forgiven and forgotten. Freddie got along with everyone for the most part. Hester, like Mom, had never forgiven Dad, but she tolerated him and admitted that he was a good grandfather to the girls.

As for Noah, he was a crusty old Vermonter. He and Gran met when they were seventeen, married at eighteen, and stayed in love for thirty-nine years. Noah viewed the rest of us as somewhat retarded when it came to human relations. He may have had a point.

"Can we eat?" Noah barked from his corner, where he was busy scowling at the rest of us. "I'm so hungry, I'm gaunt. And this beer's flatter than a plate of piss."

"That's beautiful, Grampy," Bronte said.

"So now you got an attitude, huh? I just started liking you," Noah said.

"I'll get you another beer, Dad," my own father offered.

"Good, son. 'Bout time you did somethin' useful with your life," Noah returned. "Speakin' of useless, Freddie, when the hell are you goin' to graduate from that fancy-ass college of yours and stop bleedin' your parents of their life savings?"

"About five more years, Noah," Freddie said cheerfully. "I just switched my major to parapsychology. I'm going to be a ghost hunter. What do you think?" Noah, not realizing that Fred was jerking his chain, sputtered on his fresh beer. Mom, though she usually defended Fred, didn't comment, as she was willing my father to turn into a pillar of salt or something.

"I love family dinners," Hester grumbled.

"Oh, me, too," I said.

"Hey, will you chaperone some Brownie troop field trip next week?" she asked. "I have a seminar in Boston."

"Sure," I agreed. "When is it?"

"After school on Thursday," Hester answered. "Josephine really didn't want to miss it."

"Of course," I said. "Where are we going? Cabot's?" I hoped so. The creamery had a free cheese bar.

"Uh…Josephine, where are the Brownies going next week, honey?" Hester asked. Josephine, who was rubbing Bowie's tummy and sending clots of fur onto the just-vacuumed floor, jumped up.

"It's a farm, I think," she said, leaping up to clutch my waist and beg. "Can you come, Auntie? Can you? Please?" Today she was dressed in a black-sequined unitard and a purple skirt with pink Crocs.

"I sure can," I said. I had oodles of vacation time socked away, and Mark, who had no nieces or nephews, had always been great about letting me do things with Bronte and Josephine. At the thought of Mark, my heart twisted. He'd kissed Muriel when he was leaving the office today. On the cheek. "See you later, babe," he'd said. Not that I was eavesdropping. And Muriel's face had flushed even brighter than her usual consumptive look.

Babe. Mark had never called me babe. Honey, yes. But he called Karen honey, too, and she was basically a barracuda with legs. Once, he called me sweetpea, something so old-fashioned I'd melted (you're not surprised, are you?). Dad used to call Mom Bluebird, because, he said, she made him so happy. At this moment, she was fingering her knife and looking at him with great speculation in her eyes.

I herded my family around the dining room table, got drinks, fetched a clean fork for Josephine, who'd dropped hers, moved the centerpiece of zinnias and cosmos, which I'd picked that very evening, wiped up a spill and finally sat down. "This is nice," I said. No one answered, as they were all halfway done already. Seven minutes later, it was official. Dinner, which consisted of my famous garlic-roasted chicken, mashed potatoes with dill, homemade gravy, braised carrots and green beans almondine, all of which took me two hours of prep time, was consumed in just under thirteen minutes. Setting the table had taken more time.

"That was wonderful, Poodle," my father said, twinkling at me.

"I've got to get back to the shop," Noah grumbled, pushing his chair back and hopping out of the dining room.

"Where's your leg?" I asked. He didn't answer.

"It's under the table," Josephine said, peeking.

"So gross," Bronte grunted, pushing her potatoes around her plate.

"Maybe we can play Monopoly," Dad suggested hopefully, beaming at my mother, who was staring at the tablecloth, lost in pleasant fantasies about dismembering her ex-husband. "Eleanor? I seem to remember you loved being the iron. Would you like to be the iron again?"

"Is that your come-on line, Dad? It needs work," Freddie offered, glancing up from the message he was texting.

"Let's play Wii!" Josephine chirruped. "Callie, can we play Wii?"

"Who named that thing?" Mom asked, examining her manicure. Frequent exposure to formaldehyde made her fingernails quite strong and lovely. "Whenever I hear it, I imagine children playing with a urine-filled balloon."

Dad gave a booming laugh. "That's funny, Ellie! How about that Monopoly? Bronte, sweetheart? Want to play with your old Poppy and Grammy?"

"No," Bronte mumbled, folding her arms across her nonexistent chest.

"Fred, get off your ass and help Callie clean up," Hester said, kicking our little brother.

"You help her," he returned amiably. "Your own ass is bigger, so you'll probably be more help."

"I *worked* all day," Hester said. "So bite me, you lazy little bastard."

"You get women pregnant all day long. Who's to say

I don't do the same?" Freddie returned, raising his eyebrows innocently while Bronte snickered.

Ah, family. Meanwhile, no one was helping me clean up, either. Chugging a little more chardonnay, I then took a cleansing breath and smiled. "It's all good, it's all good," I whispered to myself.

"There's Callie, slowly going insane while we all watch," Freddie said. I smiled, grateful that someone was paying attention. "Hey, Cal, you find someone to sleep with yet?" he added.

"There are children in the room, Fred, in addition to yourself and your mental age of six," Hester said, kicking him again.

"If you insist on marriage," Mom said thoughtfully, "why don't you give Louis a try? He's so talented."

My brother snorted. "Yes, Callie, the man has a way with a corpse, so—"

"Fred, quiet. Mom, no talk of Louis at the table," I said. "Besides, Dad asked if you wanted to play Monopoly with him," I reminded her.

Mom slid her chilly gaze over to Dad. "What do you want, Tobias?" she hissed.

"Is there any dessert?" Bronte asked.

"Yes, yes, get out while you can, both of you," I answered. "Run. There's pie and chocolate chip cookies in the pantry. You and Josephine can cut it up, okay? Ice cream's in the basement freezer."

Dad frowned, doubtless hoping to use the girls' presence as a shield. Slightly daunted, he nevertheless forged ahead. "Well, since you asked, I was hoping we might…put the past behind us, Eleanor. Rekindle our relationship." Mom said nothing. "You're the only woman I ever loved," Dad added. His sincerity was somewhat undercut as he glanced at me and winked. Hester gagged on her wine, but he ignored her, as she was cynical and not likely to support his quixotic mission.

Mom gave him an almost fond look, sort of the way a cat looks at a baby chipmunk… *Hey, thanks for entertaining me! I'm going to chew off your legs now, okay?* "Do go on," she said.

Dad, who could be run over by a tank and not notice, continued. "Well, Eleanor, we're not getting any younger. You've never been with another man, according to our son, anyway—"

Fred made a strangled sound…unlike Hester and me, he never learned to keep his mouth shut when our parents milked us for information on the other.

"—and we have to start thinking about the rest of our lives. You don't want to end up alone, do you? We have a lot of good years left." He sat up straighter. Gave Mom the twinkly-crinkly smile. "What do say, Ellie? Shall we try again?"

Mom smiled. Fred, Hester and I leaned farther away from the imminent explosion. "Well, Tobias," she said. "You know, I'll think about it…wait a minute, wait a minute. I don't have to think about because I'm…what's the word? Sober. Yes. I'm sober. So the answer would have to be…no."

"Why not try?" Dad suggested. "If it doesn't work, well, at least you were open to something new."

Again with the almost (emphasis on *almost*) fond smile. "Why on earth would I want to be with you again, Tobias?" she asked.

Dad shot me a nervous look. "Well," he said, and I had to give him points for courage, "I love you, Eleanor. Despite my reprehensible behavior—" here he inserted his best George Clooney grin...*yes, I'm a bad dog, but check out these attractive laugh lines!* "—I've never stopped. These past two decades, I've regretted my actions deeply—" Clearly, Dad had rehearsed this "—and I've learned the errors of my ways."

"I didn't ask about what's in it for you, Tobias," Mom said in that smooth and icy voice that had struck fear into our young hearts. "What's in it for me?"

Dad paused. "Companionship?" he suggested.

"I'll get a dog," she answered.

Dad shifted. "Well, okay, if you want me to be blunt...what about sex?"

"Siblings! Shall we go?" I suggested. "Give Mom and Dad some privacy?"

My brother and sister didn't move. "This is better than *Tool Academy,*" Freddie said, taking a pull on his beer. Hester, too, seemed fascinated, though more in the way a medical examiner is fascinated by a particularly gruesome murder.

Mom, uncharacteristically, said nothing, which Dad took as encouragement. "Remember, Eleanor? It never faded, did it? The passion. The urgency." He raised an eyebrow. "It was the best thing about our marriage."

"Except for your three beautiful children, of course," Freddie said.

"That had to mean something," Dad continued, ignoring his son. "People don't feel that for each other without it meaning something."

"Too bad we didn't have Republicans for parents," I observed. "You can bet the farm they never talk like this."

"There are no Republicans in Vermont," Hester said. "They died out, like the Shakers. Is there any more wine?"

Mom and Dad just stared at each other. Hope, a tiny

seedling, sprouted in my heart. Could it be? "He has always loved you, Mom," I said gently.

Mom smiled. A real smile. "I'll consider it," she said.

"What?" Hester said. "What?"

"Holy shit," Freddie added.

"If," Mom said.

"If what?" Dad asked.

"If you introduce me to each of the women you slept with while I was gestating our son."

The blood drained from my father's face. I pictured the hopeful seedling being crushed by my mother's sturdy shoe.

"Well, uh...women...there were only, ah...two, Eleanor," Dad said.

She raised an eyebrow.

"Well, okay, three," he amended. "And, uh, I'm sure I don't know what happened to them. I barely remember them. I think they moved. Far away. To, uh, New Zealand, I believe, and uh...France."

"Actually, I know where they are," Mom said. "They all live within a hundred miles of here. I've kept tabs on them over the years." She glanced at her children fondly. "I just love Google."

Hester closed her eyes and shook her head.

"So, if you're sincere, and it's true that you've always loved me and want to rekindle anything, that's what you have to do," Mom said smugly.

Man. She really did enjoy burying people.

WHEN DAD HAD LIMPED away and Hester and the girls had gone home, and Freddie and Noah were hiding out in the workshop sanding a canoe, Mom and I stood side by side, doing the dishes.

"So that was interesting," I said, rinsing a wineglass. I set it on the dishrack, where Mom picked it up and began polishing it with unsettling vigor.

"It certainly was," she answered.

I studied her from the corner of my eye. Mom was attractive in her own way…big frame, strong features, kind eyes. She wasn't ugly, but she wasn't beautiful, either. She looked…competent. Dad, on the other hand, turned heads on women ages seventeen to ninety-four, and was fairly incompetent in many ways…while Mom could probably overpower the Nazis and then climb in and drive their tank to the Allies, Dad…Dad would just surrender amiably and hope for the best.

"So are you really considering getting back with Dad?" I asked, turning my attention back to the legion of dishes.

"Of course not," she answered. "He cheated on me, Calliope."

"Right. So…no chance of forgiveness, then?" I placed another glass on the rack.

"I forgave your father long ago, Callie," she lied, not looking at me.

"Really, Mom? Because—"

"How's *your* love life, dear? Did that slovenly man in the café work out?"

"He wasn't that sloven—"

"I'll take that as a no, then," she said. "Why the sudden interest in dating? I thought you were going to ask Hester for help on the motherhood front." She snapped the dishcloth and got to work on a plate.

"No," I said slowly. "I'd…I've always wanted to get married. Have kids the old-fashioned way. Live happily ever after."

"That chair was your undoing," Mom muttered.

"It's not the chair's fault, Mom." I paused. "Just because things didn't work out with you and Dad—"

"Sweetheart, I defy you to find me three couples who've been married for more than ten years and are living happily ever after. With each other, that is. Here." She handed me back a glass. "You missed a spot."

"Noah and Gran. Nana and Dimpy," I said, naming my grandparents on both sides.

"How about a couple born after the FDR administration?" Mom prompted.

"Annie and Jack?"

"That's one. And for number two?"

I winced. "And…let's see now…okay, you win. But, Mom, I think Dad's sincere. He's never gotten over you. You know that. And here you've been, hating him with the heat of a thousand suns lo these many years. You know what they say. Hate and love are two sides of the same coin."

She gave me a look unique to her…pity, patience and mild disgust all rolled into one. "You're so naive, Callie," she said.

"True," I admitted. I paused, remembering my father's face at my birthday party. "I just can't help remembering you two when you were happy. When I think about getting married myself, finding someone who really loved me for me and all that crap, I always picture you and Dad, dancing in the living room when he came home from a trip."

Much to my surprise, her eyes filled. "Well. He stomped all over those times, didn't he?" she said thickly.

"Right, he did. But maybe you could really forgive him, Mom."

She sighed. "When someone cheats on you, Callie, they take a piece of your heart. And I don't know that you ever get it back."

I thought of Mark, and all the years I'd spent hoping for him. Waiting for him. Imagining the two of us together on that mythical front porch somewhere. Pictured him now somewhere with Muriel.

Mom had a point.

CHAPTER EIGHT

"OH, BLERK." I LOOKED in the mirror, but it was undeniable. I turned to view my backside. Mistake! "Shit, Bowie! Look at me!" He stood up and came over, licked my knee in sympathy, then collapsed to the floor to offer me his stomach. I gave him a perfunctory scratch, then surveyed the issue at hand.

This morning at work, Muriel had received a large carton from her daddy's company. With great aplomb, she'd handed out the goodies, starting in Reception with Damien, working her way down…Pete and Leila, Karen, Fleur, and then yours truly. She'd been quite stoked, laughing with Fleur, joking with Pete, dolling out clothes like it was Christmas and she was Santa. T-shirts in various colors, all with the Bags to Riches logo (a floating plastic bag). Multipocketed hiking shorts, the cute cargo type that went down to the knees. Hiking boots for everyone. A few backpacks.

And then she came to me.

"Callie," she smiled. "Here you go!" She handed me a bile-colored T-shirt, then reached in the box and withdrew a handful of fabric. A small handful.

I blinked. "Um…" I held them up. My heart sank. These weren't hiking shorts…they were bike shorts, the kind those bony praying mantis people wear on the Tour de France. "Are there any hiking shorts left?"

She pretended to glance in the box. "No, sorry. Well, there are, but they're in my size." She didn't finish the thought...*therefore you couldn't even get your arm in here.* "Callie, please. Don't make this an issue. As long as it's Bags to Riches, it doesn't matter."

Well, it mattered to me. As I stared into the mirror in my bedroom, I sighed. Miss Muriel deVeers probably weighed somewhere about ninety-seven pounds, all sinew and ropy muscle defined by countless hours with (according to Fleur) the same personal trainer who screamed at contestants on *The Biggest Loser,* a show I often enjoyed with a pint of Ben & Jerry's. If Muriel wore these shorts, she'd look buff and bony. Me? I looked...oh, just past my first trimester, I'd guess. Unfortunately, I wasn't pregnant. Not with a child, anyway. With Betty Crocker vanilla supreme. That's right. I had a food baby.

Tomorrow evening was the mandatory corporate hike with Charles deVeers and a couple of BTR executives. Mark had encouraged us all to bring friends, hoping to show how much we all embraced a wholesome and adventurous lifestyle. If it sounded pretentious, painful and affected, I can assure you, it really was. Pete and Leila were computer geeks who often bumped into doors and walls, too engrossed in cyberworld to pay attention to the real deal. Karen's last attempt at physical exercise had been on the high school shuffleboard team, which she quit her sophomore year. Me...my dog pulled me up the steep hills when I rode my bike, and I didn't like to paddle my kayak faster than I could walk.

Add to this the fact that we were heading up to Deer Falls Trail, which twisted its way four thousand feet up Mount Chenutney. Apparently, the trail was so named because of the alarming number of deer that fell to their deaths on said trail, something I found less than reassuring.

But more than the hike was, of course, the attire. Damn that Muriel! I knew this was deliberate. She wanted me to look bulging and soft and sluggish, and since I was all those things, I would.

"Blerk!" I yelled, startling my dog. As I flopped down on my bed, the waistband of the satanic bike shorts cut into what had yesterday been a pleasant amount of padding and today was clearly *blubber.* I glanced at my rocking chair, which held no solutions and indeed, didn't seem to want to speak to me. *When you're with me,* it seemed to say, *we're not going to be shallow. Got it?*

"Got it," I said, well aware that I needed to stop talking not just to Betty Boop and Michelle Obama, but to my furniture as well. "Don't worry," I told Bowie, who was looking at me, his lovely little brow wrinkled in concern. "I'll always talk to you. Any way you can chew some of this fat off?"

My dog gave my hand a few licks, but otherwise declined. I'd already tried my Dr. Rey's Shapewear, but that type of bondage was not going to work if I was supposed to hike up several thousand feet of mountain. Even a rush order of hiking shorts from BTR was not going to make it in time for tomorrow.

I groped behind me for the phone and called Hester. "Hey," I said. "Is there some miracle drug you can pre-scribe for me that will take off about ten pounds by tomorrow?"

"No," she boomed amiably, "but I *can* come over and lop off your head. That'd be about eight and a half, nine pounds. How would that be?"

"You're no help," I said. "I have to wear these stupid bike shorts tomorrow, and I have a food baby—"

"I'm hanging up now," she said, and did just that. I really couldn't blame her. Yes, yes, I was incredibly pathetic. But still. There had to be *something* I could do. I picked up the phone and tried Annie, who tended to be much, much more sympathetic about matters like these.

"Hey!" she said. "What's up?"

"I need to drop a few pounds overnight," I said, getting right to the point. In the background, I could hear the clatter of pans. "What are you cooking?"

"Well, maybe we shouldn't talk about it, if you're trying to lose weight," she said, ever wise. "Seamus, spit that out right now. I don't care. It's raw."

"Give him a kiss for me," I said.

"Callie's sending you a kiss, Seamus. Spit that out, I said!" She turned her attention back to me. "So what's going on?"

"Corporate hike, skinny Muriel, formfitting bike shorts, food baby. Need I say more?"

"Ooh," she said. "Okay, yeah, I understand. I can help. Write this down."

We were best friends for a reason.

FORTY-FIVE MINUTES LATER, I was back in regular clothes and at a store I'd never patronized before: The Happy Herb. It was new, it was organic, it smelled funny, a cross between hay, garlic and pot.

"Can I help you?" asked the woman behind the counter. She smiled and pushed her lank and somewhat thin hair behind her ears.

"Oh, I'm fine! Just browsing!" I said, not about to admit I was a shallow dope who wanted to look good in front of her ex-boyfriend and his new woman. I figured I'd just float around the store, find the product I was looking for, possibly explain that I worked in advertising and was doing some research, hence my purchase.

Once Annie had given me the Holy Grail of weight loss medicines, I checked Google, and the online testimonials had been quite encouraging. One woman (Cindy G. from Alabama) said she lost seven pounds just before her fifteenth high school reunion. An entire dress size!

"So how's business?" I called out, pretending to check out the natural hair care products. One brand of shampoo had eggs, yogurt and honey in it. You could shower and have breakfast in one fell swoop.

"Business is great!" she answered. "Are you from around here?"

We chatted amiably as I drifted through the aisles. Personal Care. Sexual Enhancement. Memory Improvement. Attitude Modification (perhaps I could slip some into my mother's coffee). Ah, here we were! Intestinal Health. And bingo, the item I'd come looking for...Dr. Duncan's Cleanse 'n Purge Weight Loss Jump-Start Tea.

"Hmm," I murmured, picking up the box as if intrigued. "Interesting." The copywriter in me wondered if a more subtle product name wouldn't help sales. The box looked like something Dr. Duncan had assembled while watching TV...it was slightly crooked and held shut with Scotch tape. The front panel showed a blurry picture of Dr. D., a smiling, bearded and very thin man. The copy on the back was off center. Tsk, tsk. Perhaps I'd contact Dr. Duncan and pitch him.

Reading the box, I cringed. *Dr. Duncan's Cleanse 'n Purge Weight Loss Jump-Start Tea is 100% herbal all natural organic, guaranteed to detoxify your bowels from*

the modern-day poisons you ingest every day—eep!—
maximize your liver's ability to filter toxic waste—dear
God!—blah blah blah, ah, here we go...*adhering to and
flushing out your body's fat cells, allowing you to jump-
start your new weight loss and health maximization with
results that can be measured within hours!*

Okay. So tonight would be spent in the bathroom, I
got that. Wishing that I was a more sensible person, the
kind who didn't try to lose seven pounds in a twelve-hour
period, I picked up the box. *Don't do it,* Mrs. Obama
advised. Sure. Easy for her to say. There were Pilates
classes in her honor. Besides, common sense was out-
weighed by the image of my disgusting food baby. And
after all, hadn't the tea worked for Cindy G.?

I glanced around the store. No one here but the clerk.
Superb. Of course, I wasn't about to buy just the Cleanse
'n Purge... I had to hide it among other purchases. I
grabbed some beeswax-based shampoo. A little mois-
turizer, what the heck. Some green tea that Noah might
like, better than the black coffee he swilled all the
livelong day. Oh, some sassy lip balm for Josephine.
Apricot shower gel for Bronte. Organic cookies for
Bowie, who, it must be acknowledged, really preferred
Quarter Pounders with cheese. Bringing it all to the
counter, I made sure the Cleanse 'n Purge box was buried
in the middle.

"So glad you found something!" the clerk sang.

"Oh, me, too!" I sang back. "I bought some stuff for
my nieces."

"Great! I'm so happy!" she said, seeming to mean it
quite profoundly. She scanned the shampoo, humming
as she did so. Then she looked past me and beamed
again. "Hello! Welcome to the Happy Herb!"

I turned to look, then flinched. It was Ian McFarland. Crap. No woman wants to be caught buying a weight loss miracle, let alone one called Cleanse 'n Purge. And certainly not by the man who's already seen her at her worst. Leaning subtly over the counter so my arm sort of draped over Dr. Duncan's blurry, bearded face, I decided to play it friendly. "Hi there, Ian," I chirped.

"Hello, Callie," he said neutrally. His eyes met mine briefly, and he gave a little nod. That was it.

And yet…and yet he remembered my name. Which, of course, he should. But still. It felt like a compliment. And he was…I don't know. Big. Male. He was a big, strong male. And I liked big, strong males. *Get a grip,* my imaginary Michelle told me. *Yes, ma'am,* I answered silently. *Sorry.* But even as I apologized, my attention drifted back to Ian.

He wore jeans…I'd yet to see him in something other than a suit, and I was having a hard time taking my eyes off those jeans, which fit *very* nicely. His polo shirt was a faded red, and somehow he managed to look quite…dangerous in a most pleasing and (let's be honest) horny way. Like at any minute he'd get the call from a mysterious government agency and trot off to kill someone, the way Clive Owen did in *The Bourne Identity.* I'll bet Ian had some cool scar somewhere…yes, actually, there it was, up near his eye. Knife fight, I'd bet hard cash.

I'd also bet he knew how to kiss. Guys who looked like that could *kiss,* ladies. Or so my romance novels told me. Hard kissing. Kisses that started hard, anyway, then went soft and long and the woman would be pulled against his unyielding chest, his arms like bands of steel, me all soft and melting, him hard and hot…

Blerk! I was staring. And he was looking back. His eyebrow raised in an unmistakable *Do you mind, lady?* kind of look.

Blushing, I turned back to the clerk and fumbled in my purse for my wallet. I had a purgative to buy. "I'm in a little bit of a hurry," I whispered.

"No problem!" she cooed, ringing up the shampoo. "Are you looking for anything special today?" she asked Ian.

"Do you have any glucosamine in one-thousand-milligram tablets?" he asked.

"You know, I might!" she answered.

"For dogs?" I asked.

He cut those blue eyes back to me. "Yes." Then he dropped his gaze to my purchases—crap, I'd moved!—and I hurled my body in front of the counter.

"I give glucosamine to Bowie," I said, my voice a little too loud. "Every day. Dr. Kumar recommended it, even though he's young. Bowie, that is. Bowie's young. He's three. Dr. Kumar...he's what? Middle-aged? Retired, of course. His boys are out of college, anyway, so he must be...sixty? Fifty-five? Have you met the boys? They're great."

Ian didn't answer. I didn't blame him. There was something about Ian McFarland that made me blather on like an idiot. Yes, there was definitely a pattern emerging here. Closing my eyes briefly, I smiled at him and managed to shut up. Behind me, the happiest woman in the world rang up my purchases.

"That will be $97.46," she said.

"Holy Lord," I exclaimed. "Wow!"

"I know," she said, grinning like a monkey. "It's the Cleanse 'n—"

"Doesn't matter!" I blurted. "It's worth it! Because it's all organic! So worth it." I handed her my credit card. One hundred bucks? Christ! "I can't wait to try the shampoo," I said in a more normal tone, hoping to throw her off the scent of Dr. Duncan and his miracle cure.

"It's so wonderful," the clerk said, tucking her limp hair behind her ears. "I use it, too."

I tried not to flinch. "Great."

"Here you go!" she said, handing my bag over like she was giving me the Nobel. "Make it a supermagical day!"

"I...okay!" I said. "Thank you."

Clutching the bag to my chest, I walked past Ian. "Have a supermagical day, Ian," I whispered, unable to help myself.

"I always do," he murmured.

That stopped me in my tracks. I glanced behind me. Ian wasn't smiling, not exactly. His mouth was in its usual straight line, but his eyes...those blue, blue eyes...and there it was again, that hot and darting thing in my stomach.

The whole way home, I thought of that almost-smile. And I have to admit, it was a pleasant distraction.

DR. DUNCAN WAS A GENIUS, I acknowledged as I surveyed myself in the mirror the next afternoon. I'd have to write him (as Hester G. from Vermont, to punish my sister for not helping). And I hadn't even had to sleep on my bathroom floor! Not that that would've been much of a hardship. My bathroom was a thing of beauty, which was rather strange, since Noah had built this place, and a luxurious bathroom wasn't something I'd have imagined him caring about. But I had a beautiful pedestal sink, a shower area made from those big bricks of thick glass and, the *pièce de résistance,* a huge Jacuzzi tub that I never used but often meant to. Noah's own bathroom was much more utilitarian. Maybe he knew he'd need a grandchild to live with him someday, and this had been his bribe. Whatever the motivation, I was grateful. Getting ready was always a pleasure in here.

Especially now that my food baby, while not completely gone, had definitely shrunk. I wasn't sure how it happened, since the expected GI distress never occurred (God bless you, Dr. Duncan!), but I looked pretty smokin', if I did say so myself. Curvalicious, even. More like fertile J-Lo than stringy Lindsay Lohan, and thank God for that. Take that, Muriel! If I was the equivalent of, oh, let's say a really good hamburger, juicy, comforting and delicious, Muriel was a rawhide shoelace. Mark had once told me (in Santa Fe) that he liked a woman who was, well, womanly.

I gave the biking shorts a tug, smiled at my reflection, and went out into my bedroom, where Freddie was waiting for me. In my *chair!*

"Get out of that chair!" I barked. "Fred! Come on! Out, you bad dog!"

"Why? I'm a grown-up. I won't spill anything," my brother grumbled, though he obeyed.

"First of all, you're not a grown-up. Second of all, that chair is special, as you well know." I bustled over to it. Poor chair, having to support my dopey if lovable brother. "I'm saving it."

"For what?" Fred asked, flopping on my bed.

"For my happily-ever-after," I said.

"That's really pathetic," he offered.

"I know," I agreed. But that chair was for my future, and until I got there, I wasn't about to squander it on the likes of my semi-clean brother. "But you still can't sit there. That's the rule, I'm the boss of you, the end. You ready to go?"

"Yes, yes. Tragic, really, that you have no friends and have to bring me as your date."

"Don't forget Bowie." At the sound of his name, Bowie snapped to his feet and began jumping so his front feet left the ground. "Yes, Bowie, we're going for a walk! Yes, we are!" I turned to my brother. "And I do have friends. It's just Seamus had a soccer game, so Annie couldn't come, and Dave *wouldn't* come because he and Damien broke up." Dave was not only Annie's brother, but also Damien's boyfriend. The two men kept their relationship sparky through serial breakups and glorious reunions.

"Well, if you want people to like you, you picked the right sibling. I won't lecture anyone on ovarian torsion, after all. And then there's my good looks, natural charm and athletic prowess."

"No ego problems here," I said, giving him a fond cuff to the head.

"It's hard to complain when you're me," he acknowledged. It was true. He was a good-looking puppy, Freddie was, the image of our dad and, according to Noah's picture, Uncle Remy.

We clattered down the stairs. "Bye, Noah," I called into the workshop. The table saw was running, so I waved to make sure he knew I was leaving.

"Where are you going?" he asked, turning off the saw.

"I have that work hike thingie to do. Dinner's in the oven, okay?"

"What did you make me?" he asked, scowling. Dear cuddly Grampy didn't like eating alone.

"Veggie lasagna." His scowl grew deeper. "You'll like

it," I assured him. "I used lots of cheese. We have to run, Noah. Fred, say goodbye to your grandfather."

"Bye, Grampy," Fred said, smiling.

"Bye, jackass," Noah said amiably. "Keep an eye on your sister, and don't forget you're supposed to help me tomorrow, you lazy good-for-nothin'."

At five o'clock, right on time, we pulled into the small parking lot at the base of Mount Chenutney. Mark trotted over as we got out, and Bowie yipped in excitement, then licked my boss's knee. "Great! You're here! Come meet the BTR people! And Callie, thank you for bringing someone. Pete and Leila didn't. Hi, Fred."

"'S'up, Mark?" Fred said affably.

Mark was a little tense, that was clear. The three BTR people had come in this afternoon, but only Mark and Muriel went to lunch with them…a fact that caused a pang. Usually, I was in on those client schmooze fests. Then again, maybe it was more of a…I cringed at the thought…more of a family thing. Muriel. Her daddy. Her boyfriend.

We went over to the group, who looked slightly less than adventurous and athletic. Damien, who once told me that he felt Giorgio Armani was our greatest American, looked quite ridiculous in his BTR gear, as if a pin were sticking something tender. Pete and Leila, whom I rarely saw without a computer blocking their torsos, wandered aimlessly, their hands linked, their legs shockingly white even by New England standards.

Muriel, however, looked great. Long and lean, hiking boots, tan hiking shorts and a fitted sleeveless red shirt with Bags to Riches written across the back. Her black hair was pulled into a ponytail. She seemed relaxed and happy…not her usual look.

"Charles," Mark boomed heartily, steering me over to the knot of BTR people. "This is Callie Grey, our fantastic creative director. She's so excited about the new campaign, right, Callie?"

"Oh, absolutely!" I said, giving Mr. deVeers my hundred-watt smile as my dog flopped down and exposed himself. "It's great to finally meet you. I can't tell you how much I admire what you've done."

"Nice to meet you, too, Callie," he said. His eyes fell to my chest, then rose quickly back. "Very nice indeed. This is Anna, my marketing vice president, and Bill, our sales director." We shook hands all around, smiling hard. Bill and Anna were young, fit and gorgeous. They looked like twins…highlighted hair, perfectly tanned skin, glow-in-the-dark white teeth…just what you'd expect from young executives in California.

"Mark says you have some great ideas for us, Callie," Charles deVeers said.

"I think so," I said, smiling again. "I can't wait to show you."

"I can't wait, either," he murmured suggestively. Hmm. Well, my own father was a flirt, too, so I couldn't really hold that against him. He bent down to pet my dog, who immediately began to sing in appreciation. "This is one gorgeous dog you have, Callie. A beautiful dog for a beautiful woman."

"Why, Mr. deVeers! You charmer, you," I said, grinning.

"Call me Charles," he said, smiling back. It was a harmless vibe, and heck. I liked men, especially the type who liked me.

"Daddy," Muriel said, stepping between us and lacing her arm through her father's. "Let's get going, okay? We don't have time to waste if we want to make it down before dark." She gave me a cool look, then ran her gaze up and down my form, her nose twitching.

At that moment, Fleur pulled up in her British-flag MINI Cooper and clambered out. Like Muriel, she was wearing normal hiking clothes (I was the only one in skin-tight anything). Like Muriel, Fleur looked athletic and competent. She'd said she was bringing a guest...what were her words? Someone "with potential." And here he was. I did a double take. It was Ian McFarland.

"Oy, mates!" Fleur said, her British having unraveled from upper crust to Cockney.

"Hi!" I called as they approached. Fleur made the introductions. As Ian shook Mark's hand, he glanced over at me. *That's right, Ian. Me, emotional diarrhea, DMV. Yep, that's him.*

Five minutes later, we were off, down the trail and into the woods. The line was clearly ranked. First went Mark, Muriel and Charles, followed by Anna and Bill. Then came the rest of us in a somewhat tangled knot...Fred, Damien, Pete, Leila, Fleur, Ian and yours truly. Karen had been excused, claiming to have sprained her ankle while watching television last night.

"So, Fleur, how do you know the good doctor here?" I asked, glancing over at her.

"We met through Tony Blair," she said, referring to her foul-tempered and obese Jack Russell terrier. "He ate something a bit off, yeah, and wasn't his chippy self."

"Huh," I said, shooting Ian a look. Dang. I really, really wished I'd thought of something other than "The dog ate my paper." Ah, well. Water under the bridge.

The trail began as a fairly wide and lovely path through the woods. Little stencils of a deer falling from an incline were painted on a tree every fifty feet or so to mark the path. As the trail grew steeper, it also became more narrow. Our group began to string out.

It was then that my stomach emitted the most astonishing gurgle. *Squeerrrlllllerrrggghhh...* I jumped at the sound. What the heck? I'd eaten lunch...well, I had a couple of carrots, not wanting to feed the food baby anything fatty when Dr. Duncan's Cleanse 'n Purge had worked so... *Squeerrrlllllerrrggghh.*

Oh, dear. A slight cramp bit into my left side, and I flinched. Oh, no.

"Hungry?" Freddie asked.

"Um...no," I said. Not a lie. "I'm fine." *Gluuuurrrrggggghhh.* I tried to clamp my stomach muscles down on the sound. It didn't work. *Goooorrrrggghhh.* God, it was loud! Ian gave me a look, but said nothing.

Just then, Charles deVeers decided he had to have more time with me. "Callie!" he called, turning around to wave. "Join us up front and chat a bit!"

"Would love to!" I called back. *Gluuuurrrrggggghhh.* "Excuse me, guys. Duty calls."

Great. Not only was my stomach making *Exorcist*-type noises, but I had to trot up the path thirty feet or so to join the big guns, Bowie leaping at my side. And my biking shorts were making themselves known to me. The thing about clothes made from plastic bags...they don't breathe that well, as you might imagine. They smother, and right now, they were asphyxiating my thighs. Swatting at the gnats that danced around my head, I tried not to inhale any as I panted.

"How's everyone up here?" I gasped when I reached the front of our line. "Aren't these woods gorgeous, Mr. deVeers?"

"I told you to call me Charles," he reminded me, grinning. He might've been seventy or so, but the man hadn't broken a sweat. Neither had his daughter, but then again, I suspected she was half reptile. "By the way," he added, "I loved your idea for the new logo." Goodbye, long silly name with floating plastic bag, hello simple, stylish initials.

"I'm so glad," I said, not daring to look at Muriel.

"Callie, I was telling Charles about the ad campaign we put together for that ski resort last year," Mark said. He gave me a little grimace, which I read clearly. He needed help buttering up the client, and no one could pitch woo the way I could.

I smiled at Charles. "Oh, that was a great time, let me tell you, Charles." *Wwwweeerrrrrggghhh.* I quickly burst into laughter to cover the gurgling slosh of my stomach. Was that one over? Apparently not. *Boooorrr...* I talked over it, hoping no one else noticed as our feet crunched along. "Well, we like to know our products, of course, so Mark and I went up there to get the lay of the land. Now, Mark here, he grew up on skis. Me? No."

"Uh-oh," Charles said.

"I love to ski," Muriel said. "Dad, we should go to Utah again."

"That would be fun, honey. Go on, Callie," Charles said to me. Muriel's mouth tightened.

Wwwwweeerrrrrggggghhh.

"Are you hungry, dear?" Charles asked, striding manfully along.

"Oh, no! Well, I skipped lunch. Didn't want to cramp up on this lovely hike. But I'm fine!" I said, beaming, trying to suck in enough oxygen at the same time. I reached down to pet my dog, hoping the motion would somehow assuage the alien life force in my belly. Another cramp lanced through my side, making me gasp. I coughed to cover. "Anyway, Mark told me not to worry, just go up the mountain with Skip, the owner of the resort. It wasn't really about skiing." I gave Mark a look. "So he said, right, Mark?"

"I'm still sorry," Mark answered, smiling at me.

I'd worked with Mark long enough to understand his signals. He needed me to work the crowd, and work it I did. I continued with the story, which involved me, too terrified to get off the ski lift, clutching Skip so that he couldn't get off, either, riding back down the hill, then up once more, finally tangling skis with Skip, causing him to fall about ten feet onto hard-packed snow. The ski patrol had to come not only for their fallen boss, but to give me a ride down, since I could neither ski nor walk in those boots.

"Did you get the account?" Charles asked, smiling at me.

"Of course we did!" I said. *Berrrrrrroooo.* "Hahahaha! Skip was so impressed that I'd gone six thousand feet up a mountain I couldn't get down, he had to hire us."

"So you'll do anything for a client, is that it?" Charles winked.

"Anything within reason," I confirmed. Unfortunately, my stomach was seriously cramping, and the trail was becoming steeper. Hopefully, my panting would cover the occasional bizarre noise coming from my intestinal tract. I felt a little dizzy.

"That's a wonderful story, Callie. Mark, you have a gem here," Charles said, slinging his arm around my shoulders.

"I sure do," Mark answered, smiling at me. His dark

eyes were grateful. For a second, it was like the old times. Mark and me, getting our job done. A great team.

Then Muriel said, "Well, I'm dying to get to the top. Shall we stop strolling and start making time? Dad, think you can keep up with me, old man?"

"Them's fighting words," Charles said, releasing me. "Mark? Callie? You in?"

"Absolutely," Mark answered.

"Um, I'll wait for my brother," I said, glancing back at Fred and the rest of the gang, who were now maybe thirty yards behind. The stitch in my side was more like a quilt now.

"See you at the top, then," Charles said, and with that, they forged ahead, long athletic strides. Bowie whined to go with the fast people, but the second they were a safe distance off, I staggered over to a relatively flat rock and collapsed, draping an arm over my eyes. These bike shorts were awful! Would that I could peel them off and jump into a shower right about now. Curl up in some clean pj's, watch a little *Deadliest Catch* and have indoor plumbing ten feet away.

"You okay?" Pete and Leila asked in unison as they approached, Damien just behind them.

"I'm good. Just resting a little," I lied, peeking at them. Just cleansing and purging, more like it.

"You look like death," Damien said.

"And you look like a monkey in those clothes," I returned halfheartedly.

"See you at the top. Don't worry. We're almost halfway there." Leila slapped my knee and kept going.

Almost halfway there. God, take me now! And how could those pale computer dweebs be in such great shape, huh?

Bwihhhhheerrrrgggghhh. Ack! That one hurt! I pictured that notable scene from *Alien* all too clearly. If only the creature would just burst out and end my misery! Cleanse and purge, my God! Was childbirth like this? New sweat broke out on top of my old sweat, and I tried to breathe, Lamaze-like, through the pain. Too bad Hester wasn't around to slip me an epidural. Bowie looked up at me and smiled his doggy smile, and I managed to smile back.

"Hey, Calorie." It was Freddie this time. "You got a beer?"

"No, of course I don't," I said weakly. "I'm dying." Bowie licked my face, attempting revival.

"I call your car," my brother said.

I struggled to sit up. "You're such a sweet brother. If I die, everything goes to the nieces, okay? Nothing for you. Fleur, you're a witness."

"Can do," she said, sitting next to me. She was panting, which made me grateful. "I could murder a cuppa right now."

Ian, however, seemed irritatingly unaffected by our little hike up the mountain. He ignored me (and I was grateful, as I didn't want yet another person commenting on those god-awful noises). Instead, he put his hands in the pockets of his hiking shorts—L.L. Bean, not the sweaty plastic kind—and surveyed the view. I surveyed it as well…the view of Ian, that was. Nice legs. I'd guess soccer as a child. Excellent ass. Lovely broad shoulders.

"What a view," he said quietly. For a second, I thought he was referring to himself, but no. In the fun of my melting intestines here, I'd almost forgotten the lookout. Our particular stopping place overlooked Heron Lake, two thousand feet below. The water glowed a deep, dark blue, and all around, pine and fir trees rose, the thick wall of green broken only by mighty falls of granite left by the glaciers thousands of years ago. The setting sun, though still strong, turned the towering cumulus clouds a rich, creamy gold against the paling sky. It was quite a sight indeed.

Gluuurrrreeeeggghhh. I folded my arms against my gut, trying to muffle the noise, hoping the birdsong would camouflage it.

"What the hell is going on in your stomach?" Freddie asked. Once, I loved him. Now, not so much.

"I'm a little sick," I whispered, glancing at Ian. Wondered if he might euthanize me right about now, put me out of my misery. There was no way in hell I was going to make it up to the top of the trail, not with an alien chewing its way out of my abdomen. *Squeeerrrrggh.* Bowie whined in sympathy, his tail thumping the ground.

"Well, do you want me to stay? Or should I keep going?" my brother asked.

"Keep going, by all means," I said, waving in the general direction of the peak. There was no point in having him stay…he tended to laugh when people were sick or grieving, that kind of unhelpful, irrepressible, inappropriate laughter. "Get a ride home, okay? I'll meet everyone else at the restaurant for dinner."

"Okay, sis. See you later." Like a youthful mountain goat, Freddie practically skipped off the steepening trail. I should've brought Hester.

"Have fun," I said, but he was already out of earshot. Bowie yipped twice, then began licking his front paw.

"So what were you chatting about with the BTR crew?" Fleur asked.

"Oh, nothing specific. We were just schmoozing," I

said, glancing at her. "We'll have a real meeting soon, and I'm sure you'll be in on it."

"Right." She gave me a tight smile. While Fleur was a pretty decent coworker, I knew she didn't like that I was above her in the chain of command. She was five years older than I was, and there wasn't much of a ladder to climb at Green Mountain.

"Well, Ian, luv, we should push off," Fleur said. "Mark'll get all humped up if *all* of us..." she paused, clearly unable to find a Britishism for her next phrase "...wimp out." She glanced at me. "Sorry. Didn't mean to be a tosser."

"That's okay," I said. "Go on, have fun. Tell Mark I'll meet you all at the restaurant, okay?"

"Cheerio." She hopped to her feet. "Let's go then, Ian, shall we?" she asked, extending her hand. Bowie leaped up, hoping to go as well, as he was more than capable of running up and down this mountain six or eight times without feeling the slightest twinge of fatigue.

Ian turned around from where he was still surveying the view. He looked at me for a long moment. "I'll stay with Callie," he said.

"No, no!" I barked. "Go! Off with you! I'm fine."

Fleur shot me a sharp look. "We really need to catch up, Ian," she said, her accent evaporating.

"Go on, you two. I'm fine," I said, trying not to pant (or moan). *Gooorrrreeeeccchhh.*

"I'll stay," he repeated.

"I really, really don't want you to," I said firmly.

"I will anyway." He didn't move, just stood there, hands in his pockets.

"Please don't."

"I am."

Fleur's eyes darted back and forth between us. "Well, then, I'll stay, too. Keep you company, Callie."

"You go ahead," Ian said. "It's your company's event, after all."

My alien gave another squirm, and I flinched.

Fleur took a huffy breath. "Well, right-o," she said. "See you at the base, then."

"I may have to leave before then," he said. "I'm on call at the animal hospital tonight."

Her mouth tightened briefly, but she covered with a quick smile. "Well, I'll *probably* see you down there, at any rate. Great! Thanks for staying with poor Callie! You're a prince." She made a move toward him, almost like she was going to hug him, but Ian just stood, hands still in his pockets, and Fleur retreated. The sound of her hiking boots faded within seconds.

Ian sat down next to me. "You okay?"

"I'm great, Ian," I lied. "You don't need to stay with me."

"Can I take your pulse?" he asked.

"No. I'm fine. It's just…I skipped lunch. That's all. I really don't need a nurse. Or a vet."

He didn't answer, just stared off into the woods, which were lovely, dark and deep, just as Robert Frost said, and unlike the poet, I wouldn't have minded going to sleep right now.

The only sound was birdsong, the rustle of the wind in the pines and Bowie's slight snore. The alien seemed to be quieting down (please, God), and the sweet and piney breeze seemed to blow away that sick, foggy feeling bit by bit. My stomach emitted a small groan, but nothing like before.

"Maybe you could eat some grass and throw up," Ian suggested. "Works for dogs."

I glanced at him. He was still looking off into the woods, and I studied his craggy profile. "Thanks for the tip," I said. "I don't suppose you have any Tums or anything."

"Sorry," he said, cutting his eyes to me.

I felt heat rise in my face. Those eyes were startlingly direct. "So, are you from around here, Ian?" I asked.

"I moved here from Burlington two months ago," he said.

"Where'd you grow up?"

He looked back into the woods. "All over."

"Army brat?" I guessed.

"No." He didn't elaborate.

"So," I said after realizing he was done with that subject. "Fleur invited you to our little thing."

"Yes," he said, reaching down to pet Bowie, whose tail thumped appreciatively. "I was under the impression that it was more of a town-sponsored thing. Open to the public."

"Oh. Well, sorry for ruining it for you," I murmured.

"I can't believe anyone would buy something called Cleanse 'n Purge," he commented, raising an eyebrow.

Ah, dang it. Humiliation and me—no bounds. "Bowie, would you please bite Dr. McFarland?"

Bowie rolled onto his back. *Here's my stomach, in case anyone's in a scratching mood,* he was clearly saying. I obliged, since I couldn't think of anything else to do.

My GI distress seemed to have subsided. "I should probably head down," I said. "I'm feeling better. Thanks for waiting. You can join the others."

"I'll walk with you," he said, surprising me. He stood up, offered his hand and, after a second, I took it.

It was a good hand, callused and warm and strong, what you'd expect from a man who made animals better. A current of electricity ran up my arm and straight to my groin, and it took me a moment to realize that Ian had let go, though my hand was still extended. Blushing yet again, I put said hand to use, grabbed Bowie's leash and started down the path.

"This is a beautiful spot," Ian said.

"You should come back," I said. "Think that view's pretty now, wait about six weeks."

We walked along in companionable silence, my stomach still somewhat sore but without the lancing pain of earlier. Bowie sniffed and tugged until I decided to let him off the leash, so he could bound ahead.

"Nice dog," Ian said.

"Thanks. How's Angie? She's not a hiker?"

"I didn't realize dogs were allowed," he said. "But she's fine. Thank you."

I swatted at a few mosquitoes, which were attracted to my sweat, as I was clad in plastic. Something BTR's research and development might want to work on. I glanced at Ian, who looked as cool as if we were in Siberia. Those Arctic eyes were just about the same color as the sky today. Ian was tall, too, about six-two, and I had a sudden urge to see him without his shirt. Bet it was nice under that shirt. Bet he looked pretty damn—

"So. Your boss. Mark," Ian said, interrupting my lustful thoughts. "That was the guy you were crying over in the DMV?"

My jaw clenched. My stomach, too, resulting in another gurgle. "Yes," I said tightly. "Why do you ask?"

"No reason. It was a memorable day, that's all."

"Indeed," I muttered. He didn't say anything else. A

mockingbird trilled above us. My stomach twinged as if answering, but no sounds emerged, thankfully. "Do you have any siblings, Ian?" I asked after a few minutes of silence.

He glanced at me as if assessing my ulterior motive in such a devious and personal question. "Um…yes. I do. Alejandro."

"Ooh, I love that name! Wasn't Zorro's name Alejandro?"

"I don't know." His mouth pulled up one side.

"Alejandro McFarland. I wouldn't put those two names together."

"We have different fathers. His last name is Cabrera."

"Better," I said. "Is he gorgeous? He sounds gorgeous." I was rewarded by a quick smile, complete with attractive laugh lines fanning out from his rather shockingly lovely eyes. Pleased, I blushed a little and looked away.

"Callie," Ian said, "when you mentioned doing some PR for me, how would that work?"

Well, knock me over with a feather! "Is business down?"

"A little," he said, not looking at me. "What did you have in mind when you came into the office that day?"

I had nothing in mind, Ian, as I was, in fact, checking you out. "Um, well…basically, we'd make you seem really…approachable." He didn't say anything. "I'm sure you've heard people tell you over and over again how great and sweet and wonderful Dr. Kumar is, which is all absolute fact. So, of course, you're going to look a little, er, frosty compared to him. Don't worry. We'll make people like you."

He gave me a veiled look. "By which you've just implied that people currently don't."

"Oops." I laughed. "No, no. Well, we'll make them like you more. Don't worry. That's a specialty of mine."

He said nothing.

"See, we'd turn you—Ian, this standoffish guy who dislikes single women—into the human equivalent of a golden retriever. Warm, fuzzy, affectionate. The warm and fuzzy campaign. It'll be great!"

"I don't dislike single women, Callie," he said coolly. "I just don't appreciate them wasting my time by pretending to have a sick animal."

"Touché, Dr. McFarland," I answered. "Not that I'm copping to anything, of course."

"Nor do I want to pretend to be something I'm not," he continued, his words clipped. "I'm a capable vet. That should be enough."

"Right, Ian. But if business is slacking off, then you might just have to…market yourself differently. Not be different. Just try a little harder, because I'm guessing that while you're smart and know your vet stuff, maybe you're not so, um…relaxed with people."

He didn't say anything, and I got the impression that I had hit a nerve. His eyelashes, which I heretofore hadn't properly noticed, were blond. Blond and quite thick, really, which I could see as the sun was shining right on them.

"I could do it freelance," I offered. "It would cost less, and it could be our guilty secret that way." Actually, I'd have to check with Mark on that, but I was pretty sure it would be okay. The agency didn't charge less than a couple thousand per account, and Ian's little project would be far smaller than that.

He didn't say anything for a few seconds, then finally spoke. "I'll think about it," he said.

"You do that," I replied.

Ah, heaven. There was the end of the trail, and better still, the parking lot. My beloved Lancelot waited to take me home, where all the modern conveniences awaited. I'd have time to shower, beautify and change before meeting everyone for dinner. "Thanks for staying with me, Ian," I said, clipping Bowie's leash back onto his collar.

"You're welcome," he said. He stood with his arms folded, legs slightly apart, sort of like a sea captain on the deck of a frigate. Rather appealing, really.

"Bye," I said.

"Bye," he replied, and with that, I tugged on Bowie's leash and bolted for my car.

CHAPTER NINE

"Boom-boom-boom, gotta get-get!" I sang the following week.

"Boom-boom-boom, gotta get-get!" my students obligingly echoed, much to my delight. Of course, this *was* our seventh time through the song, and so far, only Jody Bingham had the moves down.

I'd taken a vacation day today; it was the after-school Brownie field trip, and I'd swung by the Senior Center for lunch (small town, not much going on, people who liked to see my smiling face...you get the picture). My yoga ladies had been clucking in dismay... Leslie hadn't shown up for the Senior Citizen Flex class. Loath to miss an opportunity to be a *jewel,* I plugged my iPod into the stereo and was teaching my very first hip-hop lesson. See, much to the pity and disgust of Kiara, my college roommate who happened to be a dance major from Trinidad, I knew a few moves—oh, yeah. Uh-huh. Clearly, I was the hippest white girl in the state of Vermont (which wasn't saying much, but still).

I crisscrossed my arms, looking very gangsta, I was sure. "Side, step, kick, back! Again! Don't forget those arms!" I said, doing my best impression of a young and very cool person. Not a *great* impression, mind you, but considering my audience, I might as well have been Soulja Boy. "Boom-boom-boom!"

"Boom-boom-boom!" the ladies echoed.

"Watch that hip, Mary!" I shouted over the music. "Don't want to lose your investment! Carol, look at you, you trashy thing! You got it, girl!"

Our rather different style of music (Leslie chose that drippy harp and flute stuff designed to make you either narcoleptic or homicidal) had drawn quite a crowd. In the back were about a dozen appreciative senior males, including, I was shocked to see, Noah. He stood in between Josephine, who was dancing quite competently and putting us all to shame, and Bronte, who was clearly suffering a moment of adolescent humiliation the likes of which the world had never seen, thanks to her auntie. I pointed at her and increased my swagger as I shuffled and hopped, earning a magnificent eye roll as a prize.

When the song was over, I staggered over to the stereo and turned off the music. "That was great, ladies! Next you'll all be dancing in some rap video on VH1!"

My peeps laughed, clearly delighted with their new status, then grabbed towels to wipe the sweat from their wrinkled brows.

"How's work, Callie?" Jody asked, stretching her arms behind her back as if they were rubber bands.

"Work's…it's fine," I said, almost telling the truth.

After the hike last week, we'd all had a merry dinner with Muriel's dad and his minions. Charles had made sure I sat next to him, and it seemed like a great success. My defection was made light of (I stuck with the no-lunch theory), and we'd all laughed and swapped stories and had a great time. Except that Muriel kept shooting me evil looks across the table, which I resented. It wasn't like I was about to wrestle her dear old dad to the floor and have my way with him…he just seemed to be one of those flirty older men who enjoyed women. When I failed to show the proper contrition, she employed a more effective strategy…kissing Mark. That one…that one worked.

I shook off the memory. Mark could be with Muriel if he wanted to. I was supposed to be moving on.

"So you're happy there?" Jody asked.

"Sure," I answered. "You bet."

"Well. Good for you, hon. See you soon, I hope." She squeezed my arm, eliciting a little wince on my part, then walked over to Noah, smiling her big smile. *Yeah. Good luck, Jody,* I thought. *Noah would eat a baby before even looking at someone who wasn't Gran.*

"That was so much fun," Elmira Butkes said, coming up for a little chat. "You'll have to teach us more next week. Yoga is such a bore compared to this. I loved that music! The Black-Eyed Susans, you said?" She fished around in her giant pink vinyl purse and withdrew a notepad and pen.

"Peas. Black-Eyed Peas," I answered, hoping her hearing aid hadn't picked up the obscenity-strewn lyrics. "But I can't really teach. That was the only dance I know. I'm a one-trick pony."

"No!" she cried staunchly. "You're so talented."

"You're really not," Bronte said as she approached. "You shouldn't ever dance in public again, Callie. I'm totally serious. Plus, you're, like, way too old to listen to the Black-Eyed Peas."

I feigned outrage. "I am not! I'm young and incredibly cool. Besides, who introduced you to them in the first place, huh? I've liked Fergie since she was first dating Leo from *All My Children,* thank you very much!"

She rolled her eyes and sighed. "Whatever, Callie."

"What are you doing here, sweetie?" I asked.

"Mom *still* won't let me get off the bus alone, so I had to go to Noah's because Grammy was, like…*working*." My niece shuddered. "And Noah had to drop Josie off with you, and I had to come because no one in this family, like, acknowledges the fact that I'm way too old to be dragged around like chattel."

I regarded my niece, impressed with both her sulkiness and her vocabulary. "What's the matter, hon?" I asked, unable to resist petting her pretty cheek.

"There's like this stupid, idiotic father-daughter dance at school this weekend, and like, of course I can't go." She glared at me in the way only a teen can manage…disdain, fury, vulnerability all rolled into one hot glare.

"Poppy would go with you, Bronte! He would love that!"

"I don't *want* to go with my grandfather. If I don't, like, have a dad, forget it." Her eyes filled. Though Bronte had never met him, her biological father had died in Iraq, and of course, Hester had not provided an alternate father figure. "Do I, like, have to go on this stupid field trip?" she asked.

"No, sweetheart. You can stay with the grumpy old man, if you want." I studied her mercurial face. "You want to talk about the dad thing?"

"No," she said, then, realizing she was treating her beloved aunt with contempt that should only be reserved for her mother, gave me a grudging smile. "But thanks, Callie."

"You're welcome, baby. I'm always here."

"I *know,*" she said. "You, like, tell me every week." She gave another eye roll and glided away. My admiration for my sister grew. One thing to have children…another to keep them when they hit adolescence.

It was nice to be away from the office. The mood at Green Mountain had changed once the BTR people went back to San Diego. Ever since, Mark had barely spoken to me; we were busy, but still. There was something about being a child of divorce…I'd always felt somehow responsible for everyone's mood. If I was cute and cheerful enough, I believed, everyone would be happy. If they weren't, clearly I wasn't trying hard enough. That was how it felt with Mark these days…like I was somehow failing him. And Muriel…forget it. What she actually did remained a mystery, though she sat at her desk each day, dressed to kill in her black and white—I had yet to see her in a color—clattering away on her keyboard.

"Are you ready, Auntie?" Josephine asked, grabbing my hand and nearly wrenching my arm from the socket. "Can we go? Please? Are you ready? Can we please go?"

"Sure, honey. We just have to swing by my place so I can change, and then we'll be on our way. You have directions, right?"

"In my backpack," Josephine replied. "Come on! I don't want to be late!"

"We won't be late, sugarplum," I said. "Come here. Are you too big for Auntie to pick you up?" I scooped her into my arms. "Oh, I see that you are! Blerk! I almost dropped you!" I pretended to let go for a second, a game she always loved, and received her musical giggle as reward.

I set her down, took her hand and headed toward Noah. And get this. He was talking. To Jody, a woman who was not related to him by blood! This was a change. Jody had worked her magic, because Noah, while not looking exactly joyful, had not run for the door, either.

"Noah?" I called. "I'm taking Josephine to her Brownies meeting. Bronte's going to stay with you."

"Fine," he grunted. He glanced over at Bronte, who was reading *The Iliad.* "You can sand."

"Oh, joy, oh rapture unforeseen," she returned without looking up.

"She's a smart-ass, that one," Noah said, unable to suppress a proud smile.

"You've got to love a child who reads," Jody agreed.

I leaned in to give Noah a hug. "You could do a lot worse than Jody Bingham," I whispered. He swatted my shoulder. "Ow. You hurt me. I may file charges," I said. "Bye, Jody! Bye, Grampy! Love you!"

"Bye, Grampy! I love you!" Josephine echoed. There. Made him look good even if he resented it.

HALF AN HOUR LATER, I was clean and sweet-smelling and wearing comfortable pants so I could eat lots of Cabot's cheese, food baby or no food baby. Josephine bounced on my bed, Bowie barking in approval. "Give me the directions, honey," I ordered.

She hopped down and dug in her backpack, then handed me a sheet of paper. "Can I wear some of your lip gloss?" she asked.

"Sure," I said, scanning the sheet. Oh, heck! We weren't going to a cheese bar...we were going to the Georgebury Veterinarian Practice. Ian's, in other words. Huh. Clearly, this must've been set up long ago by Dr. Kumar, because I just couldn't imagine Ian welcoming in a bunch of giggling five-year-old girls.

I was right, I found out twenty minutes later.

"Dr. McFarland will be right out," Carmella Landi said for the fifth time.

"Marissa, don't eat that, sweetie," I said over the din. "It's for doggies. Spit it out." I turned to Carmella. "Is he hiding?" I asked.

"I think so," she said. "He looked like he was passing a kidney stone when I told him this was on the calendar." We both laughed merrily.

"How's business?" I asked.

She sobered a bit. "Well, it's a little quiet. Dr. Kumar was so…lovable. This guy…not so much. People want someone to worship their pets like they do. Dr. McFarland's kind of an iceberg, know what I mean?"

"I do." Clearly, Ian needed my professional help.

Given that the girls weren't breaking anything yet and Michaela Oh, the other chaperone, was meting out bribes in the form of Life Savers, I took the opportunity to wander down the hall and find our host. The place seemed mostly empty. A tech I didn't know was getting ready to go…there was no sign of Earl, my old buddy.

As I passed an open door, Ian's beautiful Irish setter rose gracefully to her feet. "Hi, Angie!" I said, kneeling to pet her and, apparently unable to help myself, began channeling Mick Jagger once more. "'Angie…Aaa-nnngie…You can't say we never—'"

At that moment, Ian emerged from his office, looking much as Carmella had just described him. He wore a suit, but in place of a jacket, he had on the expected white lab coat with his name embroidered in black. His shirt was blue, his tie red, and he looked…well, formal. Stiff. But kind of nice, too. Aside from creepy Louis, I didn't know a single man who wore suits. There was a lot of Carhartt up here, a lot of flannel. Ian…he stood out. Once again, the image of a Russian assassin came to mind. I smiled up at him, and Angie's tail swished.

He did a double take when he saw me squatting on the ground with his dog. "What are you doing here, Callie?" he asked. "Don't tell me one of those…children…is yours." He swallowed.

"See, that's exactly what I could help you with," I said, my smile dropping like lead. I stood up. "A more appropriate greeting would be, 'Hello, Callie, it's so nice to see you!' And is it really so hard to imagine that some guy found me attractive enough to knock up? Hmm?" No wonder business was off.

He rubbed his jaw. "I didn't mean…I—never mind." He looked down the hall, where the noise level in the waiting room was approaching home-run-in-the-bottom-of-the-ninth levels. I took pity on him.

"I'm here with my niece. Don't worry. We'll make this as painless as possible." He looked dubious. "Come on, big boy," I encouraged. "They don't bite. Well, Mariah and Paige might, but the rest of them are completely safe.

"Girls!" I said, opening the half door into the waiting room and shouting a bit to be heard. "Dr. McFarland is here, and he's so happy that you all came to learn about how he takes care of animals! Dr. McFarland, thank you so much for seeing us!"

He looked at the girls like a wounded calf might regard a school of underfed piranhas. "Hello," he said.

"I have three dogs!" Keira Kinell shouted, lifting her skort and dancing in place. "They're purebreds! They cost $4,000 each!"

"I have a cat named Eddie and he's so cute!" Hayley McIntyre claimed.

"No, you don't!" said Josephine hotly. "You don't have a cat. I was just at your house! That cat is fake!"

"He's not fake!" retorted Tess McIntyre, Hayley's twin. "He's imaginary! And he didn't like you, so he hid!"

"I have a pony and two dogs and a hamster," Kayelin Owens said, "except the hamster died and I found it in the cage and it was all curled up into a ball and I cried and my mother said it was in heaven so we buried it in the backyard!"

Ian looked as if electrodes were being applied to various parts of his body. Again, I grinned. "Dr. McFarland is going to give us a tour, girls! You can see where he does all that vet stuff that keeps our pets healthy. Right, Dr. McFarland?" I said.

"Yes," he said. "All right. Um, please don't touch anything and follow me."

"Good luck!" Carmella said, booting up solitaire on her computer. Michaela and I herded the girls into the rough approximation of a line and followed Ian down the hall.

"This is the operating room—please don't touch that," he said, as Keira began fondling an oxygen tank. Keira looked at him assessingly—she was a piece of work, that one—and, correctly assessing his efficacy, touched it again.

"Hands in your pockets, Keira," I said, and she obeyed with a mutter.

Ian took a deep breath. "Well, this is where we operate when—"

"Do you cut out uteruses?" Josephine asked, proud of her vocabulary, given that her mommy was a doctor.

"Um...sometimes," Ian said. "We call that spaying."

"What about peniseses?"

I bit my lip, trying not to laugh.

"Well, not exactly, no."

"What's a girl dog called?" Tess asked, smiling angelically. "It rhymes with 'witch.'"

Ian, sensing that he was being led into a trap, glanced at me. I shrugged. Ian decided to ignore that question and attempted to educate the girls. "It's important that a dog or cat or any pet doesn't have a litter unless—"

"I never litter," said Caroline Biddle.

"Not that kind of litter!" Keira shouted. "Dummy!"

Caroline looked like Keira had slapped her. "Keira, apologize to Caroline immediately," I ordered.

"Sorry!" Keira sang with great insincerity, and my jaw clenched, something like hatred rising hot and ugly in my chest. Keira was the daughter of New Vermonters and new money, and a nastier, more spoiled child there had never been. And Caroline, who often played with Josephine, was a special-needs kid, sweet as a butterfly. I wasn't sure what her official diagnosis was, but since I volunteered in Josephine's kindergarten, I knew that Caroline was a few years behind her peers.

I took Caroline's hand and kissed it, and she gave me a watery smile, making me wish all sorts of misery on Keira. That the Jonas Brothers would come to Georgebury and forbid Keira to come to the concert, where Caroline would have a front-row seat. That her purebred dogs ate the heads off all her Barbies. That…well…other bad stuff. But not too bad. She was just a kid, after all. It was her parents who really deserved to be punished.

"Do dogs sometimes die in here?" Hayley asked.

"Yes," he said. We all waited for more. More never came.

"Are there ghostses?" she persisted, clearly hoping for something a little more colorful.

"No," Ian answered, jamming his hands in his pockets.

"I have to go to the bathroom," Marissa said, and Michaela led her from the room.

"Dr. McFarland," I said, "can you tell us some of the most common operations you do?"

He shot me a grateful look. "Okay, well, we neuter and spay animals so they can't, um, have babies. Sometimes, animals get something stuck in their intestinal tract, their stomachs, so we might have to operate for that. Uh...I remove tumors, set broken bones—please don't touch that," he said as Hayley began squeezing the pump on a blood pressure cuff.

"Maybe we could move on, Dr. McFarland," I suggested.

"Sure," he said, wiping his forehead with his sleeve.

"I broke my leg once," Paige offered. "I screamed so loud. Then I got candy at the hospital."

"My mommy screamed when she had my little brother," Leah Lewis said. "She said it was beautiful, but I heard the screaming and I'm never having babies. I only want puppies."

We herded the girls back into the hall. "Ian, why don't you examine Angie and sort of show them what you look for," I suggested in a low voice. "And if you gave out a souvenir, that would be great."

"I don't have souvenirs, Callie. This is not a gift shop," he said tightly.

"Tongue depressors, Ian. Cotton balls. They're five. They won't care."

He nodded. Swallowed.

"You're doing fine," I said, laying my hand on his arm. "They're just kids." He gave me a dark look, as if I'd just said, *It's just a pit of poisonous vipers, Ian,* but he went down the hall to his office to fetch his dog.

Michaela and I crammed the girls into an exam room. "Crisscross, applesauce," I called out, and like magic, all the girls collapsed Indian-style on the floor. When Ian brought Angie in, they squealed in delight.

"She's so pretty!"

"I want a dog like that!"

"Can I ride her?"

"No, you can't ride her," Ian said, but he smiled. He gently lifted Angie up onto the metal exam table. "This is Angie, my dog."

"Does she know any tricks?" Josephine asked. "Auntie's dog pulls her up the hills when she rides her bike!"

"Is that right?" Ian asked, glancing at me. His eyes smiled, and something fluttered in my stomach. "No, Angie doesn't know too many tricks, but she's very well-behaved. Now, the first thing I do when someone brings in a dog is try to make friends with it. Like this. Hi, Angie. You're a good dog, aren't you?"

"Does she ever talk back?" Hayley asked, and the girls dissolved into giggles.

Ian smiled a bit uncertainly, almost like he wasn't sure if he was included in the joke, and my heart lurched. Suddenly, it occurred to me that despite the fact that he looked like a Russian assassin and acted like an iceberg, Ian McFarland might be a little...well...shy.

It was oddly appealing.

For the next few minutes, Ian showed the girls what a routine exam looked like, holding their interest pretty well, considering that they had the attention span of hummingbirds.

"I think I want to be a vet," Caroline said, pushing her thick glasses up her nose. "Do you have to be smart to be a vet?"

"Yes, dummy, so that means you can't," Keira answered immediately.

The words were as sharp and vicious as a razor, and for a second, I was knocked speechless. Caroline bowed her head. "Keira, you're done!" I said sharply, jolting out of my seat. "Out in the waiting room, right now." Oh, would that the Brownie handbook would allow me to…I don't know…do something to change her evil little heart and make her see how cruel she was. My own eyes filled with helpless, angry tears, and my fists clenched.

"I'll get this," Michaela whispered, taking Keira by the shoulder.

"What?" Keira demanded as she was steered out of the room. "I didn't lie! She's not smart enough!"

The room was silent, the other ten girls realizing that Keira had crossed a line. Josephine, God bless her, put her hand on Caroline's back, but Caroline didn't move, just stared at the floor.

"In order to be a vet, Caroline," Ian said matter-of-factly, kneeling down in front of her, "you have to have a big heart. Do you have one of those?"

Caroline didn't look up. "I don't know," she whispered.

"She does," Josephine confirmed.

"You do, Caroline," Hayley seconded.

"Would you be very gentle? Sometimes the animals are scared," Ian said seriously.

Caroline gave a minuscule nod, still not raising her head.

"You also have to love animals. All different kinds."

"I do," she whispered. "Even snakes."

"Well, then," Ian said. "Sounds like you'd make a great vet."

She looked up at him. "Really?" she asked, her voice wobbly. Ian nodded.

My tears sloshed over, and in that moment, I loved Ian McFarland. Quite a lot, in fact. And Josephine and Hayley should get medals of honor, as far as I was concerned. I wiped my eyes surreptitiously, not wanting the other girls to see me cry.

Ian stood up and took a stethoscope out of his coat pocket. He held it out to Caroline. "Want to listen to Angie's heart?"

"Can I, too?" Marissa asked.

"Can I? Can I?" the other girls chorused.

Caroline forgot Keira's nasty remark in the thrill of using real live medical equipment, and Angie, who must've sensed that the little girl needed some extra love, licked her face. Caroline's smile lit up the room.

Half an hour later, the girls were once again shrieking with glee in the waiting room, as Ian had given them each a pair of latex gloves and my gifted niece had blown hers up into an udder-like balloon. As they played makeshift volleyball, I went over to Ian, who was watching from behind the half door that led to the exam rooms.

"You did great," I said. "Especially with Caroline."

He gave a formal little nod of acknowledgment. "Thank you for your help."

"Was it hell?" I asked, smiling.

"A bit," he admitted. One corner of his mouth rose a fraction. He could use a shave, I noted, and suddenly my knees were a little weak.

At that moment, Hester came in through the door. "Hi, Josephine!" she boomed, scooping up her daughter and kissing her loudly. "Did you have fun with the vet?"

"I did!" Josephine said. "We saw his dog!"

Hester set Josephine down and lumbered over to Ian

and me. "Guess what?" she said to me. "My fifty-four-year-old patient is pregnant! Isn't that great?"

"So great," I said. "Um, Hes, this is Ian McFarland, the new vet. Ian, this is my sister, Dr. Hester Grey."

"You know," Hester said in her loud, bouncing voice, "I thought about being a vet. But I'm not really fond of animals, and my scores weren't high enough. Had to go slumming in plain old medical school. Johns Hopkins. Where'd you go?"

"Tufts," Ian said.

"Impressive," Hester practically shouted. "Our brother just dropped out of Tufts."

"How was your seminar?" I asked.

"It was great. All sorts of new hormone therapies, just waiting to plump up Miss Egg for Mr. Sperm. Well, gotta run. See you soon, Callie. Nice meeting you, Owen."

"It's Ian," I corrected, but my sister was already halfway out the door. "She's a fertility doctor," I informed Ian.

"I remember," he said. At my look, he added, "From the DMV."

"You love to bring that up, don't you?"

He lifted an eyebrow. "Her daughter looks just like her," he observed.

"I know," I said. "Which is funny, since both Hester's kids are adopted." I looked up at him. "Do you have kids, Ian?"

He shook his head. "No. No, my ex-wife…no. We didn't."

There was more to that story, I could tell, but whatever discussion might have ensued was swallowed as the latest batch of mothers came to fetch their Brownies. One of them was Taylor Kinell, Keira the Cruel's mother.

She was clad in expensive, skintight and age-inappropriate clothing...anemic T-shirt with fabric so thin it was basically gauze, low-slung dark jeans, hand-torn by the designer, no doubt. She bent down and opened her arms to Keira, giving us a flash of her tramp stamp and thong. "Hello, baby girl!" she cooed in the general direction of her child, though she was looking at Ian. Ah. *Mother of the year parades wares in front of hottie vet.* Sure enough, she whipped off her Prada sunglasses and blasted a huge smile at Ian.

"I have paperwork to do," Ian muttered. With that, he fled down the hall to his office. I couldn't blame him.

Walking over to Taylor Kinell, I slapped on a fake smile. "Taylor, we had a little problem today with Keira," I began.

"Mommy! Mommy? Mommy!" Keira began, tugging her mother's hand. "You said we could go out for dinner! I want to go out for dinner! I hate eating at home! Can we go? Mommy! Mommy? I'm bored! This was so boring! Mommy! You said we could eat out!"

"Yes, honey, I said we could. Where do you want to go, huh?" Taylor said. Keira kept yanking her mother's anemic arm so hard I was surprised she didn't rip it off and, being Keira, start gnawing on it.

"Keira, I'm talking to your mother right now," I said patiently. She was only a kid, after all. Being evil was probably more nurture than nature.

"So? I'm hungry! Let's go, Mommy!"

"Taylor, Keira made fun of another child today, twice, and as you know, bullying isn't allowed in Brownies. Or really, anywhere else, right? Keira, saying mean things hurts people's feelings, honey."

"I don't care," Keira said.

Ooh. I turned to look at Taylor once more. "She won't be able to stay in Brownies if she doesn't learn some basic manners. Keira, would you like it if someone called you a dummy?"

"Which no one would, because you're so smart, angel-love," Taylor said immediately, shooting me a death glare. "As for Brownies, we were planning on leaving anyway. It's a little bourgeois. Come on, baby. You can have two desserts tonight. Let's go."

My blood pressure bubbled dangerously. Did Taylor think she was doing her child a favor, raising her that way? I almost felt sorry for Keira. In ten years, she'd be the despised popular girl in high school, no true friends, everyone gossiping about her behind her back as she wielded her parents' money like a weapon.

"Thanks for chaperoning, Callie," said Sarah, Caroline Biddle's mother. She held her daughter by the hand, her face bright with the joy of seeing her child again. Now *here* was a mother.

"Oh, my pleasure," I said, then paused. "Did Michaela speak to you?"

"Mmm-hmm," she answered, her eyes speaking volumes. "Please tell Dr. McFarland he's CNN's hero of the year, as far as I'm concerned."

I smiled. "Will do. Sorry I couldn't…do more." Once again, the thought of Caroline's dejected little face made my throat grow tight.

Sarah smiled. "Don't worry about it. Caroline, thank Callie for the special day, honey."

"Thank you, Callie!" the little girl said, locking her arms around my thighs and hugging tight. "Bye! I love you!"

"Bye, sweetness," I said, smiling down at her. "I love you, too." I watched as they left, Caroline chattering away, beaming, still holding her mommy's hand, and I couldn't help feeling a pang of envy at the sight of them, mother and child, so adoring of each other that nothing and no one else mattered. Caroline's dad was a prince, a builder who thought the sun rose and set on his wife and child. Annie, Jack and Seamus were like that, too. The three of them together—the essence of happiness. Everything else was gravy.

The last of the Brownies left, and the office was abruptly quiet. "Callie?" I jumped. Ian had reemerged from his office, now that the coast was clear. "Can I see you for a minute?"

"Sure! Sure, of course."

"Ian, I'll see you tomorrow," Carmella said. "Great seeing you, Callie. Nice job with the ankle biters."

"Thanks." I grinned.

I followed Ian to his office, where Angie was sleeping, curled in her dog bed. The room was orderly—that was putting it mildly—but it wasn't sterile, not like Muriel's black-and-white blank space. My own office was cheerfully cluttered, occasionally bordering on chaotic, sticky notes and photos scattered hither and yon, coffee mugs and the like. Ian's, on the other hand, was very tidy. There were his diplomas, NYU undergrad, Tufts for his DVM. Shelves with heavy textbooks, a small sculpture of a dog. On the wall was a rather nice painting of a sailboat, lots of juicy oil and texture.

But most interesting of all was the framed photo on the cabinet behind his desk. It showed a younger Ian and a very, very beautiful woman. Long blond hair, creamy skin, bone structure to rival Natalie Portman's. They were both smiling, and an unexpected twinge hit my heart. Ian looked very happy in that picture.

"Your wife?" I asked.

He glanced at it. "Ex-wife."

Not quite ex in your heart, pal, if you keep her picture here to torture yourself every day. "She's gorgeous."

"Yes." He said nothing else.

"Ian?" I said after a minute had passed.

"Yes?"

"You wanted to speak to me, remember? Though this is quite fun, too."

He closed his eyes briefly. "Right." He sighed. "I think I might need to hire you. If you think you can really do something, that is."

"The warm and fuzzy campaign!" I clapped my hands, startling him. "Good for you, Ian. This will be great!"

"Will it?" he asked.

"Oh, come on. I'm not the dentist, for heaven's sake." At that moment, my stomach growled.

"Not again," Ian said.

"Hush. I'm just hungry. I had a hard day. First I taught old women to hip-hop, then I had to herd the Brownies. Want to grab some dinner? We can talk about things while we eat."

Ian looked wary. "All right," he said after much deliberation.

"We can go to Elements," I suggested. "It's near where I live, and I can swing by and grab my laptop."

"Fine," Ian said. He looked at me steadily for a minute. Man, those eyes were so…blue. Betty Boop folded her hands under her chin and sighed deeply.

"Okay," I said, remembering that I was a professional person and this was not prom night. "Um…do you know where it is? It's a little bit hard to find, because it's down this little one-way street, then you have to sort of turn into a parking lot, but it doesn't look like a parking lot, it's more of an alley, but it leads—"

"Why don't I just follow you?" he suggested drily.

I smiled. "That, Dr. McFarland, is a great idea."

CHAPTER TEN

TWENTY MINUTES LATER, we arrived at Noah's Arks. Ian pulled in next to me, then got out of his car, looked at the sign and gave me a questioning look. "This is my grandfather's place," I explained as I fumbled for my purse. "I live with him. Come on in. You can meet him."

Bowie greeted me with the type of joy usually reserved for parents and children separated by war, singing in joy, yipping, head butting me so that my jeans turned into a sea of fur.

"Hello, Bowie!" I said in my special dog voice. "Hello, my boy! Did you miss Mommy? You did? Do you remember Dr. Ian? You do?" Bowie demonstrated that he did indeed remember, mounting Ian's leg, his yipping growing more soulful.

"Off, Bowie," Ian said. "Off." My dog took this as a sign that yes, Ian *would* rub his stomach for the next year or so and quite possibly give him a Quarter Pounder, so he collapsed on his back, revealing his…gladness. His tail waved furiously, swishing across the floor as clumps of his undercoat drifted on the breeze he created.

"Huskies need to be brushed at least once a day," Ian said.

"I do brush him every day! Do you know Eva Potts?"

Ian shook his head. "She's a knitter. She spins his fur into yarn."

"Ah," Ian murmured.

"I have a sweater made from my own dog. I don't wear it, granted, because that's a little incestuous, even for me, but still. Neat idea, I guess." The memory of Mr. Human Hair flitted through my mind, and I suppressed a shudder. "All that shedding is the price you pay for the best dog in the world? Right, Bowie? You're the best, aren't you? Miss Angie's out in the car, did you know that, Bowie? Can you smell her?" I bent to rub his exposed tummy, earning two yips and some crooning, as well as a wink from Bowie's brown eye. I winked back. "Mommy loves you!"

"Do you always talk to him in that voice?" Ian asked, a trace of amusement in his own.

I straightened up. "Yes, I do," I said, narrowing my eyes. "That way he knows I'm talking to him. Why? Do you speak French to Four D Angel's Mayonnaise out there? Mandarin Chinese?"

Ian grinned.

Oh. Oh, yes… That was nice. My girl parts suddenly felt tight and…lively. One smile, and I was fluttery. But it was some smile. Ian looked a little…I don't know…goofy when he smiled. A nice goofy. He had these unexpected laugh lines, and his cold Russian assassin looks suddenly morphed into utter likability, and he went from…I don't know, my brain was getting mushy here, but suddenly, the image of waking up with Ian and seeing that smile…waking up naked with Ian, oh, yeah, now *there* was a visual I could spend some time examining, a smiling, unclothed, warm, strong, manly—"

"Callie, thank the Christ you're home, because this fuckin' leg just won't fit and I'll be goddamned before I... Who are you?"

My dear, cuddly grampy hopped into the great room, wielding a prosthesis in one hand like a club. "Noah, this is Ian McFarland," I said. "Ian, meet my grandfather, the legendary boat builder Noah Grey."

"It's an honor, sir," Ian said. Aw.

"What's an honor?" Noah spat. "And what are you doing with my granddaughter here? You're not sleeping with her, are you?"

"Gosh, you're adorable, Noah," I said, rolling my eyes.

"No, sir," Ian answered.

"Think you can win me over with nice manners, young man?" Noah asked, ignoring me and glaring at Ian.

"No, sir," Ian said again. He looked over at me, his eyes smiling.

"Ian's the new vet, Noah. I'm doing some work for him," I said, "so get your panties out of a twist and give me your leg." He handed it over, still glaring at Ian. "Okay, Noah, where's the sleeve?" I asked, referring to the silicone sock that helped hold the prosthetic in place.

"Fuck if I know," he grumbled. "I knew I forgot something."

"It's a lot more comfortable if you use it," I said.

"How do you know? Did you cut off your leg to test it out?"

"No, but I may cut off your other one if you don't stop growling, Grampy dear," I said. "Ian, come upstairs with me, or Noah will eat you alive."

Ian followed me up the stairs. A mistake. Ladies,

never have a man follow you upstairs, as there's just no way to hide the junk in the trunk, if you will. I raced up so as to minimize Ian's view. "My grandfather is only that irritable if he's in pain," I said. "Sorry about that."

"No apology needed," he answered.

Ian waited on the catwalk as I went into Noah's room to find another silicone sock. Then I zipped down the hall into my own room to get my laptop and, let's be honest, check my hair. I closed the door behind me and took a deep breath.

My heart was beating a little fast, and not just because I'd hurtled up the stairs. Also, my cheeks were hot. I was…hmm. A little horny. Yanking off my fur-covered jeans, I opened my crowded closet and surveyed the contents. A skirt, definitely. I had fab legs. But not too flirty, because yes, I was working. Choosing a darling little pink and green plaid A-line with fun pleats at the bottom, I pulled it on, topped it with a sleeveless green silk tank, grabbed a matching cardigan, then dug out my bottle-green suede peep-toe shoes with three-inch heels.

"I'll be right out," I called to Ian as I kicked some laundry under the bed. Not, of course, that Ian would come in here. But it was strange to have him there, right outside my bedroom. Thrilling, even. They say that men think of sex every ten seconds or something. Maybe Ian was having thoughts about me…naughty thoughts. *Dirty* thoughts. Long, hot, steamy thoughts of tumbling onto my big, comfortable bed, kissing my neck, moving lower, his hand working its way…

Hellooo? Anyone home? Michelle Obama said. Right! I was doing a freelance job. Still, I went over to my laptop and typed a quick message to Annie. *Am going out to dinner with vet. Business only, but am having sex thoughts.*

I figured she'd be proud. Then closed the cover, stuffed the laptop into its case, dashed on a little MAC lip gloss, fluffed my hair, then went to the door and opened it.

"All set," I said.

Ian looked up, his eyes most definitely checking out my legs. Great choice, that cute little skirt! Indeed, he was staring.

"Is that a Morelock chair?" he asked.

"Thanks," I said, smiling modestly. "I ran track in…what?"

"Your rocking chair. Do you know who made it?"

It was perhaps the first time I hadn't been thrilled to discuss my beloved rocking chair. "Um…yes. It's a Morelock chair." I paused. "Good eye, Ian."

"Can I see it?"

I blushed. He was coming into my bedroom! Betty Boop squealed and fluttered her eyelashes. *To admire the furniture,* the First Lady said pointedly. "Sure," I mumbled.

He came in, not even glancing at my inviting bed. Hmmph. Well. The chair *was* special, and for some reason, I was glad Ian recognized that. It was, after all, my prize possession, the first thing I'd try to save in case of fire, right after Bowie and Noah (though Noah was pushing it these days).

"Where'd you find it?" he asked, not touching the chair and, bless him, not asking to sit in it.

"Actually," I murmured, staring at the chair myself, "Mr. Morelock gave it to me for my eighth birthday."

Ian looked at me in surprise. "You knew him?"

"I only met him once, but Noah knew him," I said. "In fact, this is the last chair he ever made."

Ian nodded once. "Well," I said. "We should go, I

guess, before it gets too late." I paused. "We can walk, if you want. It's not far."

"Sure," Ian said.

"Do you want Angie to come in? Noah won't mind. He loves dogs."

"Thank you. That would be great."

FIVE MINUTES LATER, we were walking down the twisting street. The sun was setting, and birds sang in the trees. Ten yards away, the Trout River rushed past, shushing and murmuring its river song. It was almost romantic, save for the fact that my laptop banged into my hip every other step and Ian didn't say a word the whole way there. Luckily, Elements wasn't far, which was good, because these shoes, while adorable, were also vices of death.

"Callie Grey!" a masculine voice purred the minute I opened the door. "My God, look at your legs, they're proof of a loving God."

Ian looked confused. I beamed and kissed the owner of the voice.

Annie's brother, Dave, was part owner and manager of Elements, and of course I loved him madly. He looked like an Alaskan crab fisherman, rough and unshaven and so, so alpha, but unlike my crushes in *Deadliest Catch,* he knew how to dress.

"So who's this?" Dave asked, scanning Ian up and down and putting a proprietary arm around my shoulders. "I'm Dave, Callie's friend and protector, half owner of this fine establishment." Dave stuck out his hand, which Ian shook.

"Hello," he said.

"Ian, this is my friend, Dave. Dave, Ian McFarland, our town's new vet. I'm helping him out on a project, so can we have a booth? I have my laptop."

"Of course! Right this way." Dave led us through Elements, which, like Noah's place, had once been part of the mill industry, meaning it had uneven floors, brick walls and lots of character.

Various River Rats were assembled in the bar (big surprise there), and a chorus arose as we passed. "Callie! Hey, girl! How's Noah?"

I waved and grinned. "Hi, gang! Can't talk now, don't want to, have better company than you bozos!"

"Attagirl!"

"Take me with you," Shaunee Cole called, lifting her martini glass.

"Marry me, Callie!" boomed Jake Pelletier, who'd actually made the trip to the altar three times thus far...he was only forty, so we figured he had six or seven marriages left in him.

"Come on, Prom Queen," Dave urged, rolling his eyes. "Ian, she's still the most popular girl in school." He waved us to our booth, which was not far from the bar and right under the large copper wall hanging (i.e., the best seat in the house) and proceeded to hand out the endless stream of menus...daily specials, wine list, martini choices, food. "And how is that ill-tempered little coworker of yours?" Dave asked. His reunion with Damien was, inevitably, just around the corner, but to mention this would undercut the drama, so...

"He's sulky, miserable and bitter," I said.

"You're just saying that to make me happy." Dave winked. Such a shame that he batted for the other team...we would've made beautiful babies. "Well, I'll let you two get to work. Enjoy your dinner! Nice to meet you, Ian." Dave took my hand, kissed it, then wandered off to find someone else to schmooze.

"You know a lot of people," Ian commented, shaking out his napkin and putting it in his lap.

"You will, too," I said, taking a sip of water. "It's a small town. Everyone knows everyone else. And you should join the River Rats. They're a…" I made quotation marks with my fingers… "rowing club."

"Yeah, join up, hottie!" Shaunee called. "We'll corrupt you!"

"Yes, they're great," I said loudly, "if you like lazy, drunken revelers with no purpose in life other than trying to drown themselves."

"Yeah!" my compadres cheered, toasting each other and high-fiving. I smiled. "Callie, we're going over to Whoop & Holler," Mitch Jenkins called. "Drop by later if you get a chance."

"Anything's possible," I said. I watched fondly as the eight or nine Rats jostled their way out of the bar, then glanced over at Ian, who was watching as well. "They're really a fun bunch," I said.

"Rowing club?" he asked.

"Drinking club, more like it, but yes. They go white-water kayaking a few times a month, go drinking a few times a week. In October, they hold this funny little regatta." I took a sip of water. "They love my grandfather. It's a little cultish, actually." Mark was a member of the River Rats, though in name only. I wondered if Muriel would join. I sure hoped not.

Ian nodded, then picked up one of the leather-bound menus. Not much of a talker, this guy. We perused our menus in silence, though I kept darting looks across the table. The whole grumpy Russian thing was really starting to grow on me.

"So, Ian, why don't we get started?" I said once we'd

ordered. "I figured we'd do a Web site, and there'd be a section called 'About Dr. McFarland,' which is pretty standard. So." I slid my laptop out of its case and popped it open. "Tell me about yourself."

"I went to New York University for undergrad, Tufts for veterinary school," he said.

"Yes, I read your diplomas. What else?"

"I did research on joint degeneration and taught at UVM before taking over for Dr. Kumar."

I typed a few lines. "Okay, well, how about some personal stuff?"

His eyes grew wary. "What do you want to know?"

"Well, for starters, why did you move to our fair state?"

He looked at his place setting, then adjusted his fork a millimeter. "I liked New England. And Laura was from Boston."

Ah, *Laura.* I was deeply interested in Laura. "Did you guys live in Vermont when you were married?" I asked. *Do you still talk? Do you still love her? Did she break your heart?*

"Yes. Burlington." He took a breath—clearly, this was not how he'd choose to spend an evening—but he forged onward. "But I spent one summer in Georgebury when I was a kid."

"Really?" The idea that Ian had been nearby was utterly thrilling.

He nodded. "I stayed with my uncle."

"Who is he?" I asked. "Maybe I know him."

"Carl Villny. My mother's brother. He died about ten years ago."

Villny. A Russian name, if I wasn't mistaken. Suppressing a smile *(Was your uncle a Soviet mole, perchance?)*, I shook my head. "Nope, doesn't ring a bell."

I paused. "So you liked it up here, and after your divorce, you moved back?"

He nodded.

I waited for more. Smiled firmly. It worked.

"Right," he said. "Um…I moved a lot when I was a kid, as I told you. My, um…my mother is a doctor, and she works in a lot of third world countries." He paused. "I think we moved fifteen, twenty times. I lived all over."

"Holy guacamole," I said. "Now *that* is an unconventional childhood!"

"Yes." He adjusted his cutlery again. "Don't put that on the Web site."

"Why?"

"It's not relevant." His jaw looked a little knotty.

"Well, here's the thing, Ian," I said. "If people feel they know you a little, they'll trust you more."

He shifted. "Right. But don't put that on the Web site."

I shrugged. "All right. Well, why do you love animals?"

He narrowed his eyes. "That's kind of a vapid question, don't you think?"

I gritted my teeth. "Not to your clients, Dr. McFarland! Can you please scrape up an answer?"

He sighed. Looked at the table. Looked back at me. "They're loyal. Next question?"

My turn to heave a sigh. "Here. Why don't I just put my laptop away and you can pretend I'm your sister and we're just having a chat, okay?"

"No."

"Why?" I demanded. "If you want me to do this for you, you're going to have to help."

"I can't pretend you're my sister."

It might've been a cute line, if, for example, it had been said by someone else. But in Ian's case, the meaning was quite literal. Rolling my eyes, I put the laptop away and gave up for the moment.

Our server brought us dinner—trout almondine for me, with this little stack of green beans and a risotto that smelled like heaven; grilled salmon and mashed potatoes for Ian. We ate in silence for a moment or two.

"Here's what we can do," I said. "If you don't want to talk about yourself that much, we'll just say you spent a summer here as a kid, fell in love with Vermont, were so excited when the chance came to move here permanently. We'll put up a really great picture of you and Angie, the smokin' hottie vet and his best girl." This got a small smile. Hello! That little flash was quite…delicious. However, I was in professional mode and barely noticed (snort). "And then we'll ask for pictures of your clients and their pets. We'll have to get releases, but that won't be a problem. We'll have a section called 'Ask Dr. McFarland,' where people can write in asking why Rover chews Mommy's best shoes, and you can answer in a friendly and approachable tone." I paused, took another bite of the delicious trout. "With me so far?"

"Yes," he said.

"I also think you should hold a pet fair," I said, warming to my subject.

"What's a pet fair?" he asked.

"It'll be like an open house at your practice. People bring their pets, you give away dog and cat and gerbil treats, maybe have a trainer there to give out tips."

"That sounds good," he said.

"And one of those agility courses. Bowie would rock that," I said. "Maybe Noah could rig up a little cart, and Bowie could pull…nah, insurance issues, forget that. Oh! You could have a pet psychic, too!"

"I don't believe in pet psychics," Ian said.

"That doesn't matter. It'll be fun. Maybe we could get a state trooper to come with one of the K-9 dogs. We could do animal tattoos for the kiddies, face painting, have a balloon guy make those little poodles… This will be great, Ian!" I was practically bouncing in my seat, I was so excited. Ian could walk through the whole thing like a beneficent duke or something, and everyone could see that he wasn't stiff and remote, just a little shy. "What do you think?" I asked.

"It sounds…" *terrifying,* I imagined him saying. "It sounds great, Callie," he said, surprising me. "I never would've thought of something like that."

Well! A flush of pride rushed to my cheeks. "We should do it soon. Winter comes fast up here." At that moment, my phone buzzed. "Oh, sorry, let me get this," I said. "It might be Noah needing something."

It wasn't. It was a text from Annie. *Glad you're feeling lustful toward the vet. Go get him, girl!*

"Is it your grandfather?" Ian asked.

He was leaning forward, a small frown of concern on his face. He had beautiful hands, Ian McFarland did. Capable. Strong. Gentle. "He's fine," I said, my voice a bit breathy. I felt my heart roll over in a slow, pleasant wave. "Just…he's great." Wouldn't mind feeling those hands on me, no sir. I sat up a little straighter and told my inner Betty to pipe down. "So, Ian, are you seeing someone?" I heard myself say. Michelle Obama sighed wearily.

Ian froze for a second, and well did I recognize that deer in the headlights look, oh, yes. "I'm not interested in a relationship at this time, but thank you," he said, in what was clearly a much-rehearsed line.

"No, no! I'm not asking for myself…it was more of

a PR thing. You know, if you had a girlfriend, I'd…but it's a moot point, right? Okay. Moving on." My face was broiling, of course.

Rescue came from an unlikely source.

"Callie! How lovely to see you! And how lucky, too, since you never come by anymore. We'll sit right here. Near our *daughter.*"

My parents, led by Dave, stood in front of me.

"Hi, Mom. And Dad! Oh! Hi, you, guys!" I stood up and hugged my parents, Mom first so she wouldn't kill me, then Dad, who felt a little damp. Mom looked the way she always did when Dad was around—cool, disdainful and mildly disgusted. Dad, on the other hand, twinkled desperately.

"How's my Poodle?" he chortled, cupping my face in his hands, as in *Clearly we did something right, Eleanor, so please don't hurt me.* "Isn't she beautiful, Ellie?"

"Mom, Dad, this is Ian McFarland, the vet who took over for Dr. Kumar," I said.

"A pleasure, young man, a pleasure," Dad said, shaking Ian's hand vigorously and slapping him on the shoulder. "Tobias Grey. Callie's father."

"Nice to meet you," Ian said. He nodded at my mom. "Mrs. Grey."

"I am *not* Mrs. Grey," my mother said, narrowing her eyes. "Eleanor Misinski."

"I'm sorry," Ian said. "Nice to meet you, Ms. Misinski."

"Call me Eleanor," she said, as welcoming as a cuddly viper.

"So what are you guys doing here?" A date between the two of them? Nah. Too much to hope for.

"Your father and I are meeting a special someone," Mom said in her silken voice.

Dad swallowed sickly.

"Oh…right." I winced. The Tour of Whores, as Mom had called it during our last phone call.

"Here are your menus," Dave said, pulling out a chair for my mom. "Can I get you something to drink, Mr. Grey? Ms. Misinski?"

"I'll just take a bottle of Grey Goose," my father said, slapping Dave's solid shoulder. "No relation. Hahahahaha!"

Poor Dad. He was terrified, and rightly so. Sensing a sympathetic soul, he looked at me sharply. "Callie! Poodle! Why don't you and your friend join us?"

"Oh, no. God, no. No, no. Nope. Never."

"Callie, you should," my mother said, slithering into her seat. "Stay and see what your father was doing while I was pregnant with your brother. Your…" she looked Ian up and down as if trying to determine his species "…*companion* is welcome, too, of course."

"No! We can't. It's business. Business dinner. Sorry!" I chirped. "Ian, shall we sit back down? To discuss things? In more detail? We have so much more to…"

To my despair, Ian was checking his phone. "I'm sorry, Callie. I have to go. I'm on call at the hospital."

"He's on call. Must be an emergency. Drat! We have to go!"

"You don't have to come," Ian said.

"Shush!" I hissed. "Bye, Mom! Bye, Dad! Dave, I'll just call you with my credit card number, okay?" With that, I grabbed my laptop and turned to my parents. "Bye!"

"Why can't you stay, Calliope? He doesn't need you," Mom said, surveying the martini menu.

"Um…" I said, my heart sinking.

"Stay, by all means," she said in an iron tone.

"I need to go, Callie," Ian said. "Thank you for dinner."

"Don't abandon me!" I hissed. "Take me with you."

"Callie, I need to leave. See?" He held up his phone, and I caught a glimpse of a text...*emergency, dog, car.* "It was nice meeting you both," he said to my parents.

"Great to meet you, son!" Dad cried, looking over his shoulder to see what was taking so long with the booze.

"You're a cruel man, Ian McFarland," I muttered, but he was already halfway across the restaurant. Dammit. There went the cavalry, off to heal the wounded. So unfair! With a sigh, I surrendered and slid into the chair between my parents. "So," I said. "I'm guessing this is round one in the Tour of Whores?"

"Exactly," Mom said.

"Oh, gosh, that's a good one!" Dad laughed, glancing around frantically, checking all possible exits.

Mercifully, Brittany, who'd just served Ian and me, bustled over at that moment. "I'll have a huge dirty martini," I said. "Very big."

"Make it two," Mom seconded. For an instant, something flickered through her eyes, but it was gone before I could tell what it was.

"It's unanimous," Dad twinkled desperately. "Three big-ass dirty martinis for our little family gathering."

"How nice," Brittany said. "Okey-doke, I'll be right back with your drinks!"

I took a deep breath, mentally girding my loins. "So how did you get the...what's her name, Dad?"

He looked at me blankly. "Who?"

"Your—the woman who's coming today."

"Oh." He looked at Mom nervously, but she radiated calm, the same way a lizard does, cool, unblinking. "Her name is—"

"Tanya," Mom interrupted. "Which I think is a fitting

name. Tanya the Whore. It works just as well for a stripper or a drug dealer, don't you think?"

"Mmm," I murmured. "So, why did she agree to meet with you and Mom?"

"Oh, she doesn't know I'll be here," Mom said.

"Where are those drinks?" Dad barked.

Ten minutes later, when I'd almost finished my martini and was feeling a bit better, Dad stiffened. Stood up. Glanced at Mom, who gave an imperious nod. "Tanya!" Dad called weakly. "Over here."

She wasn't what I expected in a home-wrecking trollop, that was for sure. Weighing in at well over two hundred pounds, her plump cheeks quite red, hair in a long, graying braid, Tanya wore a purple peasant dress that made her look like an extra in some dreadful Woodstock retrospective. She completed her look with Hobbit-esque Birkenstocks and blue-tinted granny glasses.

"Well, well, well," she said, thumping her way over. "Tobias Grey. You haven't changed a bit."

"And you!" Dad said, trying to hit his usual Clooney sparkle. "You…it's… Hello!"

Tanya leaned in to kiss Dad's cheek, but he flinched. Her gaze drifted to Mom and me. "Hello," she said uncertainly.

"Hi," I muttered, draining my drink.

"Hello," Mom said, giving her a John Malkovich smile. You know the type. Sure, it's a smile, but you just know some serious shit is about to rain down.

"Uh, Tanya, have a seat," my father said, his face a little ashen. "This is my daughter, Calliope, and, um…my ex-wife. Eleanor."

"Oh," Tanya said. "Hi." She gave Dad a dry look.

"Isn't this nice," Mom said, and if I'd had testicles,

I'm quite sure they would've retracted in terror. Dad swallowed. "Tobias, tell Tanya…oh, isn't that charming? Tobias and Tanya, Tanya and Tobias. So *cute*. Tobias, tell her why she's here."

Dad and Tanya sat down. It was beginning to dawn on Tanya that this was not going to be the evening she'd expected. *Run, lady,* I mentally urged her. *Run fast.*

"Well," Dad said, trying to smile. "My wife here…she…back when we were, ah, married…"

"Who wants bread?" Brittany, our chipper server, plopped down a basket in front of us. Even though I'd just eaten with Ian, I pounced on it, tearing off a hunk of the still-warm sourdough and stuffing it in my mouth. Almost as good as cake batter.

"Would you ladies like some?" Dad asked, wiping the sweat from his brow. He pried the basket out of my hand and offered some to Mom, who shook her head, then to Tanya.

"Who wants to order? Oh, should I bring more menus?" Brittany asked.

"You know, Brittany," I said, chewing, "we need a little privacy."

"That's fine! Call me when you're ready! My name's Brittany!"

"We know," Mom said icily, staring at her nametag. Brittany backed away.

"So what's going on here, Toby?" Tanya said. Mom's eyes narrowed even more. "I take it you didn't want to just catch up."

"Well, see, Eleanor and I…we…well, we're thinking about reconciling. But she wants a little…closure, might we call it, El?"

"We might," Mom said. "You see, Tanya, is it? You

were sleeping with my husband when I was pregnant with our third child. Which I found quite…unsettling."

"You gotta be kidding me," Tanya muttered, giving Dad an evil look. "You cheated on your pregnant wife? You shit."

"Very bad of me, I realize that. I'm deeply sorry," Dad babbled.

"Very bad, I'll say. I would've strung you up by your balls," Tanya said. Dad's face drained of its last bit of color.

"But let's not forget your own role in this," Mom said. "You slept with a married man." Each word was an acid-dipped razor. "Tobias said you knew he was married."

"Yeah. I did. So sue me," she said.

Dad stiffened. Mom stiffened. I grabbed another hunk of bread.

"I mean, I didn't know you were *pregnant*," Tanya continued, "and if I had, I would never have gotten near him. He *said* he was separated." She nailed Dad with a look nearly as terrifying as my mother's reptilian gaze and continued. "My husband died the year before. I was looking for a meaningless fling, had dinner with Toby here once, slept with him, and that was that." She paused. "It wasn't my proudest moment, but I was lonely. And I wasn't married. Your husband couldn't keep it in his pants. I think you should blame him."

"Oh, I do," Mom said. "Believe me, I do." But she looked slightly daunted, perhaps realizing that the first stop on the Tour hadn't been quite the trashy slut she'd imagined.

"So." Tanya looked around the table at each of us. "Anything else?"

I couldn't help it. I kind of liked Tanya. "Well, now, Tanya's got a point," I said. "You wanted to meet her, here she is. Can we be done? Is everyone happy now?

Yes?" I glanced at the aging hippie, feeling more than a twinge of pity for her. "I think we're done, Tanya. Sorry for this." Then, in my need to make everyone on earth think well of me, I added, "I love your, uh...shoes."

Tanya stood with great dignity and surveyed the three of us. Very deliberately, she picked up her full water glass and tossed the contents in Dad's face. Then she snatched up the bread basket *and* the little bowl of chilled butter and walked out, right past Dave, who didn't say a word.

My parents sat in silence. Water dripped off Dad's hair and down into his collar.

"Thank you so much for making me stay," I said. "I'm getting cheesecake. And you guys are paying."

CHAPTER ELEVEN

ON MONDAY MORNING, I came into the office full of my usual sunshine and butterflies (or so I liked to think). I pretty much had the corner on the market for sunshine and butterflies… Pete and Leila were so wrapped up in each other, they almost had their own language, like children raised by wolves or whatnot. Karen was best left alone until after ten…it was only safe to go past her office if you were planning to toss in a hunk of raw meat or a double-shot cappuccino. Damien, of course, felt it was beneath his dignity to be cheerful. Fleur preferred to burst into the office, always ten minutes late, talking about hangovers and weekends in New York City and needing a smoke before she could reasonably be expected to function.

"Right," she said now, barreling down the hall. "Cheerio, old bean. What's the news?"

"Not much," I said. Fleur was much friendlier when Muriel wasn't around, something I'd noted and filed away. Mark and Muriel hadn't arrived yet, hence the "old bean" bit. "How was your weekend?"

"Went out with a total wanker, Callie, you'd simply die if I told you." She then proceeded to slay me by launching into a story about a man, a largemouth bass and a thong, but between her colloquialisms and nicotine buzz, I couldn't quite keep up. Still, I nodded cheerfully when I guessed it was appropriate.

"So, Callie, it must be hard, seeing them together all the time. They're really in love, aren't they?" Fleur asked. Before I could find a way to answer that, she went on. "Anyway, I've been meaning for us to have a chat. You ever see that bloke? The vet?"

"Um, yes, actually. My niece had a field trip to his office. I might be doing a little work for him on the side."

"Really? Oh." Fleur flashed a quick smile, then began reapplying her lipstick, and mussed her short hair. "Right. Seems like a sweetie, yeah?"

"Sure," I said, though *sweetie* felt a bit left of center when I thought of Ian. Which I seemed to be doing a lot. Over the weekend, in between sanding a canoe for Noah, trying out some new hip-hop moves while Bronte howled with horrified laughter, babysitting for Seamus and taking Josephine for a kayak ride, I'd started work on Ian's Web site. E-mailed him a request for a picture of him and Angie and was still waiting for an answer. Called a bunch of people for the pet fair, which would be held in two weeks.

"I saw him as well," Fleur said. "Down at Toasted & Roasted, yeah? Had ourselves a coffee. He was sending out signals, yeah?"

"Really? He told me…uh, never mind."

"What?" she demanded.

"Well," I said hesitantly, "he said he wasn't looking for a relationship right now. But of course, he may be feeling differently with you."

She smirked. "Differently, is it? Could be. Well, I'd best get on. Cheerio!"

I definitely could not see Ian and Fleur as a couple. Wondered just what that coffee meant. Knowing Fleur, they could've just passed each other on the street—God knew the woman exaggerated her love life. But on a real date? No way. Not the way she talked a mile a minute, always with the crazy stories and... *Now, now, Callie,* said my inner Michelle. *Don't be catty.*

Right. Besides, I had work to do. I set down my coffee and turned on my computer, staring into space as it warmed up. Well, not space, exactly. At a picture of Mark and me at the Clios. My dress had been absolutely adorable...this plum-colored A-line number with lighter purple flowers sewn on the bodice. Lots of great cleavage. I looked so happy. Mark did, too. We *had* been happy...

Might want to toss that one, Mrs. Obama offered. She was, as usual, right. But not just yet.

I forced my attention away from the photo and smiled. Fake smiling can lead to real smiling, I once read, and real smiling is good for a person. Still, my heart sighed.

Around ten, there was a ruckus in the hallway. "Give me ten minutes, Damien!" Mark snapped. Uh-oh. He rarely lost his cool in the office. Trouble in paradise? Betty Boop perked up.

Mark strode right into my office, which seemed to shrink instantly.

"Hey, Mark," I said, giving him a big smile.

He didn't smile back. Instead, he closed the door and put his hands on his hips. "What's this I hear about you doing some freelance work for some vet?"

"Oh, yeah," I answered easily. "A little PR for the guy who came on the BTR hike. Not big enough for the agency. Web site, stuff like that. I'll probably charge him two hundred bucks." I paused. "I e-mailed you about this over the weekend."

"I'll be the judge of whether it's big enough for the agency, Callie," he growled.

I blinked in surprise. "You never minded me doing little jobs before, Mark," I pointed out. "The seniors' center, the nursery school…"

"Right," he said. "But…well, you should've asked."

"I did, Mark. I e-mailed you."

"Right," he said again. He took a deep breath, then sighed and sat down on my couch, running a hand through his tousled hair. "Are you two seeing each other?"

I nearly choked. "Um…no! No, Mark."

He looked at me for a long minute. "Are you seeing anybody these days?" His voice was velvety soft. The same voice he'd used in Santa Fe.

I took a quick breath. "It's…I…it's not really your business, is it?" My heart rolled.

Mark glanced through the wavy glass wall toward Fleur, who was clicking on her computer and probably straining to overhear us. "No, I guess not," he said, dropping his eyes to the floor. "It's just…I'm sorry, Callie. Didn't mean to be a prick."

"It's okay," I said, my voice cracking a little. My stomach felt hot, my knees tingled.

I heard Muriel's voice then, and the sound of her office door closing. Swallowing, I took a breath— seemed like I'd forgotten to for a few minutes. "Anything else, Mark?" I asked in a normal tone.

"Actually, yes." He looked down at the floor. "I just took a look at your idea for Hammill Farms. I have some problems with it. You need a new concept."

My mouth dropped open. "Seriously?"

"Seriously. You need to rethink it."

"I...I... Really?"

"Yes, Callie," he said in a harder tone. "Really."

Hammill Farms was one of our biggest accounts, second only to BTR. They'd made syrup here in Vermont for 150 years and wanted to do for syrup what Grey Goose had done for vodka—have people appreciate the good stuff, basically. They were also willing to fork out the cash to do so. The owner, John, was obsessed with syrup—he'd nearly gotten Mark and me drunk on the stuff when we'd visited. That was the week before Muriel came. The week before my birthday.

We were showing John the concept this week, and honestly, I thought it was one of my best campaigns. In the television spots, we'd hear the narrator say: *John Hammill is a man obsessed.* Then we'd show John, like a master winemaker, holding up a glass of syrup to the light as he waxed poetic, extolling the thickness, the clarity, the grade, the subtleties of flavor. Then we'd go to footage of John in action, tramping through the woods, kissing his maples, talking about ideal conditions and the tradition of syrup-making as he checked the sap lines and boiler, talking nonstop. We'd end with him pouring syrup onto a stack of pancakes, taking a bite of pancakes and, as he did when we visited, practically falling out of his chair in near-orgasmic pleasure. The voice-over would say: *It takes a guy like that to make syrup like this.* Fade out to a picture of the farm in winter, the newly designed label and the words *Hammill Farms Maple Syrup: Six generations of perfection.* The print and Internet ads would echo that theme, as would the radio spots.

The *pièce de résistance* and my huge home run was the narrator—Terry Francona, the manager of the Boston Red Sox. When we first visited the farm, I'd seen a picture of Mr. Francona in John's office. Apparently, he'd visited with his family last fall just before the post-season. So I wrote to Mr. Francona's agent, sent a huge basket of Hammill Farms goodies…maple syrup, maple sugar, gourmet pancake mix, T-shirts—the whole shebang—and said what an honor Terry had bestowed upon the farm with his visit, expressed the importance of family farming here in Red Sox Nation, yadda yadda, and the upshot was that Terry said yes. Every Red Sox fan in New England would recognize that voice.

The concept was fantastic.

"It's just not what we're after," Mark said in the face of my stunned silence.

"Well, what…what are you looking for, Mark?" I asked. This was the first time *ever* that Mark had dis-agreed with a concept of mine. He'd tweaked, made sug-gestions, sure…but he'd never rejected anything of mine before. Well. Any of my work, that is. He'd rejected me just fine.

"I think we're looking for something a little more…whimsical," Mark said now.

"Whimsical?"

"Yeah." He didn't meet my eyes.

My heart raced sickly. There was another word he used that gave me pause. "And who's 'we,' Mark?"

His expression hardened just a little. "Well, Muriel pointed out that…she thought it was a little… It just wasn't what we wanted."

Muriel. "Well, I stand by it. I think it's a really good idea."

"That's fine, Callie, you're welcome to think that." His mouth tightened. "But I want something else. We have a meeting with John on Friday morning."

"And did you and Muriel have anything specific in mind?" I asked.

"Look!" Mark barked. I jumped. "You're not infallible, okay? You do great work, Callie—we all agree on that—but could you just give us another concept? I need something by Thursday afternoon, if it's not too much of a problem, okay?"

I swallowed hard. "Yes, of course, Mark. I just…I'm on it." I paused. "What time's the meeting on Friday?"

"You don't need to come," he said harshly, and with that, he left my office, the door gaping open so I could see straight into Muriel's black-and-white splendor across the hall. She was on the phone, but she gave me a nasty smile.

My computer chimed with an instant message. *He's jealous!* Fleur wrote. I didn't even know what she was talking about.

My hands were shaking, and my heart stuttered in my chest. So Muriel was weighing in on my work, huh? And Mark was listening. There was nothing wrong with the Hammill Farms ad. Not a damn thing. I'd be hard-pressed to come up with something better than that.

And I wasn't going to the meeting. That was a first. A very bad first.

For the next three and a half days, I worked furiously. Pete and Leila stayed late, laying out the storyboards for the television spots, finessing the PowerPoint presentations, designing new print ads. For three nights in a row, I worked at both the office and at home, staying up past 1:00 a.m., setting my alarm for 6:00 a.m. I kept my door closed at work, and everyone pretended things were normal. Mark said hello, Muriel pretended to smile, Fleur sent me encouraging e-mails and schmoozed with my nemesis, playing both sides.

By Thursday, I had two more ad campaigns. Neither was as good as the original, but both were still pretty solid. At one o'clock (because Mark had said afternoon, right?), I knocked on the open door to his office. He waved me in, though he was on the phone.

"Okay, Mom. I should go. See you for dinner Sunday, right? Oh, great, I'm glad you liked them. Love you, too." He smiled and hung up. "Hey, Callie." As if he hadn't chewed me out the other day. As if things were peachy keen.

"How's your mom?" I asked.

"She's great, Callie. Thanks for asking. What's up?"

"Is now a good time to go over the new Hammill concepts?"

His mouth fell open. "Oh," he said. "Well, actually, I...um...I'm glad you're here." He got up and closed the door, then turned to me, his hands clasped behind his back. "I'll take a look at those later, but...actually, we came up with something else."

I blinked.

"Yeah, and we'll show it to John tomorrow. But leave those there, just in case." He ran a hand through his hair and looked at me, his expression sheepish.

"What do you mean, you came up with something else?" I asked faintly.

He winced. "Well, Mure and I were kicking it around at home and—"

That was the last straw. "Really, Mark? I just spent three days on these. And so did Pete and Leila—your employees, in case you forgot. We've been busting our asses on this, while you and *Mure*..." My voice broke. "Here. Keep them." Tossing the comps and CDs on his coffee table, I turned to leave. My hands were icy, and I was dangerously close to tears.

"Callie, wait. Wait, honey. Don't go."

He was using that voice. That low, smoky, intimate voice and I felt a flash of anger so hot and sharp, it was like a razor left in the sun. I *hated* him in that moment. Wanted to punch him in the teeth.

But more than that, I hated myself, because that voice still had an effect, dammit all to hell.

He came a little closer. "Callie, come on," he whispered.

"What?" I snapped.

"Callie, look. Turn around. Please."

I took a slow breath and obeyed.

Mark tilted his head and looked into my eyes. "Muriel is not a threat to you. She's just cutting her teeth. She's got some talent, she really does."

Right, I thought. *I'll just bet she does.*

"Please don't be upset. I'll be taking your ideas, too."

"Whatever, Mark. You own the company."

"Yes," he said. "I do." There was a warning in his voice. "But, Callie, you're an important part of this place, you know that."

"Yes," I answered, my fists clenching. "I *do* know that. And I just spent three and a half days coming up with two new campaigns, pulling the art department off everything else, just to replace a perfectly good ad campaign because your girlfriend wants to play creative director."

Good for you, Mrs. Obama cheered. I didn't feel so triumphant. Christ, what if he fired me right now? I never talked like this! I never had to.

Mark stepped closer to me. Unlike the rest of us, he didn't have glass walls. My heart rate kicked up, and I felt my cheeks prickle with heat. "You're right," he said softly. "And I'm sorry. About a lot of things, Callie."

My throat tightened in helpless anger...and other things. Sorrow. Heartache. Memories of feeling so stupid for so long. *Don't cave now,* the First Lady urged. *You're doing great.*

"Look at me, Callie," Mark said softly.

Ah, shit, Michelle sighed. *Here we go again.*

Mark's eyes were ridiculously appealing. Dark, dark brown with thick, long lashes. It wasn't fair. I totally understood the old expression, *damn your eyes.* As if reading my mind, Mark smiled, just a little bit, and that was what broke me. For a flash, it felt like we were back in that closet in Gwen Hardy's basement, and a hot wave of longing surged over me. It just wasn't fair.

"No one can replace you, Callie," he said quietly. "No one."

I took a shaky breath. Confusion and anger and, yes, hope—dopey, immortal hope—churned around in my heart. "I appreciate that," I whispered, blinking back tears. "But I'm not sure this is going to work for me, Mark."

"Don't you even think about it," Mark said, taking my hands. "Trust me. Things will settle down. Muriel will find her place. Be patient, okay? Please?" His thumbs rubbed the backs of my hands—gently, slowly, before he let go. "Now I've made my best girl cry," he murmured, going over to his desk. "Let me find you a tissue or something."

He's using you, Michelle told me.

The thing was, I already knew.

MARK AND MURIEL LEFT FOR their meeting with Hammill Farms at 9:00 on Friday morning. Damien went, too, to help set up the presentation and take notes. The morning seemed to last forever. I fussed, I did busywork, I e-mailed clients and subcontractors, I deleted old files. I could barely sit still.

Finally, around two, they returned. The rest of us fell silent, waiting for the verdict while pretending to work. Our first indicator was Muriel, who stomped down the hall in her tight black skirt and slammed the door to her office. She didn't spare me a glance. Mark and Damien came along next and went straight to Mark's office, closing the door behind them.

A half hour later, Damien crept out of Mark's office. A few minutes later, he sent me an e-mail. *Callie shoots, Callie scores. Hammill went with your original idea.* ♥ *Damien.*

CHAPTER TWELVE

AFTER WORK THAT DAY, I dragged Damien to the Whoop & Holler, ye olde Vermont townie bar. "I'm not sitting there," he said, giving our booth a disdainful once-over. "I'll get crabs."

"Oh, stop," I said. "We couldn't go to Elements, because Dave works there, and since you guys are still broken up…" Damien sighed, and I continued. "Besides, I'm meeting someone here later." Another attempt at eCommitment's offerings. "And," I continued craftily, before he could insult me over my anemic love life, "they have the best apricot sours ever."

Damien's perfectly groomed eyebrows bounced up at the mention of his favorite drink. "Okay. For you. On this day of days," he said, sitting down gingerly.

"Two apricot sours, Jim!" I called, doing a double take when I saw my brother at the bar. "And don't serve Freddie! He's underage!"

"You little shit," Jim said, cuffing Freddie. "How dare you come in with a fake ID!"

"I turned twenty-one in April!" my brother yelped. "My own sister might not remember, but it's still true!"

I paused and did the math. "Oh, that's right, Jim. Sorry!"

Freddie gave me the finger and grinned.

When our drinks came, Damien took a sip and then,

mollified by the yumminess, told the whole story, with plenty of embellishment and snark, just as I'd hoped.

First, John Hammill had been surprised not to see me, as he was under the (correct) impression that I was the genius of the operation. Secondly, he'd been confused and slightly disturbed by Muriel's idea.

"It was a cartoon, Callie," Damien said, slurping more apricot sour. "Of a squirrel, okay? So her little squirrel, which is apparently named Squeaky the Squirrel, climbs up on a barrel of syrup, jumps in and starts lapping it up. And then comes this scary little high-pitched voice, and I'm pretty fucking sure it was Muriel...'So good even a squirrel will eat it!'"

"What does that even mean?" I asked, covering my mouth in horror.

"Who the fuck knows?" he said, laughing so hard he practically choked. I couldn't help joining in. "So John says, 'I'm really uncomfortable with this...who'd want to buy syrup when a rodent's been swimming around in it? What are you gonna do next? Rats?' And M&M, they give each other these looks, like they can't fucking believe he took a pass."

"So what happened after that?" I asked, sucking up the last of my girly-girl drink through a straw.

"So Mark said something like, 'Well, we do have another idea,' and shows yours, and John practically wets himself, he loves it so much. Came out of his chair when he heard that you already got Terry fucking Francona to agree."

I sat back against the booth. "That's great. I'm so glad John liked it. He's such a good guy," I said, pleased beyond words. Still, the fact didn't escape me that I'd just spent the past three days frantically working, all on a Muriel whim. That was not cool. Not at all.

"So. You win, Callie," Damien said, slurping down the rest of his drink. "What next?"

I took a deep breath and let it out slowly. "I don't know, Damien," I admitted. "Do you…" I hesitated. "Do you think Muriel's going to…last? With Mark, I mean?"

Damien sighed. "I don't know," he said. "She's not the one I'd pick for him, that's for sure."

I didn't say anything else. Annie had just come in, and she'd skin me if she knew I was talking about Mark's love life. She was here to eavesdrop on my meeting with Ron, my latest attempt at finding The One. I wasn't *always* sitting around mooning after my boss, my vet and other emotionally unavailable men.

Damien glanced at his watch. "Well. Must run. I have much better plans than hanging out here with you and these townies. No offense, of course. Toodles!"

"You're going to get beat up if you don't stop saying that," I advised. "And I'll be leading the mob, carrying a pipe."

To my surprise, he kissed my cheek. "Thanks for the drink, Callie. And well done. Oh!" He looked over at the door. "Is that the someone you're meeting? He's looking around, has a desperate, furtive, rat-like demeanor…"

"Shut it, Damien," I muttered. I looked over and waved. As if electrified, Annie hurtled over, followed closely by Freddie.

"Hi," she said. "Is that him? The guy you waved to? Is he cute? He's not bad. At least he's tall."

"Go sit where you can eavesdrop," I instructed. Annie took the booth directly behind me. "Come, Fred," she ordered. "Sit. Stay."

"He looks unwashed," Damien murmured. "Must flee. Tra-la!"

My date began making his way over. The Whoop &
Holler was a dark and cavernous space, excellent for al-
coholics and clandestine hookups. As he got closer, my
heart sank. *No, no, don't do that,* I told the pesky organ.
He's got...hidden depths? He might, anyway...

"This is gonna be great," Freddie said in a stage whisper.

"Fred, don't you dare..." Ah, there was no point.
Little brothers were created to mock, torment and steal
from their sisters, and Fred was a shining example.
Besides, Ron was here.

Damien was right. He wasn't quite...clean. Not that
he was filthy, mind you. But here I was, in a wicked cute
dress, a green-and-white pattern with flattering belt and,
yes, darling orange suede high-heeled shoes for that pop
of color. I'm just saying. And Ron... Ron wore faded and
stained blue work pants, matching shirt. "Callie?" he
asked, frowning fiercely.

"Yes! Hi, Ron! It's so nice to meet you!" I chirruped,
hoping that this would soon be true. He had an earthy,
not exactly unpleasant smell about him. "Have a seat."

He obeyed. Ron was a large, solid guy in that reassuring manly man way. We'd done the whole tennis volley of
e-mails, and he'd actually seemed pretty nice. Friendly.
Asked questions, gave answers. Our knees bumped, and I
quickly shifted so as to avoid any unintended signals or
dirt.

"Sorry, I'm late," he muttered. "It was my night to
milk."

"Oh! Milk the, um...cows?" *No, Callie. The monkeys.*
I heard the telltale wheeze of my brother's laughter
already, Annie's little snort. Super. "I mean, you said you
were a farmer. I guess a dairy farmer, right?"

He nodded.

"That's great. I love cows," I said. It was true. I did. Especially the kind on the side of the Ben & Jerry's truck.

Ron's eyes dropped to my chest. Damn! My adorable dress was quite low-cut…not slutty low, but low enough. If one has a great rack, one must use it to distract from food babies and the like. Or so I'd thought before now. Ron looked very…assessing, as if calculating my own potential in the dairy department.

"You don't happen to supply Ben & Jerry's, do you?" I asked. It could never hurt to have an in…

"No."

"Cabot's? I love their cheese."

"No."

Freddie squeaked.

"So, anyway," I said, determined to charm. "It's nice to finally meet face-to-face."

Ron said nothing.

"Want to order something? A drink? Nachos?" I asked.

He glanced over to Jim, who called out, "What can I get you, pal?"

"Beer," Ron answered.

"What kind? We have Coors, Coors Light, Bud, Bud Light, Amstel, Amstel Light, Miller, Miller Light…"

"Bud." Ron looked back at me. Took a deep breath. Let it out. Dropped his eyes to the girls again.

"So, Ron, tell me about yourself," I said, tipping my head so my shiny hair might distract him from my bosom.

"I'm a farmer," he said, not looking up.

"Yes! We covered that, I think. Have you been a farmer long?"

"Yup."

This guy made Ian look like Joy Behar in the chat department. The peanut gallery was having fun, anyway. I reminded myself to remember this at Christmas and not buy them so many presents.

"That's great." Tick. Tick. Tick. "And…uh, you said you were divorced?"

"Yup."

Nothing more. The Betty Boop in my head rubbed her hands together. *He's a challenge, that's all. We are not going to admit defeat here. He will like us. We are adorable, let's not forget!*

I glanced around. Above the bar, the Sox were on. Poifect. Man-talk. I could fake baseball chatter with the best of them.

"Ron, do you watch sports?" I asked. He was still staring at my chest. I *did* wear this dress, so I couldn't exactly be irritated. "Ron? Up here, pal." I snapped my fingers. Ah. Finally. Eye contact. I smiled to show I understood. "Do you like baseball? How 'bout them Sox, huh? Second place. That's not bad. Those damn Yankees, right?" I smiled ruefully. I often checked the sports page for just this sort of chatty tidbit. He still said nothing. Maybe he was diabetic or something, having a blood sugar crash. I often felt the same way when I went too long without cake batter. "Ron? Do you like baseball?"

"Nope," he said. His eyes dropped back to my chest.

"Everything okay, Ron? You feeling all right?" I asked.

"I'm fine."

Freddie wheezed behind me. Could I smack him from this angle? Alas, no.

Well, clearly Ron wasn't going to stop looking at my

chest unless I made him, so I picked up the little napkin that had come with my drink, unfolded it and held it in front of the girls. "Ron? What's the deal?" I asked. "You were very nice in your e-mails…can we please have a conversation here?"

He shrugged. "Well…the e-mails…" His voice trailed off.

"What?" I asked.

He scratched his head vigorously. "My aunt wrote them."

Behind me, Annie and my brother sputtered and choked. "I see. Well. Tell your aunt she seems very nice. Maybe she'd like to go out with me, hmm?"

Nothing. No reaction.

"I think we're probably done here, Ron," I said gently.

"Great," he answered. "Want to go back to my place and watch porn?"

Holy Lord in heaven! "I…I…I'm gonna have to pass on that one, Ron," I finally managed. "You take care."

Thirty seconds later, when Ron was a memory (though the smell of manure still hung in the air), Fred and Annie staggered to my booth and collapsed across from me. "I hope you're gonna marry him." My brother sighed.

"You really should let me screen them," Annie said, wiping her eyes.

"You picked the human hair guy!" I reminded her.

"At least he was clean," she said.

"Ish," I corrected. I sighed. "Fred, buy your best girls drinks, what do you say?"

"Sure, Calorie," he said amiably. "Jim! Another one of those candy-ass drinks for my sister, okay? Annie, what do you want?"

"I have to go," she said regretfully. "Tonight's Family Fun Night. We're playing mini golf."

"Rub it in, O happily married woman and mother of perfect child," I said. She smiled modestly. "I don't get it, guys," I continued. "I'd want to date me. Why is it so hard for me? I'm wicked fun, I dress nicely, I'm friendly... I'd *love* to date me. Wouldn't you?"

"The whole incest-sister thing aside?" Fred asked. I nodded. "Sure," he said.

"I'd date you," Annie agreed. "If I was gay, I would. Definitely."

"Thank you," I said. She smiled and gave me a quick hug, then went off to Perfectville.

Freddie and I ordered nachos and talked about work as we ate—my work, his lack thereof, and what he might do with his life. "You could always be a lawyer," I suggested. "You do love the sound of your own voice."

"True, true. Not that the universe needs another lawyer," he said. "Hey, completely meaning to change the subject, I guess the next stop on the Tour of Whores is coming."

"So much fun," I murmured. "Poor Dad. All this for nothing."

"Oh, I don't know. I think they'll make it," Fred said, draining his beer.

"Who?" I asked. "Mom and Dad? Really?"

"Yeah. They're gonna make it. I could be wrong, of course. There's always a first time."

I rolled my eyes. "You and that little ego of yours," I murmured. My voice trailed off.

Mark and Muriel had just come into the bar.

In the olden days, Mark used to take the gang to Whoop & Holler after a particularly successful pitch or a long week. Muriel hadn't changed from the black skirt, white shirt and killer heels she'd worn to Hammill Farms today. Mark's hand was on her back as he guided her to a table on the other side of the dimly lit bar. As she sat down, she looked up at him and laughed at whatever he was saying.

They looked…happy. My Hammill Farms presentation had kicked Muriel's in the butt, and she was laughing, and gorgeous, and on a date. With Mark.

My heart rolled over like a dead turtle, then sank to the pit of my stomach. Whatever triumph and pleasure I'd felt over work today faded. *I'm going to slap you,* Michelle said. *No one can make you feel inferior without your consent. So snap out of it.*

Easy for you to say, I told her. *Are you the one who was just invited to watch porn at a dairy farm? Huh, First Lady who lives at the White House? And stop stealing Mrs. Roosevelt's lines.*

"Callie? Wake up," my brother said. "You're muttering to yourself." He turned around to look where I was staring. "Why, it's Mark! The guy you've been mooning over half your life! Want to give me a piggyback ride to show how cute we are?"

"Shh!" I hissed, kicking his shin.

See, way back when I was a teen and in fact mooning over Mark, I would often take Freddie on my rounds. I thought it would make me look adorable, loving and mature, that pretty Callie Grey and her sweet little brother whom she so obviously loved. Of course, I *did* love Freddie (much of the time, anyway) and he was always thrilled when I took him out of the funeral home for a spin on my bike or yes, a piggyback ride. One day, I made the mistake of informing my prop that I loved a certain boy. "That one,"

I whispered when we actually caught a glimpse of Mark at a soccer game. The little shit never forgot.

"I'm going to the ladies' room," I said. "Back in a flash."

"Oh, desperation. So ugly," Freddie said, grinning.

The mirror over the bathroom sink showed that my cheeks were flushed. My hands were shaking. My heart seemed to be shaking, too.

For some reason, I thought—with absolutely no evidence, of course... Well. It had crossed my mind that after the little speech in Mark's office about how irreplaceable I was...combined with the reinforcement of my creative talent...that Mark would...that things would...

Oh, God. Michelle Obama was right. I was an idiot. "Idiot!" I said to my reflection.

"Excuse me?" said a woman coming out of the stall.

"Oh, sorry, sorry," I said. "Just talking to myself." I gave her a quick look. "I *love* your bag. Kate Spade?"

She smiled. "Yes, actually. Isn't the color cheery? Hey, is it my imagination, or are those Jeffrey Campbell shoes? Absolutely gorgeous!"

I smiled back. "They are."

Ah, accessories. Always good for a bonding moment.

She was very pretty...no. She was beautiful. Short, honey-blond hair, big smile, green eyes, Michelle Pfeiffer beautiful. She was also vaguely familiar, but I couldn't place her face.

"So who's the idiot?" she asked in a friendly tone, washing her hands.

"I am. Or he is. I don't quite know. Maybe we both are."

She smiled and pulled a few paper towels from the dispenser. "It's him, I'm sure of it."

I grinned. "Thank you. You're clearly brilliant."

She laughed and tossed the paper towels into the trash.

"So what brings you to our fair city?" I asked, knowing she wasn't from around here.

"Oh, I was driving through. Dropped in on a friend, but he wasn't home." She fished her car keys out of her adorable purse.

Booty call gone wrong, I thought. "Well, have a safe ride home."

"Thanks," she said. "Nice talking to you."

"You, too." I felt a warm and fuzzy glow in my heart. People were just the best. I *loved* people. Most people, anyway.

Taking a deep breath and smiling determinedly at my reflection, I left the ladies' room. Whoop & Holler was crammed tonight, and of course I knew nine-tenths of the people there. The River Rats were packed around the bar, as they saw it as their sacred duty to support both alcohol-serving institutions in town. Shaunee Cole was fending off a pass from Harmon Carruthers; Harmon was sweet-talking her, undeterred. Jim O'Byrne had fallen asleep, his forehead resting on a shot glass.

"Callie! How's your grandfather?" Robbie Neal asked. He was this year's River Rat president, a nice enough guy who was married to my eighth-grade gym teacher. "Is he coming to the regatta? It's the weekend before Halloween, don't forget."

"I'll work on him," I said, waving to a few other Rats.

"We'd be honored to have him," Robbie said. "Do you think he'd donate a kayak for a raffle we're doing?"

"Is it a good cause? Because if it's for your booze fund, then probably not." Noah had been known to give a canoe or kayak to various fundraisers over the years, though he pretended to be disgruntled when asked. Five years ago, he donated a beautiful cedar rowboat with caned seats to a children's hospital fundraiser. It sold for more than twenty grand. Noah had been equal parts proud and disgusted.

"Sorry to say, Joey Christmas was just diagnosed with cancer," Robbie said. "No insurance."

"Count Noah in, then," I said instantly. Sure, I'd have to whine and plead for an hour, despite the fact that Noah and I both knew he'd give in…it was just tradition. "I'll give something, too, if you want."

Robbie winked. "How about ten minutes alone with you? We'd get a lot of bids on that one," he said, dropping his gaze to my chest and sighing appreciatively.

"Ten minutes, Robbie? Is that all you'd need? How disappointing." He smiled. "So how's Joey doing?"

"You know. You can't kill a guy that mean. Want a drink, Callie?"

I noted that Shaunee had let Harmon's hand stay on her ass. They'd been pretending not to date for years. "No, thanks, Robbie," I said. "I have to go sprinkle fairy dust." He nodded as if that made perfect sense. "Don't let Jim try to drive home," I added. "Or walk, for that matter. He'll fall in the river and drown."

"You bet, Callie. Tell Noah we said hi."

"Sure."

I wound my way through the sea of tables toward my destination. Muriel was facing away from me, and Mark's face was serious as he leaned forward. They were holding hands. *Fairy dust,* I reminded myself. As I approached, Muriel's voice cut through the crowd. "It's just that she's so smug."

My footsteps halted.

"No, Mure, she's really not," Mark said. "She's just more experienced. You'll get there."

"Then why does she have to gloat? I mean—"

Gloat? I didn't gloat! Not one bit (which had taken some serious self-control, let me tell you!). "Hey, guys! How are you?" I said, lurching back into action.

Mark's face lit up. "Callie! What are you doing here?"

"I had a drink with a friend," I said. "Hi, Muriel."

Two spots of red burned on her white, white cheeks, practically melting them.

"Do you want to join us?" Mark said easily.

"Sure. Just for a sec." I pulled up a chair and sat. "Heard it was a little tricky at Hammill today." I may have heard Muriel hiss, and I turned to her magnanimously. "I thought the squirrel idea was pretty cute. Not bad for the first time out."

"Gee. Thanks," she replied, acid practically dripping from her mouth.

"If you ever want to bounce some ideas off me, my door's always open," I said.

She narrowed her eyes to glittering slits. "Thank you."

I took a deep breath. *You're behaving very well,* Michelle affirmed. "Well, I'll leave you two alone. Have a great night."

"Thanks, Callie," Mark said, his eyes warm. "See?" I heard him say as I walked away. "She's not out to get you, sweetpea."

The last word hit me like a poison dart, and I had to force myself to keep going. *Sweetpea.* Mark had called me that once. In Santa Fe, in front of an antique jewelry store, when I'd paused to admire a charm bracelet. *Come on, sweetpea. We have better things to do than shop.* A hundred points for guessing what those better things were, but here's a hint. Hotel. Bed. Two consenting adults.

So. Muriel was sweetpea now.

Freddie and I hung out for another couple hours, as neither of us had other plans. We ordered burgers, I switched to water, Freddie guzzled beer and we watched the Red Sox lose to the Angels in the tenth. M&M left in the sixth, I noted. They were crap fans. Didn't even care about the Sox. Not that I really did, either, but still.

"I'll drive you home, pal," I said, as my newly legal brother was tipsy.

"I'll walk," he slurred.

"Nah. I'll drive you. But I won't tuck you in. You're on your own from the driveway on."

"'Kay. Thanks, sissy."

Five minutes later, my brother had made it through the front door of the funeral home, and my forced good cheer dropped with a thud. The street was quiet; it was nearly midnight, and Georgebury wasn't exactly known for its nightlife. For a few minutes, I just sat in my silent Prius and breathed.

Sweetpea.

Then, my heart both stony and sore, I put Lancelot into reverse and headed out again. But not toward home. Silencing my inner First Lady, I headed down Main Street, past Georgebury Academy. Took a left onto Camden Street and just before the hill veered steeply downward, came to a stop. Turned off my headlights and sat there.

Lights were on downstairs, warm and mellow. I rolled down my window. There was a chill in the air…autumn came fast to Vermont. Despite what the calendar said, summer had already left us. The slight breeze carried a snatch of music toward me... I couldn't quite make it out, but it sounded...sophisticated. Jazz, maybe.

Then someone turned off a light in the kitchen, where, one time, I'd cooked dinner for Mark. A person passed by the living room window. Mark. He stopped, turned and looked back. Then Muriel's wraith-like figure passed by the window. She pushed back some hair, then leaned over and clicked off a light, enshrouding the downstairs in darkness. A few seconds later, an upstairs light went on. Mark's bedroom.

Their bedroom.

My throat was thick with tears, and self-disgust churned in my stomach. Why did I still love him? After the hell he'd put me through this week, I just shouldn't. Why couldn't I get over him? What had been lacking between us? Santa Fe had been the happiest time of my life. Why wasn't it enough for Mark? What did he see in Muriel deVeers, who had all the warmth of one of the bodies in my mother's basement, that he hadn't seen in me? If I was so irreplaceable, if he was still using that velvet voice on me, why wasn't I the one in that house right now?

Callie, get a grip. You are parked on his street, alone, while he's upstairs with another woman. Is this who you want to be? a voice asked. And this time, she didn't even sound like Michelle Obama.

She sounded a lot like me.

CHAPTER THIRTEEN

"EASY THERE, GIRL, we're not in this for exercise," I warned Annie as she paddled vigorously.

"We're not?" Annie asked.

"Nope. This is scenery appreciation only. Oh, look! A loon! Hi, loon!"

It was Saturday morning, a week after my little spying gig, which had left a bad taste in my mouth for quite a few days. A paddle on a lake was just the sort of soul cleansing I needed, so when Annie called this morning, begging me to get her out of the house before she (in her words) "slaughtered every living thing," I suggested kayaking. Then, of course, when I zipped over there, I had to pry her off her child as she covered Seamus's ridiculously cute face with kisses, then made out with her husband in the front hall. "You people disgust me," I said, finally dragging her off.

"Bye, Callie," Jack called.

"Don't you have a twin?" I'd asked. "No? Then save it, bub."

Alas, Annie was a jock...as opposed to my lackadaisical paddle, she was quite the little engine that could, propelling us along at a good clip and expecting me to keep up.

"It's nice to have human company," I said, turning my head a bit so Annie, who was in the back, could hear me.

"Bowie's not jealous?" she asked.

"Of course he is. I had to give him three chew sticks and a pancake."

Kayaking...at least, *this* type of kayaking, was just breathtaking. The let's-see-if-these-rapids-will-kill-me type...not for me. But Annie and I were just circling Granite Lake, following the shore, where small waves slapped at the rocks in a rhythmic, soothing beat. A snapping turtle broke the surface a few feet away, then ducked back under the water with barely a ripple.

Today, the air was soft, the sky gray and gentle. It had been chilly at first, but now that we'd been at it a while, we were warmer. The lake was spring-fed and so clear I could see to the bottom, which was lined with the rocks that gave the lake its name. Surrounding us was a nearly unbroken wall of green—pines and hemlocks, maples and oaks. Overnight, the leaves would start to turn...the few tinges of yellow and red that had been flirting with us since August would suddenly engulf the foliage in fiery, heart-stopping color that would light up our countryside, a shock of beauty so intense it dazzled the eyes and made you wonder how you'd last another year without it.

"So how are your parents?" Annie asked.

"Um...hmm," I said, taking yet another opportunity to stop paddling and turn to talk to my friend. "How to answer that. Let's see. The Tour of Whores made its second stop, apparently. I wasn't there this time—thank you, Jesus—but according to Hester, this particular home wrecker was blind, and when Mom saw the white cane and guide dog, she just lost heart. Left the table and had Dad buy the woman a drink."

"Figured she'd been punished enough? God struck her blind, that sort of thing?" Annie asked.

"Well, apparently she's always been blind," I said. "Which makes me wonder a little."

"About what?"

"Well, the first woman was a widow. This one was blind. What's the next one gonna be? A refugee from a war-torn country? Maybe my dad was—"

"Don't say it," Annie warned.

"Say what? How do you know what I'm thinking?"

"Because we've been friends for a thousand years, and you're always Polly Sunshine when it comes to people—"

"A positive quality, some would say," I interrupted.

"—especially when it comes to men, and especially, *especially* when it comes to your father, and you were about to say something along the lines of 'My dad was performing a public service,' am I right?"

"No! I'm well aware that he broke my mother's heart. But, Annie, you have to admit…"

"I should slap you."

"You and Michelle Obama," I muttered, then, in a normal voice, said, "The thing is, Mom's just torturing him. She's like a shark who just…I don't know…just ate a walrus, sees a baby seal and eats that, too. Not because she's hungry…just because she can."

"She has a right to be mad, Callie."

"Twenty-two years of being mad?"

"I don't know," Annie said, huffing away behind me. "If Jack even thought of cheating on me, I'd slice him up good."

I grinned. "I love when you talk all tough like that, you gangsta, you."

"Get paddling," she retorted. "Or I'll slice you up, too."

I turned back around and obeyed. A thumb-size mosquito whined near my face, taunting me before coming in for the pint or so of blood it would take. The water sluiced gently against the bow of my kayak. Our speed was pretty good…certainly much better than when Bowie and I went out, since the stubborn beast refused to help.

"Oh, look!" Annie said, nudging me with her paddle. "A man!" She pointed into the distance. Sure enough, a human figure was visible on a dock about a hundred yards away.

"Let's kidnap him and force him to marry me," I suggested.

"Okay!" Annie laughed. "Ooh. I think he's drawing! That's so hot, don't you think?"

"Only if I'm naked and wearing the Heart of the Ocean and Jack Dawson is intently sketching me mere hours before his hypothermic death in the North Atlantic," I said with a happy sigh.

"You've got to stop watching those sappy movies."

"I will not! And don't get sanctimonious on me, young lady! Didn't your own husband use the phrase *You complete me* during his marriage proposal? Hmm?"

"I still regret telling you that," she murmured. "Let's go check him out."

As we drew near, we could see the figure more clearly. It was indeed a man. And not just any man. It was Ian, sitting cross-legged on an old wooden dock, Angie at his side. And yes, he was drawing, a sketchpad on his lap. He looked up as we approached.

"Hi!" Annie chirped.

"Hi, Ian," I seconded.

"Hello." He watched as we pulled up to the dock, our intentions clear—to interrupt his lovely morning.

"Ian, this is my friend, Annie Doyle. Annie, the new vet, Ian McFarland."

"Hi there," she said, making me blush furiously,

because Annie had this voice, you know? The voice she used when a particularly good meal was served…that *oh, God, yes, yes, come to me, fettuccine Alfredo* type of voice. "It's…*really* nice to meet you." I considered smacking her with my paddle.

"Are you drawing, Ian?" I asked.

Ian glanced down at his pad, the pencil that he held in his hand, then back at me. *Wow. Those are some powers of deduction.* "Yes." Angie's tail wagged.

"Can we dock here for a sec? I could really use a good stretch," Annie said, subtle as a charging wildebeest.

Ian hesitated a second. "Sure."

We paddled up to the dock. Ian came down to steady the kayak as we twisted and lunged our way out.

"So!" Annie said, pushing her glasses up her nose. "Do you live around here, Ian?"

"Yes. Over there."

He pointed to the woods. A little path twisted through the pines and over the granite rocks. I could make out a clearing, but not a house. "Is this your dock?" Annie asked. It would probably be easier if she just asked for a financial statement. Knowing her, that would be next.

"Yes. It's mine." Ian's eyes flicked over to me.

"So Callie tells me she's doing a little work for you, Ian," Annie said, nodding approvingly. "She's the best. So talented. You're very lucky to have her. She's great."

"That's enough, Annie," I said. "I didn't know you drew, Ian." I could've put that on the Web site. *Hobbies include painting, drawing and being too polite to get rid of intrusive visitors.* "That painting in your office…your work?"

He looked at me, mildly surprised that I guessed. "Yes, as a matter of fact."

"I love that picture," I said. "Nice and juicy with all that squishy paint."

"She doubles as an art critic," Annie said with mock seriousness. Ian smiled. My uterus twitched in response. Dang. To cover my blush, I knelt down to pet Angie, who wagged politely.

"You know what?" Annie said abruptly. "I have a soccer game! Actually, Seamus—my son, Ian—he has a soccer game. But I have to go to it! I forgot! So I'm just gonna call Jack and he can come and get me! Okay?"

"I thought Seamus and Jack were going to the movies," I said.

"No, he has a soccer game," Annie ground out, widening her eyes at me as she pulled her phone out of her pocket. "Hi, Jack, sweetie, can you pick me up? No, I'm fine. I just remembered the game. The *game*. Never mind. I'm at…what's your address, Ian?"

"75 Bitter Creek Road," he answered, glancing at me. "Will you be able to get back alone?" he asked, looking down at the kayak.

"Sure," I said, resigned. Annie was matchmaking, a disastrous hobby of hers that had resulted thus far in zero happy couples and two estranged cousins.

"Shall I just scamper down this path and wait for my husband at your house, Ian?" Annie asked, snapping her phone shut.

"Please. No scampering," I said.

Ian didn't seem to know what to say. "Uh… Sure. I'll show you the way."

Annie beamed and started off. "So, Ian, tell me about yourself," she said merrily, then proceeded to fill him in on the wonder that was me. "Callie and I have been friends since we moved here when I was in fourth grade. She came right up and said hi, and the rest is history!"

The path from the lake was lovely, just wide enough for two people. The clouds had blown off, but the pines were so thick here the sunlight only broke through in patches, spilling gold on the forest floor. Ian's dog padded silently beside me. "How are you, Angie?" I asked, petting the dog's silky head. "Are you a beautiful girl?" She wagged her tail in confirmation that yes, indeed she was. "'Angie... Aaaangie. Ain't it good to be ali-i-i-ive?'" I sang in a whisper. It was, after all, our tradition.

Ahead of me, Annie was yakking away. Ian rubbed his neck with one hand, trying to answer Annie's prying questions, such as...

"So, Ian, are you married?" My friend blinked up at him.

"I'm divorced," he said, glancing back at me as if in a plea for help.

"How sad!" Annie sang. "How long has it been?"

"Two years."

Annie turned and pulled a gruesome face meant to indicate joy and hope. "Well, I'm sure you'll find a special some—"

"Look! A deer!" I barked. The deer fled, white tail flashing as it leaped neatly into the woods. I took the opportunity to trot up to Annie and pinch her. Hard. "Stop it," I mouthed.

"What are you talking about?" she mouthed back, then said aloud, "Is this your place? It's beautiful!"

Ah. We were here. I stopped in my tracks.

The woods thinned out to a backyard. The grass had

recently been cut, the fresh, sweet scent filling the air. The house was a green two-story farmhouse with a beautiful gray slate roof…a classic New England design, but, if I wasn't mistaken, recently overhauled. New windows, I thought. Fresh paint.

"This is very pretty, Ian," I said.

"Thanks," he said. "Um…would you like to come in?" It was clear he didn't know how to avoid asking us.

"Sure! I'd love some coffee," Annie said, shooting me another joyful look.

We walked around the side yard, which had a bank of mature lilac trees along one side. I could only imagine the smell in the springtime. Then we came to the front, and once again, I stopped short.

We were on the edge of a large field thick with goldenrod and late-blooming black-eyed Susans. Dragonflies dipped and skimmed, and finches flew in and out of the long grass. A stone wall ran along one side…a real stone wall, the Robert Frost variety, uneven and sincere. The gravel driveway led out to the unseen road—it would be hell to plow come winter, but who cared? About two hundred yards off was a large stand of maples, already topped in red. Ian would be in for quite a show in a few more weeks.

"Come on in," Ian said. Did I mention he was wearing faded Levis? I suppressed a lustful sigh and followed him onto the porch, then turned to take in the view (of the natural scenery, not his ass, though both were compelling). The wide porch wrapped around on the western side. Perfect for sunsets. No railing, just an unobscured view of the field. A person could spend all day sitting on a porch like this, listening to the birds and the wind in the grass, the smell of pines rich and sharp in the air…

"You coming, Callie?" Annie chirped.

"Sure," I said distantly, tearing my eyes off the view.

"This place is gorgeous!" she hissed. "And he's not so bad himself! Oh, my God, those eyes!"

"Can you keep it down, please?" I asked. Ian was already inside.

"I wish I wasn't married," she murmured. "I'm serious. I'm leaving Jack."

"Super. I've always had a thing for him. Now's my chance," I said, stepping into the house.

The interior of the house was pretty damn impressive, too. Clearly, an architect had done this, because it had that sleek, perfect feeling…smooth, shiny hardwood floors, streamlined bookcases, funky steel light fixtures. The overall effect was very modern, and maybe a little stark. And beautiful, because it was that, too. Expensive-looking furniture was well placed throughout, reinforcing the slightly chilly tone—I didn't see a place where slumping and flopping could be executed too well, a far cry from the sofa I'd brought to Noah's, which was aging leather and deliciously broken-in, a piece that seemed to invite a running start. But the house was beautiful.

And it was clean. Immaculate, even. I was a fair housekeeper myself, but not like this.

Off the great room was the kitchen, which had more steel light fixtures and slate countertops. Ian was already there, measuring out coffee beans.

"How long have you lived here?" Annie asked, gesturing me to heel.

"Not that long," he answered, not looking at her. "Four months."

"How old is the house?" she asked. Honestly, I was

surprised she didn't whip out her phone and start taking pictures.

"It was built in 1932," Ian answered. "My uncle bought it in the sixties, and after he died, I bought it from the bank. Had it redone when I bought the practice."

Dropping her hand so that Ian couldn't see (and making sure that I could), Annie rubbed her fingers against her thumb. *Money.* She nodded at me and smiled. I sighed.

Angie's ears pricked up as a car slowly came down the driveway, the gravel crunching under the wheels.

"Oh, drat, Jack's here," Annie said. "Well, great meeting you! Have to run!"

"What about your coffee?" Ian asked, his brow wrinkling in confusion. "Your husband's welco—"

"See you soon!" she said, then hurtled out the door and ran toward Jack's car.

"I thought she wanted coffee," Ian said, staring out the window as Jack turned the car around and headed back down the driveway.

"She has psychological problems. Sorry about that." I looked around the room again. "This is a very nice place, Ian."

"Thanks," he said, opening a cupboard. Inside looked like a Pottery Barn display—rows of neatly arranged mugs, all the same color and style, unlike my own motley collection, which ranged from the thick and uneven mug Josephine made me in preschool to an antique porcelain cup my gran had used each day for tea. Nope, Ian had only a row of mugs, six in all, pale green, very pleasing. Glasses, all the same model, six of each size, three sizes in all, stood like obedient soldiers.

The same thought that had been niggling away at me

all week popped into my brain. "I heard you and Fleur had coffee the other day," I said.

He looked up. "Who's Fleur?"

Say no more, Ian. Question answered. "Um...my coworker? Tony Blair's mommy? The one who took you on the hike?"

"Right. I think I saw her in town." He returned his attention to measuring the coffee.

"Can I look around a little?" I asked.

"Sure." He may have sighed.

I wandered into the great room. On the walls were three large prints, all the same size, all matted in white and framed in black, a series of photographs of leaves...maple, fern, oak, close-up studies in sharp detail.

"Did you take these?" I asked. "They're really nice."

"Yes. Thank you," he said in that formal way of his. It was starting to grow on me. The coffeepot gurgled.

So Ian McFarland had an artistic streak. That was kind of nice. Quite nice, really.

The bookcase held mostly science-related tomes...here was a page-turner—*Flynn's Parasites of Laboratory Animals.* Blick! *Small Animal Medical Differential Diagnosis.* Along with the textbooks were scattered a few manly novels... *Call of the Wild, The Old Man and the Sea.* And aw! He had *All Creatures Great and Small* by James Herriot, the charming story of the English vet.

"I loved this book when I was little!" I exclaimed, taking it out.

He looked up and almost smiled. "Me, too."

I replaced the book and continued my perusal, coming to a picture of Ian, an older woman...attractive, lean, very blue eyes…and a *gorgeous* man. Hello! Might this be *Alejandro?* Lord, I got a little turned-on just thinking his name. "Your family?" I asked, picking up the photo.

"Yes."

"Is your brother married?"

"Yes."

Figured. There was another picture of his mother…with a face I quite recognized. "Is this *Bono?*" I yelped, snatching the photo off the shelf.

"Yes," Ian said, smiling. "They met at a fundraiser in Africa… Nigeria, I think."

"Wow. I always thought we'd end up together, Bono and I."

"He's also married," Ian said.

"Rub it in," I said. A few of the books were not in English. "So you speak Spanish?" I asked, wandering back over to the kitchen area.

Ian reached into another cabinet, which showed the same ruthless organization as the first. He took out a small pitcher in the same shade as the mugs, as well as a matching sugar bowl.

"Yes," he answered. "I moved to Latin America when I was eight, spent a few years there, a couple in Chile, three in Africa. I speak passable French, too. I knew a little Swahili, but I've forgotten most of it."

"That is so cool!" I exclaimed. He didn't answer. "Or not," I added. He gave a grudging smile, then got out some spoons. I was beginning to feel like I was at a Japanese tea ceremony…everything so precise. I had some cute pitchers and sugar bowls, too, though they were of the "high on a shelf, covered in dust" variety. My own formalities usually ended at sniffing the half-and-half to make sure it wasn't sour. Ian opened the fridge—

Good Lord, it was as anal retentive as the rest of the house, neatly wrapped foil packages lined up in a row. "Do you like to cook, Ian?" I asked.

"I don't really have the time," he answered. "I get most of my meals from Kitty's Catering."

"I'm having you over for a home-cooked meal, then. One of these days."

He made a noncommittal sound, glancing up at me, almost meeting my eyes.

"So did you like moving around, living in so many parts of the world?" I asked.

The coffeepot beeped, and Ian seemed glad to have something to do while he answered. "I appreciate it now," he said carefully. "It was a little hard back then." He handed me a mug and took a sip of his own coffee. I noted that he took his coffee black. All that cream and sugar prep, just for me. It was rather flattering.

"Thanks, Ian. Sorry about intruding like this."

"It's fine. It's nice to have company," he replied.

"I think you're lying." I smiled as I said it.

"Only a little," he answered, and my smile grew. Ian McFarland, making a joke! Angie seemed to approve, because she chuffed softly next to him. "Have a seat," he said, and we moved to the living room area. Ian sat in a sleek white chair (white? With an Irish setter? Clearly she wasn't the leg-humping, lap-sitting variety of dog, like my own beloved fur ball). I chose the couch, which was pale green, taking care not to slosh any coffee.

Outside, a chickadee sang repeatedly. Angie lay down next to Ian's chair and put her head on his foot.

"You should have a party here," I observed. "Have you had your staff over?"

"No," Ian answered.

"You should. Dr. Kumar used to. And your staff is so great. I've known Earl and Carmella for ages." No comment from my host. "My own boss has us over every now and again. It would be part of your warm and fuzzy campaign." I smiled and took a sip of the joe, which was dark and nutty. Maybe his mom sent it from Colombia or something.

Ian set his cup down. "I'm not sure if you've noticed, Callie," he said slowly, not looking at me, "but I'm not exactly warm and fuzzy." He straightened the coaster so it was exactly aligned with the edge of the coffee table.

"Well, sure, I've noticed, Ian," I answered. "You're kind of…formal. But that's okay. We're not trying to lie. Just make people like you more."

"I don't really care if people like me more, Callie. I just want to maintain my customer base." His jaw was getting a little clenched.

"Which you can do by being a little warmer and fuzzier," I said, smiling to show this would not be at all painful.

"You're good at that, aren't you?" he said after a beat.

"Good at what?"

"Working people over."

I blinked. "Ouch, Ian!"

"What?" He gazed at me impassively, unaware that he'd just stuck a knife in my heart.

My mouth opened and closed before I could actually form words. "Well, if you mean I'm good at talking to people in a polite and interested way, Ian, then yes, I *am* good at it. Perhaps you can learn by my example. And thank you for the compliment."

"It wasn't a compliment," he said. "It's an observation."

"Why are you being mean to me?"

"I'm not being mean, Callie. I'm just…being honest. You try very hard to make everyone like you, and not everyone needs that kind of…affirmation. I don't."

"No, of course not. You're perfect in every way."

He rolled his eyes. "That's not what I'm saying at all."

"Well, what are you saying?" My voice was getting a little loud, and my face felt hot.

"Just…you seem to try very hard at something that maybe you shouldn't."

"And how would you know anything about me?" I asked tightly.

He shrugged. "I've seen you in action. That older woman in line in the Department of Motor Vehicles. The guy who made things out of hair. All those people at Elements. The older man on the hike that day. You work people."

I slapped my cup down on the coffee table, getting a gratifying twitch from my host as the coffee sloshed nearly over the rim of my cup. "I do not *work* people, Ian. I'm nice. I'm cheerful. I'm smart and I'm cute. People like me because those are likable qualities. Much more so than, oh, I don't know, frosty and anal retentive, wouldn't you say?"

He just looked at me, unblinking, and I couldn't tell if he was mad or amused or just unfeeling. Unexpectedly, a lump rose in my throat.

"I think I should head back," I said, standing up. "Thanks for the coffee. It was delicious. And your house is beautiful."

"There you go again," he murmured.

"I'm just being polite, Ian! It's how my mother raised me! I'm sorry if you think I'm some insincere phony!"

He stood up quickly, took a step toward me and then stopped, pushing his hands into his pockets. "I don't,

Callie. I don't think that." He gave his head a little shake. "I don't know how we got into this conversation."

"Me, neither," I muttered.

"Look, Callie," he said quietly, "I didn't mean to insult you, but it's clear I did. I meant only that..." His gaze drifted to his dog, then to the bookcase. "You don't have to try so hard." He paused, then met my eyes with some difficulty. "Not with me, anyway."

Oh. *Oh.*

Suddenly aware that my mouth was open, I shut it. What should I say? Thank you? Bite me? I don't mean to try so hard, it's just ingrained? *Why don't you just kiss him?* Betty Boop suggested.

"I'll walk you back to your kayak," Ian offered.

"Okay," I said faintly.

The walk back to the dock didn't seem nearly as long as the walk in had. We didn't talk. I was still trying to sort out what Ian had said, if there had been...something. He was not the easiest man to read.

The clouds were back, though a few shafts of gold pierced the lake. Rain was about an hour off, if I interpreted the signs correctly. Not that I ever did.

"Well. See you soon," I said, looking at my kayak.

"Okay," Ian said. "Need a hand?"

Ah, blushing. Ever reliable, those cheeks o' mine. "Sure," I said. He held out his hand, and I took it, and it sure did feel safer, that warm, strong hand holding mine. Alas, the second I was in the kayak, he let go.

"Next weekend's the pet fair," I reminded him. He stood on the rocks with his hands in his back pockets.

"Yes," he answered.

"I'll...I'll call you, but everything's pretty much in place," I said.

"I'm sure it is," he said, looking at me with those dis-concerting blue, blue eyes. *Say something,* I urged him silently.

"Do you need a push?"

Not what I was hoping for. "Okay."

And with that, he gave the boat a strong shove, sending me out past his dock.

"Thanks, Ian," I called, giving him a wave.

"Nice seeing you," he said, then turned and walked down the path, disappearing almost at once into the woods. I took a deep breath and started paddling unchar-acteristically hard, both glad and relieved to be away from him.

You don't have to try so hard. Not with me, anyway.

If it meant what I wanted it to mean, it was the nicest thing a man had said to me in a long, long time.

Then again, I was excellent at misinterpretation.

CHAPTER FOURTEEN

IN A VERY RARE MANEUVER, my sister came over one night. "Hi," I said, opening the door as Bowie leaped and crooned. "Did someone die?"

"No," she answered. "Why? Did someone die here?"

"No." I shook my head. "It's just…you never come over."

"Does that mean you're thrilled to see me and want to pour me a glass of wine?"

"Yes! Yes, it does, Hes."

"Keep it down!" Noah bellowed from the living room.

"We have company!" I yelled back.

"I don't know how you live with him," Hester said. "Dog, get off my leg or I'll castrate you so fast you won't know what hit you."

"I'm trying to watch *America's Next Top Model!*" our dear grandfather shouted. "Go upstairs, you two!"

"He's very dedicated," I told Hester, grabbing a bottle of wine from the fridge. "He thinks Tenisha's going to win, but her pictures last week…train wreck."

Hester sighed. "Callie, I need advice," she said.

I paused as I reached for the glasses. This was new. "Um…okay. Sure. Let's go up to my room."

"Finally," Noah muttered as we passed his chair. "Hello, Hester."

"Hi, Grumpy," she said.

"Takes one to know one," he returned.

Upstairs, Hester sat on my bed, well aware of the ban on the Morelock chair, and poured herself a glass of wine 'til it hit the brim. "How are you?" she asked, then chugged half the glass.

"Um, I'm good," I said. "And you?"

"Great. Just great," she said.

"So what can I advise you on, Hes?" I asked, sitting in my office chair.

"Bronte's been having a rough time lately."

I nodded. "More than just adolescence?"

"Well," Hester said, "she says she feels like a misfit up here…adopted, mixed race, single mother, funeral home in the family."

"Right," I said.

"So this morning she comes down to breakfast and gives me a list of all the reasons she doesn't fit in, from her skin color to that wonky toenail on her left foot."

I smiled. "It's always freaked me out, I'll be honest."

Hester smiled back a little, and then, abruptly, her eyes filled with tears. "So she said if there was one thing on the list that she could actually change, it would be having a single mother."

"What?" I breathed. "She wants to be put back in foster care?"

"No, idiot. She wants me to marry someone."

"Oh! Okay, yeah, that makes more sense." Or not. "Wow, Hes."

"I've tried so hard, Callie," she wept. "You know. Don't end up like Mom, avoid men, adopt a child who needs a home, be stable and normal and strict and loving, and here she shoots me right in my Achilles' heel!"

"That's what kids do, I guess," I murmured, handing my sister a box of tissues.

"Exactly. All my life I haven't needed a man. Never wanted to, because look how it fucked up Mom, right? Now my kid needs a father, and it just sucks!"

"Well, just tell her it's not for you. Tell her how much you love her and all that—"

"I already have!" Hester said, wiping her eyes. She blew her nose so loudly Bowie jumped up and barked. "Bronte said she had to make a huge adjustment to become my daughter, and the least I can do is try to make one for her."

"She's good," I murmured.

"I know," Hester said.

Bronte had been seven when Hester adopted her, living with her fourth foster family in Queens, New York. She hadn't wanted to leave the city; it took her months to sleep through the night. She'd barely spoken that first year.

"So," Hester said, flopping down on my bed, staring at the ceiling. "Can you help me find a boyfriend? I was thinking of that vet guy."

"Oh." I hesitated. "Um, Hes, I kind of…like him."

"Okay. Do you know anyone else?" Obviously, my sister didn't care who it was.

"Do you really want a boyfriend, Hester?" I asked.

"No," she said. "But I'll give it a shot." She glanced at me. "It's what you do when you have kids. And then, when Bronte sees what a clusterfuck dating is, she'll drop it, I'll take her to get her hair straightened, and maybe that will be the end of it."

"Oh," I said. "Good plan, in a freakish, insincere way."

"Exactly. So? Any names? You know everyone in town."

"Do they have to be good-looking and employed and normal?"

"Nah," Hester said. "Just single."

"Okay, then. Yes, I know lots of men," I said. "I'll make a list. I have a guy who makes macramé out of human hair, a farmer who doesn't talk or bathe, Jake Pelletier and his three ex-wives…" I looked up at my sister. "Plenty to choose from."

"Perfect. That'll set Bronte straight. Thanks, Callie," my sister said sincerely. "I knew I could count on you."

THE MORNING OF THE PET fair dawned bright and beautiful, a perfect fall day, the air crisp, the sun warm, the leaves abruptly unbelievable. Honestly, the trees glowed as if lit from within, Nature's personal cathedral.

"Do you want to go see Dr. Ian? Do you?" I asked Bowie, who leaped onto his feet at the very thought. Then again, he tended to leap to his feet for anything.

I got dressed…no skirt or dress today, alas, but still, I wanted to look good, as I was sort of running this thing. And I'd be busy: There was the dog agility course, face painting, refreshments. Josephine and the Brownies would be dressed like cats or dogs, collecting for the Vermont Humane Society. The Senior Center had a choir—the Merryatrics (I thought of the name, thank you very much…they'd been high on my chocolate chip cookies that day and had nearly voted in favor of One Foot in the Grave) would be performing animal-related songs, such as "Barracuda" and "Eye of the Tiger" (they were a frisky lot). I'd confirmed with Sergeant Davis of the state police K-9 unit yesterday. Bethanne, the pet psychic who also worked as a nurse in Hester's office, was thrilled at the chance to use her sixth sense. I had even—and this had been the hardest sell of all—I had even convinced Noah to come and whittle little cats and dogs to sell, the proceeds of which would go to the local animal shelter. Ian's three-person staff would all be there to help as well.

If the advertising career didn't work out, I could always do event planning, I thought as I surveyed myself in the mirror. "You're very cute," I said aloud. Smiled to prove it. Remembered what Ian had said about not needing to try so hard. Sighed.

Going into the bedroom, I glanced at my rocking chair. The sunlight poured through my window, illuminating the honeyed tiger maple. I ran a finger over the back, gave it a little push to see it rock, its smooth, gentle movement never failing to charm me. It was waiting, I thought. Waiting to be used for more than the occasional comfort session. But the time wasn't right. Not yet.

"Let's go, Bowie!" I said, earning a high yip and three whirling-dervish circles from my beloved.

Noah was waiting in the kitchen, scowling, a sweater vest over his flannel shirt—his version of dressed up.

"You look very nice, Grampy," I said.

"What do you know?" he retorted. Then he recalled that he loved me and pinched my chin. "So do you, sweetheart. So do you."

"You haven't been hitting the sauce, have you?" I asked.

"That's what I get for being nice," he said, limping for the door. "Get in the damn truck. I'm driving."

When we pulled up to the vet practice, there were already people milling about, a few Brownies and Scouts, the DJ, Bethanne, the pet psychic. Hester was there, sitting under a tent, booming into her phone. "No, it's completely normal, it's the injections. Just tell your husband to lock up any weapons, okay? Let's be on the safe side." She jerked her chin our way.

Fred, whom I'd bribed and blackmailed into being my helper, was running an extension cord to the PA system. He waved. "Hey, idiot!" I called, grinning.

"Hi, dumb-ass!" he returned.

"Have you seen Ian?"

"He's inside," Freddie answered.

Indeed he was. Gnawing on his thumbnail, staring out the window as if watching Mongol hordes descend. He was wearing a suit.

"Come on, Ian," I said, not bothering with pleasantries. I grabbed his arm and towed him down the hall to his office.

"Take off the suit," I ordered.

"This is unexpected," he said.

"Very funny. A suit, Ian?"

"Well, I thought it would—"

"Take off your tie," I said, jerking the knot loose, "and get rid of the jacket." I shoved it off his shoulders. His broad, manly shoulders. My movements slowed. Ian smelled good. Really, really good. Like rain, somehow, sharp and clean. I could see the pulse beating in his neck, slow and sure. Felt the heat from his body, which was just a fraction from mine. Those unexpected eyelashes, so blond and somehow sweet, softened his severe looks. There was a little smile in his eyes, and his mouth was very near. If I stood on tiptoe…

"Doc?" Earl, my old vet tech buddy, appeared in the doorway. "Oh. Sorry."

Suddenly aware that I was basically undressing my client in his office, I jumped back a foot or so, maybe three, and cleared my throat loudly.

"What do you need, Earl?" Ian asked.

"The police officer was wondering if you could float him some etogesic," Earl said.

"Sure. I'll be right out," Ian answered.

"Sorry again," Earl said.

"No, no!" I chirped. "Just a little…wardrobe malfunction."

"Whatever you say," Earl said, winking. With that, he left.

"Sorry, Ian," I muttered, my legs still a little weak. "I just…you know. A suit is not quite the look we're going for. Dockers would've been perfect, a nice blue oxford to match your eyes…"

I was blushing. Big surprise.

"Being male, I generally don't think about matching my eyes," he said, a note of amusement in his voice.

"Well. You should. You have gorgeous eyes," I said, taking a shaky breath. "Bowie has an eye the same color as yours, very clear blue, like the sky. But his other eye is brown. Like mine. Funny. One like yours, one like mine. Not that I mean anything by that. Okay. I'm gonna stop talking now."

Ian laughed, and the sound caught me right in the reproductive organs. Resisting the urge to pull a Bowie and flop on my back and offer myself up, I slapped my gaze out the window. Lust twisted hot and hard in my stomach. That was some laugh. Wow. Low and seductive and completely unexpected, that laugh.

"How's this?" Ian asked.

I looked back at him. Swallowed. "Very nice. Much better," I said. He'd taken off his tie and jacket, rolled up his shirtsleeves a few times, unbuttoned his shirt a couple. Would it be inappropriate to lick his neck? It probably would be. I cleared my throat. "Well, you'd better get out there," I said. "It starts in ten minutes."

A FEW HOURS LATER, IT was clear that the pet fair was a huge success.

Dogs of all kinds bounded in the area Freddie and I had designated as Dog Land. The obstacle course hadn't worked so well, as none of the dogs seemed to get the concept and wanted only to mark their territory, but the Brownies had taken it over for their own purposes... Tess McIntyre had the best time thus far. The Merryatrics gave a rousing version of "Who Let the Dogs Out?" Bethanne's readings confirmed just how much everyone's pets loved their owners. Noah carved animals, which Jody Bingham took upon herself to hand-sell. Kids ran around with their faces painted like tigers or dogs or Scottish warriors (that would've been Seamus, my dear godson, who wanted to look like William Wallace from *Braveheart* rather than Tigger). The drug-sniffing dog had found Freddie a "person of interest," but Freddie made a compelling catnip argument, and the cop let Freddie pass after a quick lecture on the continued illegality of marijuana. Bronte had been in charge of Cause for Paws, which rescued cats. By telling people that she herself had found a new and wonderful life thanks to the wonders of adoption, she'd managed to pawn off fourteen felines thus far.

And Ian had been great. Honest. A little stiff, sure, but he'd really tried. Shook hands, admired pets, fielded questions from Elmira Butkes, who was concerned that her twenty-two-year-old cat, Mr. Fluffers, wasn't feeling "perky." When Ian brought up the average lifespan of housecats (it's thirteen), I gave him a sharp elbow to the ribs, and he changed his tune a little, saying maybe some B12 would do the trick. He even took the mike for a painful moment and thanked everyone for coming, encouraged them to have fun, not to forget to give what they could to the Humane Society. A little brief, a little formal, but quite…nice.

"So how are you?" Annie asked, coming up beside me to survey the fair.

"I'm feeling…ruttish," I answered. She snorted appreciatively.

"Who wouldn't?" she said. "He's hot. All dangerous and growly."

"Like a Russian assassin," I murmured.

"Exactly," she nodded. "I'll bet he could kill you with one finger." We were best friends for a reason.

"Hey," I said, tearing my eyes off Ian, who was admiring a little girl's newly adopted kitten, "Damien wants it floated to Dave that he's ready to reconcile, okay? So consider it floated." Damien had cornered me in my office yesterday with the aforementioned information, tired of being single after all of two months.

"Roger that," Annie said. "How many well-dressed gay men live up here, anyway? They have to be together. It's just a numbers thing."

"Calliope, you look absolutely edible," came that silken voice from behind me. I jumped. Sure enough, it was Louis, looking pale and damp and smug, like Gollum smiling over the sleeping Frodo Baggins.

"Oh! Louis! Annie, you remember Louis, right? Oops! Gotta run! Bye. Sorry! I have…things. To do. Things to do. Annie, help me! Help me do the things, okay?"

"Absolutely," Annie said.

"I'll help, too," Louis said. "I'm very handy." He raised an anemic eyebrow. "Very. Handy."

I paused. "You know what, Louis? My sister needs help. Over there." I gestured toward Hes, who appeared to be dozing in a lawn chair.

"If it would please you, then I will help your sister," Louis said, gliding away.

"That wasn't nice," Annie said. "Oh, here comes Ian. Hi, Ian! You look *really,* really nice." Back to her fettuccine voice.

"Hello, Annie," Ian said. "Um…thank you." He turned to me. "Callie, the K-9 unit has to go now. Did you want to say goodbye?"

"Sure. I have the check right here." I peeked into my leather backpack purse. "Yup. Right here."

"I hear Seamus calling me," Annie lied. "Must run. Bye, kids!"

Ian and I walked over to where the cop was still holding court with his beautiful German shepherd under the elm tree. "So how are you doing, Ian?" I asked.

"I'm fine," he answered. He glanced at me. "You really did a nice job on this. So many people came."

"I thought you did great, too," I said, risking a quick squeeze to his arm. Ooh. Nice arm. Nice and strong with all that dog-hefting or whatever. Cat hurling. Whatever.

We gave the good sergeant a donation to the cops' union and thanked him. The fair was winding down, though Josephine had found the microphone and was serenading the stragglers with her favorite song. "'Don'tcha wish your girlfriend was hot like me,'" she sang as Seamus head-bopped agreeably in the background. Annie and I had high hopes for a marriage between them someday.

"Callie, I'm headed home," Noah said. He was rubbing his leg, but he gave Ian a terse nod.

"Sure, Noah," I said. "I have to stay a little and make sure everything's settled, but don't worry. I'll catch a ride." I wasn't in a horrible hurry, to be honest. It was 4:00 p.m. on a Saturday. I didn't have plans, though the River Rats had invited me to hang out with them. I believed it was their monthly mojito night, not to be confused with their monthly martini night, beer night, wine night, mint julep night...

"I'll drive you home," Ian said.

"Thanks," I said. "That would be great."

"I'll bring Bowie," Noah said, then hobbled off toward his pickup truck, his uneven gait more pronounced than usual.

"His leg must be hurting," I said. "He hates wearing the prosthesis. We've tried eight different models." I frowned. "Can we stop at the pharmacy on the way home? He's out of Lanacane, and I'll bet he won't remember to pick some up." Glancing at my watch, I winced. "Shoot, they're closed already."

"I have some in the office," Ian said.

"Really? Thanks, Ian," I said. "See? You're getting good at this nice thing. Just like me."

He gave me a tolerant look, and I smiled.

As we approached the office, a new-model Saab pulled into the lot. The driver got out. I recognized her immediately—it was the woman from the ladies' room at Whoop & Holler. The one who told me I wasn't an idiot.

"Hey!" I exclaimed. "How you doing, Kate Spade?"

"Hi there, fabulous shoe woman!" she called right back. "How are you?" Then she looked at Ian, and her expression softened. "Hi."

"Hi," he said. I sensed a tremor in the Force, if you know what I meant. Ian had gone very still.

"I didn't realize you had an...event," she said, gesturing to where the rental folks were taking down the tent.

"Yes," he said, offering no more. They looked at each other for a moment, the air suddenly was crackling and brittle.

"Got a minute?" she asked.

"Sure," he said, then, turning to me, added, "Callie, though I take it you've already met somehow, this is Laura Pembers. My ex-wife."

THOUGH I OH-SO-CASUALLY circled the building with Angie, I was unable to find a spot where I could eavesdrop on Ian and Laura without climbing a stepladder and pressing my ear against the window...and sadly, I didn't see a ladder anywhere.

The last of the pet fair people left, trickling away with waves and compliments. I kissed my nieces and managed to catch Seamus and kiss him as well, though he was getting to the age where he kind of hated, kind of loved that sort of public display. With a sigh, I flopped on the grass under a pear tree, the silvery leaves rustling slightly in the breeze. Angie joined me, lying down with her front paws crossed daintily as if she were the Queen of England. I stroked her silky fur and was rewarded when she put her head in my lap.

So. Ian's ex-wife was gorgeous, friendly and most important, had great taste in accessories. I remembered thinking that night in the ladies' room that she looked familiar, and now I knew why. Her picture was still in Ian's office, though her hair was shorter and darker now. *I don't think he's over his ex-wife,* Carmella had told me the first day I'd come to check Ian out. Ian himself told me he wasn't looking for a relationship. So I guess I knew what he'd meant that day, when he'd told me I didn't have to try so hard with him. It didn't mean he was interested in me. And heck, he'd made that clear, hadn't he? Actions spoke louder than words. He'd never touched me, except to help me into the kayak. Certainly didn't flirt. So what if he laughed this morning? I was easy to laugh at.

I heard a car door close, then an engine start. As Laura drove down the driveway, she slowed. I stood up and waved. "Nice to meet you, Callie!" she called. Angie woofed softly.

"Same here," I shouted back. Then I headed back toward the building where Ian stood looking where Laura's car had been, his hands in his pockets, face more than a little grim.

"Hi," I said, and he started.

"Hi," he said, not looking at me. "I'm sorry, I forgot the Lanacane. Come on in."

I followed him into the office and waited while he disappeared down the hall. A few seconds later he was back, his suit jacket and tie over his arm, the tube of cream in his hand. His face was tight, and he didn't look at me.

"Everything okay, Ian?" I asked gently.

"Yes."

"Do you want to talk about it?" I offered.

"No."

"Okay. Well, I appreciate the cream. Noah will, too."

A muscle in his jaw clenched, and he managed to cut his eyes to me, then looked away once more. "She's getting married."

I bit my lip. "I'm so sorry."

He shook his head. "No, it's fine. I knew already…she

wrote to me about a month ago. I just haven't seen her for a while." He paused. "They should get married. They're…right for each other." He shrugged unconvincingly. "Let's go."

Angie came the nanosecond she was called, jumping into the way back of Ian's Subaru, where there was a dog bed for her comfort. I got in the passenger door. "Thanks for the ride," I said, buckling my seat belt.

"You're welcome. Thank you for today. It was very nice."

I could tell his mind was elsewhere. For a change, I managed to keep my mouth shut as we drove home. Autumn was here, brilliant and blazing. The fields glowed with good health, and black-and-white cows lined the fence at the edge of the road at the Valasquez farm. But my heart hurt for Ian.

When we pulled into Noah's Arks, Ian spoke again, though he stared straight ahead. "Callie," he began, taking a deep breath. He didn't continue, just exhaled slowly.

"Yes, Ian?" I prodded (gently, I thought).

"Laura wants me to come to her wedding." He turned to look at me.

"Ah," I said. He didn't say anything else. "Well, do you want to go?"

"No," he answered. "But I probably will." He dropped his gaze to his hands.

"And how do you feel about going?" I asked, trying for armchair psychologist.

"Really crappy, Callie."

I gave a little laugh, almost surprised at the honest answer. "I would, too," I said.

"It's next weekend."

"That's...soon."

He took another deep breath, then seemed to grit his teeth. "Will you come with me?"

Lordy! I certainly didn't see that coming. Well, of course he'd want a date! Especially (not to toot my own horn) but especially one as pretty and charming and in possession of such fabulous shoes as I was. "Sure, I'll come!" I said. I could see it already. I'd flirt with him, be utterly gorgeous, we could dance, everyone could see that he'd moved on... "You can say I'm your girlfriend, I'm a great date, Ian, and I'll—"

"No!" he blurted, looking stricken. "I don't want you to pretend to be my girlfriend," he said more calmly. "I...I don't even want you to come as my date."

"Oh," I said, deflating. There went that plan. What did he want, a driver?

"Just come as my...friend." He turned to look at me, his eyes steady.

My heart seemed to stop beating for a second. *Oh.* Somehow, coming from this man, the word was huge. His *friend.* "Okay," I whispered. "I'd be honored."

Ian reached into his pocket and withdrew a folded up piece of paper, handing it to me. "It's just outside Montpelier," he said. "We'll have to stay overnight, but I'll pay for your room."

"Or we could bunk together," I said, glancing at the invitation. "Save some money. We could have a slumber party. Order room service, watch movies, jump on the beds."

"I'll pay for your room," he repeated, but there it was, that little smile in his eyes.

I opened the car door. "Okay. See you next week."

"It's black tie, by the way."

"Oh, I love black tie!" I exclaimed. "I have the best dress! How cool! This will be so much fun, Ian!" Then, remembering that Ian's poor heart was probably breaking and his wife was in love with another man, I hastily added, "Actually, this is going to suck, and it won't be any fun at all."

Ian rolled his eyes. "I know I'm going to regret this," he murmured.

I got out of the car and pointed at him. "You won't, Ian. I'll make sure of it."

CHAPTER FIFTEEN

"BRONTE, TELL YOUR aunt why you got sent to the principal's office," Hester said on Wednesday. Hes and I were being summoned to Elements…third and final stop on the Tour of Whores…and I'd offered to pick my sister up, since she hated to drive at night.

Bronte sighed and slumped in her chair. "I told Shannon Dell I was Barack Obama's love child. And when she didn't believe me, I told her the Secret Service had, like, already tapped her lines and knew she was a snot who should totally mind her own business." She glanced up at me. "I also swore."

Hester raised an eyebrow at me.

"You could do a lot worse than the President," I said to my niece, putting my hands on her shoulders. "Though I was fond of the Morgan Freeman version myself."

"Callie!" Hester barked.

"It's very wrong to lie," I hastily amended. "Tsk, tsk, Bronte." She grinned up at me. From upstairs came the sound of Josephine singing another age-inappropriate song…Shakira's wholesome little ditty, "She-Wolf." "Shouldn't we censor Josephine's songs?" I suggested.

"I figure she'll outgrow it," Hester said. "All that Baby Einstein's gotta kick in sometime. God knows I spent thousands of dollars on those fricking DVDs."

"So are you two meeting one of Poppy's girlfriends?" Bronte asked, casually studying her nails. Hester, who'd just taken a sip of water, sputtered.

"How do you know?" I asked.

"I eavesdrop and spy," she answered.

"My admiration continues to grow," I murmured. "Yes, we are. Speaking of that, let's get going, Hester. I'll need a drink first." I glanced at my niece. "Just one glass of wine, as I would never drive while intoxicated. Ever. And nor would you."

"I'm thirteen years old, Callie," she said patiently. "Try to, like, pace yourself on the lecture circuit, okay?" She favored me with a kiss, then hollered up the stairs to see if Josephine wanted to eat ice cream and watch SpongeBob.

"She's the greatest kid," I told my sister as we drove over to Elements.

"That she is," Hester agreed. "But this father thing at school…not the first time. Last month it was Denzel Washington."

I laughed. "Well, she has excellent taste."

"So. I have a date," Hester boomed.

"Oh, fun! Who is it?"

"Louis."

I sucked in a breath of pain. Granted, I'd kind of orchestrated that by sending Louis over, but it still wasn't a pretty mental picture. "Good luck."

"Ayuh." She didn't comment further, so I changed the subject.

"What do you think about the, uh, Tour of Whores?"

She shrugged. "I don't know. Seems like a lot of scab picking to me. You want to turn up here," she said, pointing at a street sign.

"Yes, Hester, I know. I live a quarter of a mile away.

Have lived in this town most of my life. Eat at this very restaurant twice a week or so."

"Go left at the firehouse. So why did you agree to come tonight?"

"I'm afraid of Mom and don't want to disobey her."

"Mom's such a pussycat," Hester said. "You have this skewed image of her… I don't know. Always making her the bad guy."

"Well, what about your image of Dad?" I asked, in that sibling way one never outgrows. *No, I didn't. You did!*

"Dad's a shit," she said calmly. "Mom, pregnant. Dad, fucking around. Do the math, Callie."

"I know," I muttered. "I do know. But twenty-two years is a long time to atone."

We walked into the restaurant, where Dave greeted me in his usual way. "Callie! You look incredible tonight." He took my hands in his strong grasp and kissed my cheek, then turned to my sister. "Hester. Always a pleasure." She glared at him… Dave might be gay, but he was still male, and that was enough to make Hester suspicious.

"Have you talked to Damien lately?" I asked Dave.

"No, but I did get a very mysterious and romantic card yesterday," Dave said, smiling a little, looking (sigh) like Clive Owen. So unfair…the good ones were always gay or married. Then his expression changed. "Listen, ladies." His voice dropped. "They're here. Your parents and the…other woman." He looked at me seriously. "Prepare yourselves."

He walked us to the table, and before we even got there, my steps slowed.

My parents were both in their early sixties… Fred was

a surprise baby, born a week before Mom's fortieth birthday. But even turning back the hands of time twenty years…even so…Dad's, er, special friend here had to have been…oh gosh…older than God's dog. Honestly, she didn't even look alive.

A tiny, shriveled woman sat—in a wheelchair—between my parents. Mom was wiping the lady's chin with a napkin, and Dad was patting her liver-spotted hand. Her wispy hair stirred in a draft as we approached.

"No fucking way," Hester said in her version of a whisper, which was slightly louder than a shout. "Oh, my God, I have to go to the bathroom." She bolted, deserting me.

"Callie. Do join us," Mom said, pinning me with her laser look.

My mouth snapped shut. Surely there was a mistake. "Ah…I…well! Hello there!" I said, ever my father's girl when it came to putting on a good front. "Mom! Dad! Hi!" I turned to the stranger, who was indeed alive. "I'm Calliope Grey, Tobias's daughter." I held out my hand to shake hers. She raised her arm weakly, then let it fall back to the table, unable to find the energy to do more.

"Is this…are you…?" I whispered to my parents.

"What did she say?" the little old lady asked, her voice creaky and thin.

This was the other woman? Holy Lord!

"Callie's my daughter," Dad said loudly. "Callie, this is Mae Gardner."

"Very nice to meet you," I lied.

"Oh. I'm fine, dear." She smiled—no teeth, I noted, and I bit my lip. I glanced at my mother. She gave me a cool look in return, her thoughts unreadable.

"I was so happy to hear from you," Mae said, turning

her head with some effort toward my father. "To be honest, I don't remember you, but I thought it would be nice to get out. Most of my friends are dead, after all! My great-grandson drove me. He just got his license! He did very well on the way over here. No accidents!"

"That's great," I said after a beat, because Mom and Dad were staring at each other and Hester was apparently never coming back to our table. Sure enough, she was waving and gesturing to her phone, pretending a patient needed her. "Is he here?"

"Is who here, dear?"

"Your great-grandson."

"He's in the car. He has the most cunning little gadget, it's a talking camera or a radio or some such thing. He can take pictures with it! And type on it! Isn't that remarkable?"

"Oh…yes," I said. "Modern technology…amazing. So, um…how old are you, Mae, if you don't mind my asking?"

"I'm eighty-five," she said. "And I knew your father here—he's your father, you said?" I nodded. "We knew each other, oh, quite some time ago! We had some fun, didn't we, Lenny?"

"It's Tobias," my father said kindly.

"Is it? I don't know why I said Lenny. Well, I had a cousin Lenny, of course. He served in World War II, in the Pacific, and I used to send him cookies!"

With that, Mae fell asleep, her bony little chin resting on her collarbone. None of us said anything for a second. Mae gave a slight snore, assuring us that she was still in the land of the living.

"I cannot believe you cheated on me with an old woman," my mother hissed.

"She wasn't that old back then," Dad said weakly.

"Children present, no fighting, please," I interjected quietly, not wanting to wake our companion.

"Mind your own business, Callie," Mom said.

"You made me come! And where's our waiter? Could I please get some alcohol? You know, I could be home watching *Say Yes to the Dr—*"

"Hush, Callie. Tobias. Explain yourself! First that hippie widow—and I mean hippie in every sense of the word—then a blind woman...now...now... Bette Davis here! What the hell am I supposed to think?"

"At least they needed me!" Dad said, leaning forward abruptly. "Unlike you, Eleanor!"

"Oh, right. So it's my fault now," my mother said, disdain dripping from her voice.

Mae twitched in her sleep. "It's in the left drawer," she said, then resettled herself and gave another gentle snore.

"No, it's not your fault. Of course not," Dad replied in a softer voice. "I did a horrible thing, Eleanor. I broke our marriage vows, and I hurt you." His voice became firmer. "I've admitted that, and I've been apologizing for *decades* now, and I've told you again and again that I'd do anything to make it up to you...which I think I've proved by dragging these women back into our lives."

Mom didn't answer, just gripped the stem of her wineglass. Her shoulders were tense, the only indication that she was listening.

"But maybe you should take some responsibility, too, Ellie," Dad went on, his voice dropping to a harsh whisper. "The minute we moved to Georgebury, it was like I was just...some...appendage or something. You had the family business, you had the girls, you had your work, and on the nights when I was home, I was just someone who messed up your routine. You couldn't wait for me to go back on the road again!"

"Oh, Dad, nobody felt like that," I attempted. "We loved when you were home."

"Hush, Callie," he said.

"Why don't I just go to the bar and have a nice drink?" I suggested.

"Stay where you are," Mom ordered. "We might need you if she wakes up." She gave Dad an icy look. "And it wasn't like that at all, Tobias."

"Wasn't it?" he asked fiercely. "Callie, did you ever feel neglected or overlooked because your mother was so obsessed with her dead people and creating the perfect send-off and comforting and coddling everyone but her husband and kids? Did you, honey?"

"I'd like to invoke the fifth amendment," I said, waving to Dave. "Can I get a drink over here, Dave? Something large?" Dave pulled a face, rightfully wary of approaching.

"She did, Eleanor," my father said. "And so did Hester, and I'm sure Freddie has as well. And as for me, Ellie—" here my father's voice cracked "—you barely remembered who I was." His eyes were wet.

"I remembered enough to get pregnant with your child," Mom said, but her voice was not quite as certain as before.

"Yeah. The first time we'd had sex in a year and a half." I closed my eyes. Would that aliens would abduct me right about now. "And I was so happy about a new baby," Dad continued. "But you weren't, were you? This was just a great inconvenience."

Mom blinked. "I was thirty-nine years old, Toby."

She hadn't called him *that* in a long, long time.

"It was a *baby,* Ellie. Our baby. But every time I brought up the subject, what should we name him, should we take another vacation before he came, you just gave me a dirty look and left the room."

"I love Freddie," Mom said, opening her hands up in an appeal.

"I know. But you stopped loving *me.* I don't know when, but you did, and no matter how hard I tried, I couldn't make you love me again, and yes, I had three one-night stands, and I'm sorry, I'm so, so sorry, and I'm so damn tired of being sorry." My father's face crumpled. "I wanted to be needed. I wanted to be appreciated, and I was an idiot, and I'd take it back if I could, I'd cut out my heart if it would make you forgive me, but for Christ's sake, Eleanor, it didn't happen in a vacuum."

My mother was silent, her mouth slightly open, eyes wide.

My father stood up. "I'm sorry, Poodle," he said to me, wiping his eyes.

At that moment, a young man came over to our table. "Hey. You guys done with Goggy?" he asked.

Neither of my parents answered. "Um…yes! We are! She's lovely," I said, cringing as the words left my mouth. "Do you need help getting her into the car?"

"I'm all set. Thanks for inviting her out! She's usually in bed by seven. Big night for her."

He backed his sleeping ancestor away from the table and left. Without another word, my father followed. I watched him go, his shoulders slumped, then turned to my mother. "You okay, Mom?" I whispered.

My mother blinked and closed her mouth. "Yes. I'm fine, Callie."

If "fine" looked like "slapped," then I guess she was

fine. Not knowing what to say, I took her hand. She squeezed back gratefully.

"Where'd she go? Where's Dad?" Hester boomed. "Sorry about the phone call. Did I miss everything?"

"Not now, Hes," I said. "Come on, Mom. We'll take you home."

"I didn't even get to eat," Hester protested.

"So order a pizza," I hissed. "Now is not the time."

I DROPPED HESTER BACK AT her house, promising to call her later, then took Mom back home. Fred, who'd just popped open a beer, set it down when we walked into the foyer.

"Mom, you okay?" he asked, his dark eyes, so like our dad's, filled with concern.

"Rough night," Mom murmured, patting his shoulder absently. She wandered into the Tranquility Room and sat in the back row.

"What happened, Callie?" he asked, and I briefed him in low tones.

"Poor Dad," he said when I was done, then glanced toward our mom. "And Christly, poor Mom."

"Tell me about it," I murmured. "She looked like he slapped her. And Daddy... Fred, he was crying." My own eyes filled up.

"Now don't you start," Freddie said, sounding a lot like Noah. "Twenty-two years divorced, and they're still making the kids miserable. Come on." He gave me a quick hug. "Ma! You want a grilled cheese?"

"Sure," Mom said after a minute.

"Go," my brother said to me. "I'll get this one."

"Thanks, buddy," I said, kissing his stubbly cheek. Strange to have my brother needing to shave. Stranger still to have him acting like an adult.

I drove over to my dad's, but his little house was dark, and he didn't answer the door when I knocked. I sat on the porch for a minute or two. This was the same place he'd been renting all these years since he first moved out—he could well afford to buy it, but he never did. An owl called from a nearby tree, and the air was cool with the promise of some late-night rain. Cozy under other circumstances. Lonely under these. With a sigh, I got up and returned to my car.

A half hour later, I was rocking in my chair, waiting for the magic, listlessly eating some Betty Crocker Supermoist Cherry Chip batter. *Come on, chair,* I thought. *Do your thing.* I remembered those ads from my youth... *Calgon, take me away!* the beleaguered housewife would cry, and seconds later, she'd be ensconced in bubbles up to her ears, reclining in some gorgeous bathtub. Funny that I had such a tub but rarely used it. No, it was the chair for me. My happily-ever-after chair. But happily-ever-afters seemed in short supply these days.

I closed my eyes and let my head fall back against the smooth maple. Sometimes it seemed like my life was spent shoveling fog...trying so hard to be that adorable hedgehog everyone liked. Some days, optimism was an ill-fitting wool coat, heavy and uncomfortable.

Bowie whined from the floor, then raised his head and licked my ankle. "Thanks, Bowie," I whispered. "You're the best."

No matter how hard I tried, I couldn't make you love me again.

The last time I'd seen my father cry was just before my eighth birthday when he moved out. Hester was in her room, furious; she hadn't spoken to him for weeks, and Mom was in the basement, losing herself in preparing the dead, so I was the only one to see my father off.

"I'll see you Wednesday, Bunny," he called up the stairs to my sister. His voice cracked.

"Don't you fucking call me that ever again!" Hester shrieked, her voice clearly audible through the closed door.

Dad flinched, then turned to me. "It won't be so different, Poodle," he lied, standing in the hallway, surrounded by suitcases. "I'll just be a few streets over." He smiled, a horrible smile because it wasn't a smile at all, just a contortion meant to fool his child.

"Oh, I know, Daddy. I love your new house," I lied right back.

"Go play now," he said, and I knew he didn't want me to watch him go. He hugged me so hard it hurt, then gave me a gentle push toward the stairs.

I couldn't help it. I stood at my bedroom window, a Hello Kitty throw pillow pressed against my mouth as I sobbed, watching my father bent in sorrow, openly crying as he pulled his suitcases to his car, the trunk yawning, swallowing up his things. Then he looked up at the house, and I dropped the pillow and pressed my hand against the window. And I forced myself to smile, a pretty smile, a real smile, so my father wouldn't have to drive away with that image in his heart, the remembrance of his little girl crying.

But after that day, he'd been the George Clooney type...determined to have fun when we were with him, no matter what Hester's mood or, later, Freddie's fussiness. He'd taken on that sheepish bad-dog personality around my mother, who responded with icy disdain. All those years passed, and I figured my father was just fine.

I never realized he still carried so much grief. So much loneliness.

I reached over the side of the chair and fumbled in my purse for my phone, then hit Dad's name. His voice mail picked up immediately. "Hi, Daddy," I said after the beep. "I just wanted to say I love you. And you're a great dad. Also, I'm free for bowling tomorrow night, okay? I love you."

No matter how hard I tried, I couldn't make you love me again.

The words certainly struck a chord. Apparently my father and I had more in common than sparkly brown eyes and dimples. After all, wasn't that what I'd been doing with Mark? I'd tried so hard to get him to notice me, and when he finally did, tried so hard to be perfect. Even after he'd put our relationship on pause, I'd tried so hard. Tried be cheerful, tried be upbeat, tried not to let my feelings show, not to blame him, not to mind when day after day, week after week, his nonchalance eroded my heart.

Sometimes, being an optimist was quite the fucking effort.

For a second, I had the urge to call Ian, because something told me he'd understand. Then I remembered that he had his own heartache to deal with. With a sigh, I set the bowl of cherry chip batter on the floor for Bowie to finish off. He wagged vigorously as he finished up my snack. Then, because I couldn't think of anything better to do, I washed up and went to bed, petting my dog's thick fur until we both fell asleep.

CHAPTER SIXTEEN

THINGS WERE BETTER the next day. Good night's sleep and all that. Besides, all that doom and gloom last night… blick! "No more Bitter Betty," I informed Bowie, who was curled in a tight ball on his side of the bed. "And no more Debbie Downer. I killed them both in my sleep. Today is a new day, Bowie, you handsome eighties pop icon, you!" My pet licked my face in vigorous agreement. I sang in the shower, Bowie chiming in on harmony, then put on a wicked cute pink dress and paired it with to-die-for gray pumps, made pancakes for Noah and kissed his cheek as I left.

When I got to work, my mood continued to blossom. Muriel had gone to California—some BTR meeting she couldn't miss. Without her, the office had its old vibe back; Damien snarked about, lounging in my office to update me on his joyful reunion last night with Dave (their fifth). Fleur told a funny story about her latest wanker. In the art room, Pete and Leila spoke in their feral child language, laughing at jokes no one else understood but which made us all smile anyway. Mark brought in pizzas for lunch, and Karen even emerged from her cave to eat with us.

"The office is closed tomorrow," Mark announced, waving a slice of garlic and sausage in the air.

"Yankees–Red Sox at Fenway, and even though I had to mortgage my house to get the tickets, you're all worth it."

Cheers broke out, though Karen was the only true baseball fan. Field trips like this were something Mark had done from the beginning of Green Mountain Media. Once we'd spent the day at Ben & Jerry's (heaven, I tell you). Another time we'd gone skiing (or, perhaps more appropriately for some of us, drinking in a picturesque lodge while Mark and Karen skied). We'd been to Fenway once before, and it had been wicked fun.

After work, I swung by the funeral home. Mom didn't mention the Bette Davis debacle, and neither did I. She and Louis were engaged in a mutual praise-fest over the restoration work on a particularly gruesome case involving a man and a wood chipper (enough said, don't you think?), so I endured that as long as I could, then kissed my mom's cheek and left them to their work. Dropped by home, got Noah's dinner ready, called my dad and found myself at the bowling alley an hour later.

"Poodle!" Dad cried when he saw me. I could see he was back to channeling George Clooney.

"Hi, Daddy," I said, giving him an extra big smooch on the cheek.

"Don't you look pretty!" he exclaimed, and I smiled and gave a little twirl. If Dad was George Clooney, then I was Audrey Hepburn (well, a somewhat plumper Audrey) with a cute ponytail, pedal pushers and a white shirt tied at the waist. "Stan, doesn't my daughter look gorgeous?" Dad called to his buddy, who was joining us.

"So gorgeous," Stan called, winking at me as he reverently removed his bowling ball from its case.

"You doing okay, Daddy?" I asked.

"Of course!" he said. "Sometimes it feels good to get things off your chest, know what I mean? But your mother's got a lot invested in being the martyred ex-wife. I was hoping that things could be different. Gave it my best shot. Que sera, sera." He sang the last bit, took my hand and twirled me. "Now come on, pretty girl. See if you can knock over a few pins."

I chose a sparkly pink ball (to match my personality) and lobbed it with great enthusiasm and zero skill. Dad chuckled and put his arm around me as we watched the ball head inevitably for the gutter.

AROUND FIVE THE NEXT EVENING, we were all jammed into Karen's minivan, full of Fenway franks, Cracker Jacks and beer. "Those fucking Yankees!" Karen cursed, leaning on her horn as we sat in the sea of cars exiting Boston. "A total waste of fantastic fucking seats, Mark. Eleven to two. It's just wrong."

"*I* didn't think it was a waste," Damien said. "That Jeter has the best ass in baseball. *And* I heard a rumor he's gay."

"He's not gay," I said. "I got a totally hetero vibe when he looked at me."

"You wish," Damien sneered. "He was looking at *me*."

"I'll fight you for him," I offered.

"You'd win," Mark said, smiling as he checked his iPhone.

Yes. Mark and I were sitting next to each other. Pete and Leila, already entwined around each other, had claimed the seats furthest in the back and were, from the sounds of it, snogging. Damien conveniently suffered from carsickness, so he always got the front. Which left Fleur, Mark and me in the second row, Mark between us two girls.

"This was a great day, Mark," I said. "Thank you."

"Yes, thanks. Brilliant idea," Fleur quickly seconded.

He put his phone back in his pocket. "Good to be with my people," he said. His dark eyes slid to my face, and he smiled that crooked grin, then winked.

My face warmed, and to hide my blush, I turned my head and looked out on Commonwealth Avenue. Mark chuckled.

Twenty minutes later, my boss's head was on my shoulder, his soft, curly hair tickling my cheek.

"How men can sleep anywhere, anytime, is beyond me," Fleur said, shifting. The minivan was called mini for a reason.

"You okay back there, Callie?" Karen asked, glancing in the rearview mirror.

Everyone in this car knew about my crush. Everyone was also kind enough to say nothing, though Fleur raised an eyebrow. "I'm fine. I'll just give him a good shove if I get uncomfortable," I answered easily.

"I'll give him a good shove if he keeps Muriel around," Damien grumbled.

"Stop it," I murmured.

"Seriously," Damien said, turning around in his seat to whisper. "She's such a self-important little bitch." Fleur's ears pricked up, and she leaned forward to join in.

"Damien. Stop," I said. "What if Mark hears you? What if *God* hears you and puts a black mark next to your name? Okay? So shut it."

"I hate moral people," he said, turning around. "You're so boring."

"I'm telling Dave you were mean to me," I said, grinning. "You know your boyfriend adores me."

He turned around and smiled, his usually supercilious

expression gone in place of a big smile. "Thanks for helping with that," he said.

"You're welcome. Buy me something fabulous."

"You got it."

And then I was alone again, sort of, breathing in the smell of Mark's shampoo, telling my heart to wise up, despite it natural inclination to do otherwise.

ON SATURDAY, I SURVEYED my vast collection of fab shoes, wondering if bringing seven pairs on an overnight trip might be excessive, when Noah bellowed up the stairs.

"Got a second?" he asked. "I need some help in the shop."

"Sure," I called, glancing at the clock. Ian was coming at two, and it was only quarter after twelve, so I went downstairs, Bowie pattering after me, his steps light, looking up at me as if I were the most fascinating person in the world. Or as if I were about to give him some bacon, which was more likely.

Noah was working on a sea kayak, a long, beautiful boat with a razor-sharp bow and thin body. It looked like a suicide machine to me, but to each his own.

"Okay, just slide it down the side here," Noah instructed, feeding me the piece of mahogany, which was so long it quivered.

"You don't usually put trim on your kayaks, do you, Noah?" I asked, doing as I was told.

"No. But this flatlander wanted what he wanted, and he was dumb enough to pay me three grand extra, so here we go. Now can we drop the chatter and get this done?"

"Yes, Noah. And don't forget I'm going to a wedding and I still need to pack."

Ian had e-mailed me last night with our schedule, a rather matter-of-fact list of information. We'd be staying at the Capitol Hotel, a beautiful old place that was actually a former account of mine. *(The grace of yesterday, the convenience of today.)* I was glad Ian had chosen it…not that there was a lot to choose from, even in our capital city. Montpelier was only about an hour from Georgebury, but if Ian wanted to put me up in a gorgeous hotel, I wasn't about to talk him out of it. *Just come as my friend.* The memory brought a smile to my face. I would. I'd be a great friend.

"So who's gonna feed me while you're gone?" Noah asked.

"No one. I expect to come home tomorrow and find your withered little skeleton, sitting all alone at the table, still waiting for dinner. If only you could walk or talk or use the phone or make your own damn dinner…wait a minute! You can!"

Noah growled, but beneath his white beard, a smile lurked. "You're a smart-ass, anyone ever tell you that?"

"I get 'saint' a lot, especially when people find out I'm living with you," I said. "But no, not smart-ass."

"Maybe you're not listenin'," he grunted. "Now hold that there, sweetheart. Good. This is gonna take a sec."

I glanced at the clock on the wall…12:30 p.m. I had time.

Noah tapped, swore, hopped (he was going one-legged today), swore. It had been a long while since I'd helped my grandfather in the shop, and it was lovely, the smell of wood smoke and cedar, my grandfather nodding in approval, whistling tunelessly. Time seemed to stop out here, since so little had changed over the years. Ever since we were small, Noah had put us to work out here.

He was a good teacher, explaining how wood fit together, why he did things a certain way. I'd always felt so safe when I helped him. Still did.

I checked the time again. 12:47 p.m.

"Go get me a C-clamp, darlin'," he said, in a rare and fine mood today. I went to his workbench and scavenged around 'til I found it, then returned.

"Okay, hold this again," Noah instructed. We were on the other side of the kayak now, and after a few minutes, my hands tingled from staying in the same position. Noah then needed another bit of wood sanded, and I obliged. After a while, I glanced at the clock again. 12:51 p.m. But that couldn't be right.

"Noah? Is that clock broken?" I asked, once more holding a piece of wood in place.

"Oh, yeah. Been broke for a while," he said.

"What time is it? I have to pack! I haven't even showered!"

He pulled out his pocket watch. "Five of two."

"Noah! I have to go! Ian's coming in five minutes! Can't you call Freddie and have him come over?"

"You cahn't just stop, Callie! I'm almost done."

"I have to—"

"Shush, child! You let go now, I have to start over, and you don't want that, do you?"

"I don't want to be late, either..." My voice broke off as Bowie exploded into barking. Sure enough, I heard a knock.

"We're in the shop!" I yelled.

"Christly, you're loud," Noah muttered.

The door to the shop opened. Sure enough, it was Ian, wearing khakis and an oxford. At the sight of my flannel pajamas, his face tightened.

"Ian, I'll just be two minutes," I said. "Noah," I hissed through clenched teeth. "We're going to a wedding."

"Fine! One more nail…there. You can go, Princess, for God's sake." He looked over at Ian. "Afternoon."

"Hello, Mr. Grey. Nice to see you. Callie, we need to leave." His jaw was clenched.

"Yup! I know! Two minutes! Come on, follow me. You can carry my, um…my bag." Which I hadn't packed, thanks to my grandfather's broken clock. And let's be honest. I wasn't exactly the "Let me just grab my tooth-brush" type. I flew up the stairs, Bowie leaping excitedly next to me, Ian following without so much joie de vivre. "Come on in," I said, flying into my room. "Or no, just stay…well. I'm sorry. Noah needed…forget it. Two minutes!" Leaving him scowling on the catwalk, I flew into my room, then into the bathroom.

Okay, I needed a shower, that was clear. I threw the faucets on and, while I waited for the water to heat, yanked open the drawer and took out my overnight makeup bag. Foundation, concealer, powder, blush, eye shadow (three shades of course, this was black tie), eyeliner, mascara, not this stuff, the good stuff, where was my eyebrow brush, ah, here it was, tweezers, lip gloss…no, *lipstick*…no, both…okay, and which shade…

"Callie! We need to leave."

"Two minutes!" I lied. Razor. Shampoo. Conditioner, voluminizing mousse, styling cream, finishing spray, gloss.

I tore off my jammies, jumped under the spray and soaped up, washed my hair, slapped some conditioner on it. "We're going to the hotel to change, right?" I called.

"I can't hear you."

I winced, knowing he was pissed off. "We're stopping at the hotel before the ceremony, right?" I bellowed.

"Yes."

I jumped. His voice was much closer. "Are you in my bedroom?"

"Yes."

The latch on my bathroom door was broken…a minor inconvenience, unless there was a man in one's bedroom. All he'd need to see me buck naked would be a little breeze… Wait a sec. Ian. My bedroom. Of course, I hadn't made my bed today, and about eight dresses, several bras and panties and…blerk! My Dr. Rey's Shapewear, in plain sight. Shit! Shit on a shingle, shit on rye.

I slapped off the slower, toweled off and jumped into my robe. Scooped every makeup and hair care product I had into the bag, grabbed a few clean towels and opened the door. "Hi! Sorry, I'm just running a teensy bit late," I said, throwing the towels over my unmentionables on the bed.

Ian was standing with his arms folded, staring at my Morelock chair. He turned to me with a look that would restore the polar ice caps. "Your two minutes were up eleven minutes ago," he said.

"Ian, I'm just…I just have to throw these things into a bag—you know what? I'd be a lot faster if you weren't here. So out! Out you go! You, too, Bowie. I'm going as fast as I can."

Basically shoving Ian out the door, I once again closed it on his face.

"I'm leaving here in five minutes," he said.

"Hush, you! I'm coming."

Nineteen minutes later, I opened the door. He was still there, glaring.

"Thank you for waiting. But we have plenty of time, right? The wedding's at five—"

"The ceremony starts at five, Callie. It will take us an hour and a half to get to the hotel, where we have to check in, get changed, then go to the church, which is another twenty minutes out of town." He fixed me with a look that said very clearly *I can kill you with my pinkie.*

"Well, it takes that long if *you* drive," I said. "Let me drive, and we'll get there in plenty of time."

"You're not driving," he said.

"Well, try not to stress," I said, glancing at my watch. "We can still make it if we leave now. Don't be so tense."

"I wasn't tense an hour ago," he said through gritted teeth.

"Oh, wait, I forgot something," I said, dashing back into my room. He may have growled, but I emerged seconds later with a CD. "I made us a playlist for the ride."

"Get in the car before I strangle you," he said.

"Is that a romantic thing to say to your date?" I asked, heading him down the stairs. "It really isn't."

"You're not my date," he said, completely serious.

"Bye, Noah! Thanks for ruining my day!" I called through the kitchen door.

"You're welcome. Have fun," he said.

Ten minutes later, Ian pulled onto the interstate.

"Sorry I was late, Ian," I said contritely, since he hadn't spoken since my house. He didn't answer, so I took it upon myself to fiddle with the CD player. A disk slid out. "Mahler's Symphony #1? My mother plays this at the funeral home. Yikes, it's worse than I thought."

His mouth didn't even twitch.

"Ian, please don't be mad at me," I said. "I'm really sorry I lost track of time."

"I'm not mad, Callie. I'm preoccupied." He cut his eyes to me, then back to the road.

"Well, here's what I picked out for our little ride. I mean how many times do you have to go to your ex's wedding, right? So we have the classic 'Love Stinks,' of course. 'Nothing Compares to You' by that crazy Irish woman, 'Love Lies Bleeding' by Sir Elton…oh, here's a personal favorite, 'Shut Up' by the Black-Eyed Peas— remind me to tell you about my hip-hop class for senior citizens. 'Good Riddance' by Green Day. I haven't actually heard that one yet, but I liked the title."

Bingo. Got him to smile. Not much of a smile, but a little one.

"Shall I put it in?" I asked, holding up the CD.

"Sure," he said, flicking on his signal and changing lanes. I complied, and the rather elementary chords of the J. Geils Band filled the car.

"So tell me about the groom," I said, settling back and looking at my driver. He looked nice in profile, I thought. Definitely a rugged face, not quite handsome…but awfully interesting. "Have you met him?"

Ian glanced at me for a long moment—longer than I was comfortable with, since he was driving—then looked back at the road. "There is no groom," he said.

"What do you mean?" I asked. "I thought this was a wedding."

"There is no groom."

"But—"

Ian looked over again, his face grim.

I swallowed. "Oh. Oh, holy guacamole, Ian. Are you kidding me?"

"No groom."

I fumbled in my purse for the wedding invitation he'd given me last week.

The pleasure of your company is warmly requested at

the marriage ceremony of Laura Elizabeth Pembers &
Devin Mullane Kilpatrick, Saturday, September, etc., etc.

"Devin's a woman?" I asked.

"Yes."

"Oh, my God, Ian."

"Yes." He cut another glance my way.

For a second, I didn't say a word. No wonder he looked clenched all the time! No wonder he had issues with women! No wonder he didn't want a date! "So you never…"

"No."

"And she didn't…"

"No."

"How did you…"

"I found them in bed together, Callie."

"Oh, Ian." I reached out and put my hand on his leg. He glanced down, then at me again, eyes icy. Right. I carefully removed my hand—apparently there was a "no touching" rule in effect. Couldn't blame him. Crikey. Ian's ex-wife was gay.

Holy. Crap.

There was an exit for a rest stop up ahead, and Ian pulled off the highway. He parked the car carefully between the lines, despite the fact that there was no one else around, shifted into Park, then turned to me, his face expressionless. His hands still gripped the wheel.

"We met at Tufts. She was in law school. My first real love, everything I was looking for and all that. We dated for two years, got married after graduation. Devin was her friend from high school. She was in our wedding, ironically. About three years into the marriage, I came home early one day, and there they were. Any questions?"

A zillion, I thought, but I only asked one. "Do you still love her?"

"Would I be going to her wedding if I hated her?"

"Well, yes, absolutely," I said. "You could make a scene, have a hissy fit, get drunk, grope your ex-mother-in-law."

He gave a reluctant grin, and my heart twisted a little. "I don't hate her."

"You didn't answer the question." I felt my cheeks warming.

He looked down. "Sure. I married her. I'll always love her a little."

"And why *are* you going to the wedding, Ian?" I asked.

He sighed and put the car in reverse, backing out carefully. "Damned if I know. Closure, I guess."

We pulled back on the highway. Man. Ian McFarland had caught his wife cheating on him, and here he was, going to her wedding.

For some reason, that made my heart feel a little bit too big for my chest.

I MADE IAN WAIT YET again once we got to the hotel...not on purpose, honest, but I felt I needed to start my hair from scratch, so that required another shower. Plus, I wanted to look incredible. Ian might not know it (or want it) but I was about to be the best date he'd ever had, and part of that involved being gorgeous. So I fussed with my hair, used the big curling iron to make it swingy and smooth. "Callie, time's up!" Ian called from the hall.

"Two minutes! Almost ready, Ian," I lied. Did my makeup to perfection, smoky eyes, easy on the lip gloss. A little perfume at the old pulse points. My grandmother's pearl necklace and matching earrings. Then I put on the dress. It was long. It was red. It showed off the girls. And yes, my shoes were *begging* for it, slutty little strappy purple (I know!) things with three-inch heels. Oh, mommy!

"Callie, this time I'm really leaving without you."

"You definitely don't want to do that," I said.

"We're late. Again. You have five seconds, Callie, and if you're not with me, that's probably not the worst thing in the world. Five...four...three..."

I grabbed my little sparkly evening bag "...two..." glanced once more at myself in the big mirror "...one..." and opened the door. "Hi."

Oh...God. He was in a *tux*. I'd sort of forgotten to think about that. He looked like an assassin about to infiltrate a state dinner...tall, blond, dangerous, and heavens, it was a turn-on! Those eyes of his were staring back at me, and you know what, it had been a *long* time since I'd had sex, and could we please just do it right here in this hallway? Holy. Guaca. Moley.

His eyes drifted down, slowly, assessingly, then back up, pausing at the girls for a gratifying heartbeat or three, then continuing up to my face. "Let's go," he said, then cleared his throat.

I snapped out of my haze of lust. "'Let's go,' Ian? Can't you do better than that? Here, I'll give you an example." I smiled and let my eyes drift over him once more. *Frrrroooww!* "Ian, you look...amazing. Wow. Okay, now it's your turn."

He almost smiled. "You look pretty. Let's go."

I sighed. "You're a work in progress, Ian McFarland."

Still, it was kind of a thrill, walking through the lobby of the prettiest hotel in Montpelier. Heads turned, people smiled, and I felt very Julia Roberts in *Pretty Woman*, minus the prostitute factor.

Ian was quiet in the car. His GPS system guided us past the gold-domed Capitol, the charming brick buildings, inviting shops and luscious smells of downtown Montpelier.

"Nervous?" I asked as we drove over the bridge.

"Yes," he answered.

"I am still totally game to pretend to be your girlfriend," I reminded him.

"No, thanks," he said.

"That's so insulting. And to think I wore this dress for you."

Ian was not amused. His eyes looked tight, if such a thing were possible. "Sorry," I muttered, adjusting my bracelet. "Just trying to lighten the mood." I glanced at the little GPS system, which was one of those handheld thingies. "Can I look at this?" I asked. "I've been meaning to get one."

"Sure," Ian said, taking a left as instructed.

I picked up the unit. Cute. There was an arrow at the bottom of the screen. I touched it. It showed our next four instructions. Yes, I definitely could use one of these things. Vermont roads were notoriously unmarked. I hit the button to exit back to the last screen. *Escape?* the unit asked. I hit *yes*.

"When do I make the next turn?" Ian asked.

"Um, let me check here…oh. Oops, I think I…there's nothing." Ian gave me the Siberian Freeze again. "I just touched an arrow," I explained. "It asked if I wanted to escape, I said yes, that's all."

"You canceled the instructions," he said, pulling over a tad abruptly.

"Oh. Sorry," I said. "I don't think I did, actually, but—"

He took the GPS from me. "You did," he said. He

stabbed a few buttons with unnecessary roughness, I thought. Growled. Stabbed some more. Finally got it back.

"Don't touch it again," he said.

"Okay, boss," I said, sighing. "Sorry. Again."

Ten minutes later, we pulled up in front of the Universalist Unitarian Church of Willington. Cars lined both sides of the street, but everyone already appeared to be inside. The dashboard clock read 5:06 p.m. Shit.

Ian opened his car door and walked around to open mine. He looked fierce, and tension rolled off him in waves. "Pretty church," I said, and it was, a large, classic white church with a steeple, the foliage glowing around it, pretty much what you see on every Vermont postcard ever printed.

The church lawn was a little soft; I had to tiptoe so my heels didn't sink into the earth.

"Can you…kick into gear or something?" Ian said, striving for patience.

"Sure, sure," I said, almost trotting. We made it to the steps, and Ian ran up a few and held the door for me. Whatever his faults, he had nice manners.

I went into the foyer, Ian hot on my heels, then lurched to a stop, causing him to crash into me. "Callie," he growled, then drew in a sharp breath.

Laura stood there, her back to us, peeking into the church through a slightly cracked door. She wore a calf-length white dress (Vera, I was thinking), and white roses twined in her pretty hair. At the sound of our little commotion, she whirled around, and her mouth fell open. No one spoke for a second. Until I did, of course.

"Hi there," I said.

Laura's eyes filled. "You came," she whispered. Clearly, she wasn't talking to me.

Ian swallowed.

The foyer was wide and bright. Three sets of doors led into the church. "I'll...I'll just find us a seat," I said, drifting over to the farthest set of doors. Pulling on the handle, I found it was locked. I tried the next one. Also locked. The last set of doors would require me to push past Ian and Laura, who were just staring at each other.

Okay, I wasn't actually *meaning* to spy, but I seemed to be trapped here. Trying to be as discreet as a woman in a scoopalicious red gown could be, I crept over to the far corner and wished I could be invisible. It almost worked...I might as well have been a ninja on a dark night as far as Ian and the bride were concerned.

"I didn't think you'd come," Laura whispered, the foyer acoustics letting me hear just fine. "And it occurred to me while I was on the way here that I...I wasn't sure I could go through with it without you being here. Without knowing you were really okay."

Ian looked at the floor for a beat. Then he took her hand and looked at her. "Of course I came," he said gently, and my eyes filled.

"I'll always love you, Ian," she said, tears slipping down her cheeks. "You know that, right? I'm so sorry that—"

"Shh," he said, wiping her tears away. Then he took her in his arms, her head fitting right under Ian's chin. "Don't cry, honey. Whatever you needed to say to me, you already have."

Being the kind who wept at dog food commercials, I bit down on a sob. Such...*kindness!* God only knew what humiliation and heartbreak Ian had been through—cheated on, lied to, quite probably laughed at—yet here he was, forgiving her, releasing her from the guilt she still obviously felt, and giving her the blessing she seemed to need.

I wished my mother could see this.

Then Ian kissed the top of Laura's head and stepped back, still holding her by the shoulders. "You look so beautiful," he said, smiling a little.

She took a shuddering sob.

"Oh, come on," Ian murmured. "No tears. This is a happy day. Besides, you're running late."

"Leave it to you to keep an eye on the clock."

He grinned. "Well, Devin's waiting in there, so… better get moving."

Her face scrunched, and she fished a tissue out of her sleeve. "Thank you, Ian," she said wetly, wiping her eyes. Then a door opened on the other side of the foyer, and an older gentleman in a tux came in. His eyebrows bounced up when he saw Ian.

"Ian! Good to see you, son," he said, shaking hands.

"John. Nice to see you, too."

"Everything okay out here?" the man asked Laura.

She smiled, straightened her father's boutonniere. "Everything's great, Dad," she said. "Let's go." She gave Ian one more smile.

"See you in there," Ian said. He opened the door—sure, *that* one was unlocked—and ushered me in. A few people glanced back, and a collective murmur went up. Some nudging occurred. Ian ignored them. We found an unoccupied pew behind all the other guests and took our seats.

The lump in my throat was killing me. As the organ music started, I slipped my hand into Ian's.

After a second, he looked at me, as if surprised. Then he reached into his jacket pocket with his free hand and withdrew a handkerchief, because of course, I was crying.

"What you did in there was just beautiful," I whispered, taking a little shuddering breath.

"Get a grip, Callie," he muttered.

"That was the first thing you ever said to me," I said, wiping my eyes. "I'll tell our children about that someday."

He shook his head, but he was smiling, and he squeezed my hand. Didn't let go, either.

CHAPTER SEVENTEEN

IN THE RECEIVING LINE, Laura hugged and kissed Ian, then turned to me. "Callie! Thank you so much for coming! I'm so glad you did."

"Congratulations," I said, smiling. I couldn't help liking her.

"And oh, my God, that dress!" she exclaimed.

I smiled modestly, but hiked the hem up so she could see my shoes.

"Don't tell me...Manolo?" she said in the hushed and reverent tone the shoes deserved.

"Yes," I confirmed. "And I got them on clearance for only—"

"Okay, let's move along," Ian grumbled, giving me an ungentle nudge. He stood in front of the other bride. "Devin. Best wishes." His voice was cool.

"Ian. Hello."

My eyebrows raised. Well, of course they'd hate each other. Devin turned to me. She was wearing a cream-colored Hillary Clinton–style pantsuit (the horror, the horror) and no makeup, a far cry from her stylish and ultrafeminine new wife. Still, she was quite attractive in that good-bone-structure way. "So you're Ian's date, huh?" she asked, looking me up and down.

"We're friends," I corrected, suspecting he would if I didn't. "Nice to meet you."

At the end of the line, Ian introduced me to Laura's parents. "John, Barb, this is Calliope Grey, a friend of mine from Georgebury. Callie, these are my...uh, Laura's parents."

The mother shook my hand. "Well, we certainly never saw this day coming," she said, still holding onto my hand. "We were hoping for grandchildren."

"You never know. They can always adopt," I said. "My sister adopted both her girls."

"We always thought Ian would make a *wonderful* father. He was so good to Laura, and honestly, he couldn't have been—"

"That's enough, Barb," Laura's father said. "Nice to meet you," he said to me. "We'll see you at the reception."

"So," I said once we were in the car. Ian put the key in the ignition. "I take it you weren't the only one surprised by Laura's, um...sapphic tendencies?"

Ian rubbed his eyes. "No. Her parents were just as...I guess Devin was the only one who... Can we not talk about this, Callie?"

"Sure. I'm sorry, Ian. Shall we stop for a drink first? A primal scream, maybe? Want to kick something?"

Ian tipped his head back against the headrest. "Maybe you could just...be quiet for a while."

"Sorry," I whispered, chastened. "I was just trying to cheer you up."

"I don't need cheering up," he said. He started the car and pulled away from the curb, then glanced at me. "The hand-holding was nice, though."

I waved my hand in the air. "Available whenever you need it. All part of the date package," I said.

"We're not on a date," he said.

I sighed. "Right. Just friends." Then, determined to give the man some peace, I shut my mouth.

The reception was at some old mansion on a hill. A wall of windows overlooked a long, sloping field. The sun sank into the horizon with an obligingly magnificent show of color. Candles flickered everywhere, the flower arrangements were opulent and waiters circulated with trays of cocktails and hors d'oeuvres. Pretty much exactly what I'd want for my own wedding, should that happy day ever occur.

Ian knew a lot of the guests, of course, and was doing his best to be sociable. But his shoulders were tight, and he wasn't smiling or talking much. One couldn't blame him. Even outside his ex-wife's wedding, he didn't smile or talk that much. Well. Ian certainly had other qualities. Like possibly the biggest heart in all of New England, if not the Eastern Seaboard. How many men would do what he was doing now?

There was much speculation, of course. Here he was, not only at Laura's wedding, but at her wedding to a woman, to the *other* woman, for that matter. As Ian exchanged stiff pleasantries with people from his old life, I put my eavesdropping skills to use. There were plenty of "That poor slob, how could he not know?" comments. If Ian overheard any, he didn't say a word.

Some people were happy to see him. He got a few hugs, a few cheek pats. Laura's aunt, a portly woman who clutched a fox terrier in her arms, pinned us in one corner. "Kato here keeps pooping in the dining room, don't you, snooky-bear? Ian, can you take a look at him?"

"Uh…sure, Dolores," Ian said.

Now perhaps was a good time to hit the ladies' room, as my gown and Dr. Rey's Shapewear required some forethought.

"Back in a flash," I said, giving his arm a squeeze. He gave me a stiff nod, then turned back to Kato, who bared his tiny teeth and snarled adorably.

Five minutes later, as I was in the stall, wrestling Dr. Rey's Shapewear back over my thighs, I heard Ian's name again. And this time, the person wasn't quite so kind in her assessment.

"Can you believe *Ian* showed up? I mean, what the fuck is he doing here? Trying to make Laura and Dev feel guilty?"

"No clue," said another voice. "I always thought he was a cold fish."

I wasn't about to let that go unchallenged.

"He's here because Laura asked him to come," I said, coming out and staring at the two women. "It meant a lot to her."

"Is that what you think? And who are you?" the first one asked, not at all nicely.

"Yes, it is what I think…what I know, actually. And hello, I'm Callie Grey, Ian's date," I said, glad that here, at least, Ian wouldn't contradict me. "So nice to meet you."

How I wished Ian would let me pretend to be his girlfriend to show people that he'd moved on…even if he hadn't. But no, when I rejoined him a minute later, he relentlessly introduced me as his friend, didn't hold my hand, didn't smile at me, didn't indulge in any body language that said he was crazy about me. Which I thought was really too bad, because let's be honest. I was definitely *feeling* things. Any man who could do what he'd done in the foyer of that church…well. Not to mention how smokin' he looked in that tux.

We made it through dinner well enough, though of course we were seated with the snotty pair from the bathroom. If Ian was quiet, I made up for it by being my usual chatty self. He seemed to grow more and more still, tension making him almost brittle as he doubtlessly counted the seconds 'til we could leave gracefully.

The best woman gave an endless speech, riddled with inside jokes and references. When that was finally over and we'd all dutifully sipped champagne, Ian and I looked at each other. "Want to go?" I whispered.

He nodded.

Then Laura stood up and took the microphone.

Ruh-roh.

"Thank you all for coming tonight," she said. "It means so much to Devin and me to have you sharing our happy day." She paused, and Ian seemed to freeze, as if sensing what was coming. "But," Laura continued, "there's one very special person here who put aside a lot—a *lot*—to come tonight—"

Oh, God. Poor Ian, I thought, my stomach contracting in horror.

"—and I just wanted to say how overwhelmed and grateful I am, Ian—" her voice grew husky "—that you found it in your heart to be here. You are so special. Thank you so, so much. I'll never forget this."

Every one of the roughly two hundred guests swung around to get a look at Ian, who sat as if carved from granite. His face was grim, and I knew that this was just about the worst thing that could happen to him…all that attention, all that *emotional diarrhea,* aimed right at him. A swarm of fascinated whispers rose from the guests.

Well, I couldn't just let him sit there. I leaned over, a sweet smile on my face, and kissed him on the cheek. "You're right, Laura," I called, settling my head on his shoulder. "He's a prince!"

There was an "aw" from the guests, a few chuckles. The nasty bathroom woman sneered, but up at the head table, Laura beamed. "Yes, he is," she agreed. "Well, I guess that's it from me! I hope everyone dances and eats cake and has a great time! Thank you!"

The roar of conversation resumed, and I looked up at Ian. "You okay, buddy?" I whispered.

He fixed me with those blue, blue eyes. "Yes. Thank you." For what, I wasn't sure. In fact, he might have been mad. Hard to tell.

"Careful, now," said the bitchy bathroom woman. "He might turn you into a lesbian, too." Her companion gave a snort.

I just smiled at her, snuggled a little closer to my guy. "I'm not worried," I said, tossing her a little wink. Then I looked up at Ian. "Want to dance?"

"Love to," he answered. He grabbed my hand and practically dragged me onto the dance floor.

There weren't too many people out there yet, but Ian didn't seem to mind. The band was just starting their second song…"If I Ain't Got You" by Alicia Keyes, and the singer was pretty damn good. Ian slid his arm around my waist, and we assumed the position.

The wave of lust I'd been riding since I saw him in his tux seemed to swell.

"So how are you, Ian?" I asked. My voice sounded embarrassingly sex kitten, and I cleared my throat.

He tilted his head to one side. "Better now," he said, and those girl parts of mine started yowling like ruttish cats. "Thanks for rescuing me."

"Oh," I said, blushing. "It was…I…it was nothing."

"It was something." His eyes crinkled slightly, and I fought off a swoon.

He smelled so good…that clean, fresh smell of rain in the spring, and the heat from his body seemed to pull me closer. My hand was so, so happy, being held lightly in his, and when his cheek brushed mine, the faint rasp of razor stubble against my skin, my knees almost buckled.

"This is a nice place," I said.

"Yes," Ian agreed, and his voice scraped some tender place inside me.

"So, Ian," I breathed, fighting off the urge to pull a Bowie and just climb on. "Everyone's watching us. You could definitely kiss me now. End all that speculation."

He pulled back and looked at me, and his eyes seemed…warm. "I'm not going to kiss you because someone's watching, Callie," he murmured, and his eyes dropped to my mouth.

And he *didn't* kiss me, but somehow, my God, that meant even more, though why, I couldn't tell, as my blood supply was cheerfully fleeing from my brain to my reproductive organs. He pulled me a little closer, and we weren't moving so much now, but the feeling of him so close made me forget how to breathe. I wanted just to slide my hands under his coat, unbutton his shirt, kiss his neck, pull him closer, feel his mouth on mine, taste…

"Having fun, kids?"

"Yes!" I squawked. It was what's-her-name's…the bride. Laura. Her dad. Whoever. My breath shook as I inhaled, and Ian glanced at me, the slightest smile in his eyes.

"Great. Glad you're doing well, son." Laura's father slapped Ian on the back, then walked away.

Ian and I looked at each other. I swallowed. "Would you like to leave, Callie?" he asked.

"Sure," I said, my voice unsteady. "Whenever you're ready."

"I'm ready," he answered, and again, the old knees threatened to give way.

Of course, we had to say goodbye to the happy couple. "I hope we see you soon," Laura said, giving him a hug. She hugged me, too. "Thank you for coming," she whispered. "You're good for him."

"Well," I said, blushing furiously. "Um…good luck with everything."

Ian didn't hold my hand on the way to the car, simply opened the car door for me. As we pulled away from the reception, the skies opened and rain pounded down on the roof of the car. My well of snappy one-liners seemed to dry up. I didn't look at Ian, and he didn't talk. The only sound was the pattering rain, the hissing of the tires through the wet streets, and the hard, fast rhythm of the wipers.

The rain had grown heavier by the time we drove back into Montpelier. Ian pulled into the hotel parking lot, found a space, then turned off the ignition. For a second, he rested his forehead on the steering wheel. "I'm very glad that's over," he said.

"I'll bet," I murmured, looking at him for the first time in half an hour.

He turned his head and looked at me. "You were a wonderful date, Callie," he said, and with that, he leaned over and kissed me.

For a minute, I didn't move…the shock was so great that I just sat frozen. Then the reality of his mouth on mine sank in…warm and gentle and rather perfect, really. I sighed, and his hand came up to cup the back of my head, his fingers sliding through my hair, and I realized I was already gripping his lapels. I shifted so I could get closer. Then the kiss deepened, and God, he tasted so good, and his mouth felt unbelievable. I slid my hands under his jacket, up along the solid muscles of his back, then shifted, one foot pushing against the car door so I could get closer to him, to that solid heat. He seemed absolutely focused on kissing me, just that, just this lovely, long, hot kiss, and man, he knew what he was doing. I felt myself softening, melting against him, and Ian was the opposite, hard and, oh, just hard and hot and safe. A low sound came from deep in his throat, and a rush of deep satisfaction flooded through me…he *did* like me, he *did* want me. His mouth moved to the base of my neck, and my hands fisted in his shirt, practically tearing it.

Then a car door slammed, and I jumped back a little. The emergency brake (or *something*…oh, no, it was the brake) was pressing into my thigh, as I'd basically crawled on top of Ian and was now sprawled awkwardly across the seat and my driver. The rain pounded on the car, and the windows were already steamy…and let me tell you, they weren't the only ones.

Ian was breathing hard, I noticed, and his eyes were half-closed as he looked at me. He smiled, a slow, satisfied smile, and I swallowed and bit my lip. My hands were on his chest…his broad, solid chest, and I could feel his heart thudding away, gratifyingly fast.

"Want to go inside?" he whispered, tucking a lock of hair behind my ear.

I nodded, apparently unable to speak.

He gently pushed me back to my side of the car, as I was also apparently unable to move. My legs were wonderfully weak and trembling, and my skin felt feverish. Ian opened his door and got out, the rain instantly soaking him. He came around to my side, opened the door, then bent down.

"Your shoes will drown," he said, and with that, he scooped me up in his arms. The cold rain was a shock, and I yelped a little. Ian smiled, closed the door with his foot and carried me...*carried* me toward the hotel, and it was so crazy romantic that I couldn't quite believe it was happening to me. My heart felt as light and happy as a dandelion seed carried on the breeze.

"Do you like hauling women off to your lair, Ian?" I asked above the rush of the rain. "Makes you feel manly, does it?"

"Makes me feel hernia, anyway," he said, trying not to smile. Or grunt, perhaps. "And I'm carrying you to the lobby. Not necessarily my lair."

"Drat," I said.

He laughed. I melted.

Alas, we were at the front door, which a bellhop thoughtfully opened. Ian set me down just inside the lobby, then ran a hand through his wet hair. I was soaked as well, dark splotches on my dress, the soggy silk clinging to my legs. He was still smiling, and man, what a difference...from Russian assassin to, I don't know...*dessert.* There were wonderful crinkles around his eyes, and he didn't have dimples so much as these lines that slashed his cheeks, and he looked so happy, so sweet in his wet tuxedo that I'd have married him in an instant, should a justice of the peace have happened to conveniently walk by.

I pushed my wet hair behind my ears. I had a good feeling about this. Like I was about to get lucky, oh yeah. "Hope I didn't rupture any of your disks," I said. Okay, not the best come-on line, but I was still a little breathless. From being *carried.* I did mention that he carried me, didn't I?

"No, no. You can't be any heavier than the DeCarlos' bull mastiff, and I have to lift him up all the time." His grin widened.

"Ian, stop. I'm blushing."

He looked at me. At my mouth. And so here it came. That moment where we'd actually have to discuss going to his room. Or mine. If we were going to do something about that kiss in the car. As the good Lord knew, I sure as heck wanted to. And as of tonight, the feelings finally seemed mutual.

"Callie?"

My head whipped around, my mouth fell open.

It was Charles deVeers. Muriel's father.

"Mr. deVeers!" I blurted.

"Now, now, you said you'd call me Charles," he said, coming over and giving me a bear hug. "What are you doing here, sweetheart? Did Muriel call you?"

My mouth opened and closed a few times before actual words emerged. "I...I—uh, Charles, this is Ian McFarland. We were at a wedding."

The men shook hands. "We've met before, haven't we?" Charles asked. "On the hike. You're Callie's boy-friend, right?"

Ian looked at me. Didn't say anything.

"Uh...no," I stammered. "We're...we're just friends."

Though Ian had been calling me that all night—and though being his friend was something of an honor—the word suddenly seemed very...meager. Ian's gaze shifted away from me.

"So...um, what are you doing here, Charles?" I asked.

"Well, this is the best hotel around, according to your boss. I stayed here last time, too."

"It's a great hotel," I said faintly. "Definitely. We did an ad campaign a few…" My voice trailed off.

Now, granted, Vermont is a tiny state with very few people, and cities—real cities, with things like hotels—are few and far between. Georgebury only boasted a couple of bed-and-breakfast places, so it wasn't exactly shocking to learn that Charles deVeers, multimillionaire businessman, might choose this hotel if he was visiting the state. Especially if Mark had recommended it.

But it was shocking anyway.

"Daddy? Where are you?" Muriel came out of the bar. At the sight of me, her face tightened. Then she smiled an alligator's grin, all teeth and carnivorous intent. "Callie. What are you doing here? Are you stalking us?"

I attempted a laugh. "Ian and I were at a wedding, actually." I paused, wondering if I could take Ian's hand. I didn't. "You remember him from the hike, right?"

"Oh, right. *Fleur's* friend," Muriel said, smirking. "Hi, there."

"Hello," Ian said.

And then, of course, Mark emerged from the bar as well. At the sight of me, he jerked to a stop. "Callie!" His face flushed. "Uh…wow. Hi! Oh, and…Ian, is it?"

"Right," Ian confirmed.

"Nice to see you again," Mark said. "Small world." He glanced at me, looking guilty as a shoplifting teenager.

"This is silly," Charles boomed. "You two should join us! We were just having a little celebratory drink. Come in, come in!"

Mark's gaze bounced between Muriel and me. He swallowed.

"They were at a wedding," Muriel said. "And, not to blow the big surprise, but…well, you'll be going to another one pretty soon." She smiled broadly, then put her hand on Mark's chest.

On her fourth finger was a solitaire diamond big enough to choke my dog. I felt the blood drain from my face. Blinked. Nope, it was still there.

"Congratulations," Ian said.

"Come have some champagne with us," Charles said. "It's such a happy occasion!"

My eyes slid from the rock to Mark. Though he was smiling, he didn't meet my eyes for more than a drive-by.

Mark was getting married. To Muriel. She'd be here forever now. He was getting *married* to that *un*helpful, *un*cheerful, *un*friendly…

Realizing that I hadn't inhaled in some time, I sucked in some air. I tried to say something, but my vocal cords seemed to be frozen.

"We're actually pretty soaked," Ian said, and at the sound of his voice, I closed my mouth. "But thank you," he added.

"Congratulations," I said finally, though my voice sounded strange. "Best wishes. Um…well, I guess I'll see you Monday."

"Another time, then, kids. You have a great night." Mr. deVeers, all charm and conviviality, waved us off.

Ian steered me to the elevators, his hand warm on my arm. The minute we got there, he let go, making me realize how cold I was. He pushed the button, then shoved his hands into his pockets.

I took a deep breath, my mind still reeling. "That was…wow. Small world. Small state." I glanced at my companion, trying to recover. He didn't look at me, and our kiss seemed like a year ago.

"Ian?" I asked.

"Yes?"

"Um…I'm sorry about that. The interruption." Shit. I sure as heck was. Just when you think you're getting somewhere, a huge sinkhole opens up in the damn road and breaks your axle.

The elevator arrived with a ding. "After you," was all he said.

Our rooms were on the fourth floor, right across from each other. I opened my evening bag and withdrew my key card. He pulled his out from his jacket pocket. The mood from the car was as dead as roadside possum.

"Ian," I blurted. "Um… Do you want to come in? Raid the mini bar, share a Toblerone? Maybe, um…talk? Or other things, too?"

He hesitated, but the answer was already written on his face. "I appreciate you coming to Laura's wedding, Callie," he said carefully, "and you really were…helpful. But maybe this isn't the right time for Toblerones." He paused. "Or anything else."

I took a quick breath, mortified that tears were stinging my eyes. "Okay. Sure. Yup. Well, sleep tight, Ian. See you in the morning. Um, if we could leave on the early side tomorrow, that would be great. I have a lot of things to do."

"Sure," he said, and with that, he slid his card into the door and went into his own room.

"Shit," I whispered. "Shit on a shingle, shit on rye."

CHAPTER EIGHTEEN

GREEN MOUNTAIN WAS subdued the following week with the news that M&M were making it official. Mark avoided me, acting chipper and professional when we did have to talk and, on the two or three occasions when we happened to walk in at the same time, suddenly remembering he'd forgotten something, requiring an about-face. I heard him and Muriel laughing behind his office door one morning, and another day, the elder Rousseaus came in to take their son and his fiancée out to lunch. I still couldn't believe it. Not that Mark was getting married...but that out of all the women on earth, he'd picked her. That he loved her enough for a lifetime.

Though I tried to stay out of any true gossip, it was clear the rest of my coworkers weren't thrilled about the engagement, either. "He can marry her if he wants," Karen said as we walked in together on Wednesday, "but I wish to holy hell that she wasn't working here." Yesterday, Muriel overheard Damien referring to her and Mark as M&M. "Oh, that's so cute!" she said. "We should rename the company. M&M Media. What a great name, don't you think, hon?" Mark had murmured an answer, and later that day, I'd seen Muriel playing with the words *M&M Media* in different fonts on her computer.

Muriel may have been a tad more pleasant, but the sight of her running our weekly staff meeting was off-putting. Apparently, she'd given up trying to be creative director and was moving into production.

"Callie, what are you working on this week?" she asked, her eyes giving me the customary scan-and-judge. She was clad in a winter-white wool dress, wide black belt and gorgeous black patent leather pumps.

"I'm working on your dad's Web site and some of the downloads for—" I began.

"Please call the company by name," she said mildly, ticking something off her notepad. Damien snorted and went back to studying his manicure. He used to run our production meetings and was making his irritation known through deep sighs and eye-rolling.

"Anything else?" Muriel asked.

"Yep. The hospital ad for the *Globe* and the pitch for that construction company in New Hampshire," I said. "Tomorrow we're shooting the fall footage for Hammill Farms, so I'll be going to that, too."

"Do you really need to? Mark and I will be on site," she said, looking up with a fake smile.

I glanced at Mark, who was staring out the window. "Well, since I came up with the concept and wrote the script," I said calmly, "I'd say the answer is yes, I do need to go."

"Now, Callie," she said in a placating tone. "You don't need to be hostile. Everyone agrees that your commercial is wonderful. I'm just not sure if you really need to come, or if you can delegate once in a while. After all," she added, "your boss will be there. I'm sure you can trust his judgment." The insincere smile remained on her face.

"Mark?" I asked.

He snapped to attention. "Um…well, uh, I could use you here, actually."

"Okay," I said after a beat. "I guess I'm staying, then."

"Great," Muriel said, her diamond eyes sparkling with satisfaction. "Fleur? What are you up to this week?"

Fleur straightened. "Muriel, those shoes… Prada, yeah?"

"Suck-up," Damien muttered.

Fleur shot him a glare, but Muriel smiled. "Chanel," she said.

"Right-o. Well, I'm nearly done with the copy for the BTR catalog, as you asked. Anything else you'd like me to do?"

"No, that's fine, you keep at it. I love what you've shown me so far."

My stomach knotted. Fleur was smart, and political, and if it felt a bit like she was a traitor, well, she was just looking out for herself. "And, Pete," Muriel said, just as Pete was yawning hugely. "What are you working on this week?"

"I'm trying to get my USB into a certain port," he said, nudging Leila who, as usual, was fused to his hip bone.

"Maybe you need a converter," she giggled.

To my surprise, Muriel smiled, a real smile this time. "You guys are so cute," she said. "I guess love is in the air."

I LEFT WORK A LITTLE EARLY, and Bowie greeted me with his usual astonished joy that so great a miracle as my return had occurred. "Where's Noah, huh, Bowie?" I asked. "Where's your Grampy?" Noah's truck wasn't in the driveway, but my dog failed to elucidate. Noah must've had some errands to run, though he usually got me, his slave, to do that for him, as he wasn't fond of "the great unwashed," as he liked to call the public.

I wasn't alone in the house that often, and I had to admit, it was kind of nice. I loved my grandfather, of course, but I missed living alone, too. The tiny apartment I'd rented before Noah's accident had been a snug little space with sloping ceilings and big windows. My father had clunked his head every single time he visited, but I loved the coziness of it. And sure, I wanted a house someday. I didn't want to be Noah's faithful servant forever. Or, I corrected, I didn't want to *just* be Noah's faithful servant. I wouldn't mind having him live with my husband and me.

Not that there was a husband on the horizon.

I hadn't heard from Ian since our drive home from Montpelier last week, which had been a study in awkwardness and fidgeting. On my part, that is. Honestly. Me, reduced to inane chatter about the foliage. Sure, he'd responded, his answers all polite and brief. We hadn't talked about anything real. Certainly hadn't talked about that kiss, which I'd relived about three hundred times thus far.

You blew it, the First Lady said, shaking her head sadly.

How did I blow it, huh? I snapped back. *I was surprised that Mark's getting married, that's all. Is that a sin? And isn't there a kindergarten somewhere waiting for you to show up and read a book?* Betty Boop was useless, sighing mournfully somewhere in a corner of my brain. But Michelle was right. Somehow, I'd blown it. From Ian's perspective, it must've seemed like I wasn't over Mark. *Are you sure you are?* the First Lady asked.

I closed my eyes and sighed. I knew one thing. I really wanted to breach the wall between Ian and me. Too uncertain to pick up the phone, I'd written, then deleted about thirty e-mails to him, but despite the fact that I was good at making people want stuff—and making people like me, as Ian had once pointed out—every word sounded wrong. I checked his "Ask Dr. Ian" blog…he was doing fine. Carmella and I ran into each other at Toasted & Roasted, and she told me things had been really busy since the pet fair. That was good, at least. The little nudge provided by the warm and fuzzy campaign had worked. But at the memory of the scene in the church foyer, I felt ashamed that I'd ever suggested that Ian McFarland needed to be any different from how he actually was.

I slipped off my shoes and went up to my own room, Bowie at my side, the unaccustomed quiet broken only by the sound of the rain pounding the roof. The Morelock chair sat in front of the window as if waiting. Waiting to be a part of that happily ever after I'd promised it. For a second, I thought about trying to get some comfort there, but I didn't feel worthy today.

I lay on my bed, Bowie curled next to me, and wondered what to do. Work was sucky, Muriel wasn't going anywhere and I'd ruined things with Ian.

Bowie's ears pricked up suddenly. So did mine, figuratively speaking.

Any further thoughts on my romantic woes disintegrated. *It's just the rain,* I told myself. But there it was again. A sound. A thud. Not rain at all.

Someone was here. In my house. Someone was upstairs with me. Hot, liquid fear flooded my veins. Silently, I sat up.

Someone was in my bathroom.

Could it be Bronte, maybe? It was possible…she came over once in a while, but without Noah here, she would've gone to Mom's. Maybe it was Freddie, but what the heck would he be doing in my bathroom? Should I follow that train of thought? Maybe it was a mass murderer, on the run from the police, ducking into our perpetually unlocked home to hide, coldly delighted to find one more victim.

It's probably a bat, dummy, the First Lady said. The thought was calming, despite Michelle's disrespectful tone. She was probably right. Speaking of bats, well, I didn't have one. Baseball bat, that was. But I did have an oar, this old wooden oar I'd bought at a yard sale a few years ago, which I'd hung up as a very cool decoration. Taking care to be quiet, just in case the noise was indeed caused by Jack the Ripper, I crept over and took the oar off the wall.

Picking up my cell phone, I flipped it open, pressed *9,* then *1,* then kept my thumb hovering right there. If there really was a person in my bathroom, I'd press the last *1,* then toss the phone under the bed so the perp couldn't pry it from my hand and hang up. The police could then track my signal and rescue me. And surely Bowie wouldn't just twirl in gleeful circles as I was attacked, right? Surely he'd protect the woman who'd saved him from the animal shelter, right? I glanced at my faithful friend. He was sleeping. Super.

Tiptoeing across the room, I could feel my heart clattering. The thing in my bathroom was probably a bat or a bird, but…what if it *was* a serial killer? Or a terrorist? *Don't forget vampire,* Michelle suggested.

Lucky for me, the bathroom door's latch was still broken. The door was closed, but I could kick it open the way they did on *Law & Order: Criminal Intent* and thus surprise my intruder. Oar in one hand, phone in the other, I took a deep breath, then kicked the door open as hard as I could.

A naked man leaned against my shower, dripping wet, his back to me.

"Aaah!" I screamed—the door hit the wall and closed again, and I leaped backward, away, the oar clattering to the floor. Bowie bolted to his feet, barking hysterically, rushing instantly to my side. A shriek—someone else's—split the air, and I gave an answering scream. Holy shit, who was in there? *What* was in there?

"Nine-one-one operator, what's your emergency?" came a voice. Thank God, I'd hit the last *1,* bless my smart thumb. "Naked man! Naked man!" someone yelled—oh, it was me! *Hide the phone!* my brain instructed, so I hurled my cell across the room and vaulted across the bed, Bowie rocketing after me, baying in high-pitched panic, as I scrambled away from the naked intruder. Grabbing a pillow, I clutched it in front of me, my back against the wall.

The bathroom door opened again, and I screamed, long and loud.

"Christly, Callie, shut up!"

My scream choked off mid-screech.

My grandfather. Wrapped in a towel. It was *Noah.* Noah! The naked man had been leaning because he only had one leg. I threw the pillow to the floor.

"Jesus God in heaven, Noah, what the hell were you thinking?" I yelled, my entire body shaking wildly. Bowie barked, backing me up. "I thought you were a serial killer! You scared the life out of me!"

"Did I?" Noah snapped. "You're kiddin' me. And

what if I was a killer, huh? Your pillow gonna save your life, dumb-ass?"

"You… I—" My heart still thundered away, so hard my head buzzed. "What the hell are you doing in my bathroom, anyway?" I asked.

"What the hell are you doing home so early?" he countered.

"I left work a little…wait a minute, wait a minute," I said. "Who else was screaming? It wasn't just me, was it?"

"None of your business," Noah answered, but his cheeks reddened.

"Is someone else in there?" I asked, narrowing my eyes.

At that moment, Jody Bingham appeared from the bathroom, damp and…okay…wearing my bathrobe. "Hi, Callie," she said calmly. "Sorry we scared you."

In the distance, I heard the sound of sirens. "Well, *I'm* sorry I called 911," I said.

WHEN THE POLICE, THE EMTs and the volunteer fire department (half of whom were River Rats) had listened to my story four or five times, wept tears of mirth and ascertained that my grandfather was not a threat to my safety, they finally trooped out.

"Always great to see you, Noah," Robbie Neal, president of the River Rats, said, shaking my grandfather's hand.

"Get outta here, Mister Man," Noah grumbled.

Robbie winked at me. "Sorry for your troubles, Callie," he said.

"Not as sorry as I am," I returned. He closed the door behind him, already pulling out his phone to share the love.

"Noah, Jody, once again, I'm wicked sorry," I said.

"But maybe you've learned an important lesson about not using other people's bathrooms, huh?" I stirred the soup I'd whipped up during my little police interrogation. Jody and Noah sat at the kitchen table, looking rightfully sheepish.

"We weren't doing anything too…" Jody paused. "Nothing *that* improper, Callie," she assured me. "Your grandfather's leg hurt, I suggested he take a little Jacuzzi, and the tub's in your bathroom."

"Uh-huh. So, Noah, the next time your truck's in the shop and you feel like getting a booty call, maybe you could leave a note?"

"What's a booty call?" he asked.

"What do you think?" I muttered, still a little ticked off. One does not often see one's grandfather naked in one's bathroom, after all. And thank the merciful Christ for that.

"A booty call is when you visit someone for sex," Jody said matter-of-factly. "Callie's teaching us hip-hop. It's very enlightening."

"So," I said, bringing the pot of soup to the table and going back for a pack of Ritz crackers and some cream cheese, "how long have you two been…getting it on?"

"Oh, we're not really getting it on," Jody said fondly. "Just two kindred spirits, right, Noah?"

"Let's not get hysterical," he muttered, but his cheeks were pink, and when Jody reached across the table to hold his hand, he didn't pull away.

At that moment, the back door opened, and in poured the entire rest of my family—the parents, the siblings, the nieces.

"We just got a call from Robbie Neal," my father said, his forehead wrinkled with concern. "He said there was a break-in involving a…a pervert, honey?" Dad came right over to me and gripped my upper arms.

"There was," I confirmed. "And it was terrifying."

Once again, I told the story of Naked Grampy, which was sure to become a Hallmark Hall of Fame movie.

"That is *so* nasty," Bronte said, her face a little gray.

Freddie was rocking back and forth, wheezing, Hester wiped tears from her eyes, Josephine played with a one-armed Barbie. And my parents sat next to each other on the bench.

There was enough soup for everyone, and I whipped up a little peach crumble while we were all talking, and despite the fact that work sucked and I'd almost had my grandfather arrested for a sex crime, it turned out to be the nicest family meal we'd had in a long, long time.

Maybe ever.

CHAPTER NINETEEN

THREE DAYS LATER, realizing I'd crushed any fledgling romance between Ian and me, I was fighting the blues. I wanted to call him, but kept losing my nerve. I thought about posting a question on his Web site… *Dr. McFarland, if a guy kisses you and then, through no fault of your own, you run into an old boyfriend, how do you get things back on track?*

But all the dating manuals and Web sites warned fiercely against such an act. According to *Slicing the Carotid: Fatal Mistakes Women Make in Relationships* as well as *Why the Man You Love Hates You,* the very last thing I should do was pursue. *Men are genetically predisposed to be the hunter/gatherers,* one book said. *Think of yourself as the woolly mammoth. Let the hunt come to you.* I wasn't sure about that advice, knowing just what happened to the woolly mammoths, but I got it. Besides, Ian had my home, office and cell numbers, my e-mail, my Facebook page and my street address. He was ignoring them all.

In other news, eCommitment showed that I'd had some interest from a fifty-three-year-old lumberjack with two ex-wives, seven children and nine dogs. Clearly, I'd run through all the available men in northeastern Vermont. Human Hair was looking better and better.

On Tuesday, Annie and I met for lunch at Toasted &

Roasted, which was mobbed with senior citizen leaf peepers, and it was only because I'd danced with Gus at our eighth-grade mixer that we got a table. After hearing about my godson's triumphs in the classroom, athletic field and dentist's office, I brought my friend up to speed on my lack of a love life. "Are you sure I shouldn't call him?" I asked, toying with my soup.

"Give him some space." She took a bite of her French dip sandwich and chewed wisely.

"I hate space," I muttered. "I'm much better at smothering, pestering and stalking. Space sucks."

"Trust me," she said, smiling. "I know everything."

By Thursday, I decided that Annie in fact knew nothing and stalking was indeed the way to go. Hence, I decided to take my kayak for a little spin that evening on Granite Lake. Wasn't like I'd never kayaked here before, was it? Sure, Ian's dock was on the far side of this same lake, but that was hardly my fault. I'd been kayaking here long before any vet moved in.

I unloaded the boat, got my paddle from Lancelot's hatch and clicked on my life vest. "In you go, Bowie," I said. My dog leaped neatly into the front seat of the kayak, pleased as punch.

Twenty minutes later, I sighted Ian's dock. He wasn't there, and his house was too far to see from the water. Too bad. I'd rather hoped he'd be sitting out here, mooning after me. I bobbed there a moment, the waves slapping the side of the kayak. Then, with a gusty sigh, I turned my trusty vessel around and headed back. But the fresh air and exercise soothed my soul a little nonetheless; it was hard to be blue with Bowie, who sat in quivering attendance upfront, his head turning sharply whenever he sensed a fish or a turtle or an amoeba.

Vermont was at its most beautiful this week, the height of leaf season, the foliage so pure and brilliant it was almost a physical sensation. The early October evening was soft, the setting sun cutting in golden shards through the gray clouds. In just a few weeks, all this would be gone, just an achingly beautiful memory 'til next year, and the long, white winter would be upon us.

Another kayak came cutting across the lake. A couple about my own age paddled vigorously, their cheeks glowing with the cool air and exercise. "Beautiful night, isn't it?" I called.

"It sure is!" the man answered. "Guess what? We're getting married! She just said yes!" The woman flapped her left hand, ostensibly to show me her ring.

"Oh, mazel tov!" I called merrily, though a quick vision of them capsizing flashed satisfyingly across my brain. They waved, in love with life, and continued on their happy way.

"Want to be my boyfriend, Bowie?" I asked, huffing away. He did, of course. He twisted neatly out of his seat and took a step or two to lick my face. "See? You're very attuned to my moods. You don't snore. You're quite attractive. Okay, that's probably enough, boy. You're a dog, after all, and this sounds perverted. Go sit down."

Bowie returned to his seat and continued his search for minnows. As the twilight thickened, I made it back to shore. Bowie jumped out and watched as I hauled the kayak onto the roof of my car and took off my life vest. With one more look across the lake, I opened the car door. "Come on, boy," I said, then buckled him into his doggy seat belt and kissed his furry head.

My melancholy returned as I started Lancelot and trundled down the dirt road away from Granite Lake.

Work wasn't horrible, but it wasn't the same. Last night, I'd scouted out Craigslist, but there'd been nothing, just a sales position for a dying newspaper in New Hamster. I'd be kind of dumb to quit in this economy, give up all those nice perks and bennies. "Maybe I'll go into the family business," I told Bowie. "Not that I want to be around dead people all day, but I would have job security."

Suddenly, a huge wild turkey came running out of the woods to my right. The thing was enormous, and it was sprinting as if being chased, its wings flapping, clearly preparing for takeoff. And on a collision course with my car! "Watch out!" I called, slamming on the brakes. I flung my arm protectively in front of Bowie, who barked in surprise, and we jerked to a stop, our seat belts locking.

"Oh, shit," I whispered. There'd been a thud. I was almost sure of it. Heart pounding sickly, I got out of the car, my hands over my mouth, prepared to see turkey carnage.

There it was, lying on the side of the dirt road. One wing flapped weakly, then stopped.

"No!" I cried. "Oh, no, I'm so sorry!" I wrung my hands as I approached. The turkey didn't move again. I couldn't tell if it was breathing. "Please don't be dead," I squeaked.

Sobs jerking out of my chest, I went to the back of my car and opened the hatch. Stupid Lancelot! Why did I buy a Prius? If only it made some noise, the poor bird would've been warned. "Please don't be dead," I repeated.

I grabbed the tarp I always kept in the car for my dripping paddles. Bowie whined in inquiry. "We hit it," I said wetly, then returned to the turkey.

It was horribly still. Like all turkeys, it was an ugly brute...a tom, a male. In the fading light, its feathers looked dull and black, the bald, rough-skinned head in shades of red and chalky blue. The bird's legs were long and strong, with spurs on the back for defense. Not that it did much good against my car.

My hands shaking with fear and adrenaline, I lay down the tarp next to the bird, then got the paddle from my car. Closing my eyes with the horror of the job, I used the paddle to gently push the huge bird onto the plastic, gagging at the flopping sound its body made. "I'm so sorry, so so sorry," I wept, then gathered up the ends of the plastic, making a sling so I wouldn't actually have to touch the bird. Half dragging it—it was heavier than I expected, maybe twenty pounds—half swinging it, I got it over to the trunk, still crying, then sort of swung it inside. One talon stuck out from the tarp, making me cringe. Poor, innocent thing. "Please don't be dead," I said, tears sluicing down my cheeks. Then I closed the hatch, ran to the driver's seat, threw the car into Drive and floored it, my tires slipping on the rough road.

In all my life, I'd never hit an animal before. Not even a squirrel. Not even a chipmunk! It was quite a feat, living up here in the boonies, and something I'd always been proud of. I could hear myself crying, a long, low whimper that caused my dog to howl softly as well. "Don't be dead, don't be dead," I chanted, ignoring Bowie, who tried to twist around to get a better sniff at our quiet passenger. We came onto pavement, and I pressed the accelerator harder, the trees whipping past in a blur of color. Bitter Creek Road, a hard left. "Don't be dead, don't be dead."

There. Number seventy-five, a black mailbox marking the nearly hidden driveway. I turned so hard and fast the car fishtailed, causing Bowie to yip and scrabble to keep his footing on the car seat.

Thank God! There were lights on. He was home.

I hurtled out of the car, popped open the trunk, grabbed the tarp edges and swung the package out, then ran awkwardly up the steps, cringing as my shins bumped the turkey.

Ian was already opening the door. "Callie? What's wrong?" he asked.

"I killed it," I blurted, my tears flowing anew. Pushing past him, I staggered through the great room and slung the tarp onto the table. "I killed a turkey."

"Callie, I *eat* there," he said, eyeing the bundle. "And have you ever heard of avian flu?"

"That was just a scare tactic used by the Bush admin— Ian, can you just check it? In case it's maybe still alive? Or not quite dead? Please?" I took a shuddering breath, then ran to the sink to wash my hands. The bird might not have avian flu, and I didn't actually touch it, but Ian had a point.

"Sure," he said, following me into the kitchen.

"If it needs to…you know. To be put down, do you have the stuff here?" I said raggedly, wiping my hands.

"Yes." Opening a drawer, he took out a pair of latex gloves, then passed me a box of tissues. "If you hit it, Callie, it probably is dead," he said gently, pulling on the gloves. "They don't have much chance against a car."

I nodded, tears still leaking out of my eyes. I had no great love for turkeys, but I didn't hate them, either. I certainly didn't want to kill any. Even at Thanksgiving, I always felt a pang…sure, I ate heartily—I loved turkey— but…there'd always been that pang.

Ian went over to the table and lifted the tarp-wrapped bird down onto the floor. He knelt beside it and pulled back the plastic. "Wow, this is a big one," he murmured. I approached, standing just behind Ian, and without thinking, I reached out and gripped his shoulder, biting my lip hard. The bird's eyes were open and unblinking, and it didn't appear to be breathing.

"Is it dead?" I whispered, tears dropping onto Ian's shirt.

He looked up at me. "It seems to be."

My face scrunched. "Oh, dammit," I squeaked. "Dammit, dammit, dammit."

"Now, Callie, come on," Ian said, rising. He took off his gloves and dropped them on the floor, then took my shoulders. "You couldn't help it." His eyes were kind. "It happens all the time."

"I never hit an animal before," I whispered, fighting off sobs, though my breath still hitched in and out.

"I'll bury it," he offered.

"Oh, thank you, Ian," I said.

Suddenly, there was a great flutter and a scrabbling. Instinctively, I ducked, and Ian whirled around.

The turkey wasn't dead. No, it was quite alive. It flapped and heaved, then managed to get onto its huge taloned feet. It gave a weird sort of throaty growl... *Gooooorrr... Gooorrrr,* and tilted its head suspiciously.

"You said it was dead!" I hissed.

"It must've been in shock," he answered. "Don't just stand there. Open the door so it can get out."

I backed away so as not to startle it, then opened the door through which I'd just come. Ian slowly approached the bird.

"Easy, turkey," Ian murmured. "Out you go." He circled behind it, and the bird took a few steps toward the front...and me... "Good turkey," Ian said soothingly. "Out the door with—"

Suddenly the bird burst into another great flutter of wings and sprinted right at me. I screamed, the bird veered to the left, dodged around a chair, knocked into an end table, tipping it. There was a crash, and the bird went airborne. *"Glooglooglooglooo!"* it screeched. *"Glooglooglooo!"*

From the den came a blur of red. Angie. "No, Angie!" Ian yelled, but Angie, after all, was an Irish setter, bred for just this thing, and she sped after the bird, which landed awkwardly on the kitchen table. Angie leaped, the bird flew, hitting the chandelier and causing it to sway crazily. The turkey tried to land on the bookcase, but there wasn't enough room, and flapped toward me. "No! Get away!" I yelled, collapsing to my knees and covering my head. "Kill it, Ian! Kill it!"

"Callie, stop scaring it away from the door!" Ian barked. "And I'm not going to kill it! Weren't you just bawling over this thing?"

The bird landed on the couch, then fluttered down and ran into the den. Angie lunged and Ian tackled her, managing to grab her collar. "No, girl! Stay! Callie, open the sliders, for God's sake!"

I power-crawled across the floor and opened the sliders that led to the deck. Angie was whining, trying to get away from Ian, who was half lying across her. From in the den came some more crashing and turkey growls.

"Here, turkey, turkey, turkey," I called. Laughter wriggled dangerously in my stomach.

Goooorr...gooorrr... "Go in there and flush it out," Ian said.

"Yeah, right," I snorted. "I'm not going in there. You go." *Goooorr...*

"I'm holding the dog."

"Well, I'll hold the dog, then," I said, crawling over to Ian and Angie. "I'm not going in there. It's a man job. Testosterone required. Besides, it might peck me."

"It *should* peck you. You're the one who hit it," Ian muttered, but once I had the dog by her collar, he stood up. "Don't let go of Angie," he warned.

"Yes, Doctor," I said. "Now good luck in there. I'll take a drumstick." A wheezing laugh burst out of me.

"Great," Ian muttered, giving me a look. He went in, and Angie wagged her tail, wishing her master luck. I waited, burying my face in Angie's silky fur. *One... two...three...*

"Gloogloogloogloo!"

"Watch out, here it comes!" Ian yelled.

The bird came sprinting out, wings flapping, and Angie lunged again, barking for all she was worth. I caught a glimpse of hideous bird legs, felt the wind from its wings and couldn't help but shrieking. "Ian! Get it out of here!"

"Easy for you to say!" he called, scrambling after the bird.

Then the bird must have finally smelled freedom, because it turned its ugly head, spotted the great outdoors and sprinted through the front door, down the porch steps. I heard Bowie's explosion of barking. "Is it safe?" I called after a minute.

"Yes," Ian answered, so I let his dog go. She immediately began sniffing all the good turkey smells. I hoisted myself onto my feet.

Ian stood in the great room, breathing hard. I went over and stood next to him.

"I don't think it's dead after all," I said. Ian cut his gaze to me, and I doubled over with laughter, clutching the doorframe.

"Very funny," he said drily. "Why don't you let Bowie out of the car? He can go in the backyard with Angie. It's fenced in." He turned and went into the kitchen.

I obeyed, still laughing. "I'm sorry you missed all the fun, Bowie," I giggled, unclipping my dog. "But now you can play in the back with Angie, how's that?" I followed my dog inside, and the smile slid off my face.

Ian's house, his perfectly ordered, beautifully furnished house, was a wreck. Two tables were overturned, a vase or wineglass or something had broken, and shards of glass lay in a puddle. Feathers littered the floor here and there. A few books and a picture or two had fallen from the bookcase. The kitchen table was askew, and one of the chairs had tipped. A glimpse into the den showed similar damage.

Angie was already in the backyard, so I ushered my dog through the slider, then closed it behind me. "I'll clean up, Ian," I said, biting my lip as I surveyed the wreckage. Several envelopes were scattered about, and I picked them up. Interspersed with the expected phone bill and such were a few other addresses... Heifer International, Doctors Without Borders, Hole in the Wall Gang. "Pledge week?" I asked, setting them down.

"Guilt," he answered. He was rolling up his sleeve. His bloody sleeve.

"Ian, you're cut!" I exclaimed, leaping over to him.

"Yes," he said.

"What happened? Was it the turkey?"

"No," he answered, glancing at me. "I caught it on the edge of the bookcase."

I took his wrist and turned it so I could see. It wasn't too bad, a long scratch, but it was bleeding a fair amount.

"Where's your first-aid kit?" I asked.

"I can do it," he said.

It suddenly occurred to me that I was standing close enough to him to feel his warmth. That he was wearing jeans and a white oxford. That his lashes were long and straight and somehow tender. That he was looking at me steadily, and that even though he could probably clean up this cut in a New York minute, I really, really wanted to take care of him.

"I insist," I said, my voice a little husky.

Ian reached for a paper towel and held it against his forearm. "In there, then," he said, nodding to a cabinet.

There it was, a blue plastic case, neatly labeled *First Aid*. I took it out and looked at the patient. He was leaning against the counter, still holding the paper towel against his arm. Watching me. Intently.

My knees started to tingle. Face felt warm. Girl parts on the alert.

I opened the first-aid kit, which contained a small bottle of hydrogen peroxide, a roll of gauze, some ointment, Band-Aids, the usual. "So," I said, then cleared my throat. "Um, let's wash it off, okay?"

"Okay," he said, a trace of amusement in his voice.

I took his hand—it was such a good hand, big and strong and capable, just like you'd want a vet's hand to be. And holding his hand meant I was close to him, which was definitely having an effect on me. My heart thudded harder as I turned on the water and held his arm under it, our sides pressed together. He felt awfully wonderful, all warm and big and… *Focus, Callie. First aid, remember?*

Yes. Well. The bleeding had stopped…it really was just a scratch, but you know what? I was going to take good care of that scratch.

Ian didn't talk as I poured some hydrogen peroxide on a cotton ball, patted the scratch, then blotted his arm dry. It was disconcerting, being so close to him that I could see the steady rise and fall of his chest. His forearm was perfect, muscled and tan, sprinkled with blond hair, the tendons moving under his smooth skin as he moved his hand.

"I'll just…um…just put on a little of this…gooey stuff…how's that?" I asked, reaching for the…gooey stuff.

"Sounds good," he said.

I sneaked a peek at his face. There was a hint of a smile in those blue eyes, and I looked down quickly, feeling my cheeks prickle with a telltale blush.

Still holding his hand, I smeared some bacitracin (that was the name!) on his cut, running my forefinger from just above his wrist to his elbow. The skin was perfect, the muscles solid beneath. Lovely. The inside of his elbow was soft and tender by comparison, and I ran my finger across the skin there.

Realizing my first-aid application had morphed into vet-fondling, I yanked back my hand and groped for the roll of gauze. It was either use the gauze or use about nine Band-Aids, because the scratch was pretty long. But my hands were clumsy, and it was harder than it should've been. I wrapped his arm up firmly, then began tying the gauze ends in a knot.

"That's a little tight," Ian said. I looked up. His mouth pulled up in the corner, and he held out his hand, which was turning quite red, the veins in his wrist starting to bulge.

"Sorry!" I said, hastily untying the knot and unwrapping the bandage. "Okay. Ian's boo-boo, take two."

This time, the gauze was too loose and kept slipping down. Plus, it was a little soggy from overapplication of the gooey stuff, so I grabbed a Band-Aid, tore it open and used it to hold the gauze in place. Added another one. This bandaging job was starting to look like Josephine— or Bowie—had done it. Not to mention that those Band- Aids were going to take some arm hair with them when Ian took this thing off. And still it was droopy! I adjusted the gauze wrap a bit, but it slid right back down, so I just patted his arm instead.

"How's that?" I asked, looking up at him.

He was smiling. Not a lot, just a little, and more than enough. "Perfect," he murmured.

Without another thought, I wrapped my arms around his neck and kissed the living daylights out of him.

His arms, injured and otherwise, went around me, pulling me against him. One hand slid through my hair, and he kissed me back fiercely. He was solid and, oh, just wonderful, his arms strong, his body hard, and he smelled like soap and rain. I leaned into him, my hands going through his soft, short hair, and deepened the kiss, getting a most satisfactory groan in return. My God, he felt so good, so…reassuring, somehow, so real and warm and safe, and his mouth was soft and hard at the same time, and he kissed me with such heat and intensity that I could barely stand. In the turkey struggles, my shirt had come untucked, and Ian's hand slid under it, hot against my skin. My leg, my ruttish leg, was wrapped around his, and in another minute, I'd be pulling a Bowie. His mouth lowered to my neck, his hand moved to cover my breast, and my knees buckled and my head fell back, and for a second, I thought I might just slide to the floor in a boneless heap, pulling him on top of me.

Then his mouth found mine again, and oh, that kiss, that life-changing kiss, because really, that's how it felt, a kiss that meant something, promised something, made you want all sorts of things. It took me a minute to realize he was looking at me. My breath came in short little gasps, and underneath my hand, I could feel Ian's heart thudding fast and hard.

He didn't say anything for a second, just tucked some hair behind my ears and looked at me, right into my eyes.

"Would you like to stay?" he asked, running his thumb over my lower lip.

I swallowed. Then I nodded. "Should we clean up first?" I whispered, glancing at the devastation the turkey had wrought.

"No," he said, then he took my hand and led me upstairs.

CHAPTER TWENTY

I WOKE UP ROUGHLY twelve hours later, completely and delightfully unrested. Oh, no. Not a lot of sleeping going on last night, no sir.

I was smiling before I even opened my eyes. Purring, too, a bit. Felt like maybe I should be given a medal. And Ian...he *definitely* deserved one, too.

I rolled over and opened my eyes. Ian's side of the bed was empty, and the clock said 7:32 a.m. New day, new boyfriend, new world. Sigh! Ian McFarland was a thorough man, let me tell you. Made sure I was a very happy woman, know what I'm saying? Made sure a couple times.

And I made him *smile,* and just the memory of that had my girl parts tightening. A smile from Ian really meant something. It was worth waiting for, that wonderfully goofy, melting smile.

Somewhere around ten last night, we remembered that our dogs were outside and a turkey had made a huge mess. It was oddly cozy, cleaning up together, laughing, me figuring out where things went. Then Ian made peanut butter and banana sandwiches on whole wheat bread, poured us some milk, put everything on a tray and we had a little midnight snack in bed, the dogs sitting quietly in attendance, waiting for a crust or two to be tossed their way. And then Ian and I made each other *very* happy once more.

So…what now? I wondered, climbing out of Ian's big bed and looking around. Ah. A bathrobe, a rather old flannel robe I thought I'd look quite cute in, as it was Ian's and Ian was now my honey. I pulled it on and breathed deeply. It smelled like him, giving my knees a pleasant wobble.

Checking my reflection in the bathroom mirror, I tousled my hair a bit and grinned. There. Sex kitten. Meow! I fairly skipped downstairs, the smell of coffee rich and dark in the air. I couldn't wait to see him smile again, because those smiles were gifts, they were sunshine after the storm, they were flowers bursting into bloom, they were Betty Crocker Supermoist Triple Chocolate Fudge. A giddy ribbon of happiness danced through my stomach. Ian McFarland *liked* me. Possibly more.

At the bottom of the stairs, I sneaked a peek at my *lover.* What a delicious word! He stood in the kitchen, already dressed in a suit, complete with jacket. He looked…um…well, a little tense. His arms were folded, and he stared out the kitchen window at our two dogs, who were frisking and frolicking. Aw! Maybe they were in love, too. But Ian…Ruh-roh. His face was kind of…grim. Well. Maybe he was just tired. He'd brighten at the sight me, Callie Grey, wanton woman.

"Good morning," I said, leaning against the wall and smiling.

His head jerked around. "Oh. You're awake. I didn't hear you." He shoved his fists into his pockets. He didn't smile. He looked, in fact…scowly.

"Hi," I said again, pushing my hair back. Sort of a reminder… *I'm all tousled and unkempt because we did it three times last night.* It seemed to miss its mark.

His jaw was knotty. Probably not a positive sign. My smile felt a little less confident.

"You probably need to get going, right?" he asked, swallowing.

I sucked in a breath, my excellent mood falling to the ground, shot dead. "Wow. That is *not* what I expected."

He withdrew a hand from his pocket and scrubbed it over his jaw. "Well," he said to the floor, "what…what exactly do you expect?"

There was the smallest note of uncertainty somewhere in that question. Or I thought so, anyway. "Oh, gosh, Ian," I said slowly. "How about 'Good morning' or 'Last night was incredible' or 'Would you like some coffee?'"

Ian didn't answer. Just stared at the floor, as if…well, as if last night had been a huge mistake and he was trying to figure a way out of whatever expectations I might (and kind of did) have. Certainly I had time to wonder about what he was thinking, because he didn't say a damn word.

Crap. A lump wedged itself in my throat. Emotional diarrhea could not be far off.

"There is coffee. If you want some," Ian said carefully. And that was it. Jeez Louise. He looked at his watch.

"You know what?" I said tightly. "I don't want coffee. I'll just get dressed and leave you alone, since that's clearly what you're after."

I turned to go back upstairs.

Before I made it to the first step, he grabbed me by the waist. I squeaked in surprise, held there against his chest. "Wait," he said in a low voice.

I waited. Swallowed. Waited a few seconds more.

"I'm sorry," he whispered.

"You should be," I said, my voice a little breathy.

"Are you crying?" he asked.

"I'm very close." Still, I couldn't help feeling a bit turned on, hurt feelings or not.

His hands slid up to my shoulders, turning me around to face him. "Maybe I should start over," he said, completely serious.

"You think?" I asked.

"Yes. I didn't…I should've thought of something to say. Something different." He frowned, but his eyes were steady on mine.

"Well, okay, then," I said. "Start over."

He gave a little nod. "Good morning."

I nodded back. "Good morning."

"Would you like some coffee?"

"Not right now, thanks," I said.

"Last night was incredible." He swallowed. Didn't smile.

Well, he'd have to do more than echo me to gain back some ground, after all. Just because he had beautiful eyes and a rumbly voice didn't mean I should just…melt. Though it *was* getting a little…melt-ish in here.

"Callie," he said, taking a deep breath. "I just don't know…I'm not sure…I don't know what…last night… meant to you, and I don't—" His voice broke off in frustration, and he ran a hand through his hair. "I'm not usually an impulsive person."

"You're kidding," I muttered.

He didn't smile, just looked at me. "I don't believe in flings," he said, his expression bordering on somber. "I don't want just a fling."

My knees softened. My heart did, too. "Me, neither," I whispered.

He gave a half nod and squeezed my shoulders just a little. "Callie," he said, looking down. He hesitated, then went on. "I know you were in love with your boss. At the hotel that night, it seemed... Well, if you still, uh...have feelings for him, I need you to tell me." He raised his eyes back to mine, and it was like a shock, those eyes and what was in them.

"I'm not," I said in a half whisper. "That's...that's done." And it was true. I wasn't sure when it became finalized, but it was true nonetheless.

"Are you sure?"

I nodded. "It's done."

He let out a breath. "Good." His gaze dropped to my mouth.

"So," I said.

He waited, but I said nothing more. "Well then," he said after a few beats. "Do you want to...go steady?"

I couldn't help it. I laughed, then slipped my arms around his waist. "Yes, I'll go steady with you, Ian," I said, smiling broadly.

"Good. That's good." Then he kissed me, softly, gently. "Callie, I'm sorry I'm so..." His voice trailed off.

"Socially retarded?" I suggested.

He gave a surprised laugh. "I was going to say nervous, but I guess yours works, too."

I pulled back to look at him more clearly. "I make you nervous?" I asked. For some reason, that pleased me beyond measure.

"You make me terrified," he answered, smiling a little. Oh, *melt!*

"Make you anything else?" I whispered, standing on my tiptoes for a kiss.

"Yes, now that you mention it," he said, then he slid his arms around me, hoisted me up, and I wrapped my legs around him as he carried me back upstairs.

Quite a while later, he finally rolled out of bed. "I'm going to be late for work," he admitted as he reached for his clothes.

"First time?" I asked, lounging ruttishly against the pillows.

He grinned. "Yes, actually."

"Do you think the world will keep spinning?"

He leaned down and kissed me, then pulled on his shirt. "I'm finding I don't really care," he said, and he gave me a smile that kept my heart warm for the rest of the day.

WHEN I GOT TO WORK WELL past the appointed hour, Damien took one look at me and the box of doughnuts I was holding and said, "Well, well, well. *Someone* got laid last night."

"Hi," I breathed. "It's a beautiful day, isn't it?"

"Who? Who is he?" Damien asked. "I command you to tell me."

"Want a doughnut?" I asked dreamily. "I got chocolate just for you."

"Hey, Callie," Mark said, walking into the reception area. He glanced at his watch. "Everything okay? You're not usually late."

"I'm fine," I said.

"She's postcoital," Damien said, raising an eyebrow.

Mark's head jerked back in surprise.

"I'd better get to work," I said. "I'll skip lunch to make up the time, Mark."

"That's not necessary, Callie, you put in more than enough—"

I barely heard him as I floated down the hall to my office.

Yep. I was in love.

About time.

CHAPTER TWENTY-ONE

IAN AND I WERE A COUPLE. Sigh! Granted, my honey seemed to have just a splash of Asperger's, but I generously forgave him, as he was an excellent kisser and had many other nice qualities. Besides, given how he'd grown up, bouncing all over the world, and after finding his wife in bed with a woman, Ian was allowed to have some quirks. On Saturday, I took him kayaking…Bowie sulked, but then, being half Husky, decided he couldn't sustain it and went into Ian's yard to sing to Angie, then tried to mount her.

Under a leaden gray sky, we paddled out to a small island filled with pine trees and rocks and a few squirrels. I spread out a blanket and retrieved the bag I'd packed with two thermoses of coffee and some cookies.

"How do you think those squirrels got out here?" Ian asked, watching them scurry on the rocks.

"They have tiny boats," I answered. "They make them here, on the island. Cottage industry."

"I take it you don't know," Ian said drily.

"You are correct. Come, my dear boy," I said, patting the blanket next to me. "It's a soft day in autumn, we live in the most beautiful state in the union, and I baked chocolate chip cookies, just for you. Though I did have to leave a couple dozen for Noah. Let's talk about you."

Ian winced, but obeyed. "What do you want to know?"

"Well," I said, taking a bite out of my cookie, which was, admittedly, excellent. "How'd you get this incredibly hot scar?" I reached up and traced it. "I'm thinking knife fight with a pirate. Am I right?"

He laughed. "Shockingly, no."

"Well?"

"I fell off a swing when I was six."

"Let's run with the pirate story, shall we?" I grinned and leaned my head against his shoulder. "So tell me about your childhood and all the places you lived," I suggested.

Ian glanced at me. "Right. Um…well, I mentioned my mother and brother, right?"

"Yep. *Alejandro.* That's fun to say."

He nodded. "Actually, he's not really my brother. He's my cousin. And Jane is my aunt. My parents died in a small plane accident when I was eight."

"Oh, Ian," I said, sobering instantly. "I'm so sorry! You poor thing!"

"Well, it was…hard. But Jane took me in. I'd only met her once before, and Alejandro is nine years older than I am. Jane…she did her best, dealing with her brother's kid while doing her work."

"Doctors Without Borders?"

"Basically, yes. She's a plastic surgeon. Fixes cleft palates and stuff like that. Alé is also a doctor."

"Are you guys close?"

He hesitated. "In some ways," he answered carefully.

"Why didn't you live with your uncle here in Georgebury?" I asked.

Ian nodded. "I would've liked to, but he was an alcoholic. Nice man, but not someone who could raise a kid."

There was a story there, I was sure. I was also sure Ian didn't want to go into it. Not now, anyway. "How's your family?" he asked, changing the subject and confirming my suspicions.

"They're good," I answered, slipping my hand into his. "Bronte, my thirteen-year-old niece, is pressuring my sister, a man-hater, to get married, so Hester's dating the mortician at our funeral home. My other niece wants to be Lady Gaga when she grows up. My parents may hate each other, may love each other, depending on the day. My brother smokes pot, gets laid and has no ambition, and I found my grandfather in the tub with his girlfriend last week."

Ian grinned, thrilling me, cheap date that I was. "Speaking of your grandfather," he said, "There's a museum down in Greenledge, do you know it?"

"Oh, sure. All of us Vermont kids get dragged there in fifth grade. The American Craftsman place?"

He nodded. "They're doing a show on David Morelock. I bought tickets to the opening. Thought we could go with your grandfather."

I looked up at him, my mouth opening slowly. "Ian...thank you!"

"You're welcome."

"No...thank you! This... Noah will be...you know what? You're getting laid. Right now, mister."

"Well, if you insist," he said, and with that, he pulled me close and slid his hands under my fleece coat, and though it was cold and started to rain halfway through, we managed to stay quite warm. Quite warm indeed.

"SO YOU'RE DATING HER," Noah said a few days later. We were having an early dinner before heading to the David Morelock retrospective.

"Yes, sir," Ian replied.

"Honorable intentions and all that crap?"

"Noah," Jody chided. She'd been a frequent guest around here lately.

Ian said nothing, just looked at me. His eyes crinkled a little, and my girl parts gave a happy squeeze. *How many hours 'til bedtime?* Betty Boop wondered. *Too many,* I answered.

"Just treat her right," Noah instructed, pointing at Ian with his fork. "And no kissing in front of me. This is my house. I have rules, young man."

"Oh, please," I said. "I have rules, too, and they include not using my bathroom."

"You never use that tub," Noah said, glancing at Jody with a little smile.

"And now I never will," I answered.

Jody laughed. "We should probably get going, don't you think? Ian, what time does the show open?"

"Seven," Ian answered. He looked at me. "Thank you for dinner, Callie."

I smiled, reached out with my foot to touch his leg. Oops. Got Noah's prosthetic instead, shifted to the left...there. Ian didn't get too many home-cooked meals. I was hoping to change that.

LIKE SO MANY MUSEUMS, the Museum of the American Craftsman had a still and sacred quality about it. In the large foyer, a huge black-and-white photo of Mr. Morelock was on display, his lined face intent as he hand-planed a piece of wood. *Thank you again for my chair,* I said silently, a lump in my throat. *I hope you can see how much it still means to me.*

Glancing at Noah, I saw his face was somber. "Well," he said, not looking at me. "Jody and I will wander off, then. See you two young people in an hour?"

"Sure, Noah," I said. I reached out and put my hand on his arm, and he gave my hand a squeeze.

"This was a nice idea," he said gruffly, nodding to Ian.

"My pleasure," Ian replied.

We watched them go, Jody's hand on Noah's elbow, Noah using a cane, for once. "I'm glad he's with Jody," I said quietly. "He doesn't have a lot of friends left anymore."

"How old is he?" Ian asked.

"Eighty-four," I answered, that melancholy tightness still clamping my throat.

"He really loves you," Ian said.

I looked up at him and smiled, shaking off any melancholy. "Well. Let's go see if there's anything as pretty as my chair," I suggested, and off we went.

Each piece of furniture was lit from above, reinforcing the churchlike atmosphere. The show was well attended, and people murmured with the appropriate amount of awe. Little placards described each piece—*Butler's table, 1984, cherry & oak, made for the Glidden Family of Bennington, Vermont, mortise and tenon joinery… Dining room table, tiger maple with mahogany inlay, 1993, made for Edwin Whitney, New York, New York.*

There were benches, small cabinets, kitchen chairs, end tables. Each one was unique, each one seemed to glow, the clean lines and innate strength creating a sense of surety. Mr. Morelock had really had a gift.

At the end of the exhibit was the show's crowning glory…the rocking chairs. Four of them, arranged as if they were on a porch, waiting for a family to sit down and relax.

"They're beautiful," Ian murmured. I nodded. "None as nice as yours, though," he added with a little smile.

"You're right," I said. "And mine's also the last one he made, apparently."

A short, gray-haired woman suddenly materialized at my side, quivering like a hummingbird. "Did you say you own a David Morelock rocking chair?" she asked.

"Yes," I answered, a tad smugly.

"The last one he made?" she answered, then glanced at Ian. "I'm sorry to interrupt. I'm Colleen McPhee, the curator of this museum."

"Nice to meet you," I said. "The exhibit is beautiful."

"So you own the last chair? Are you sure?"

"I think so," I said. "Mr. Morelock gave it to me three days before he died. My grandfather told me it was the last one."

"There'd be a number on the bottom," she said.

"Fourteen," I confirmed.

"Oh, my God," she breathed. "That's it. You do own the last one." She took a deep breath, as if overcome with the news. "We'd be very, very interested in acquiring your piece."

I smiled. "I'm sorry. I'd never sell it."

She smiled back firmly, a woman on a mission. "We have quite an endowment, Miss…"

"Grey," I said. "Callie Grey. It's not for sale."

"I could offer you $25,000 for it right now."

"Holy guacamole!" I blurted. Twenty-five grand was a down payment on a house! But even as staggering a number as that was, I knew I'd never do it. "That's really generous, but it's not for sale," I told the curator. "But thank you." Ian smiled at the floor.

Her face fell. "All right," she said, her voice considerably less enthusiastic. "Well, if you ever change your mind, we'd really appreciate the chance to acquire it."

"You know," I said, "you might be interested in meeting my grandfather. Noah Grey of Noah's Arks. Have you ever heard of him?"

"You're kidding! Noah Grey is here?"

I pointed over to where Noah and Jody were standing, admiring a dining room chair. "The man with the white beard and the cane," I said.

"Thank you!" she said, springing away. "Lovely meeting you!" We watched as she approached my grandfather, said something, then clasped her hands to her chest, no doubt gushing.

"You're very good with people," Ian commented.

"Was I working the room?" I asked.

He gave a half smile, acknowledging our little discussion a few weeks back. "I've never seen you sit in your chair," he commented. "Why is that?"

I glanced up at him, then back at the display. "I'm sort of saving it, I guess," I said.

"For what?" he asked.

I hesitated. "Um…just for…I don't know." *For when I've earned it.* I slipped my hand into Ian's, and he looked at me, always seeming a little startled—and happy— when I showed him some affection. My heart gave a nearly painful squeeze. Standing on tiptoe, I kissed his cheek. "I like you, Ian McFarland," I said.

His eyes crinkled a little. "I hope so."

"And you like me, too, of course," I prodded.

"Yes," he agreed. "You're fun to look at."

"Like a circus monkey?"

"Exactly."

I punched his shoulder. "I'll bet you never expected to be with the crazy woman from the DMV."

"You would win that bet," he answered easily.

I paused. "What did you think of me, that day?"

"I thought you were a junkie." He grinned.

"Nice, Ian! I have to teach you to lie a little bit."

"Well, it was logical. You were clearly agitated and very…kinetic."

"Got it, Mr. Spock," I muttered.

"You couldn't stop moving, couldn't finish a sentence. I thought you needed a fix."

"Flatterer," I muttered.

He squeezed my hand. "I also thought you had pretty hair. And I liked your ears."

Ears. Who knew what men would fixate on next? There was that smile again, starting in his eyes and staying there, making that pure blue seem as warm and lovely as a September sky.

"And what about my horrifying propensity to blurt out my feelings, Ian?" I teased. "My 'emotional diarrhea,' as you called it. You seemed quite disgusted, I remember."

"Yes," he said, lifting my hand and studying it. "I was. At first, anyway."

I waited for more. Another couple passed us, cooing over a chest of drawers they wished they could afford.

"But then?" I prompted when too much time had passed.

"Then I wondered…" He hesitated.

"Wondered what, Ian?" I said. He didn't answer. "Wondered what it would be like to cry in the DMV? Because I'm sure they'd be happy to arrange that. Most of us do cry, in fact. Leaving dry-eyed…that's a fluke."

He met my eyes abruptly, giving me the full force of the pure blue. "I wondered what it would be like to just…let everything out." He glanced past me. "Even though I thought you were a little crazy, I sort of admired you, too. For being so…open. And honest." His eyes came back to mine and softened. "And…well…so full of life."

Realizing that my mouth was open, I closed it.

That day had been one of the worst days in my adult life. And Ian had found something admirable there.

"Thank you," I whispered.

"You're welcome," he said quietly.

"Callie! Did you send that pit bull over to talk to me?" Noah came hobbling up, Jody at his side.

I shook myself out of my haze. "Um, yes, I did. I take it you're overwhelmed."

"Some granddaughters should learn to keep their mouths shut," he grumbled. "But they don't."

"Some granddaughters should smother their grandpas in their sleep," I returned. "But they don't. But they might, so watch it, old man."

"They want a canoe for their collection," Jody explained. "Noah, it's a compliment."

"I didn't ask for this," he grumbled.

"Oh, boohoohoo," I said. "You're flattered. Admit it."

"Hush you. Mind your elders." He glared at me, but his beard twitched. I knew the truth. He couldn't have been more pleased.

Ian held my hand the whole way back, and just the simple sensation of his warm, strong hand holding mine so firmly had me quite ruttish. My heart felt swollen and tender after what Ian had said. That my worst moment had, in some way, shown something good about me. It was somewhat astonishing.

When we got to Jody's house, a muttered conversation took place in the backseat. "I think I'll be stayin' here, Callie," Noah said.

I turned around in my seat. Even in the near-dark, I could see my grandfather blushing. "Okay," I said, opting not to tease him. "See you tomorrow."

Noah looked at Ian. "Thank you," he grunted. "And if you stay over, make sure you're gone by the time I get home. You may be a good man, but she's my grand-daughter, and I don't want my face rubbed in the fact that she's all grown up."

"Two words, Noah," I said. "Bath. Tub. Okay?"

Jody laughed, and Noah opened the door. "How you put up with her is a mystery," he growled at Ian, but he reached over and pinched my chin. "G'night, young-sters."

"Thanks for an absolutely wonderful evening, Ian," Jody said.

"My pleasure," Ian answered. We waited 'til they got inside Jody's house, then headed to my place. Upon our arrival, Bowie twirled and sang, then sniffed Ian's shoes with religious fervor.

Ian hadn't stayed over here yet…well, obviously, since Noah was usually in residence. A gentle quiet fell as we looked at each other. The refrigerator hummed. Wind gusted outside, and a shower of yellow leaves flut-tered against the window.

"Well, it's pretty late," I said, the universal code for *make your move, sonny.*

"Yes," Ian said. Right. Forgot who I was dealing with.

"Would you like to stay?" I asked, my heart rate kicking up a little.

"Yes," he said simply.

"Will Angie be okay?"

He nodded. "I fed her before I left, and there's a dog door to the backyard."

Of course. Ian would have all the angles covered. "Well," I said, suddenly shy, but then he kissed me, his mouth gentle and warm. I didn't know why, but I never expected the man who looked like a Russian hit man to kiss me so…tenderly. If I was a person who read into things—and God knows I was—I might think that Ian could only kiss me this way if it really *meant* something, because the way Ian kissed me made me feel…cherished.

Then the kiss changed, became hotter, and harder, and his hands slid down to pull me tighter against him, and he was so warm and delicious—

"Come on upstairs," I whispered, and taking his hand, led him to my room, shutting it before Bowie could come in. "Go sleep on Noah's bed," I told my dog through the crack, and he whined, but then trotted off.

My room was dark except for the moonlight spilling in the eastern-facing windows. Ian stood, waiting, looking at me. I slipped off my shoes. "Have a seat," I whispered. He went toward the bed, but I took his hand, stopping him. "Have a seat," I repeated, pointing to the Morelock chair.

Ian looked at it, then back at me. My heart thumped. I gave a little nod, then bit my lip as Ian walked over to the chair. He sat down, his hands on the smooth, carved arms. God, he looked good there! As if reading my mind, he smiled, and my heart lurched toward him.

"Come here," he said, and I obeyed, sitting on Ian's lap. The chair didn't protest, having been made by the master, and Ian slid his arms around me, rocking gently, his cheek against my neck, against my throbbing pulse. We just sat like that for a long moment, wrapped around each other in the Morelock chair, my fingers smoothing

Ian's soft blond hair, tracing the lines that fanned out around his eyes. Then Ian's hand moved up, and he unbuttoned my shirt slowly, kissing the exposed skin. My hands went to the thick, hard muscles of his shoulders, that sweet, melting feeling spreading through me as he slowly pushed my shirt off my shoulders, his fingers tracing the lace of my bra. When our lips met, the mood changed, suddenly hot and urgent and hungry. Ian scooped me up and stood, the chair gliding silently as he rose and carried me to bed, the moonlight pure and bright and perfect, the only noise from the wind and the two of us, together, the soft and gentle sounds of two people falling in love.

CHAPTER TWENTY-TWO

"GOOD MORNING," IAN said the next day as I staggered into the kitchen. My legs were still a little weak from all that happiness. Bowie crooned me a morning song, and I petted his big furry head.

"Hi," I said to both my guys.

"Would you like some coffee?" he asked, already opening a cupboard for a mug from the mishmash selection therein.

"Sure," I answered.

"Last night was incredible." He smiled at me, and my heart practically rolled over onto its back, like Bowie offering himself up.

"Yes, it was," I said, grinning back.

Ian poured me some joe, then added cream and sugar. "Even though you're already so sweet," he said, stirring the coffee.

"Oh, my God. Are you *flirting?*" I asked.

"This is what I get for trying," he grumbled. But his eyes were happy.

Just then his cell phone rang. Ian glanced at the screen. His face froze. Laura? I wondered. We hadn't talked about her since the wedding… He picked up the receiver. "Hi, Jane."

I went on full alert. Could it be his aunt?

"I'm fine, and you?" Ian said, not looking at me. "Okay. Great. Sure. Seven o'clock. Do you need directions? Okay. See you then." He closed his phone and stared at the counter for a second. I waited, not saying anything. My patience was rewarded.

"That was my aunt," he said. "She's in Boston and wants to come up and have dinner tonight."

"Great," I said, nodding. "Is *Alejandro* coming?" I couldn't resist saying that with a full-blown Spanish accent, and Ian gave a little smile.

"No, just Jane." He shoved his hands into his pockets, his smile fading. "Would you like to meet her?" he asked.

"Yes! Absolutely!" I said. "Want me to cook?"

"No, no. That's fine. I'll pick something up."

"Ian, you can't give her dinner from some store. Would she rather eat out? We could go to Elements. Dave would treat us like royalty."

"She doesn't believe in restaurants. Too much waste."

"Oh. Well, then I'll cook. I'd be happy to, okay?"

He took a deep breath. "Callie," he said slowly. "I know you're going to try to make a good impression and do your thing—"

"My thing?" I asked.

"Make her your new best friend."

I snorted. "Ian, I don't *try*...people just like me. Because I'm so nice, remember?"

"I do. But she won't like you."

That gave me pause. "Why?"

He squinted. "She's...a very passionate person, and...well, she doesn't really approve of me, and she'll think you're...uh..." He winced.

"Okay, forget me for a second. How can she not

approve of you?" I asked. "You're her nephew, her brother's boy. I'll bet she adores you."

He took a sip of his coffee. "She wanted me to become a doctor, and the fact that I didn't is tough for her."

"Well, I'm sure she's very proud of you anyway, Ian," I said, giving him a hug. "You're so smart! And so handsome! And you have all those special skills, like making dogs love you and killing people with your little finger—"

"You're babbling," he said, but there was a smile in his voice.

"Well, whatever the case may be, I'll make dinner, okay? Give me your key, and I'll come over and get everything ready, and it will be wonderful. Is she a vegetarian?"

"Vegan, I'm afraid."

"So tofu it is. I can do tofu." I kissed him on the cheek. "Don't worry. We'll have fun."

TWELVE HOURS LATER, we were not having fun.

My first impression had been good—I watched as Ian greeted his aunt on the driveway, giving her a hug, which she returned. She held his face in her hands and smiled hugely…the *Look how you've grown* thing I did on an almost daily basis with Bronte and Josephine. See? I mentally told my honey. *She's crazy about you.*

And then they came in, and the impression started to head south.

"Jane, this is Callie Grey," Ian said. "Callie, my aunt Jane."

"I wasn't aware you were seeing anyone, Ian," his aunt said, glancing at him as if startled.

"It's so nice to meet you, Dr. McFarland," I said, smiling. She was small and very lean, pleasant face, gray hair, somewhere in her late sixties. "Ian's told me a lot about you."

"Mmm," she said. She wandered into the great room, taking a look around. "So, Ian, this is your home. My, my. Very…expensive-looking."

Okay…a veiled compliment at best.

"Would you like some wine, Jane?" Ian asked.

"I'd love some," she said, not looking up from her perusal of his bookcase. "What is that strange smell?"

I bit my lip. "Um…dinner?"

"Ah. And what are we having?"

I brightened, sure my dinner would impress. "Well, I made sure everything was vegan, since Ian said you were—"

"Not anymore, actually," she said, taking her wine from her nephew. "Too difficult, given where I'm living. Côte d'Ivoire. There's just not enough agriculture in the area, so I've been eating eggs and dairy."

"Oh," I said. "Okay, well, we're eating vegan tonight. Beet ravioli with a fava bean sauce, sweet and sour cauliflower…" Nothing that a human would willingly eat, in other words "…and, um…a salad. And chocolate cake."

"Sounds like we could feed an entire African village with that," she murmured.

"Here you go, Callie." Ian handed me a glass of wine. His face was neutral.

"So! Ian! Tell me how things are with you," Jane said, settling on the couch and ignoring the guacamole I'd made.

"Things are good," he said, sitting across from her.

"Any plans to finish your education?" She smiled brightly.

Ian glanced at me. "I did a year of med school before switching to the vet program," he explained. "No, Jane. No plans to go back."

She shook her head. "That's such a shame," she said. "Cassie, let me ask you. If you could choose between healing sick children or treating an overbred golden retriever, which would you pick?"

Youch! I set my own wineglass on the coffee table. "Actually, my name is Callie," I corrected, glancing at Ian. "And I'd choose the profession I really loved, I guess."

"Mmm," she said. "And what is it that you do, Callie, is it?"

"Yes. Short for Calliope. I'm the creative director at an advertising agency."

"Do you find that rewarding? Getting American consumers to buy more…stuff?" She raised an eyebrow.

I paused. "Well, I do, actually. I love my job."

"Mmm."

Now, not to toot my own horn, but the number of people who didn't like me were…well, Muriel and now Jane McFarland. If Muriel and I had met without both loving the same guy, things might've been different. We both loved shoes, after all, the basis of many a female friendship. But Jane…she was tough.

"So Ian told me you don't get back to the States too often," I offered. Angie came over and sat faithfully next to me.

"That's right. Too much to do, too little time, too little money to fund the programs that could save lives. It's a shame." She looked around the room. "The cost of your dog alone, Ian, would've probably fed a family for a year."

"I didn't pay for Angie. She's a rescue," he said. "As is Callie's dog." He glanced at me with a little smile.

"You rescued Angie?" I asked.

He nodded. "Her first owner abused her."

"You poor thing," I said to the pretty dog. She wagged her tail. Jane didn't comment.

"How's Alé?" Ian asked. "I haven't talked to him in a few weeks."

"He's wonderful." Jane turned to me. "My son, Cassie, is a *doctor* in a small village in Honduras. You should visit, Ian."

"I'm planning to," he answered. I looked at him, but he didn't elaborate. Then he said a few lines in rapid-fire Spanish—it was strange, hearing him burst into another language just like that. Jane answered, and then Ian said something else. I didn't catch anything (the only Spanish I knew was from watching *Sesame Street* when Josephine was little, and since Ian and Jane didn't seem to be counting to ten, I was lost). I did get one word, however...*Callie*. I hoped Ian was setting her straight on my name.

"Sorry," he murmured to me when they were done.

"Ian, how's...what's-her-name...Laura?" Dr. McFarland asked.

"She's fine," Ian answered. He hesitated, then said, "She got married a few weeks ago."

"Well, I hope you learned something. Don't go rushing into anything. Marriage ties you down. Limits your options. And in case you did finally have a change of heart, you'd be able to finish medical school, no strings attached." She gave me a look, making it clear just who the strings were.

"I don't see a change of heart in the future, Jane," Ian said.

"Never say never."

"Were you ever married, Dr. McFarland?" I asked, hoping to shift gears a little.

She looked at me as if just remembering I was there, then took a sip of wine. "Very briefly."

Okay. This was indeed a challenge. "So," I offered, groping for a more neutral topic. "Ian told me you met Bono."

Jane raised an eyebrow. "Yes. Why? Do you want tickets to a concert?"

"Can you get me some?" I returned instantly. No smile from either McFarland. Okay. No jokes, then. "Just kidding," I muttered. "It's just that he's very… um…famous."

Ian's cell bleated softly. "Excuse me. I'm on call," he said, checking his phone as he walked to the den, shutting the door behind him. Maybe he'd arranged for Carmella to call him…God knows I would have.

I eyed Ian's relative a bit warily. "I really admire what you do, Dr. McFarland," I said, hoping we could bond with Ian out of the room.

"No need," she said, waving her hand.

"Um…no need for what?"

"No need to stroke my ego." My mouth opened, but she kept talking. "Listen. I'm sure you're very…adorable and whatnot, but if you're looking for my blessing, you won't get it. I still have high hopes for Ian, despite his… choices…thus far. He's not meant to be a vet. He's certainly smart enough to be a physician. So you'll have to forgive me if I want more for him, Cassie. He has a destiny."

"It's Callie," I said, a bit tightly. "As in Calliope, Homer's muse. Just to clarify."

"Mmm."

I took a breath. "Were you and your brother close?" I asked, figuring a change in subject couldn't hurt.

She gave me an assessing look. "We were close as children. As adults, not so much."

"It must've been hard, taking in a little boy when—"

"It wasn't hard at all, Callie. Ian was no bother, and Alejandro, my son—" *I know who he is, lady,* I wanted to say, but held my tongue "—was already nearly grown. Ian just came along and never made a peep."

I was well able to picture Ian as a kid, not making a peep, lonely and scared after his parents died, leaving behind everything he knew. My throat tightened.

Jane sighed and took another sip of wine. "Who could believe that after all I showed him he'd end up…here?"

I glanced at the closed door to the den. "Dr. McFarland," I said carefully, "after losing his parents and, um…moving so much as a kid, maybe Ian just wants a normal life. And just because he didn't become a doctor doesn't mean he's a bad person. He—"

"Dear, I don't need a lecture on my nephew from someone he met, what…a month ago? Two?"

I bit my tongue. Hard. Wondered when the hell Ian's phone call would wrap up. God forbid he was called out and left me alone with Jane.

As if answering my silent prayer, Ian emerged from the den. "Sorry about that," he said. "Callie, would you help me in the kitchen for a minute?"

"Absolutely," I said, faking a smile. I followed him into the kitchen as Jane got up to once again peruse Ian's décor.

"Look," Ian said quietly, "you don't need to defend me or explain anything or win her undying love. Okay?"

"Well, it's very hard to listen to this," I whispered.

"I told you she wouldn't like you. And she won't, unless you become a doctor and move to the third world. So can you just try to get along?"

"I *am* trying, Ian!" He said nothing, just stared at me. "Okay. Fine. I'll try harder."

"Thank you," he said tightly.

We returned to the living room. This time, I made sure to sit next to Ian on the couch.

"So you love it here," Jane said.

"Yes," he answered.

"The foliage was incredible on the drive up," she commented.

Ian glanced quickly at me, then turned to his aunt. "If you want to stay for a few days, we could see the sights. Go hiking, maybe," he offered, and it might've been my sentimental streak, but for a second, I thought I saw a flash of the little guy who'd lost his parents, hoping to find someone to love him.

"You could use my kayak," I said. Maybe if Jane stayed, she and Ian could have a nice day or two, and her disapproval would ease. "There are so many incredible rivers and lakes up here. It's really beautiful. Well, we Vermonters think so." Ian gave me a small, quick smile.

"I won't have time. I'll be leaving tonight, in fact," she said, ignoring both offers. "I'm trying to get Pfizer to donate more antibiotics to our program, and I have a meeting in New York tomorrow." She raised her eyebrows meaningfully at her nephew. "Want to come? See how the drug companies rape the poor?"

Ian's face went back to neutral. "I'll have to pass."

"Mmm," she said.

Okay. While it was undeniable that Jane McFarland

did great things, she wasn't the easiest person to like. My left eye started to throb as I listened to her continue with her thinly veiled criticism. Ian just sat there, seemingly unaffected, but the urge to defend him swelled in my heart. I actually had to clamp my lips shut to keep from saying anything.

Dinner was painfully awkward, not to mention *nasty*...the ravioli tasted like a combination between burnt coffee scrapings and rope. As for the sweet and sour cauliflower...need I say more? It was definitely a culinary "don't." Jane was on her fourth attempt to convince Ian to return to medical school so he, like Perfect Alejandro, could follow in her holy work. The thing was, her work *was* holy, there was no denying that. But she couldn't seem to accept that Ian didn't want the same thing.

She didn't touch the cake I'd baked. I couldn't blame her for that. Note to self—tofu and chocolate do not a happy marriage make. Sighing, I stirred a spoonful of sugar into my coffee.

"Dear, you should read about what conditions are like for sugarcane workers," she said, finally addressing me. "Well, that's condescending of me. Perhaps you already know."

"I don't," I admitted, suppressing a sigh.

"No, I don't suppose you do," she murmured. "Most Americans don't." Strike 10,006 against Callie/Cassie... she put sugar in her coffee, the ignorant, disgusting American.

And then...and then we heard a little chirp. For a second, I didn't realize what it was...not until my sister's voice boomed into our lovely evening.

"Callie! Guess what! I just had sex! It was amazing!"

"Excuse me!" I lunged from the table. Shit! Earlier today, I'd used the *push to talk* feature, as the walkie-talkie method tended to work better out here by the lake. Alas...oh, alas!...I'd forgotten to turn it off.

"I mean, sure," Hester continued, "I've, you know, *felt* things. I own a vibrator, after all. But this was *much* better than anything you can buy online, you know?"

Where was my purse, dammit all to hell? Counter? No. Desk? No! Ah, right, over there by the back door. Hester's thunderous voice continued to detonate from the depths of my vast orange bag. "Seriously! I thought I was going to end up clinging to the ceiling by my fingernails! I know you said you were doing the vet, and he does seem hot, but listen... I hope he's *half* as good as Louis."

"Holy crap!" I blurted. I jerked open my purse and shoveled through the debris for my phone. Tampon, paperback, picture of Bronte and Josephine, wallet. No phone. Come on!

"Callie? You there? Well, anyway, just wanted to share the big news. I'm screwing a mortician and yes, it really is true. They do it stiffer." My hand closed around the phone. "Gotta go. I think I'm up for round two! Bye!"

I stabbed the off button. The quiet was deafening...not that I could hear anyway, the way my pulse was roaring in my ears. I returned the phone to my purse and took a breath.

"Guess what?" I said. "My sister has a boyfriend."

Neither of them said a word. Angie, however, wagged her plumy tail. I was grateful.

Back to the table I went, face flaming. Finished off that glass of wine, oh, yes I did. It was the only friendly thing at the table. "Sorry about that," I muttered.

"What a lovely family you must have," Jane said, raising her eyebrow.

"You know what?" I snapped. "They are lovely. I have a *great* family. We love each other, we accept each other, we don't sit around once a year talking about how disappointed we are in each other."

"Callie," Ian said in a low voice.

I ignored him. "My sister may be a little, well…weird, but she's a great mother to both her kids. She'd never try to make them feel like they'd let her down."

"Callie," Ian said again.

Jane, however, simply looked amused. "Oh, no, speak your mind, dear."

I swallowed and unclenched my fists. "I just think maybe…maybe you should stop telling Ian what he should do with his life. He lost his parents when he was little—"

"She knows what happened, Callie," Ian said quietly.

"—and maybe you should stop trying to convert him to your mission and just back off."

Ian closed his eyes briefly. The kitchen clock ticked. Angie sighed.

"Well," Jane said, unfazed. "I guess we know where Cassie stands."

I waited for Ian to correct her. He didn't.

"Okay," I said, standing. My hip bumped the table, sloshing my untouched, sugary coffee. "Um, I have to run. It was good to meet you, Dr. McFarland. Have a safe trip back. Ian…" My heart was thudding so hard I thought I might barf, and not because I'd eaten beet ravioli (though surely that didn't help matters). "See you soon, I'm sure."

He cut his eyes to me, and for the first time since I met him, I saw that he was angry. My chest tightened. How could he be mad at *me*? I defended him! *I* thought he was pretty damn wonderful.

"Actually, I'm the one who should go," Jane said calmly, rising from the table. "I'm heading to Manchester Airport. That's not too far, is it?"

"I'll get you directions," Ian said. "Come in the den, Jane." He glanced over at me, his eyes still hot, and led his aunt into the other room.

Was I supposed to stay? It didn't seem right to just walk out right now, while they were looking up directions on Google. Because I wasn't sure what else to do, I cleared the table, tossing Jane's untouched cake into the trash with more force than was necessary. Loaded the dishwasher. Ian always put all the forks in one quadrant of the silverware holder, all the spoons in another, the knives in a third…you know what? I mixed them all up. So there. Swallowed against the sharp lump of tears in my throat. Listened to them talking in Spanish. Point taken. *We don't want you to know what we're talking about.*

They came back into the great room a few minutes later. "Well, it's certainly been interesting meeting you, Callie," Ian's aunt said matter-of-factly.

"Same here," I said. *Interesting* didn't come close.

"Thank you for cooking, dear." She didn't *seem* to be making fun of me.

"You're welcome."

"I'll walk you to the car, Jane." Ian held the door, and out they went. I took a deep breath, felt the tears sting my eyes. Figured emotional diarrhea was just around the corner.

From the light over Ian's garage, I could see the two of them, Ian a good eight or ten inches taller than his aunt. They talked for a minute or two, then Ian gave her a hug, picking her up a little as he did. Jane reached up and tousled his hair, then got into her rental car and backed around, her tires crunching on the gravel driveway.

Ian was very quiet when he came back in. His dog, sensing her master's mood, slunk into the den. I wished I could follow.

"So," I said, swallowing.

He folded his arms across his chest and stared at the floor, practically burning a hole in it. "Was I somehow unclear when I asked you not to...*campaign* for me, Calliope?" he asked, not looking up.

Crap. Things were never good when my full name was used. "Nope. Not unclear."

"But you did anyway."

I took a shaky breath. "Well, Ian, I'm sorry, but I just felt she should be...proud. Of you. Is that such a bad thing?"

"She's not going to be proud, Callie. I don't need her to be. And I *don't* need her to approve of you. What really bothers me about tonight is that you didn't respect the fact that perhaps I know more about my family than you do."

"Well, don't we sound all Jane Austen," I said. "Although it's funny, you and Mr. Darcy have a lot in common."

Ian failed to appreciate the comparison. "I'm also a little uncomfortable with your view of me as a tragic orphan. Jane did her best with a child she didn't expect or want. That was more than anyone else was offering."

My eyes filled. Poor Ian! Of course, he'd smite me for thinking that, but come on!

He wasn't done. "I think tonight had more to do with your need for people to adore you than with my relationship with Jane."

"It is not about that, Ian!" I said. "She was mean to you! I stuck up for you!"

"She's not mean, Callie, and I don't need defending. Believe it or not, I can handle my aunt."

"Then why didn't you straighten her out on my name? Couldn't you have done that, Ian?"

He raised his hands in frustration. "She knows your name, Callie. She was baiting you, and you bit. I understand my aunt. I know what she wants for me, and she's not going to get it. Okay?" His voice rose. "You're the one who had the problem. Not me. This whole night...this is just the way things are, and you being Little Miss Sunshine was not going to change that, and I told you that, but you couldn't leave it alone, could you?"

I grabbed my purse. "You know what, Ian? I'm sorry I have so many inconvenient human emotions. I know you hate that sort of thing. I wish I could be more like your dog, who's perfect in every way. I'm sorry I want people to like me, since I know you don't give a rat's ass about that sort of thing. I'm also sorry—" here I hiccupped, so dignified "—that I care about you enough to get upset when someone treats you like shit. I'm sorry that Hester called, and I'm sorry I actually voiced an opinion." I dashed the heels of my hands across my eyes.

"Don't cry," he added tightly.

"Sorry," I bit out. Then I opened the door and ran down the porch steps.

"Callie, wait," Ian called, sounding defeated.

"You know what, Ian? I'm gonna go," I said. "Talk to you soon." With that, I got in my car and drove off into the dark country night.

CHAPTER TWENTY-THREE

ONCE IN THE CAR, I wasn't sure where to go. Noah had told me that he had, in his words, "romantic interests." Clearly I didn't want to run into him and Jody in a compromising situation again. Hester, too, was busy, though my brain shied away from the thought of her with Louis. God! There'd been enough carnage tonight. I knew Annie would take me in, but it was late. Besides, she and Jack were probably cuddled on the couch, cooing at each other.

That left Mom or Dad, and as usual, I picked Dad. His house was dark, and no car was in the driveway. He might be on the road…his bowling club did little overnights to different alleys throughout the Northeast. I unlocked the door and went in. "Dad?" I called softly, just in case he was home.

"Who's there?" a voice called from upstairs.

I turned on the stairs light. My brother blinked and covered his eyes. "Christly, Callie, turn that fucking light off."

"Sorry," I said, obeying. "What are you doing here?"

"Mom's been on my ass lately. Figured I'd hide out here. What about you, sis?"

I sat down on the stairs. A thin beam of pinkish light from the streetlamp sliced through the front windows. "I had a fight with my boyfriend," I said.

"Mark?"

I glanced up, startled. The idea of Mark and me seemed like a long, long time ago, a foggy memory best left untouched. "No. Ian. The vet. We've been…seeing each other."

"What did you fight about?" Freddie asked.

"I had emotional diarrhea," I said glumly.

"Now there's a pretty image," he muttered. The stairs creaked as Fred came down. He sat next to me, slung his arm around my shoulders. "Tell your brilliant child prodigy of a brother," he said.

"Seriously? You won't tweet this or anything?"

"Fine. Steal my fun. I won't tweet. Or blog. Or put you on YouTube."

Odd, to be telling my cute little brother my romantic woes, but he listened mostly in silence, except for the strangled noises of appropriate horror he made when I mentioned Hester's interruption.

"So what should I do?" I asked, feeling the prickle of tears yet again.

"You should've stayed and shagged him," my brother advised sagely. "We men are very basic. We'll forgive anything for a little action."

"You're not a man, Freddie my love. You're a mere child." My voice was a little hollow. Freddie didn't answer. "So how are things with you?" I asked.

He sighed. "I don't know, Callie. I lack direction."

"I think we're all aware of that, honey." Slipping off my shoes, I tipped my head against the wall. "Is there anything you love to do?"

"Other than get laid, you mean?"

"Yes, Fred, and I'd rather not discuss your tomcatting, okay? I changed your diapers and all that."

Freddie was quiet for a minute. "I like having fun. Sounds stupid, right? I like to hike and kayak and fish. I don't think the market is great for river guides, though."

"Wanted: Mountain Man," I said. He chuckled, and I patted his bare foot. "Well, what are you best at? You're a math whiz, your blogs are hilarious, you have a huge following on Twitter, you built a computer when you were twelve, you're as charming as Dad, so you'd be great in some kind of schmoozing job…"

"See, that's the thing," Freddie said. "I'm good at everything. The crushing price of genius."

"Okay, brat. I'm going to bed. How about you?"

"I'm gonna stay up and watch TV and eat all Dad's ice cream." He put his hand on my head. "Want to keep your little brother company?"

"Sure," I said, and fifteen minutes later, I was wearing a pair of my dad's pajamas, watching *Evil Dead III* and doing my part to support Ben & Jerry. And trying hard not to think of Ian.

I RAN HOME THE NEXT morning to change. Noah was up (and alone), Bowie quivering at his side as my grandfather absentmindedly fed him bits of bacon and perused the local paper. "Well, well, well," I said, getting a cup of coffee. "You made your own breakfast. I'm so proud." I looked around. "Or has Jody replaced me as your slave?"

"Pipe down, youngster, I'm reading." He glanced up, then frowned. "What happened? You look awful. You have a fight with that vet of yours?"

I blinked. Most of my conversations with Noah went something like *Find my leg, dammit!* and me replying *Yes, Master.* "Wow. Yes, I did."

He stared at me a minute longer. "Well. Things'll work out. Don't you worry."

"I'm worried anyway." My throat tightened.

"Ah, Callie. You had a fight, you'll make up." He slipped Bowie some more bacon, which my dog inhaled. "Give the boy some time. He's not used to the likes of you."

"What's that mean?" I asked.

"Means you're…big."

"Thank you. I feel much better."

"You fill up the whole room, sweetheart, try to fix everyone's problems, be everyone's friend. You don't have to try so hard. We'll love you just the same."

Not the first time I heard that, was it? "You just implied you loved me, Noah. What's next? A Hallmark card? This Jody Bingham thing is transforming you."

He grinned. "You never know."

WORK SEEMED ENDLESS THAT day. I kept my office door closed, ground out copy and tried to stay away from other people. And, of course, obsessed over Ian, trying to figure out how to smooth things over, how to say the exact right thing so we'd be back to where we were. Because where we'd been…that was a nice place. A *very* nice place. As for Ian himself, he didn't call or e-mail…the only personal message I got all day was from my mom, summoning me to a family meeting at the funeral home after work. My guess was a career intervention for Fred.

Nothing from Ian. Half a dozen times, I picked up the phone to call his office, and half a dozen times, I put the phone back.

You don't have to try so hard. The problem was, I didn't know how to do anything else.

At five-thirty, I tidied my desk and said goodbye to Pete and Leila. Damien and Karen had left already, as had Fleur. Muriel was once again in California. At least there was that.

"Have a good night, Mark," I said, pausing at his door.

"Hey, Callie. You, too." He stood up and smiled. "You look pretty today. Well, you look pretty all the time. If I'm allowed to say that, that is."

I hesitated. "Uh…sure."

"Callie, do you have a sec?" he asked, indicating the two empty seats in front of his desk.

"I have plans, actually."

"Just for a minute?"

We both sat down. Mark looked at his hands. "I miss us talking," he said, his voice quiet. His eyes dropped to my mouth, then rose back to my eyes.

"What did you want to talk about?" I asked, shifting slightly away from him.

He sighed and ran a hand through his hair. "I don't know," he said. "I just miss you, and I hope that…I don't know." He sighed. "We've been friends a long time, haven't we?"

"I guess so," I said.

He was silent a minute. "What do you think about Muriel and me, Callie?"

The question caught me off guard. "Oh…I don't know, Mark, and I…I don't want to have this conversation."

He shook his head and held up his hands. "No, no. You're right. I'm sorry. I just…I could use a woman's opinion. That's all. I didn't mean to put you on the spot."

"Ask your mom," I suggested.

He grinned. "Yes. Much more appropriate. You

just…" He looked down at his hands, then gave me the James Dean look, lowered head, sheepish grin. "You have a way about you, Callie. It's…special. You're special. I hope you know that." His smile faded. "Very special."

The air in the office seemed to change. My knees prickled uncomfortably. Mark's eyes dropped once more to my mouth and stayed there. When he spoke next, his voice was very quiet. "I seem to be thinking about Santa Fe a lot these days."

My breath caught. "Excuse me?"

He raised his eyes back to mine, gave a little smile and shrugged. "I don't know. It was…special. A special time."

Couldn't the man think of another adjective? I stood up fast. "I have to go, Mark. See you tomorrow."

"Callie…" I waited, but then he sighed. "See you tomorrow. Have a great night."

Out on the street, I took a few cleansing breaths, my breath fogging in the darkening evening. Stupid Mark. What was *that* all about, huh? I knew Santa Fe was special, I'd spent practically an entire *year* getting over how special it was, I *told* him about its specialness the night he dumped me and he dumped me anyway! And how dare he look at my mouth that way after all he'd put me through?

I took a few more breaths, the sharp scent of autumn leaves and woodsmoke finally calming me. Jake Pelletier pulled into a parking space in front of Whoop & Holler, saw me and waved. I waved back, then headed up the hill toward the funeral home.

I was over Mark. I was. I just didn't appreciate him stirring up the muck of my feelings from the past. Especially the day after my very first fight with Ian.

Speaking of my fight with Ian, it was time to fix that.

Time for some wild monkey make-up sex. Last night had been awkward, we'd fought, now we'd make up. Because a day without hearing from him or seeing him was just not acceptable.

You go, girl, Mrs. Obama said, and I smiled at the thought. But first, my family.

"Callie, you're here!" Mom declared as I walked in the family entrance of the funeral home. My sibs, nieces and parents were all here.

"Hey, everyone," I said, unwinding myself from my Pashmina (on sale, a deep shade of rose, so soft!).

"Where's your grandfather?" Mom asked.

"I came straight from work. And contrary to popular belief, I am not my grandfather's keeper," I said.

"She's more like his slave," Freddie said.

"You are correct. And Fred, since you're shiftless, unemployed and have yet to graduate from college, why don't you take over?"

"I just called over there, and no one answered," Mom said.

"He's probably with his lady love," I suggested. "Hi, Josephine! Your hair looks so pretty!" My niece held up her arms, and even though she was getting big, I picked her up, sniffing her neck, making her giggle. "You smell like fairy dust," I told her, and she grinned back at me, then wriggled down to go pick my father's pocket, a life skill if ever there was one. Dad tossed me a wink and pretended not to notice his granddaughter digging in his back pocket. Her little hand emerged clutching a twenty. "Poppy, I robbed you!" she said happily.

"Hello there, Callie," came the silky voice of Louis. Louis who was banging Hester. That's right! I'd almost forgotten.

"Louis," I said, taking my customary step backward.

"No need to retreat," he murmured. "I've moved on."

"So I heard," I said, swallowing.

"Yeah, so, we're a freak show," Hester said, coming up and handing me a glass of wine, good sister that she was. "No atheists in foxholes, you know?"

"Yes," I said, not wanting her to clarify that statement. Besides, Hes was beaming. Beaming! I hadn't seen her look so happy since Bronte's adoption was finalized.

Speaking of my elder niece, Bronte came up, noted that her mother was holding hands with Louis and made a gagging sound. "Now, Bronte," I said. "You're the one who wanted a father figure."

"I was picturing Denzel Washington. Not Dwight Schrute here."

"I love Dwight Schrute," I said.

"Yes, but do you want him sleeping with your mother?" she demanded.

"Good point." Hester and Louis were staring at each other, all sorts of icky pheromones flying. "You can come live with Noah and me," I whispered to Bronte.

"I probably will," she said huffily. But a little smile played around her mouth.

"Okay, kids, gather 'round," Dad said. "Well, I wish my father were here... Callie, where'd he go?"

"He slipped out of his collar and ran off! I don't know, Dad! He has a girlfriend. Can we leave it at that?"

"Sure, Poodle," he said, all sparkly and Clooney-esque. "Well, Bluebird, would you like to tell them?"

Bluebird. *Bluebird.* My breath caught.

"You go ahead, Tobias," Mom said.

Dad looked around at us all. "Your mother and I..."

His voice grew husky. "We've reconciled. And we're getting married." His gaze rested on me a long second.

My eyes flooded. I covered my mouth with one hand, absolutely stunned. He got her back! He did it.

For a second, I was right back in that upstairs window, watching my father leave, and the memory of that wrenching, twisting heartache made me dizzy. Back then, I would've given twenty years of my life for him to come back. And now he was. They were getting married. Married! My God! My heart felt so big I thought it might pop out of my chest.

"Way to go, Dad!" Freddie said, applauding lightly.

"Aren't you married already?" Josephine asked.

"No, honey. Do you want to be a flower girl? You can have a sparkly dress," Dad said.

"Ooh! Sure, Poppy! Can it be black?"

"Whoa, whoa, whoa," Hester boomed. She shook loose of Louis's hand. "Are you kidding, Ma? You're not serious, are you?"

Mom glanced at the girls. "Ah, Louis...would you mind taking the girls elsewhere for a few minutes?"

"Of course," he said. "Girls, would you like play vampires in the showroom?"

"Typical," Bronte muttered. "I am so old enough to hear this, but I get booted anyway."

"I call the Windsor!" Josephine said happily, grabbing her sister's hand. "I love bronze."

"I'll be Van Helsing," Bronte said, resignation dripping from her voice. Louis closed the door after them.

"I'm sorry," Hester said, "but uh...this is fucking ridiculous."

"Hes," I began.

"Please, Callie," she said. "I'm not like you, singing rainbow songs and letting fucking bluebirds flutter around my head. Dad. You cheated on Mom when she was pregnant. I think we can see that I'm emotionally scarred from that. I mean, I've spent my whole life avoiding men like the bubonic plague because, *Mother,* that's what you taught me!"

Mom's mouth was hanging open. "Oh, honey... I never meant to—"

"But you did!"

"And yet here you are, sleeping with the Prince of Darkness," Freddie commented.

"Shut it, little boy," she snarled. She turned to my parents, who'd been beaming just a few seconds ago. "And now you're marrying him? Again? Are you insane? What if he cheats on you again?" Her breath came in jerking little fits, and I could honestly say I'd never seen her so upset.

My mom's face was pale, and Dad's smile had vacated the premises.

Then he put his glass down and walked over to stand in front of his eldest child. "Hester, I want you to forgive me," he said gently.

"No fucking way," Hester answered.

"Forgive me," he repeated.

"Dad..." Her voice broke a little. "No."

"Please." He stared right in her eyes, no smile on his face, no twinkles, his eyes steady and sad. "Everything you said is true."

"I know that!" she sputtered.

"Please forgive me, Hester. Give me another chance. Please, Bunny."

At the sound of her long-ago pet name, my sister's

mouth wobbled. Her eyes were no longer dry. She looked at my mother, then at Fred and me.

"Come on, Hes," Freddie said gently. "It's true, they fucked us up, but isn't that what all parents do? Imagine what the girls will say about you. Stop stepping on kittens and let Mom and Dad be happy."

My sister looked at me, and our eyes locked, sunshine and butterflies against the rhino. Then I smiled, gave a little shrug, and the butterflies won. My sister heaved a sigh. "Fine. I'm outranked, anyway." She looked at my father. "You're taking the girls and me to Disney World. God knows you owe me."

"Name the day," he said. Then he put his arms around her, and after a second, she hugged him back, and if it was awkward and less than wholehearted, it was, nonetheless, a start.

"This family is not normal," Hester said, releasing Dad to wipe her eyes. "Not fucking normal."

I found that I was crying (surprise!). Going to my mom, I hugged her long and hard, then went to my dad, my dear old dad, and wrapped my arms around his neck. "You did it, Daddy. You got her back," I whispered.

"Thank you, Poodle," he said, tears in his own eyes. "Thank you for never giving up on me."

CHAPTER TWENTY-FOUR

IT WAS FULLY DARK when I left the funeral home, as we'd all ordered celebratory pizzas and started planning the wedding.

The night was cold…cold enough for frost, maybe. A thin slice of moon hung in the sky, and leaves rustled and fell from the trees as I walked down the hill. I checked my phone. No messages. I wasn't sure what that meant regarding Ian and me, but as I said earlier—time for wild monkey make-up sex. Heck, if my parents could get together after all that, Ian and I could certainly get past this bump. I'd just nip home, check on Noah and Bowie, throw on some slutty underwear, then trundle out to Bitter Creek Road.

The lights of Georgebury were dark, as the sidewalks rolled up around 8:00 p.m. The Whoop & Holler showed signs of life, but the other storefronts were dark. Only Green Mountain Media had its lights on. Mark was still there. I could see his dark head in the window as he sat at his desk in the apex of our iron-shaped building.

I stopped, looking up at the office, the light golden and inviting. And then, just like that, I decided. Tomorrow, I was giving notice.

It was time.

A weight lifted from my heart. Yes. It was definitely

time. I'd find something else soon enough. Could even start my own business, maybe, or help Noah for a few months 'til another opportunity presented itself. But it was time to cut whatever tattered strings kept me near Mark. He'd been in my life forever, always clouding the waters one way or the other, and finally…finally!…I was sick of it.

"What do you say to that, Michelle?" I asked aloud. The First Lady didn't answer, but that was okay. I didn't need her voice of reason when I'd finally found my own.

When I got home, Noah's truck was in its customary space. As I went into the kitchen, I snapped on the light…the house was pitch black. And quiet. Where was my doggie? He usually greeted me at the door, alerted to my presence at the first whisper of my footsteps, quivering in joy. Tonight, though, there was nothing.

"Bowie?" I called. "Mommy's home, buddy!"

There was only silence.

"Noah?" I said. My voice seemed to echo.

He must be out with Jody, I thought. *And he took Bowie, that's all.*

But bile rose in my throat. My purse slipped from my suddenly sweaty hand. "Bowie?" My voice was quavery and weak.

Then came a small sound. *It's probably Noah,* Betty Boop said. *He's in his bedroom with Jody, and they're having geriatric sex, so make a lot of noise.*

But I knew it wasn't that.

The sound came again, a small, keening cry. It was my dog.

Turning on every light as I walked, my legs wobbling—because I knew, I already knew—I made my way through the kitchen, the great room. Then, my hands shaking violently, I opened the door to the workshop. Bowie whined again, louder now.

My hand hesitated as I reached for the light switch. I was absolutely certain I didn't want to see what was in here. Without turning the overhead light on, I stepped into the workshop. I knew the way, after all.

"Grampy?" I whispered. Bowie's tail thudded against the floor, the only answer.

Slowly, carefully, I made my way to the worktable in the corner and then, after a moment's hesitation, turned on the old copper light. Its gentle light was more than enough to show what I already knew I'd see.

My grandfather sat in his old recliner, Bowie lying at the foot of the chair. My dog's tail thumped once, but he didn't get up.

Noah's eyes were closed. More than ever, he resembled a skinny Santa Claus, the white beard and hair, the gentle, capable hands. Without his customary scowl, his face was sweeter and more relaxed. Those lines around his eyes…they were laugh lines. My grandfather had a wonderful smile. He'd always tried to pull off that grumpy old man persona, but I'd never bought it—not really. A person couldn't hide a good heart, no matter how hard he tried.

He really looked as if he were sleeping. Such a cliché, but reassuring, because even though I'd grown up in a funeral home, I'd always been afraid of the dead.

Bowie whined again. "You're such a good boy," I whispered. "Such a good dog, Bowie."

I covered Noah's cold, stiff hand with my own and knelt by the chair, hot tears slipping down my face. He must've been here for a while, because the shop was chilly, no fire hissing in the woodstove. It was so quiet. "Oh, Noah," I whispered. "I'm so sorry I wasn't here."

Don't be an idiot, I could almost hear him saying.

"Mom and Dad are back together," I told my grandfather, my voice wobbling. "So you don't need to worry about your son anymore, okay? And I'll look after Freddie. He'll be fine. He's just young. He's growing up, though. I know he'll make you proud."

I thought of my grandmother, the love of Noah's life. Thought of Mr. Morelock and my uncle Remy, gone for so long. I hoped they were there for Noah. I was so glad I got to live with him and tease him and help him. Glad he'd found a little fun with Jody in his last weeks. Glad he died out here in the shop he loved so well, working until his last day, because an old Vermont Yankee wouldn't want it any other way. Glad my excellent dog had been here, because Noah had so loved Bowie.

I kissed my grandfather's forehead, then rose. "Come on, Bowie," I said. "You did a good job. Come get some bacon."

My dog, released from his duty, followed me into the kitchen.

Funny. I didn't really know what to do, despite my upbringing. I gave Bowie his reward, then picked up the phone. Dialed a number almost without realizing it. *Please be there,* I thought.

He wasn't.

"You've reached Ian McFarland. Please leave a message and I'll call back as soon as possible."

"Ian?" I said, my voice small. "I know you're a little mad at me, but I was wondering if you could come over, because my grandfather just died."

Two hours later, I was alone again in Noah's house.

My parents had come almost immediately. Dad

standing silently next to his father for a few minutes, then kissing his head. Mom took Dad in her arms then, murmuring softly. Robbie Neal, River Rat and paramedic, had come to confirm that Noah was indeed gone, and Shaunee, another ambulance volunteer, gave me a hug.

"Looks like a massive heart attack," she said.

The police asked a few questions…when I'd seen him last, if he'd had any visitors, the usual. They did a routine check, but it was obvious that Noah's heart had simply stopped. Louis came, quiet and efficient, and for the first time, his voice didn't seem creepy…instead, he seemed only kind and capable.

Both my parents were concerned about me, wanted me to stay over, offered to stay here. They figured Hes and Freddie could wait 'til morning to hear the news… Freddie had gone out with friends, Hester always went to bed early. I offered to tell Jody tomorrow. Poor Jody.

"You sure you don't want to come home, sweetheart?" my mother asked, petting my hair as I sat at the kitchen table. Dad was out with the EMTs.

"I'm fine, Mom," I said. "Just, you know…sad." Bowie, who was definitely putting in some overtime, put his head on my lap and winked his blue eye. I smiled at him and gave him half of the sandwich Mom had made for me. I looked up at my mother. "I'll just stay here tonight, have a good cry."

She looked at me sternly, assessing my truth-o-meter. "Okay. I'll call you in the morning."

"Thanks, Mom. I guess you have all the arrangements and stuff?"

She nodded. "Yes. He gave them to me after your gran died. He never thought he'd live so long without her."

I looked up at my mother. Her face was contemplative. "Mom?"

"Yes, honey?"

"I'm so glad you and Daddy are back together."

Her eyes filled with tears. "Me, too," she whispered.

"You sure you want to be alone, Poodle?" Dad asked, coming back into the kitchen.

"I'm sure, Daddy."

I hugged them both, assured them once more that I'd be fine, watched as Dad held the door for Mom. As he got into the car next to her, she took his hand and kissed it.

Then I turned away from the window and went upstairs to wash my face and brush my teeth, change into pajamas. My throat was tight and hard with tears, and the house was so horribly quiet.

There, in the corner of my room, by the window that overlooked the river, sat my Morelock chair. On the shelf above it sat seventeen little wooden animals, carved over the years by my grandfather, and at the realization that he'd never make another, a sharp pain stabbed my chest.

I came back down to the great room, sat on the couch. Bowie leaped up next to me. Maybe *Deadliest Catch* was on, but the thought of watching it without Noah made my throat ache even more. I could've called Annie, but I didn't, just sat in the quiet, quiet house. When a knock came on the door, Bowie and I both jumped. I let out a breath I didn't know I was holding. He was here. Finally.

It wasn't Ian.

"Mark," I breathed. "What are you doing here?" I glanced past him to see if there was anyone else coming… Ian, for example.

His face was solemn. "I just heard," he said, taking me in his arms. "I'm so sorry, Callie."

It was a full-body hug…not just the lean-in type, but a full court press, thighs to faces. His cheek was against mine, smooth and warm and clean-shaven. He smelled like he always did—that Hugo Boss cologne that I'd loved so much, I'd pathetically bought a bottle after our breakup. Many maudlin hours were spent sniffing the stupid cologne and analyzing those famous five weeks.

I disentangled myself. "Thank you, Mark. Um…who told you?" I stepped back, letting Bowie go through his ritualistic *sniff the visitor* routine. My face felt hot.

"I just stopped by the Whoop & Holler," he said. "Shaunee Cole told me." Word did spread in a town this size. "Are you all alone?" he asked.

"Yes," I said, hesitating. "Um…come on in. Would you like something to drink?"

"Sure. Let's raise a glass to old Noah."

Part of me bristled. *Old Noah never liked you, Mark. Thought you were pompous.* But Mark was being kind. Besides, I guess we needed to talk.

A minute later, we were seated on the old leather couch in front of the fire, each of us with a finger or two of whiskey.

"To your grandfather. A better boat builder there never was," he said.

"Cheers," I returned, dutifully clinking my glass against his. Took a sip. I never liked whiskey. Mark drained his, I noted.

"Take as much time off as you need," he said.

I took a deep breath. "Actually, Mark, I need to talk to you about work." I traced Hello Kitty's face on my pajamas, then took a deep breath. "I'm giving notice. Might be best if it was effective immediately, given the circumstances."

Mark didn't move. Didn't even seem to breathe. Then

he blinked and inhaled abruptly. "Callie, sweetheart, don't be rash. That's crazy. You can't leave."

I paused. "Well, actually, I can."

"You're upset. Your grandfather just died. You shouldn't make this decision now."

"I didn't. I made it earlier today."

He blinked, then rubbed his forehead. "All right, let's be blunt. Is this about me?"

I considered his face, his eyebrows drawn together in a frown, those lovely dark eyes, the ever-rakish hair. The face of Lord Byron or something…romantic and expressive and ridiculously handsome. Ian's face wasn't quite so good-looking, but it was far more interesting, full of hidden nuances and almost smiles. Mark might embody male beauty, but Ian…Ian's face told quite a story. Mark was simply blank perfection.

"Callie," Mark whispered, taking my hand.

I took it back. "You know what, Mark? You're right. It *is* about you." I took a throw pillow and clutched it against my stomach. "I want to be honest here, because it's just dawning on me that I haven't been honest with you. Ever, maybe."

He pulled a face. "Don't be silly."

"No," I said. "I haven't been. The truth is, Mark, I…I was in love with you for years. A long time. Well before the Santa Fe thing."

Mark opened his mouth, started to say something, then reconsidered. "Uh…okay. Go on."

"Well, first there was high school, Gwen's basement, all that." He smiled a little, and I continued. "Then later on, ever since the day I interviewed with you, I just sort of sat there like some hopeful puppy, waiting for you to notice me." Bowie yipped in support.

"Of course I noticed you, Callie," Mark said impatiently. "I've always thought you were great."

I snorted. "Right. But it took three years and a near-death experience for us to hook up. And the thing was, I didn't mind. I was completely head over heels, and at long last, it seemed like you felt the same way. For a few days, anyway. When we got back, you got all squirrelly and I thought, okay, well, he just needs some time. So I waited some more, thinking any day you were going to realize you loved me, too." I shook my head. "That night…the night you broke up with me, when you made that nice dinner—I actually thought you were going to propose, Mark."

He looked at his hands, and a slight flush colored his cheeks.

"And then you gave me that bullshit line about timing."

"Callie, that wasn't bullshit."

"Um…bullshit, Mark."

He exhaled in exasperation. "All right, fine, Callie. Look. You and me…Santa Fe, that was a mistake. It was special, but the timing *was* wrong, and I should never have slept with you. I'm sorry."

Even though I was over him, the words stung like little bees.

"But, Callie," he continued, "that doesn't mean you should quit! You love what you do. And you're great at it!"

"I know," I said. "I just…I just want something different now. And quite frankly, I don't like the way Muriel's steamrolled everyone at the agency. I just want to move on and make a clean break. I've wasted enough time on you, Mark."

He shook his head. "I had no idea you felt this way," he muttered.

"Yes, you did!" I barked, making him jump. "And you played me! You're still playing me! Just tonight, you told me how *special* I was. You knew how I felt, and you used it, and you've been using it for years." He shot me a guilty look, and I sighed, suddenly exhausted. "Mark, my grandfather died today, and to be honest, you're the last person I want here. I quit. Please go. We'll talk next week, okay?"

He stood up. "All right. But we're not done. And I don't accept your resignation, because I think you're upset and sad and you shouldn't make a big decision right now. Just think about it, okay?"

"I don't need to."

"Well…do it anyway." He took a ragged breath. "Look, I didn't mean to make your day worse, Callie. I just wanted to say how sorry I was about Noah. I know how much you loved him."

That was always the problem with Mark. He was never all bad. "I appreciate that," I said more gently. I got up and walked him to the door. "Thanks for coming."

"You're welcome," he answered, opening the door.

Ian stood on the porch, wearing scrubs and no coat, despite the cold autumn air.

"Ian," I breathed. Bowie began crooning with joy.

Ian looked at me, then Mark. "I was in surgery," he said hesitantly. "A dog was…well." He swallowed. "I just got your message now, Callie."

"I was just leaving," Mark muttered. "Good night." He trudged out to his car, got in and drove away, his taillights harsh in the dark night. Behind me, Bowie whined, then flopped on the floor, offering his belly for a rub, should anyone be so inclined.

"Is it too late?" Ian asked.

"For what?"

"For company?"

"Not for yours," I answered, and with that, Ian wrapped his arms around me and kissed me on the forehead.

"I'm so sorry about Noah," he whispered.

"Thank you," I said, and he was so warm and strong and gentle that tears once again sloshed out of my eyes.

"Do you want to talk?" Ian asked.

"I just want to go to bed," I squeaked, my face pressed against his chest.

"Okay, sweetheart," he said. He'd never called me anything but Callie before, and it made me cry harder. Ian closed the door, said some kind words to Bowie, and led me upstairs, turning off lights as he went. "Need to brush your teeth or anything?" he asked.

"No," I wept. "I'm all set."

He tossed all my little throw pillows over the side of the bed and turned down the quilt. "In you go," he said, and I obeyed, feeling so heavy and tired all of a sudden.

Ian pulled the covers up to my chin, then bent to kiss my hair. I caught his hand, and he sat at the edge of the bed, his thumb gently stroking the back of my hand, and the thought came to me that Ian McFarland would make a great husband, a great father, a great anything.

"I'm really sorry about last night," I whispered.

"Well," he said, smoothing back my hair. "Your heart was in the right place, I guess. I'm sorry, too." He looked down at the quilt, traced a piece of fabric. "She's never going to be easy, Callie."

"I guess not," I said.

"Are we done with that, then?"

I nodded.

"I thought you broke up with me last night, when you left," he said, not looking up.

My breath caught. "Oh. No, Ian. We just…we just had a fight."

"Okay." He swallowed, and my heart seemed to swell abruptly.

"In fact, I was going to come over for some wild monkey make-up sex. But then I came home and found Noah, and…and…well…" My face scrunched up.

"Oh, hey," Ian said, and honestly, nothing on earth ever felt as good as those solid arms around me. He pressed my face against his neck and let me cry.

"Can you stay with me tonight?" My voice sounded small.

Ian pulled back and looked at me with those summer-blue eyes. "That's why I came," he said simply.

Then he pulled off his scrubs and came into bed with me, holding me so close that my cheek rested over his heart. Within seconds, I fell asleep.

CHAPTER TWENTY-FIVE

THE DAY OF NOAH'S burial was cold and gray. We gathered at the funeral home in the morning. There would be no church service, as per Noah's orders…just two hours for a wake, then on to the cemetery.

In an oddly beautiful tribute, the River Rats had asked my mom if they could bring in one of Noah's kayaks, which they set up behind the casket in the Serenity Room. The boat was one of Noah's most beautiful designs…a long, sleek vessel, the red cedar inlaid with white oak. As it always had, the dichotomy of my grandfather struck me…the rough-talking old man with callused hands who could produce such a thing of lightness and grace. Quite a legacy he left behind.

It was strange, all of us here in the funeral home—our home—all of us together, this time as mourners. I wished Noah could've seen Mom and Dad together again. Maybe he knew now. Freddie looked somber and mature in his suit, standing next to Bronte, slipping Josephine butter rum Life Savers and telling the girls jokes when they got too weepy. Mom let Louis run the show, and Dad, handsome as ever, greeted the people who paid homage to his father.

Jody was in the receiving line, too. I'd gone to see her the day after Noah died and broke the news, then asked her to stand with us. "I'd like that," she'd said in a small voice. Then she gripped my hand with surprising strength. "Thank you, Callie."

"Well. Anyone who can do a full split *and* put up with my grandfather deserves some recognition," I murmured.

"He thought the world of you," she said.

"Right back at you," I said, and then the two of us had had a good cry.

Ian was here, too, standing in the back of the room like a mastiff…quiet and calm and protective. He brought me a glass of water, fished a handkerchief out of his pocket when I got a little tearful.

"Who even carries these anymore?" I asked, wiping my eyes.

"I stocked up after I met you," he said, looking down at me. He gave my hand a squeeze, then returned to his post in the back of the room, bending slightly as Elmira Butkes asked him a question about that Methuselah of cats, Mr. Fluffers. All the hip-hop yoga ladies had come, as well as the River Rats, not to mention at least a dozen people who'd bought their boats from Noah's Arks.

"I'm so sorry, hon," said Annie, Jack and Seamus in tow. She was teary-eyed, too. "You doing okay?"

"Doing okay," I confirmed.

She wiped her eyes. "Okay. I'm around. I'm on call for you. Will drop everything at a moment's notice. We can get drunk, eat cake batter, curse, whatever you need."

I smiled damply. "I know. Thanks, Annie."

"Sorry for your loss, Callie," Jack said, giving me a hug.

"The least you can do is cop a feel, Jack," I said, hugging him back.

"Sentimental fools, both you girls," he said, winking. They moved on to my parents.

"I'm very sorry, Callie," came a cool voice. Muriel.

"Oh, hi, Muriel," I said. "I didn't know you were back from California."

"I got back yesterday," she said, scanning my outfit. I'd worn a sunshiny yellow dress for Noah. Red peep-toe pumps that were killing my feet but an homage to his life force. Such are the musings of a shoe fetishist.

"Well, thank you for coming." I looked around for the rest of the Green Mountain gang, all of whom had called me since Noah's death.

"They're coming later," Muriel said, answering my unspoken question. "I, uh, had an errand and figured I'd stop by now." She tipped her head. "Well. Sorry again."

It was clear she was itchy, and I couldn't blame her, here in the lair of my family and friends. "Thanks for coming, Muriel. That was very nice of you."

"You're welcome. I…I'll see you around," she said.

"You bet," I said. I wondered if Mark had told her I was quitting, but then Dr. Kumar gave me a big hug, and thoughts of Muriel slipped away.

"My dear girl, I am so very sorry for the loss of your grandfather," he said, his lovely brown eyes moist. "I know you were very close."

"Thanks, Dr. Kumar." I smiled wetly at my old friend. "How was Branson?"

"Oh, Callie, it was lovely! We had a very wonderful time indeed. Next, we are hoping to go to Dollywood. But tell me, my dear, how do you like Dr. McFarland?" Dr Kumar smiled sweetly.

"I like him very much, Dr. Kumar."

"Yes, I had it in my mind that you would. I'm glad." With that, Dr. Kumar winked, hugged me again and moved on.

When the time came, Louis herded everyone out so

we could head for the cemetery. "Can I have a second alone, Dad?" I asked.

"Of course, Poodle," he said. "We'll just be outside." Louis thoughtfully closed the door behind my dad, leaving me alone in the Serenity Room.

The quiet fell heavily. I went up to the casket and looked at my grandfather's face. "I guess this is it, Noah," I whispered. For all his curmudgeonly ways, he'd always been a rock in the river of my life, and it hurt to think I'd never talk to him again.

Then I opened my purse and fished out the little tokens I wanted him to have. A curl of cedar shaving from the floor of his shop. A tuft of Bowie's fur. A chocolate chip cookie.

And one more thing. A card from me, one of the weekly drawings I'd sent him after Gran died. This one was typical child's artwork...a heart and tulips and a rainbow of thin, wobbling Crayola lines. Along the bottom, written as neatly as I could, were the words *I love you Grampy! xoxoxoxox Calliope.*

I'd found it yesterday at the bottom of his sock drawer. Each one of those sixteen cards, tied with a faded ribbon. He'd kept them for twenty-three and a half years, and he saw them every day. That knowledge made my heart feel thin and fragile, as if the slightest nudge would break it.

A few tears slipped down my cheeks. One plopped onto Noah's flannel shirt, and I thought he might like that, because despite all that growling and cussing, Noah had been quite the softy.

"Thank you, Noah," I whispered, touching his scratchy white beard for the last time. "Thank you for letting me be useful. Thank you for everything."

THE FOLLOWING SATURDAY was the River Rat Regatta, a raucous affair that involved lots of locally brewed beer, hot dogs and an occasional race down the Connecticut. Not your typical regatta, mind you, in which people cared about the results…nah. This was more of a good-spirited romp. Some of the events included Ugliest Boat, Best Use of Cardboard and How Long Can You Last, a breath-holding competition usually won by Jim, owner of the Whoop & Holler, who'd been a Navy SEAL in his youth.

The late October sun was bright and strong, though more than likely, this was our last gorgeous weekend. The foliage was mostly gone, a few brave ash trees clinging to their yellow leaves. It had been a drier-than-usual September, so the river was slow and placid, winding its way between New Hamster and Vermont in graceful curves.

This year, the River Rats had asked me to present the Most Beautiful Boat award, which they'd just this week renamed the Noah Grey Award of Aesthetic Excellence. In years past, they'd always asked Noah to present it. He'd always declined, though he usually showed up for a peek. I was touched that they'd asked me.

I waved and smiled to the many people I knew. Soon I'd meet up with Annie, but for now I was solo, as Ian was at work. At the thought of my honey, my heart squeezed. I was in love, and for the first time, it was the kind of love that made me feel like a better person. Mark may have been all I'd thought I ever wanted, but Ian…Ian was what I needed.

"Hey, Callie," my brother said, appearing at my side. He was wearing one of Noah's shirts, and he hadn't shaved in a couple of days. The resemblance to our grandfather was a bit surprising, especially as he knelt to pet Bowie. "Where's Ian?" he asked.

"He's coming a little later. Saturday hours," I answered.

"You guys serious?" Fred asked. Bowie sang in near-orgasmic pleasure as Fred found an itchy spot.

I blushed. "Sort of. Yes."

"He seems cool," my brother said, rising and brushing off Bowie's fur. "Callie...I was thinking."

"What? Are you okay?"

"Be serious." He folded his arms over his chest and looked over my shoulder. "Noah left the rights to all his boat plans to us three, did you know that?" I nodded. "I was thinking I might try boat-building," he said. "Continuing the tradition."

My mouth fell open. "What about college?"

"I've changed majors six times in three years, Callie. I'm guessing that says something."

"Weren't you thinking of becoming a lawyer?"

"Yeah. But only because I'm good at bullshitting," he said. "But...well, I've just been thinking about it, and the truth is, I can't think of anything I'd rather do. Helping Noah out in the shop...that was always the time I felt best. Less like someone going over jackass hill, more like I was doing something...meaningful. Whatever." Freddie rolled his eyes, embarrassed, but I could hear the sincerity in his voice.

"I think you'd be great," I said.

"Could I make a living at it, do you think?" he asked.

"Well, Noah did just fine. You might have to cut your prices at first, do some marketing...hey, I could help you! Noah never did let me advertise, but this would be so nice. Noah's Arks would be a family tradition. Multigenerational. We could do a Web site, a photo gallery…"

"I won't do as good a job as Noah, though," Freddie said, looking for a minute like the little boy I had so loved.

"Maybe not at first. But you'll do great. I know it." Bowie, in complete agreement, licked Freddie's boot as encouragement.

Fred gave me a quick hug. "Thanks, Calorie. I hope Mom won't freak when I tell her."

"She's too busy rediscovering Dad," I said.

"Which is disgusting," Hester said, coming up with the girls.

"Yeah, right. Like you're any better," Bronte said. "Callie, guess who's coming to dinner? Louis. He wants to, like, 'get to know us.'" She made quote marks with her fingers. "Freak." Hester rolled her eyes and gave her daughter a fond nudge.

"Louis made me a death mask," Josephine said, letting Bowie lick her chin. "It's in my room. I'm wearing it for Halloween. I named it Mooey."

"That's a great name," I said. "What do you think of Louis, Josephine?"

"He's nice," she announced, then, apparently finished with that subject, said, "Grammy's taking me shopping for my flower girl dress. I can pick out whatever I want."

"Leopard skin, I'd say," Freddie recommended.

"Buy me popcorn, Uncle Fred," she commanded.

"Yes, my liege," he said, taking her by the hand. "See you guys later. Bronte, you coming?"

"Sure. You're my only cool relative," she said.

"I resent that," I called after her.

"Then stop singing the Black-Eyed Peas in public," she retorted over her shoulder.

"Love you!" Hester called. Bronte didn't answer, but she held up her hand, her pinkie, forefinger and thumb sticking out...*I love you* in sign language.

"Aw!" I said. Hester smiled. "So," I continued. "Louis is..." *shudder* "...good to you?"

She shrugged. "The sex is amazing. We did it in a casket the other night—"

"Oh, my dear God in heaven, please strike me down right now!" I blurted, causing Bowie to bark in sympathy. "Hester! Come on! I'm a normal person. I'm disgusted with that kind of information."

"What? You and Ian haven't done it anywhere...unexpected?"

"Well." I paused, feeling my cheeks warm. "He has this dock, you know? And we went out there the other night to look at the stars, and we had blankets, and things got...romantic."

"Yawn," said Hester.

"It wasn't yawn, okay? He made me happy. Twice. It was..." Special. Beautiful. Meaningful! Betty Boop and I sighed happily, dopey grins across both our faces. I'd been having quite a few dopey grins these days. I paused, looking up at the achingly blue sky. Thought of my honey's eyes. Bowie nudged my hand, reminding me just who my true love really was, and I scratched his ear obediently.

"Well, whatever. Don't rule out the caskets. When Mom's out, of course. Oh, look. Speaking of Mom, there they are now." Hester shook her head. "Look at them. Who the fuck would've guessed?"

Our parents were wandering along the riverbank, holding hands. "Are you glad they're back together, Hes?" I asked.

She sighed. "Not sure if *glad* is the right word. But what the hell, right? Their lives to fuck up."

"I guess we know who'll be making the toast at the wedding," I said. "That was beautiful."

She smiled at me again. "I'm starving. Want a chili dog or something?"

"Nah, I'm good," I said. "See you later."

No sooner had she left than someone called my name. Aw! Damien and Dave were here, also holding hands. They waved in unison, looking like an ad for *Wholesome Alternative Lifestyle*. There were Pete and Leila, ever absorbed with each other, two and yet one, like conjoined twins, which wasn't the most romantic image, but it did seem to work for them. Apparently, the whole Green Mountain Media gang had come together and was heading toward me. We were—oops—*they* were one of the sponsors of the regatta, and we'd always had fun in the past. The good old days. A pang of nostalgia bounced around my heart. Not for Mark the man…but a little for Mark the boss.

"Hi, guys!" I said, waving.

Just coming past the little ticket booth was Fleur, smoking a cigarette, possibly the last person in our fair state to do so and earning quite a few glares and fake coughs. Karen snatched the cigarette from Fleur's fingers and ground it out, and I couldn't help laughing.

And here was Mark. His face brightened at the sight of me. I hadn't seen him since my grandfather's funeral, but I'd have to go in soon. Pack up my stuff and get my vacation pay and all that. "Hey, Callie," he said. "How are you?" He knelt down to pet Bowie, who licked his hand appreciatively.

I smiled back, carefully. "I'm fine. How are you?" The rest of the gang swarmed around.

"Cheerio, mate," Fleur added.

"We sure miss you," Leila said. "The place is just—"

"—not the same. Not as fun," Pete finished.

"And no one else bakes," Karen muttered. "We really do miss you."

"So do the clients," Damien said pointedly. "We've lost three since you left."

"Right, but no worries," Fleur said. "They were mostly done anyway." I wondered if she'd been promoted to creative director with my departure. Muriel had that job, more likely. And speaking of the ice princess...

"Where's Muriel?" I asked.

Silence fell. Awkward silence. Pete and Leila exchanged looks, Fleur raised an eyebrow. Bowie flopped on the ground and offered himself to the first taker.

"Callie, walk with me," Mark said, taking my arm. "We should talk." Bowie leaped to his feet—I had him on a leash, so he had no choice—and trotted at my side as Mark steered me past the Lions Club grill.

"Hi, Callie!" Jody Bingham called, standing in line for a burger.

"Hi, Jody!" I called back. "How you doing?"

"Pretty good, thanks," she answered. We were scheduled to have lunch next week. Noah's girls.

"Guess what, Callie? I can do a cartwheel!" Hayley McIntyre demonstrated her skill, and I tugged my arm free from Mark's grip to applaud.

"That was wonderful, honey," I told her.

"I know it!" she affirmed, then ran off to her family.

"Can we continue?" Mark asked, his voice on the impatient side.

"What's the deal, Mark?" I asked. "And why do we need to go way over here?"

"I'd like to talk privately."

We came upon the back lawn of the library, which was closed today. The grass was still green, and a few leaves still clung to the branches of the crabapple trees that enclosed the yard. I used to come here to read after school when I was a kid, wishing I were Anne of Green Gables or Jane Eyre. A stone bench in memory of some long-ago patron overlooked the river, which shushed and gurgled past.

"Have a seat," Mark said. I obeyed, and Bowie flopped at my feet, curling into a tight ball. The bench was hard and cool, despite the sunshine, and I fidgeted, not sure I wanted to be here.

Mark didn't sit with me. He stood, hands on his hips, exhaled sharply and looked at the sky.

"Speak, Mark," I said irritably. "You dragged me here for a reason, after all."

He looked down at me. "Right. Okay, first of all, Muriel's gone. So you have to come back to work."

"What?" I exclaimed.

"She and I are done. It wasn't working out."

"Wow." I paused. "She came to Noah's funeral."

"Yeah, well, she left just after that." Mark's mouth was a straight line, and his shoulders were tight. "The BTR account went with her."

"I'm not sure what to say, Mark."

"Say you'll come back to work. You wanted me to choose, so I chose. I chose *you*."

"I didn't…I'm not sure what you're talking about."

Mark ran a hand through his dark hair, then sat heavily next to me. His shoulders slumped, and he turned to face me. "Callie, you said some things the night Noah died. And I listened, okay?"

"Uh…apparently not, since I quit that night. I won't be coming back, Mark."

But then Mark took my hands in his and just stared at them. "Callie, if I could turn back time—"

"As Cher would say," I couldn't help interjecting, reclaiming my hands and folding them primly on my lap.

He grinned, and suddenly he seemed more…normal. "Okay, that was funny." I gave a half nod, as he was right. "But listen, Callie." His voice lowered, and he gave me the James Dean look. "I screwed up. I didn't see what I had in you, and I…" He shook his head. "I want you back. At the company, and you know, if you want to give a relationship another shot, that would be…that would be nice. Great, in fact," he amended hastily. "So. Let's get you back in the office and see where things go on the, uh, personal front."

Bowie, an emotional whore if ever there was one, instantly forgave Mark and sprang to his feet, licking Mark's hand. Me… I'd become a little more demanding. "That was the lamest offer I've had in my entire life, Mark," I said.

"I'll give you a raise," he said earnestly.

"Gah! Come on!"

"Callie, please. I'm making a mess of this, I see that, God knows, but…well, Callie, you're great. And I could…I could definitely see us working out. Really. You said you've loved me for years. Give me another shot. Let's go back to the way things were in Santa Fe."

"You told me that was a mistake, Mark."

"Well, I was wrong. You're incredible, Callie, and I was so stupid not to see it before."

Granted, I'd waited a long time to hear those words. Would've sold a kidney—maybe two—to have heard them at one point. Now, though…they didn't have the same impact. They were, in fact, an overcooked noodle in the pasta salad of love.

"Listen, Mark, that's really…uh…flattering to hear and all, but I have to ask. How much of this has to do with the three clients who left?"

"Okay, you bring up a good point," he said quickly. "Work and…us…we're intertwined. I think the thing I'm proudest of in my whole life is Green Mountain, and you're a huge part of it, Callie. The way you are in life, the way you are at work, with clients, with the whole gang, it's all the same, isn't it?"

"I…don't know, but I still quit," I said, glancing at my watch. Ian was due to meet me pretty soon.

"We make a great team, we really do," Mark persisted. "At work and…otherwise. That's undeniable."

"That was undeniable, Mark," I said. "It's not true anymore."

"Look, I'm sorry," he blurted. The wind rustled in the branches, and a shower of small brown and yellow leaves fluttered down like cautionary notes. "I admit that I was an idiot, Callie, but the thing is, what we had…it scared me. It was so intense—"

"Seriously?" I asked, raising a dubious eyebrow. "Because you didn't seem scared or intense at all back then."

"No. I was." He gripped my hands again. "Callie, I just panicked. That's why I hooked up with Muriel. She was so different from you—"

"Mark, stop," I said firmly, tugging my hands free once more. "I don't care. I've moved on, okay? I'm sorry."

Mark stiffened. "I know. The vet."

"Ian. His name is Ian."

"Right." Rather than discourage him, the mention of the other man seemed to strengthen Mark's resolve. He slid to one knee in front of me.

"Oh, get up. Up you go! Right now," I said, looking around a bit desperately. Bowie smiled and yipped. "I'm not going to marry you, for God's sake."

"I'm not asking," Mark said, grinning. "I just want to see your face."

I grimaced. "This is very uncomfortable, Mark."

"I know. For me, too." He leaned forward, bracing his arms on either side of me. "I just want you to think about this, Callie," he said quietly. His face was way too close to mine, and I pulled back. "I want you to remember our time together. How it was between us. I mean, I've been thinking about it recently, and it was…We were two halves of a whole. We completed each other." I snorted, but he kept going. "Great at work, great in bed—" here he cocked an eyebrow and gave that famous crooked grin "—great just talking. Do you remember, how it was when we were together?"

Blerk! Had he always been so smarmy? "We know each other, Callie," he continued. "We've known each other so long. I was the first boy you kissed, remember? Give us another chance. Please, Callie. I think we're worth it."

I stared back at him, almost fascinated. I did remember, of course. Oh, yeah. I remembered being positive that Mark Rousseau wouldn't have kissed me a second time in Gwen Hardy's closet without it really meaning something. Remembered waiting for him to break up with Julie Revere, carting Freddie all over town as my prop. Remembered waiting for him to see me as more than a great coworker. Remembered those five sickening weeks when he inched a little further away each day. Remembered my desperation and frantic rationalizations as I tried harder and harder to remind him of why he *had* to love me.

I remembered falling apart in the DMV.

Helpless in love, that's what I'd been.

I wasn't helpless anymore.

Besides, he's an asshole, Betty Boop said calmly from within my conscience, and I couldn't have agreed more.

But Mark mistook my silence for happy nostalgia, and he leaned forward and kissed me. I didn't move. Not because I was shocked, or thrilled, or disgusted… I sat there almost scientifically, wondering if that old melting magic would wash every smart thought away. No magic came. The smart thoughts…they stayed.

"Okay, that's enough," I said as I pulled back.

"Oh, bollocks," came Fleur's voice. "Didn't mean to intrude. Ian was looking for you, Callie. Bit awkward, yeah, Ian?"

I lurched to my feet, practically knocking Mark over. "Ian! There you are!" My dog raced over to Ian, keening with joy. Ian didn't move.

They were standing in the side yard of the library…obviously, they'd come from the street. Fleur was smirking. Ian looked…oh, God. He saw me kissing another man, and he thought I was cheating. Just like his ex-wife.

He looked like the deer, and this time—for the first time ever—I was the truck.

I unfroze and ran over to them. Ian looked away abruptly, toward the river. "Ian, I know this looks bad," I began, twisting my ring. "But I can explain."

"Seems like your little scheme worked brilliantly,

Callie," Fleur said easily. She fished a cigarette out of her purse and fumbled for her lighter.

"Ian," I said again. With difficulty, he looked back at me. "This is not what it seems," I whispered.

"What little scheme?" Ian asked, shifting his eyes to Fleur.

"Oh, sorry. Thought you were in on it." She lit the death stick and took a deep drag, then exhaled, smiling at me through the smoke. "Date another man, make Mark jealous."

Her words were a sucker punch. "That was never my plan, Fleur." My voice cracked.

She tilted her head "No? Funny. Could've sworn we discussed it. At length." She took another drag on her cigarette. "And now it's worked. Well done, you."

"Ian," I said in a low voice. "I'll explain this. It's just…it's not what she's saying."

His eyes sliced back to me. Otherwise, he didn't move. Shit.

Fleur turned to Mark, who was approaching us, tucking in his shirt. As if I'd pulled it out in a moment of ruttishness or something, making me look guiltier by the second. "Mark, what gives?" she asked. "Have you finally come to your senses and seen the little diamond Callie is? Now that Muriel's left you?"

That caught me off guard. "She left *you*, huh?" I said. "Funny, you made it seem like the other way around." Should've known, not that it made any difference. "Ian, if you could—"

"So you and the boss are back together," Fleur said. "You must be thrilled."

"No! And I didn't scheme anything," I hissed. "Ian, there was no plan or scheme or anything." Bowie barked, backing me up. Would that he could talk and bear witness. I bit my thumb. "Can we talk alone?"

He didn't answer. Hadn't said anything to me, in fact.

"We'll go," Mark said. "Callie…we'll talk soon. Think about what I said." Another James Dean look, this time with brow furrowed meaningfully, and then off he went, Fleur trotting at his side like a sycophantic rat terrier.

Which left me alone with Ian. A great wave of fear sloshed at my legs, making them weak and sick-feeling. "Um, do you want to sit down?" I asked, indicating the bench.

"No."

"No, of course, not there, anyway." I took a shaky breath and looked up at him. His face had lost that slapped look and now seemed carved in stone. It was not encouraging. "Okay, Ian, here's the thing. Mark wants to get back together with me, and I don't want to. That's it." I tried to take his hands, but he pushed them into his pockets, his arms straight, fists clenched.

"You were kissing him," he said.

"Um, well, technically, he was kissing me."

"You didn't seem to mind."

"It wasn't like that. I don't want to get back with Mark. I really don't. Please believe me. I'm sorry you saw us kissing, and I know that must bring back some bad memories—"

"Yes, Callie. It does."

"But I wasn't cheating! And I wouldn't, Ian. I never would."

He shook his head. "What about what Fleur said? Your plan to make Mark jealous."

"I didn't… It wasn't… I never planned to…"

Except, of course, I had.

I took a deep breath, started to speak, then stopped.

"Tell me the truth, Callie," Ian said, his voice low.

I bit my lip. "Well, you remember that day, right? In the DMV?" He nodded. "Well, after that, Annie and Fleur and I...we were talking and basically thought the best way for me to get over Mark would be to...find another fish to fry. Or whatever. Not a great metaphor, but..."

"And that's why you came to my office that day? When Bowie ate the newspaper?" At the sound of his name, Bowie barked. *Yes, I am here and will eat whatever you have on you!*

"Um, yes."

"So you lied about that."

"*Fibbed* is a better word, I think." At his dark look, I nodded. "Yes, I lied. As you suspected. I'm sorry."

Ian looked at the ground. In the distance, the sounds of the regatta drifted toward us in snatches, laughter and music, a baby crying. "So you needed a distraction," he said slowly. "To get your mind off Mark." He lifted his eyes to me, and my heart shriveled.

"I wouldn't put it that way, Ian," I whispered. Tears pricked my eyes, because I knew...I just knew...this conversation was not going to end well.

"I asked you, that first morning after we...I asked you if you were over him."

"And I am! Ian, I'm not using you to get over Mark."

"But you are," he said. "You just admitted that."

I swallowed. "Well, technically, to be perfectly honest, yes, I guess it started that way. But the turkey, that day...that wasn't... You must know I care about you, Ian! Let's not get caught up in details here."

"The details happen to be very important to me, Callie," he barked, causing me to jump. "I've already been with a woman who had a hidden agenda. I've already been with a woman who wanted to be with someone else." His voice rose. "I've already been someone's second choice. Every time I turn around, there he is. Jesus, Callie, you were kissing him!"

"Ian, stop!" I blurted. "I don't love him anymore. You're not going to find us in bed together!"

"I didn't expect to find you kissing him, either!" he yelled. "But I just did! And you know what, Callie? Maybe you do still love him. Maybe once the newness of—" he flapped his hands in the space between us "—of *this* wears off, you'll realize that Mark is the love of your life. And you know what? I don't want to hang around to find out I'm the runner-up."

"Wait," I said, my voice breaking. "I'm..." My stomach twisted. Oh, shit, this was hard to say, and this was not the time to say it, but I was desperate. "I'm in love with *you,* Ian. Not Mark."

"You were in love with Mark just a couple months ago."

"This is different," I whispered. "I promise."

He shoved his fists back in his pockets. "How do I know? How do *you* know, for that matter, Callie?"

"I just know." Oh, Christ, talk about a lame answer! "Ian," I whispered, "please don't do this."

But he'd already decided. His face fell back into that distant, reserved expression I'd seen too many times before. "I think it's best if we just end things now," he said quietly.

"I don't. I think that's a horrible idea," I squeaked, tears splashing out of my eyes.

"I'm sorry," he said.

And with that, he turned his back on me and walked away.

CHAPTER TWENTY-SIX

LIFE REALLY SUCKED. You know? I had no job, my grand-father was dead, I'd finally fallen into a good love, and he dumped me.

Of course, my first instinct was to feel completely blameless. I had, in point of fact, done nothing wrong. Not one thing. Should I have kneed Mark in the groin? Would *that* have made Ian happy? I wasn't really the groin-injury type, a fact I now deeply regretted. I never *needed* to kick a guy in the nuts, quite honestly. I'd always been able to *(work, play, manipulate)* deal with men before.

And as for the whole idea of scheming and planning and using Ian…I knew I hadn't done that. There was nothing wrong with wanting to move on from a helpless, hopeless love, was there? Was it a sin to want something better?

"Not a sin," Annie confirmed as we swilled cheap chablis the night after the stupid regatta. "Though this is why all the dating books say to give yourself a year after a breakup."

"Well, I didn't give it a year," I said, wiping my eyes and throwing the tissue on the floor, where it joined its half-dozen brothers. "I never got to that chapter. And I think Ian would be honored. You know? Because he's the healthy, stable, good man I chose over Captain Asshole."

"Honored. You're right." She nodded wisely. She was

spending the night, and though we had rented several Gerard Butler movies, they all sat untouched. "I guess he just doesn't feel that...chosen. And therein lies the problem."

"So how do I prove my love and all that crap?" I asked.

"No clue." At my dark look, she added, "But we'll find something. We will."

I already missed Ian. How could I get through the day without that smile? He was so easy to tease, and when he smiled, it was like the sun coming out from behind the clouds. Stupid, stupid Mark! *He* smiled all the time, like some slavering village idiot. Meaningless, empty, supermodel smiles, not that supermodels ever smiled, but you know what I mean.

"So what about Fleur?" Annie asked.

"I just ordered a voodoo doll on eBay," I muttered.

"She's always resented you. I can't believe you never saw it."

"Not helping," I muttered.

"Well, let's get her back, the jealous hag," Annie said. "I know people."

"You're a school librarian," I pointed out, pouring more wine for both of us. "You don't know people. Not those people."

"She's a bitch."

"Yes. She is. And her empty, bitter life will be punishment enough."

"Not for me," Annie said. "Let's key her car."

"The thing is," I said, wiping my endlessly leaking eyes once more, "I know how Ian is. He's like cement. This is just going to sit there in his heart and harden, and I'll never..." A little sob squeaked out... "I should call him. Don't you think?"

"Shit, no. You're not calling him. Give me your cell phone. Oh. Oh, no." She closed her eyes. "You called him, didn't you?"

"Um…well, yes. Three times. And I, well, I e-mailed him. Twice. And I drove by his house at ten last night, but it was dark."

"Wow. Restraining order material," she murmured. "Did you try the door?" she added. Yet another example of why we were friends.

"I was afraid the dog would out me."

"Right." She ate a potato chip, chewing contemplatively. "I guess you have to wait."

I swallowed. "I just feel that if I could say things the right way, he'd understand. But he won't talk to me."

"Did you tell him you loved him?" she asked.

My eyes filled again. "Yes. It didn't work."

Annie sighed. "I don't know, Callie. Seems like you have to…ride it out. I mean, if it's meant to be…" Her voice trailed off. "Right?"

"Right," I said, blowing my nose. "He's just not the kind of guy who…overlooks things. He saw Mark kissing me. He's not going to forget that."

"That was a nut-kicker, I'm sure," she said.

"Thanks."

"Well, come on. The man walked in on his wife in bed with someone else. Now he sees his new girlfriend kissing her ex-boyfriend."

"If I wanted this kind of talk, I'd have called Hester, okay? Can't you be more sympathetic?"

"Sure," Annie said easily. "Maybe it's time for Gerard, don't you think?" I nodded. "Do we want *300* or *P.S. I Love You?*"

"*P.S.* The other one is just homoerotic dreck."

"It's Dave's favorite movie," she said. "So you're probably right."

THE NEXT FEW DAYS DRAGGED. Ian didn't call. He did, however, respond to my fourth e-mail—*Callie, I'd appreciate a little space. Ian.* Try as I might, it was hard to put a positive spin on that, though I guessed it was better than *Leave me alone, hag.*

What I'd said to Annie had been true. If I could just get Ian to see what I meant…and what I felt. Every time I thought of that stupid line—*I'm in love with you, Ian. Not Mark*—I cringed and reached for more cake batter. Though my statement had been true, it just sounded…shallow.

I hadn't realized how much noise Noah made, the saws and sanders out in the shop, the odd rhythm of his uneven gait, his barked curses and demands for dinner. Though I was glad he'd gone the way he had, I missed the old troll. Bowie did, too, often going into Noah's room, then returning to lie quietly at my feet.

The golden light of October faded into the gray skies and cold rains the Vermont Tourism Board doesn't want you to know about. With the foliage stripped by a windstorm and the three rivers brown and churning, Georgebury looked bare and weary, hunkering down in resignation for a long, long winter.

Freddie was moving in…it made sense, given that he'd be working here. Somewhat surprisingly, my parents had been thrilled that Fred wanted to take over Noah's Arks, shrugging off the small fortune they'd already spent on his education and sending him for yet another round, this time for a week at the WoodenBoat School in Maine. He'd be back in time for the wedding.

Ah, the wedding. It would be a civil ceremony, followed by dinner, at Elements. My parents were so happy it was surreal…the laughter, the flirting, the affection. Hester still looked at them with a mix of horror and amusement, but then again, that's how we were all looking at her these days.

"Think you and Louis will tie the knot?" I asked her one day as we shopped for the girls' dresses…red for Josephine, cream for Bronte.

"Nah," Hester answered. "The girls and I do great together. Maybe when Bronte goes off to college, but if it ain't broke, don't fix it, right? And Louis likes having his own place. He has this collection of antique mortuary tools—"

"Okay, we're done. Glad things are working out, Hes."

"Thanks, Callie," she said, slugging me affectionately on the shoulder, hard enough that I'd be sore in the morning. "Hey. Sorry you and Owen didn't work out."

"Ian. Thanks," I said.

"How's the job hunt going?" she asked, kindly changing the subject.

I sighed. "Not much out there," I admitted, then glanced at my watch. "Shoot. I have to run, Hester. I'm supposed to clean out my office today, and I wanted to do it at lunch. Avoid a few people."

"Good luck with that," she said.

My mood was bittersweet as I walked to Green Mountain. I'd miss Damien's sniping and gossip, miss Karen's growling and Pete and Leila's symbiosis. And I'd miss the work most of all. But I was done. I'd sent Mark an e-mail saying when I'd be in to clean out my office, asked him to have Karen settle my insurance and all that. I didn't mention his idiotic declarations or stupid kiss.

As I struggled through the door with my empty boxes, Damien jumped up to help. "We're interviewing for your position," he whispered. "But Mark would take you back in a heartbeat. Probably double your salary, too."

"Gotta pass, buddy," I said. "But I'll still see you, right?"

"All the time," he said.

In a way, it was soothing to pack up my office and see the evidence of years of my work. As I looked at the hospital poster, the boy's remarkable eyes, I thought about taking that home. After all, it was one of my best pieces ever. But it was also the poster that had brought me to Santa Fe, and I didn't want to be reminded of Santa Fe anymore.

I packed up my books, my plants, samples of my work over the years. Quite a few clients had e-mailed when they'd heard the news of my departure, and Damien, in a rare fit of thoughtfulness, had printed them all out for me. Several clients had sent gifts, too…a complimentary stay from a B&B in Burlington, a gift certificate for a car detailing from the dealership in Stowe. John Hammill, my maple syrup zealot, had sent a gallon of each of his eight strains of syrup, so I'd be all set in terms of pancakes for some time.

He'd also offered me a job—director of marketing, which he admitted wouldn't be a huge challenge for me. "You'd get as much syrup as you can hold," he said hopefully, and I laughed and pointed out I had eight gallons to go through as it was.

"Let me know. The job's yours if you want it," he said, and a lump had risen in my throat. People were awfully nice, but Hammill Farms was a little too far to commute. Then again, a move might not be the worst thing for me.

A soft knock came on the door. I looked up. Mark. "This is a tough day for us," he said quietly. "Losing you."

"Thank you," I said, turning back to my packing.

"Is there any way you'd stay, Callie?" His voice was forlorn.

"No."

He flopped on the couch where he'd sat so many times these past four years. "I wanted to apologize for the other day, Callie."

"Go right ahead," I said frostily, wrapping a picture of Bronte in tissue paper.

"To tell you the truth, I'd have said anything to get you to stay here." He toyed with his cuff and didn't look at me.

"Yeah. I got that." I reached for the lumpy mug I'd always used for coffee.

Mark sighed, leaning forward and clasping his hands between his knees. "I'm sorry I didn't fall in love with you, Callie. I wanted to. Back then, I mean." He looked at me, but I just kept packing. "I wanted to feel the way you did, but I…didn't, so I said it was a timing thing. Figured it would be easier that way."

"What about Muriel?" I asked. "Did you really love her, or was she just part of the BTR account? Because that would make you a whore, of course." I felt an unexpected wave of sympathy for the ice princess.

"I…I thought I loved her. She was…" He paused. "Different. Confident. In California, she seemed really…well, smart, and she didn't seem to care about anything except work. Like me. I thought we were kindred spirits. I didn't expect her to be quite so…clueless." He looked down. "Maybe the only thing I've ever really loved is this company."

"Don't forget your reflection," I said.

"Touché," he muttered. "I deserve that."

I sat down in my chair and looked at Mark, the first boy who'd ever kissed me. He was so handsome. And shallow. And heartless, not in a ruthless way, but just…lacking heart. At least now he was being honest.

And just like that, I decided to forgive him. Because I'd learned something from Ian. Forgiveness is what really sets a heart free.

"You were a great boss, Mark, and I really loved working here. Thank you for the opportunity."

He looked up, startled, and after a second, his eyes grew wet. "You're welcome. Good luck with everything, Callie."

Then he stood up, extended his hand. I shook it, and then there was nothing left to say.

As I was just about ready to go, Fleur returned to her office, smelling like a wet ashtray and clutching a container of yogurt. She pretended not to see me, despite the fact that our work areas were separated by glass. I grabbed the gift I'd brought her and knocked loudly. "Hi," I said.

"Callie! Right! Someone said you'd be in today. Well. Best wishes and all that." She smiled, remorseless as a great white. Just following her instincts.

"Listen," I said. "I know that scene at the regatta was awkward, but…well…" I faked a smile. "I always enjoyed working with you. So here's a little farewell gift. I know living in Britain got you hooked on tea." I handed over a little basket containing a china cup, a tea ball and a little bag of loose tea, all wrapped in cellophane and tied with yellow and orange ribbons.

"Wow, Callie, thank you!" she said, forgetting to sound British. Her face flushed. "That was really nice of you."

"You're welcome. Good luck with your career."

"Same to you," she replied, untying the ribbon. "I'll have some right now." She seemed to remember her accent. "Right. Could murder a cuppa." She sniffed the tea. "Yummy. Herbal, is it?"

"It sure is," I replied. "One hundred percent, all natural organic."

Then I hefted my box into my arms and left Green Mountain Media for the last time, somehow forgetting to mention that the tea just happened to be Dr. Duncan's Cleanse 'n Purge Weight Loss Jump-Start. When Fleur discovered an alien in her stomach about twelve hours from now, I hoped she'd think of me.

"BOWIE, DO YOU FEEL OKAY?" I asked my dog as I got dressed a few days later. "Do you need a checkup? Huh, buddy? Feeling a little off?" Bowie leaped in a circle, howling with joy, then froze, motionless, quivering with attention. *Do I smell bacon? Somewhere, someone is cooking bacon!*

Okay, apparently my dog was just fine, so no excuse to see Ian. Drat. Last night, clearly desperate for affection, I'd scanned YouTube for huskies who could say "I love you," and then tried to teach Bowie to do the same. "Say you love Mommy," I said now as my dog wagged furiously. "I love you! I love you, Bowie!"

Rehrahruuu, Bowie attempted gamely.

"Good boy! I love you! Say you love Mommy!"

"Jesus, Callie, this is sick! Can't you just find a prostitute like everyone else?" my brother demanded, stomping into the room

"You're more and more like Noah every day," I said. "Not that he ever encouraged me to seek out a hooker."

"Just go to Ian's and do him, for crying out loud."

"And he never said that, either. But the spirit is the same."

"When are you moving?" Freddie asked grumpily.

"I'm looking for a place this afternoon," I answered. "Just keep in mind that Noah left this place to *me,* young man, and just because I'm renting it to you doesn't mean you get to be all bossy like Hester."

This got a smile. "Okay. You can stay as long as you want. Just try to be out by next week."

As tempting as sharing a house with Fred was…well, it wasn't tempting at all. And though I loved Noah's place, I didn't want to live there without the old grump.

One of Jody Bingham's many hobbies was real estate, and she was taking me house-hunting after lunch. "Okay, Bowie, I have to go, buddy," I told my dog. "I'll find the bacon. And I'll bring it back! Yes, I will! I love you! Can you say that back? I love you!"

Rrrroooruh! was the best he could do. That's what I got for adopting a mutt.

The first place Jody took me was a condo. It had a lovely kitchen and a sunny little deck, but it was too close to the highway for me. The second place was basically a hovel, and the instant we'd opened the door, the odor had turned us right around. "Sorry," Jody said. "This third one is a winner, though. From the sound of it, anyway."

"How are you these days, Jody?" I asked as we drove north out of town.

She sighed. "Well, I'm fine. I really enjoyed sparking with your grandfather. Miss him more than I ought, probably."

"Nah," I said. "You miss him as much as you want."

She smiled fondly at me, and a warm glow of affection filled my chest. Nice to have a new friend, even if she had pirated my bathtub.

The third place was just off a twisting little road up Mount Kiernan. It was indeed a winner—a tiny, fairy-sized house with faded green shingles and a blue tin roof, hidden in a clump of massive pines. Some brave little marigolds were still toughing it out in a pot by the yellow front door. Yellow was my favorite color...a sign, maybe? There was a minuscule front porch...big enough, however, for my rocking chair and a little table and a cuppa joe.

"Sold," I murmured before I even got out of the car. There were no neighbors, just the pines and the view...woods and fields, the glint of Trout River to keep me company, the spire of St. Andrew's marking my town.

The inside was snug and cozy, a far cry from Noah's echoing forty-foot ceilings and arching beams. Ample counters in the small but well-designed kitchen, a little table overlooking the backyard, which was just a scattering of pine needles and a decrepit stone wall. Two tiny bedrooms (I could use one for a closet), a serviceable bathroom, a sleeping loft above. "I'll take it," I said, smiling at Jody.

"Excellent," she said. "Callie, have you found a job yet?"

"Oh, I can afford it, don't worry. I have savings," I assured her. "And Noah left me a nest egg."

"No, I was just wondering about work, if you'd found anything."

I grimaced. "No. Not yet."

She nodded. "Well, listen up. There's an opening at the Senior Center. Director. Timmy McMann left for bigger and better things, so we're looking. You'd have to deal with the town, draw up the budget, manage the entire staff of two, apply for grants...the usual garbage. But I think you'd be wonderful. Not nearly enough people use the place, and you're good at drawing people to you. Care to apply?"

I blinked. "Um...yes! Thank you, Jody!"

"You're a shoo-in with my recommendation, so make sure you want it, honey. The description's online."

And so it was a productive afternoon... I had a new friend, a new residence and, most likely, a new job. Noah's was empty when I came home, as Freddie was out with Lily Butkes, Elmira's daughter. I set my purse and keys in their usual spot and picked up the phone. Almost before I realized what I was doing, Carmella answered. "Georgebury Veterinary Practice, how can I help you?"

"Hey, Carmella, it's Callie Grey."

A second or two passed. "Hi, Callie," she said.

"Um...is Ian there, by chance?" I could just about picture the index card taped to Carmella's phone: *Callie Grey—No.* That and a picture of me with a big X through my face.

Another pause. "He is here, Callie, but he's with a patient. Can I take a message?"

"Do you know if he's busy later?" I asked, cringing. *Hi. I'm pathetic. Want to be my friend?*

"Uh... He's actually going out of town for a couple days, Callie. Maybe you could call him at home?" *And leave me alone?*

"Okay. Sorry, Carmella. Didn't mean to bother you."

"No bother, sweetie."

Great. She was being nice. Ian must really hate me. Or maybe not. Maybe he just got sick of me. He was a man who was trying to make order out of the chaos of his life, and I was a messy addition, after all, with my crying and blubbering and lateness and slutty shoes and a sister who announced middle-aged impregnations all over town and a brother who attracted drug-sniffing dogs. Ian was…well, he was probably looking for something else.

It was pretty clear he wasn't looking for me…not when I was just sitting here, waiting to be found.

Rreehhhrruuhrrooo! Bowie nudged my hand with his nose.

"I love you, too, Bowie," I said, then wiped my eyes and took a look in my closet to see what I'd need to purge.

CHAPTER TWENTY-SEVEN

THE DAY BEFORE MY parents once again pledged themselves to each other was my last day at Noah's.

I'd already moved most of my stuff to my tiny house. My big old leather couch, my many houseplants and pictures of my nieces, my shoe collection. I bought café curtains for the kitchen in a green fern print, scavenged a couple of things from my parents…an end table and lamp from Dad, an old brass tub from Mom that looked really sweet outside the front door.

Next week, I'd start at the Senior Center. As Jody predicted, I was offered the job almost immediately. Who knew one feeble hip-hop class would generate so much goodwill? It paid less than I made at Green Mountain Media, but that was okay. Something Ian's aunt had said had stuck in my brain…my job in advertising had been to make people buy more crap. And let's be honest; most people didn't really need more crap.

The Senior Center, on the other hand, gave the older people in Georgebury somewhere to go, something to do. It fostered community and usefulness. The idea of working there just felt better. Cleaner. More karmic or something. Maybe all those yoga classes hadn't been for naught, after all. I already had great plans. Adopt a Brownie Troop. Memoir classes. Field trips and blood drives. More hip-hop, and this time, by someone who knew what she was doing.

So it was all good. We Greys were better than we'd been in a long, long time. After all these years, my father had gone from bad dog to good man. And Mom…no longer was she the bitter betrayed. Instead, she had done that most difficult and generous thing a person could do…she forgave the man who'd hurt her. Forgave him so deeply and truly that she could even love him again. Tomorrow would be beautiful indeed.

But for now, I had to leave Noah's and go to my new home. Freddie had thoughtfully made himself absent, and Bowie and I sat for a minute in my nearly empty bedroom, the afternoon sun streaming in through the windows, belying the chill in the air.

It seemed like I'd been here a lot longer than two and a half years. The day I'd moved in here, Noah had yelled at me. "I don't need a fuckin' nursemaid, and don't you forget it, young lady!" He was still in a wheelchair back then, and he slammed it into the doorframe three times before he made it into the workshop, where he sequestered himself for the rest of the day. That night, I found a little whittled chickadee on my bureau as an apology. That bird now sat on the windowsill of my cottage's kitchen.

The only thing left to bring over was my chair, as I hadn't wanted it to be scraped or jostled with my other belongings.

I stood up, let Bowie out and then approached my prized possession. Taking it gently by the arms, I carried it downstairs, being sure not to let it bump against the railings. Out the front door, into the back of Hester's minivan, which she'd lent me for just this purpose.

Funny how it felt to be driving out of town, past the

little shops and buildings of downtown, past the railroad station and mill. Past Green Mountain Media, past Toasted & Roasted, past Elements. I wasn't leaving Georgebury, but I was leaving a lot behind.

When I arrived at the cottage, I let Bowie out, sucked in a few breaths of the cold, piney air, then got the chair. With great reverence, I carried it to the porch and set it down. My own home. This was what my chair and I had been waiting for. I smiled in anticipation and looked at the chair.

Huh. It wasn't… It didn't look quite right. I moved the chair to the left a few inches. No. How about here, to just right of the window? Not there, either. I tried angling it, first west, then east. Put it in the far corner, then moved it over near the door.

Something was off. After all this time, the chair was too…much. Too beautiful, too full of grace.

The thought came to me so fast and hard that almost before it was fully formulated, I had loaded the chair back in Hester's car. Fifteen minutes later, I turned off Bitter Creek Road.

In the late afternoon sunlight, Ian's house was even lovelier…and lonely, somehow. No car was in the driveway, no dog barked from within. Maybe Ian was still at work…maybe he was truly out of town, as Carmella had said. Heck, maybe he was in Russia, buying a wife. I just didn't know.

I popped the hatch and took out the chair once more. When I set it on the porch, I knew it had found its home. The happily-ever-after chair belonged here, whether or not Ian and I were together.

I went back to the car, rummaged in the glove box and found a pen and a napkin, which would have to do. I sat for a moment, thinking of all the clever things I'd written over the years. Nothing clever came to me now, nothing perfect or transformative. After a minute, I gave up and just wrote what I meant.

Ian, I want you to have this. Keep it, sell it, donate it somewhere worthy. It's yours now.—Callie.

I tucked the napkin under the rocker and then, with one more long, grateful look at the chair that had meant so much to me for so, so long, I went home.

TWENTY-SEVEN HOURS LATER, my parents were once again married. The wedding was held at the funeral home, which was just sick, but the furnace at Elements had conked out. Dave sent over the food, but yes, my parents got hitched in the Tranquility Room. Fortunately, there were no wakes booked this day, and Mom had a point…we already had flowers, a damn good music system and plenty of room for dancing.

As my father pledged to love and honor Mom all the days of his life, I sobbed into a hankie. Ian's hankie, actually. I'd kept it. My crying was kind of a given, I guess, but Hester cried, too, which was not. Freddie mugged dreadfully as best man. Bronte looked beautiful in her dress, so grown up and stunning that the sight of her alone had brought me to tears. Josephine looked startlingly wholesome, and Louis looked…well, he still looked damp and creepy, but he smiled at my sister throughout the ceremony, and Hester seemed to appreciate that.

"Make a toast, Poodle," Dad said, beaming and sparkly and in love.

"No. Freddie should do it."

"Right," Dad snorted. "Or Hester. Or maybe your

dog. No, honey, you do it. Come on. Do it for your old dad. And Mom."

Mom drifted up, her face luminous with serenity and, er, tranquility. "This is a happy day, isn't it, Calliope?" she asked, resting her cheek on my dad's shoulder.

"It is," I said, my eyes welling yet again. "I'll make a toast. Sure. You bet, Daddy."

And so I did, saluting persistence and love, faith and forgiveness, and yes, I did a great job, feeling it was only fair for everyone to shed a tear since my own eyes were working overtime. Then Josephine got the microphone and Bronte did something with her iPod and seconds later, little Josephine was wailing away, "Don't cha wish your girlfriend was hot like me," and somehow that became the first song my parents danced to.

It was something, I thought, dancing later with my father. Today, there was a lot of happiness in this room of sorrow. Twenty-some-odd years ago, I'd watched my father leave this very building, and now he was back, married to Mom once again, and that sad little girl who'd waved from the upstairs window…she could go jump rope or play hopscotch or Wii or whatever it was that made her happy. Mommy loved Daddy and all was right with the world once more.

Almost.

No. Check that. All *was* right with the world. Period. If Mark had taught me anything, it was that I lacked the superpower to make a person love me. I could be friendly and helpful and cute, but I didn't get to control everything. If Ian wanted me, he did. And if he didn't…well, that was harder. But I'd be okay.

"Thank you, Poodle," my father whispered into my hair.

"What for, Daddy?" I asked.

"For thinking I was a good man all these years." He kissed my temple.

"You are a good man, Daddy," I whispered. "A good man who made some mistakes, and that's all in the past now."

"Yes, I was right," Dad mused. "You're a genius. Hello there."

"Callie?"

I stopped abruptly, causing Dad to step on my foot. "Hi," I breathed.

Ian stood in front of me, his face looking creased and tired and...worried.

"I'll just bow out here," Dad murmured, winking at me.

Ian didn't seem to know what to say. He just stood there, looking at me. "Hi," I said again.

"Hi, Dr. McFarland!" Josephine said. "Guess what? My mommy's boyfriend is giving me a kitten! Bronte says it's a bribe, but I don't care! I'm gonna name her Stephanie! Isn't that a beautiful name?"

"They're busy, honey," Hester said, winking so that her entire face appeared to be in some grand mal seizure. "Let's give them some privacy."

Apparently, *privacy* meant *let's all stop talking and listen,* because that's what happened.

"Callie," Ian said. "I...I was in Honduras with...and I... When I got back..." He took a frustrated breath and didn't seem to know what to do with his hands. "See, I always thought I knew what I was looking for," he said. "First it was Laura, and obviously...then I figured I knew what I should look for, but it was supposed to be...well, not you. But when I was away, I kept thinking about you, and God... I've missed you, Callie." He seemed stunned by this fact.

"Shall I get everyone out of here, Callie?" Annie

muttered, coming up beside me. I didn't answer, as speech seemed to have abandoned me.

"That's okay," Ian said, swallowing. "I don't care who hears."

My heart rate tripled. The words *emotional diarrhea* flitted through my mind—not the most romantic words, perhaps, but then again, under the circumstances, maybe they were. I heard a panting, breathy sound, realized it was coming from me, and tried to stop. "Hi," I said for the third time.

"Callie," Ian said, "when I saw you kissing Mark—"

"Oopsy," Jack said, grunting as Annie elbowed him in the ribs.

"I...I panicked. Because I saw that you could...shit, I don't know. Break my heart."

"He swears like you, Mom," Seamus said.

Ian shook his head, closing his eyes, then opened them and took my hand. "I don't want the chair. Not unless it comes with you. That's what will break my heart. Not having you."

"Oh," I breathed.

Ian swallowed audibly. "I just...you know, I have to say, you're the last person I'd picture myself with, Callie, but I can't...I don't... Life is messy and hard to figure out, but all I know, Callie, is that you make me...better. Happier. You bring a lot of life wherever you go, and I...I'd be an idiot if I let you go. So please, Callie, don't let me be an idiot." He took a shaking breath. "I love you. Even if it doesn't make sense."

"Okay," I said, and then I was kissing him, and he felt so, so good, and so right. He hugged me so hard I couldn't breathe, and I vaguely heard clapping and perhaps Bronte saying how gross this all was, and maybe my brother whistled and Josephine saying she'd like a black dress for our wedding.

I didn't really care. All I knew was that right here in this room, in this moment, with this man, I had all I ever wanted.

And then some.

EPILOGUE

Eight months later

JANE MCFARLAND COULDN'T come to our wedding, as she was in Nigeria. But Alejandro had arrived this morning, and tomorrow he'd be standing up for Ian as best man.

"So you'll take good care of Manito, *si,* Calí?" he asked, making my name sound incredibly exotic with that accent of his. We were sitting on Ian's porch…it was a beautiful June evening, and the birds were singing full force. The wind blew gently, and the smell of lilacs drifted to us. From the backyard, we could hear Bowie's happy yipping as he serenaded his lady love. As Alé had to leave tomorrow night, we'd decided to skip a rehearsal dinner so he and Ian could have more time to catch up. The wedding was going to be small, anyway.

"Manito?" I asked in a somewhat dreamy voice. Just because I was in love with Ian didn't mean I couldn't enjoy the visual feast in front of me.

"That one," he said, jerking his chin toward Ian. "Her-manito. My little brother."

Oh! His little brother! Not cousin…*brother.* Sigh! I sat on the porch floor, leaning against the post so I could see both men. "I will, Alejandro, but let's not talk about it now. I'm kind of crushing on you, and I want to soak it all in." I sighed à la Betty Boop, and Ian grinned into his drink.

"Crushing on me...what is that?" Alejandro asked, and Ian answered in Spanish. Alé chuckled. He looked like Antonio Banderas. I am not lying about this.

"Your home is beautiful," Alé said. "I will picture you here, being so happy."

Ian smiled at me, and I reached up and took his hand. I had every intention of making Ian happy.

"So how are things with La Tormenta?" he asked Ian. "My mother," he said to me, widening his eyes. "Yikes, you know?"

"I do," I said, grinning.

"She's fine," Ian said. "Happy for us." This may have been a stretch, but I let it go.

"She told me about the, how you say...the donation. Good move, Manito. You were always smart, for a quiet little guy."

"Callie's idea, actually," Ian said.

Alejandro raised an eyebrow. "Even better."

The thought still gave me a pang, but it had been the right thing to do. I thought so, anyway.

We sold the Morelock chair.

Colleen McPhee at the Museum of the American Craftsman had been ecstatic. "You're sure?" she'd said on the phone. "Not that we don't want it, of course! We do! But you seemed so...adamant."

"I'm sure," I said.

The museum paid thirty grand for it. Though I was granted special visitation rights, when the time came to actually say goodbye, I couldn't help but cry a little. "You don't have to do this," Ian said, frowning. "Callie, if it makes you cry—"

"No. It's fine." I smiled and wiped my eyes. "I'm sure."

And then I sent a check to a very good charity. *Bono*'s charity. Uh-huh. That's right. And guess what else? I got a letter. From Bono! *And* a signed picture. And guess what else? The next time U2 went on tour, I'd be getting free tickets *and* backstage passes, though I'd probably take Bronte, because Ian was sticking to his Mahler symphonies and wouldn't fully appreciate my favorite Irish band.

The thing about my beautiful Morelock chair was, well…it had done its job. All those years of comfort were deeply appreciated, let me tell you. But I didn't need a chair that symbolized what I could have one day, because now I had it. Maybe Jane McFarland had rubbed off on me a little, too, because the chair became…well…just a chair. A beautiful chair, a special chair, but it wasn't my happily-ever-after. Ian and I were making that on our own.

And if it was a blatant suck-up move to the woman who would be as close to a mother-in-law as I'd get, well, so be it. Ian was worth it.

"You two, you're making, how do you say? You're making the eyes, *si?* So sweet." Alejandro winked at me. "He loves you, Calí."

"Which is lucky," I murmured. "As the feeling is mutual." I stood up and brushed off my jeans. "I should go, boys. Leave you two *hermanos*—" thank you, *Sesame Street!* "—alone so you can visit. Plus, I have to get some beauty sleep and all that."

"Perfection, you cannot improve it," Alejandro said, rising to kiss me on both cheeks.

"I hope you're taking notes," I said to my fiancé.

Ian smiled, and my knees wobbled. That smile…it just did things to me.

"Next time, I will bring my wife and my little ones so they can meet their new aunt," Alé said.

"I'm so glad you came, Alejandro," I smiled.

"Of course I came! But, Ian, this one, this has to stick, *si?* No more weddings."

"No more weddings," Ian agreed.

"*Hasta mañana,* Calí," Alé said.

"Bye, *hermano,*" I said. My almost brother-in-law smiled.

Ian took my hand as we walked toward my car. "So you have a new best friend," he murmured.

"He's really great," I said.

He gave that half nod. "He is. Thank you." Still formal, still a little quiet, still a little reserved. "Don't go falling for him," he added.

"My heart is spoken for," I said. Ian smiled, and happiness so overwhelming and so deep seemed to lift me off the ground. "I'll see you tomorrow," I whispered. "I'll be your wife tomorrow, as a matter of fact."

He kissed me then, and kissed me some more, then leaned his forehead against mine. "I can't wait," he said. My heart was so full, the air so sweet, and the sky…the sky never seemed so blue.

* * * * *